THE ROOMIE RULEBOOK

CRYSTAL KASWELL

Copyright

This is a work of fiction. Similarities to real people, places, or events are entirely coincidental.

Also by Crystal Kaswell

Inked Love

The Best Friend Bargain - Forest

The First Taste - Holden

The Roomie Rulebook - Oliver

Inked Hearts

Tempting - Brendon

Hooking Up - Walker

Pretend You're Mine - Ryan

Hating You, Loving You - Dean

Breaking the Rules - Hunter

Losing It - Wes

Accidental Husband - Griffin

The Baby Bargain - Chase

Dirty Rich

Dirty Deal - Blake

Dirty Boss - Nick

Dirty Husband - Shep

Dirty Desires - Ian

Dirty Wedding - Ty

Dirty Secret - Cam

Pierce Family

Broken Beast - Adam

Playboy Prince - Liam

Ruthless Rival - Simon - coming soon

Sinful Serenade

Sing Your Heart Out - Miles

Strum Your Heart Out - Drew

Rock Your Heart Out - Tom

Play Your Heart Out - Pete

Sinful Ever After – series sequel

Just a Taste - Miles's POV

Dangerous Noise

Dangerous Kiss - Ethan

Dangerous Crush – Kit

Dangerous Rock – Joel

Dangerous Fling – Mal

Dangerous Encore - series sequel

Standalones

Broken - Trent & Delilah

Come Undone Trilogy

Come Undone

Come Apart

Come To Me

Sign up for the Crystal Kaswell mailing list

For every girl who's ever been told she's too much.

Chapter One

OLIVER

Here's something no one tells you about sobriety: it's boring as fuck.

Old hobbies, old friends, old lovers?

They're arranged around a bottle.

They're for that fun, life of the party, always-has-the-good-shit guy.

The sober asshole with a chip on his shoulder?

Not welcome.

So here I am, sweaty and exhausted, after a full day of work and a long session at the gym.

I should be spent.

Instead, my body aches for release.

A rush. Any rush.

I don't have a motorcycle. I don't like sweets. With old lovers no good—

My hand is a friend most of the time. It serves me well when I sketch, tattoo, toy with a gorgeous woman.

But lately?

My right hand is my new best friend.

Six p.m. and I'm ready for session number three today.

Might as well make it count.

I turn on my fan—even though it's October, it's hot as fuck upstairs. Then I spend a few minutes looking for a video.

School girl/professor.

Pizza boy/customer.

Boss/secretary.

Pages and pages of over-the-top bullshit.

Not what I need.

I need real. A gorgeous woman on my bed, legs spread, hips bucking as she comes on my face.

Someone new. Different.

Someone like Luna.

No. I'm not going there. I'm not fantasizing about my sister's best friend. No matter how much my self-destructive streak screams *yes*.

My cock ignores my reasoning.

Why not Luna?

Why not the gorgeous college student, with her smart mouth and her perfect tits?

Could anything really be more important than hearing her come?

My thoughts disobey me.

They flit through images of Luna.

Long legs. Tan skin. Teasing smile.

That sexy black bikini. The one that barely covers her tits.

My cock roars to attention.

There's no arguing with the fucker. I might as well savor the next few minutes.

The anticipation. The rush. The release.

The only fucking satisfaction I get these days.

I wrap my hand around my shaft. Let my head fill with memories.

2

Luna at the beach in that tiny swimsuit. Jumping into the waves.

Emerging all tan and tall and soaking wet.

Shooting me that *you wish you could* look.

Then fantasies.

Her against the wall, my hand between her legs, my name on her lips.

A sound downstairs—

What the fuck?

Dad is at work for another few hours. Daisy is hundreds of miles away. No one else has a key.

No one except—

Shit.

"Hey," a familiar voice calls. "Ollie? Your car is out front. Are you here? Or did you walk to the gym? Oh god, don't tell me you're running now."

Fuck. Am I lost in some porno fantasy? Did my cock develop magic powers? Somehow, it summoned the object of its affection.

It would be nice. If it helped me out for once. Instead of daring me to detonate my entire life.

"Ollie?" Footsteps move in the main room. Then up the stairs. Luna mutters something about my terrible music being too loud.

I grab a towel. Wrap it around my hips. Fail to hide my hard-on.

Thoughts of baseball fail to cool me down.

My mantra—*I will not fuck up the only thing in my life that matters*—does jack shit.

The risk only makes me harder.

Fuck, why is the door open?

This house is too goddamn stuffy.

"Ollie?" Luna moves down the hallway. Three steps from the door. Two. One. "Oh. Shit. Sorry."

3

In the mirror, I catch her reflection. Damn, I might as well turn around and point to my dick.

She stares at the towel straining to cover my hard-on. "I, uh…" Her cheeks flush. Her gaze shifts to the floor. "I'll let you get to it."

"What are you doing here?"

"Maybe we should talk when you're finished."

"Right. I have to shower."

"Yeah." She stares at the towel like she's willing it to disappear.

If you keep staring, I'm gonna go right now. You want to watch me finish, baby? How would you like to come on my hand? I'm dying to hear you groan. "Fifteen minutes."

She looks at me like she's going to make her question explicit—*are you going to fuck yourself*—but she doesn't.

Chapter Two

LUNA

I will not think about Oliver's cock.

I will not think about Oliver's cock.

I will not, under any circumstances, think about Oliver's cock.

A door opens upstairs. Then footsteps. His bare feet. His jean-clad legs.

Those same black jeans he always wears. Slung low around his hips.

Low enough I could unzip them and—

Nope.

Not.

Going.

There.

Not.

Thinking.

About.

His.

Cock.

Period.

End.

Of.

Sentence.

Yes, it's a much better subject than the one currently occupying my brain.

Yes, I much prefer sexual fantasies to the blinking light screaming *love is over*.

Yes, even unfortunately timed sexual fantasies. (Oliver is Daisy's older brother. And Daisy is the only person I trust. So, sleeping with Oliver... not in the cards).

This isn't the time. I need to figure out where I'm sleeping tonight. Tomorrow. Next week.

Someplace that doesn't reek of betrayal.

Okay, I'm not in physical danger. There's no practical reason why I can't stay at my parents' place.

But I can't.

Even if that means I spend the night at some twenty-four-hour diner, drinking shitty coffee to stay awake until Mom's at work.

Anywhere else.

Anyplace I don't have to look at her traitorous face.

"You okay?" Oliver steps onto the main floor. His bare feet pad the hardwood. Slow, steady steps. The steps of a man who isn't hiding an awkward boner.

Did he finish in the shower? Did he think of me? Did he let out a groan so low it blended into the shitty grunge song emanating from his room?

Maybe grunge isn't so bad. Under that context.

Or maybe I'm imagining things. Maybe he was getting ready for a shower. Period. End of sentence.

His gym shoes are sitting by the door. And he does look clean and relaxed.

Like he finished.

Fuck. I need to stop thinking about his cock. For the next ten minutes at least.

"I need a favor." I smooth my high-waist jeans.

"Shoot." He nods *hey* like this is a normal day. Like he came downstairs for a snack while Daisy and I were watching TV on the couch. Like I didn't interrupt his... release. "You want coffee?"

"It's getting late."

"Is that a no?"

"Depends whether or not you'll make it right." I just manage to tease him. It feels strange on my lips. So light it's begging to escape.

He flips me off. Half-smiles. It's not quite there for him either. But then Oliver isn't really a happy-go-lucky guy.

Only when he's drinking. No. Even then, he's more... even. Not miserable, but certainly not the life of the party. He still hangs out on the sidelines, watching the action, enjoying the company of his favorite flask.

God, he looks good. Like he's spent the last few weeks working out.

Broad shoulders. Narrow waist. Tattoos covering his strong arms.

Has he always been this hot? Or is it the war zone in my heart?

"Luna?" He moves into the kitchen. Sets the electric kettle to two hundred degrees. "Your favor?"

"Can I stay here tonight?"

He looks at me like I'm crazy. "Since when do you ask?"

It's true. For the last ten years, Daisy and I have been best friends. I've spent hundreds of nights here. I practically live on this couch.

But now she's at Berkeley. And I'm still in Venice. And it's weird spending the night at my best friend's house without her.

"You're usually really fucking rude." His voice is teasing. Until he catches my expression. It must be bad, because he shakes his head. "Fuck. Sorry. Is it serious?"

"Just my parents."

"They forbid you from dating some loser?"

"When have I dated losers?"

"That Sean guy." He rolls his eyes *what a tool.* Grabs a bag of dark roast coffee. Scoops beans into the grinder.

"Sean's at USC." And he's an incredibly handsome water polo player with rich parents. He's an asshole, sure, but he's not a loser.

"Maybe they're really into the rivalry."

"Neither of them went to UCLA."

"Still."

"Still?" I manage to look him in the eyes. For one second. Then my thoughts drop to the gutter. "He's going to be an investment banker or something." Part of his explanation for needing a supportive woman. And not a difficult one. *Honestly, Luna, you're hot, but you're too much work.*

"I don't like him." Oliver turns to the grinder. He almost looks jealous. Then he hits the button. The machine roars as it breaks the beans into tiny pieces.

"It has nothing to do with him." And why does Oliver care about my ex-boyfriend?

"Is it serious?" His voice softens. Just barely, but it does.

I don't know how to answer that, so I dodge the question. "Is it okay if I stay? For a few days?"

"Of course. I'll check with Dad, but he'll say yes."

"Thanks."

Again, he looks at me like I'm crazy for asking. Then he shrugs and turns his attention to the kettle.

I pretend as if there's something interesting on my phone. And not a message from Mom checking if I'm okay.

Allison Locke: I know you're upset, Luna. I know you hate me right now, but I'm still your mother. I need to know where you're staying.

She doesn't need to know.

I'm a college student. An adult. An adult who cannot afford Los Angeles rents, much less ones near school.

It's true. I need a place to stay. I can't support myself financially.

But, in all other ways, I can take care of myself. If someone dropped free rent in my lap, I'd have no problem living alone—or with a roommate. I can cook and clean and manage my schedule.

And keep my pants zipped.

She is the one who cheated.

She is the one tearing our family apart.

She is not treating me like the troublemaker.

Uh-uh.

No way.

I should make her sweat it. Make her nervous. Make her wonder what Divya felt when she came home late. Or took fake business trips.

An executive with her secretary.

A pathetic cliché of a mid-life crisis.

Fuck her and her bullshit excuses.

"You want cream or sugar?" Oliver interrupts my train of thought.

"I'm pretending you didn't say that."

"You don't always drink it black."

"I do too." I stare at the message on my cell. No apology. She is not apologizing for breaking up our family. She is simply reasserting her role as my mother. As if she owns the role more than Divya does because we share the same gene pool.

"Isn't it hard on your stomach?"

"Sometimes."

9

"And that's when you have cream?"

"Yeah." I tap out angry reply after angry reply.

I'll come home when I want.

Leave me the fuck alone.

Why don't I make like you and find some guy's bed for tonight? Does that make you proud?

I delete them all. Send a simple text to Divya instead.

Luna: Staying at Daisy's tonight. I'm sorry.

At least someone is apologizing to her.

Ugh.

I hate everything.

Since I was a kid, I watched a million families fall apart.

I always thought I was okay. That I'd never hear tales of a cheating spouse or a younger woman. Sure, that type of behavior is normal from men.

But women who went through hell to be together—

Who made a very conscious choice to have a child—

They're better than that, aren't they?

"You don't look okay." Oliver sets a mug on the table. One marked with the logo of the tattoo shop where he works. *Inked Love.* "If it's about earlier…" He almost blushes. "It's not a big deal."

Maybe I should give into my lust. Better than other considerations. And I have the okay to stay here. That's the deal, right?

Place to sleep.

Then lust.

Maybe I should go to the shower and fuck myself. It worked for him. He's different than usual.

Looser and stiffer at the same time.

Not that I'm thinking of him stiff.

It's just—

I haven't seen him much. With Daisy in school, I don't

have reason to come here. And the last time I saw him was our trip to Mexico. A week in the sun, swimming, drinking, dancing.

Oliver in only his swimsuit, all tall and broad and tempting.

"Luna?" he asks again. "Tell me you're okay and I'll go."

"It's not about earlier." The mug is warm against my hands. That feels good. Safe. Comforting. I take a sip. Let out a soft groan. Mmm. Dark, rich, a little bitter. "This is good. Thank you."

"Do you need anything?"

"A drink." I stifle a laugh. "You got any bourbon?"

He looks at me funny.

Which is weird. Oliver carries a freaking flask. A twenty-one-year-old with a flask. Like he's in a noir flick. He's always drinking. And now he's looking at me funny for asking for booze.

"You don't like bourbon," he says.

"You have gin?"

He lets out an Oliver huff that means something between *whatever* and *okay, sure*. "Daisy wouldn't like it."

True, but—"Since when does that stop you?"

"Do you need anything else?"

Yes. Take off the jeans. Distract me. Please. Can you go again so soon? "Coffee is good. Thanks."

"Dad said you'll talk after dinner."

"Oh. Cool." I swallow another sip. Try to assess the situation.

Oliver only stays here for Daisy. He promised her he'd stay at home her first year of college. Even though she's five hundred miles away at Berkeley.

I guess he wanted her to know she could find him anytime.

It's sweet. They're close. He's protective of her. Too protective, but it's hard to blame him.

There's something about Daisy. This sweetness that demands protecting.

Oliver, on the other hand—

He's all hardness and rough edges.

Fuck, I'm losing track of my point.

My heart is still heavy. My blood is still surging. I need to do something to ease the fury racing through me.

I can booty call an ex. I can beg Oliver to distract me. I can march home, break glasses, call Mom all sorts of things I can't take back.

That isn't it.

Even pissed as hell I know better.

Which leaves Oliver.

No. I can't. That's going to ruin everything outside my house.

I have to think about something else.

Anything else.

Not his cock.

I am not thinking about Oliver Flynn's cock.

That's possible.

Totally and completely possible.

Chapter Three

OLIVER

For a while, I give Luna space.

She sits on the couch, watching reality TV, her attention somewhere else.

Through my headphones, Kurt Cobain whines about his emptiness. The lithium or the heroin or some other drug of choice?

Why is it shrinks complain about self-medicating then prescribe something else to numb the pain? Is bourbon really so much worse than sertraline?

At least bourbon is fun.

As usual, my thoughts scatter. I try to pull them back with another mock-up. That Latin quote from *The Handmaid's Tale*—it's all the rage with smart women—surrounded by curving red fabric.

It's a nice idea. Applicable to any situation, really.

Don't let the bastards grind you down.

It's not *glory fades* or *I came, I saw, I conquered*. But it's solid.

I trace the lines on my forearm.

ex favilla nos resurgemus

From the ashes, we rise.

One of my first.

I still remember the day I got it. The rush of adrenaline. The one thought racing through my brain *I can't believe I did this.*

This job used to be everything. I used to sit outside Blacklist, waiting for one of the artists to take pity on me. Show me something, anything.

I've wanted to be a tattoo artist since I could remember.

I only graduated from apprenticing a year ago. I have so far to go. So much to learn.

But it's not the same now. Something is missing. Something I can't find.

ex favilla nos resurgemus

From the ashes, we rise.

At the time, it sounded badass. Optimistic in a twisted way.

Now—

Is it better to burn my life to the ground and start over?

Or hold on to what matters?

I don't know. But I can't keep thinking about it.

I give up on work. Stand. Move downstairs.

Luna barely looks up from her cell. She's staring at the thing like she's trying to destroy it with her glare.

"You talk to Daisy?" I ask.

She shakes her head. "I guess I should, huh?" She wipes her eye. Not a tear, but something close.

"I won't say anything. If that's what you want."

"Really?"

"Do I look like a narc?"

Her eyes meet mine. "Your loyalty is with her, isn't it?"

Yeah, but I have principles. Not snitching is one of them. "I won't." I release her gaze. Move into the kitchen.

"You hungry?" It's still early. Dad isn't due home for another hour. But I need something to occupy my hands and my mind.

"I could eat."

"Pasta?"

"What kind of psycho would say no to pasta?" She half-smiles.

"Lots of girls are watching their figure."

She laughs. "Is that really what they say? 'I'm watching my figure.'"

I shrug. "Sometimes. It's Southern California. I don't question. Everyone is on some diet." It's none of my business. And I know better. Pushing people who have a problem. That does more harm than good.

"Pasta is good. With a lot of garlic." This time, she offers a full smile. It's not as bright as her usual smile. There's a strain to it. "And spicy. As long as you're taking requests."

I flip her off.

"Please."

I shoot her a really.

"Pretty please."

"Shit, that's the magic word. Gotta do it now."

She laughs *you're ridiculous*. "You know you love garlic."

And spicy too. I want to give her shit for trying to boss me around, but I don't mind it. Hell, I love it.

Luna tells me what she wants. That makes it easier to give her what she wants.

She's like family. I want to take care of her. To make sure she's safe, fed, happy.

Her expression darkens and it overwhelms me—this desire to comfort her.

It's not like me. I stay out of things. I don't comfort people. Only Daisy.

15

But Luna…

She's different. My friend. Maybe the only friend I want to see at the moment.

"Are you going to help?" I ask.

"Wouldn't it be more fun if I ordered you around?"

Yeah, order me to take off your pants and dive between your legs. Say my name when you come on my face, baby. Fuck. Maybe I should tell her I've got it handled. Better to have the fifteen feet between us. "You can help. Or you can take whatever I make."

"Okay." She stands. Slips her cell into the back pocket of her jeans. Moves into the kitchen. Into my space.

She's three feet away. In front of the fridge. I'm in front of the stove. Close enough to touch.

Close enough, I can make all those fantasies come true.

Close enough, I feel something.

That surge of lust. And something else. A flutter in my stomach. A thump of my heart.

A craving.

For her touch, her kiss, her fuck.

And her smile, her laugh, her love.

It's strange. Unfamiliar. But it's something. It's not the endless grey of sobriety. Anything is better than that.

"You want an apron?" I motion to her light top. It's sexy as fuck—tight around her lush tits—and easily stained.

"Are we doing tomato sauce?"

"Nah. Pasta aglio e olio."

"Oil and garlic?" she asks.

I nod. "Oil can stain."

"I'll live." She doesn't wait for instruction. She turns to the fridge. Pulls it open. Grabs tomatoes, fresh pasta, arugula, Parmesan. "You have good shit here."

"Yeah."

16

"Usually it's all TV dinners and dried pasta."

"I'm an excellent cook," I say.

"You are. But you're usually… more efficient."

I shrug. "I have time now."

"With Daisy in Berkeley?" She tosses it out as a possible explanation. Half statement. Half question.

"Yeah." That's part of it.

"That's funny. I don't usually cook for myself. It's so much effort for one."

"Dad too."

"Still." She bites her lip. "You two aren't exactly…"

Not going there. I pull out a cutting board. Motion to the knife.

She nods. Gathers the ingredients. Starts slicing tomatoes.

I put a pot of water on the stove. Find the garlic. The other cutting board. The mincer.

She watches closely as I peel. When she catches me watching her, she raises a brow. *Really?* "Fresh garlic."

"And?"

"That's next level effort."

"Do you not want me to cook for you?"

"No." She gives me a quick once-over. Not like the one in the bedroom. Not like she's savoring the lines of my body. Like she's trying to find a missing piece of a puzzle. "I appreciate it. And I know you appreciate my help."

"I do. Thanks."

"You're welcome. And thank you." Her smile gets easier. "I just… fresh garlic is serious cooking."

"Everyone needs a hobby."

"True." She finishes slicing the tomatoes. Moves on to peeling Parmesan. Thick slices tumble into a clean white bowl. "I miss Daisy too."

It is hard, having my sister hundreds of miles away.

Worrying about her. Not being able to protect her. Not being able to make her dinner, help her study, warn her about guys with bad intentions. "She loves Berkeley. And she's doing great. Thriving."

Luna nods *right*. "And you?" She looks up from her work for a second, then her eyes are on the bowl. The cheese is so light it nearly blends into the ceramic.

"And I…"

"Are you good?"

"Good enough. You?"

"Uh… I think I need wine before I answer that."

"You don't drink wine." And she doesn't lust for booze either. Why does she keep bringing it up? Does she know?

"Pasta. Wine. It goes."

"Dad got rid of everything."

She nods, accepting the explanation.

But the question refuses to leave my head.

How could she possibly know?

———

WE MAKE SMALL TALK. THE WEATHER, TO START. THEN the Dodgers. The state of things at Inked Love.

The shop is buzzing. Plenty of clients. Some famous. Some rich. Some incredibly hot.

Under different circumstances, I'd take some home. Share dirty stories with my friends until I find better dirty stories.

Right now, I can't.

Sex and booze are tangled in my head. Not drinking means not fucking.

Mostly it means keeping to myself. Since all my friends are soaked in booze.

It fucking sucks. But I'm not sharing that with Luna.

It's hard enough not touching her.

I'm already picturing her naked. I'm already buzzing from the proximity of her body, the smell of her shampoo, the warmth of her skin.

She always smells like sunscreen. All those years on the swim team. They give her those sculpted shoulders, those strong legs, the tan limbs—

I push past mental images of her in a tiny practice suit long enough to finish dinner.

We bring everything to the table as Dad strolls into the house.

He looks at the scene with a curious expression. Unsure what to make of it.

"Luna, hello." He sets his messenger bag on the coffee table. Then his keys. "How are you?"

"Good. Thanks." She looks from me to him. "Did Ollie text you? I'm hoping to stay here a few days."

"Of course." He gives me that look that says *we're going to talk about this*. "And you helped with dinner. Thank you. Give me five minutes to change."

She nods. More polite than normal. No mention of my dad's hotness. She brings it up to tease Daisy. Sometimes to tease me.

All the women who meet my dad bring it up. I guess he's an attractive guy. Tall, built, well-dressed.

I can't look at him without seeing his bullshit orders. But I have to admit: good looks run in the family.

If I grow up to act like him, shoot me.

But if I grow up to look like him, minus the slacks, I won't complain.

Luna takes a seat. Smooths her pants. Stares at the fancy balsamic vinegar.

True to his word, Dad returns a few minutes later, in

jeans and a grey t-shirt. Casual in his clothes but not his manner.

Luna smiles. Nods to the Latin quote on his right arm. "You really rock the ink, Mr. Flynn. I can see it runs in the family."

He laughs. "You know I prefer Gabe, Luna."

"Right. Gabe. It looks good on you. That's all," she says.

I shoot her a *what the fuck* look.

She ignores it. "Oliver made dinner."

"We made it," I say.

"Thank you. Both of you." Dad takes a seat at the table. Motions for me to follow.

I do.

He eyes the glasses on the table. Water. Plus the carafe. He looks at me for a moment, but he doesn't say anything. "This smells great." He picks up his fork. "Shall we?"

"Yeah. Right." Luna nods. She shifts in her seat. Uncomfortable.

I guess this is weird. Sure, Luna's here all the time. But not by herself. Not with Daisy hundreds of miles away.

"I haven't seen much of you, Luna. Is school keeping you busy?" he asks.

"Yeah. It's a lot. My chem class is moving really fast. And the ones in the humanities"—she sticks her tongue out —"why is there so much reading? I don't know how people can say math is hard then read three hundred pages on European History like it's nothing."

He lets out an easy chuckle. "Those textbooks can be dry."

She nods. Goes quiet as she takes a bite. Then she lets out a small groan. That *fuck this is good* groan.

It's about the food, I know. But my head goes other places.

He asks about dinner. How we made it. She launches into an explanation. Then they're talking about Daisy's favorite TV show, makeup, fashion, all sorts of shit that isn't in my wheelhouse.

Her posture softens. Her tension fades.

By the time she's finished with dinner, her smile is warm. "Are you sure it's okay for me to stay?"

Dad nods *of course*. "I'll have to talk to your parents. To make sure they know you're safe."

In an instant, the ease disappears. She shakes it off. "Of course. They… uh… they're separating."

Fuck.

"That's why I don't want to be there," she says.

"I'm sorry, Luna." Guilt streaks Dad's expression. "I won't give you the lecture about how it's not you. I'll just say… I'm sure they love you and want you to be okay."

"Yeah. I'm sure. I just… can't really look at Mom right now. Allison. She's the one… it's, uh… do you mind if I go up to Daisy's room? I'll text. Make sure it's okay with her."

"You can take the spare," he says. "It's fine."

"You sure?" She looks to me. "And it's okay with Oliver?"

He doesn't let me answer. "Yes. It will be good for Oliver. To have company. In fact, we need to talk." He offers her a sincere smile. "Make yourself at home. I'll bring towels and blankets in a little while."

"Sure, yeah." She offers him a weak smile, then she moves away from the table.

Dad waits until she's all the way up the stairs to speak. "Are you going to say it? Or should I?"

Chapter Four

OLIVER

Are you going to say it or should I?

Which of my fuckups does he want to discuss? I never know with Dad.

The drinking? The screwing? Some other sin I need to confess?

He places his hands on the table. Looks me in the eyes. Adopts a paternal tone. "You've barely left your room."

Since when does he care about that? "Okay."

"Are you talking to anyone?"

"I'm going to the court-appointed therapy."

"No, Oliver. Are you seeing your friends?"

No. My friends know me as the guy who brings a bottle to every occasion. Who fixes every drink. How am I supposed to hang out with them as the sober buzzkill? "I'm working a lot."

He studies me carefully. "It could be a good idea. To have someone around."

"A babysitter?"

"A friend."

I swallow hard. Yeah, in theory, a friendly roomie is a good idea. But in practice?

I already want to fuck Luna.

Having her across the hall—

Not helping me keep my dick in my pants.

Like he can read my mind, he asks, "Will it be a problem?"

"No." I *can* control myself. Even if it's hard.

"She likes you," he says.

"We're friends."

He doesn't buy it, but he doesn't press the issue. "I know it's not fair to remind you of that. With your sister dating your best friend."

It's not. I should complain. I should tell him to fuck off with the hypocrisy. But what good will that do? "Do you have a point?"

"I'm proud of you, for trying. But you're not going to make it if you white-knuckle your way through it."

That's his opinion. "It's been four weeks. I've made it so far."

He frowns. "Oliver…" He says my name in that tone of his. The one that means I'm a constant disappointment.

"Yeah?"

He makes that *hmmm* noise of his that means *you're clearly full of it.* "We have a deal. I won't tell Daisy what happened if you complete the program. Ten weeks of alcohol education. Ten weeks without a drink."

"I know." I thought I was numb to my father's disappointment—it's all I've earned for a long time—but I can barely stomach the way he looks at me. I can't take Daisy seeing me as a fuckup too.

Yes, I fucked-up. I did a very stupid thing. And now, I'm paying the price.

I don't need more on top of this bullshit.

Sobriety is enough torture.

Stupid classes about blood alcohol level and liver damage and healthy partying—

Seriously, it would be easier if I had to die for Daisy. Less painful.

"I want to make this easier for you. Not harder. Will this make it harder?" he asks.

He's giving me an out. The chance to say *fuck this, I can only handle one temptation at a time.*

The chance to kick her out when she needs comfort.

I remember my parents' divorce. If I could have gotten away from that. If I could have stayed somewhere else, away from their fights and anger and turbulence—

"No. It will be good. Having a friend around," I say.

He nods *good*. "And it won't be a problem?"

"No problem."

"She trusts you."

"I know."

"Don't take advantage of that trust," he says.

"I said it won't be a problem."

Whatever.

"Is there a question in here somewhere? Or is it just a lecture?"

"She's Daisy's best friend."

And he's the one who went through the ugly divorce that destroyed Daisy. But I don't throw that in his face every three minutes. "We're friends."

"She's going through something too. She needs a friend too."

How much of an asshole does he think I am?

"I know you promised your sister you'd stay here. I know you want to honor that. But you're only welcome here if you—"

"I know." If I stay sober through the rest of this fucking program. After that…

It's pretty clear he expects it to stick. But he hasn't issued any ultimatums yet. None of the *stop drinking or else* shit he tried a few years ago. I guess he learned from that mistake.

"I want you here, Oliver. I love you," he says. "I don't like playing this role. But I will if you force my hand."

"I got it."

He nods, accepting my response. "Thank you. For fixing dinner. I'll clean up."

That's our usual arrangement. I cook. He cleans. With Luna here… I guess we can alternate.

"This is an opportunity, Oliver. Treat it like one."

Whatever. I stand. Move toward the stairs.

He says, "I love you," again.

I know I should reply. Say it back. Tell him I appreciate that he puts up with my bullshit.

But I keep my mouth shut until I'm in my room, my music loud enough to muffle any fucking sound.

Six more weeks of sobriety.

Six more weeks of torture.

After that, I don't fucking know.

I'm not sure it matters. I don't know how the hell I'm going to survive another six weeks.

Chapter Five

LUNA

My brain is fried. I'm completely unable to finish my European History reading. Even my chem textbook is incomprehensible.

I look for something to do. Anything. Stay busy rearranging the minimal decoration in the room.

Mr. Flynn's old office. He worked from home a few days a week for a while. Not anymore. Now, the space collects dust.

There's a couch. A desk. A bookshelf with a mix of business texts and thrillers.

Oliver's books or a shared love? It's hard to imagine the two of them sharing anything beyond a willingness to die for Daisy.

I text my best friend. Ask if she minds if I crash at her place. Tell her I already have Oliver and Gabe's permission. Offer a vague explanation about my parents fighting.

She says yes immediately. She doesn't push for details. Just leaves one of those *we can talk whenever you're ready* notes.

I can tell her anything. That is true. But I can't dive into this. It's too heavy, too painful, too fuzzy.

Finally, Mr. Flynn knocks on my door with towels, blankets, a roll out bed.

"Your parents understand," he says as he arranges the bed on the hardwood floor. "They'd rather have you home. But they understand."

"Sure."

He nods. "As far as I'm concerned, you can stay as long as you like."

"Oh." My stomach flutters. "That's very generous. Are you sure?"

"I'm glad to have someone here. To keep an eye on Oliver."

Oh.

He opens his mouth like he's going to continue his explanation. Then he stops. Shakes his head. "He needs the company. And he won't take it from me."

"It's different. With parents."

"Yeah." He lets out a knowing chuckle. It's more sad than anything. Wistful, maybe. "I'm sorry. About your parents."

"Thanks."

"Can I offer advice?"

"Depends what it is." I sit on the couch. Pull my legs into my chest.

Mr. Flynn, I mean Gabe leans against the wall. The same way Oliver does. "With your mother's assets, it might get ugly. Especially if it's not a mutual decision."

"She didn't tell you?" I swallow the bile that rises in my throat.

His voice softens. "I didn't ask."

"She's found a younger woman. Allison has. Her secretary."

He just nods. Not surprised. Or upset. Or filled with the fire of a thousand suns. "You're angry?"

"Of course."

"I understand that. But, as someone who's been on the other side—"

"That was different."

"Maybe," he says. "But I still stood there, watching it tear my kids apart, completely unable to help."

I bite my lip. I'm not going to feel bad for her. Under any circumstances. She made her bed. She can lie in it.

"I just… know it's got nothing to do with you. Or how they love you."

"Yeah."

"I'm sure you'd rather talk with Oliver. You can whisper secrets about evil parents."

"He doesn't think you're evil."

Gabe makes that *hmmm* noise. So much like Oliver's but so different too. "If you do need anything, let me know. You're part of our family, Luna. You're always welcome here."

"Thanks."

"Are you going to be okay on the mattress pad? You can take my room if it's not—"

"It's good, thanks." I'm already imposing enough. Even if he wants a free babysitter.

He nods *sure*. "I'll tell you what I tell my kids. If you ever need anything, call me. I might be mad. I might be disappointed. I might call the police in the morning. But I'll do whatever it takes to help."

"Thank you." My chest tenses. The parental affection is too much. Too familiar. "Good night, Gabe."

"Good night." He closes the door. Moves to his bedroom.

Quiet noises fill the space. The soft murmur of traffic outside. The low mumble of Oliver's grunge music. The light breeze.

All these thoughts racing through my head.

I try to focus on studying for my chem test, but my head keeps racing.

Eventually, I give up, gather a towel, head to Daisy's bathroom.

It's immaculate. Everything in shades of pale pink and light turquoise. Her dainty collection of makeup. And the massive red bag I keep here.

My silver shampoo and conditioner.

I practically live here. I did. All summer.

But this is different. My best friend isn't here. Oliver is.

He's across the hall. In his room. In his bed, maybe.

He might be reading or drawing or working or thinking of me.

I run the water. Step into the shower. Close my eyes and will my thoughts to abate.

That blinking sign keeps flashing in my head. So I recall the sight of Oliver in his bedroom. In a towel that failed to hide his hard-on.

That look in his eyes when he's teasing me.

The citrus smell of his shampoo.

The deep tenor of his groan.

My other thoughts slip away. Bit by bit, I fade into a familiar fantasy. The two of us at a party. Outside. In some beautiful backyard.

His hands on my skin.

His lips on my neck.

Fuck, I come fast. Too fast.

It's not enough. I need more.

I absolutely, positively, can't have more.

He's across the hall. For the next few weeks. Maybe even the rest of the semester.

I have to get used to it.

———

THANKFULLY, I HAVE HALF A DOZEN OUTFITS HERE. IN Daisy's closet.

She makes space for me.

We're practically sisters.

So it's pretty messed up that I step onto the stairs and see Oliver on the couch and immediately think *damn, he looks like he's waiting to be mounted.*

He really does, though.

He's lying back with his Kindle in his hands. All long and tall and comfortable.

His t-shirt is even pulling up his torso. Showing off that sliver of skin above the low waist of his jeans.

The tattoo on his hip. Lyrics to some grunge song. It sounds like a love song, but it's really about heroin.

He looks up at me and nods *hey*. "If you want to watch something, I can go upstairs."

"Or you can pretend you're staying because you're here when it's really because you love *The Bachelorette*."

He chuckles. "They usually pick a hot chick."

"And she has all these men vying for her attention."

"Is that your dream?"

"No." My fingers trail the railing as I move down the stairs. My feet pad the floor. It's cooler than usual. Different. This is all different. But it can be normal. Just me and Oliver teasing each other on the couch. We've done that a million times.

Usually, it's after Daisy goes to sleep. Or while she's showering. Or doing homework.

But it's the same thing.

No. Big. Deal.

"The guys are always scrubs," I say.

"You love scrubs."

I shake my head. "Is this about Sean again?"

He shrugs *maybe*.

I move past him. To the kitchen. Fill a glass of water. "You want one?"

"You're asking?"

"I'm very polite."

He makes that *hmm* gesture. Motions to a mug on the coffee table. "I'm good."

"Is that coffee?"

"Decaf."

"You're drinking decaf?" I ask.

"Desperate times."

"No better way to hide your bourbon?"

That same *maybe* shrug. But different. Stiffer. "There was that other guy. Before Sean."

"James?"

He nods *that's it*. "He was a loser."

"You know, some girls would take offense to you calling their exes losers."

"'Cause they dumped you?"

I flip him off.

He laughs, but there's still a tension to it. "He did, right?"

"I was fifteen. We dated for three months. I'm not sure it really matters who dumped who."

"Did you fuck?"

"Oh my god!" I set my glass aside. Slide onto the counter. Cross my ankles.

"You did." His expression shifts. His shoulders soften. His deep blue eyes fill with interest. "Was it good?"

"None of your business."

"Was he your first?"

"You didn't eavesdrop on me and Daisy?" I ask.

"Believe it or not, Luna, but I have more interesting things to do."

"I choose not," I say.

He chuckles *of course you say that.* "Was he? Or was it Sean? Fuck, have you only been with Sean?" He shakes his head *sad, so sad.*

"Why do you want to know?"

He stands. Moves across the room. To the kitchen island. Takes a seat on the opposite side of the counter. "Making conversation."

"Is it that unfathomable, the idea of being with only one person?"

"For you? Yeah."

"Excuse me?"

He chuckles. "You know that's not what I mean."

"It sounds like you called me a slut."

"No." His eyes flit to my chest. "But you like to show off. You like to flirt. You impart wisdom."

"I thought you didn't eavesdrop."

"You're loud," he says.

True.

His smile lights up his blue eyes. It's so beautiful. Too beautiful. It makes my heart race and my stomach flutter. Oliver's smile is rare. A treat. An incredibly delicious treat.

"You know what you want," he says. "Usually, that takes trial and error."

"Maybe I have a rich inner life."

"Maybe you've fucked a few different guys." He leans back on his hands. "No shame in that."

"You couldn't talk if there was."

He laughs as he picks up one hand. Points to his chest. "Biggest slut in the state."

"Are you? Or do you want people to think that?"

He makes that *a little* motion. "You?"

"I?"

"Want people to think you're experienced."

Sort of. "I want men to know they can't fuck with me. Otherwise, I don't care."

"Hmm." So much like his father's. But so different too.

"Hmm? Why are you so interested?"

"I'm not." His gaze flits to the TV. "Just figured you'd rather talk about something else."

"Oh."

"Yeah." He runs his hand through his hair. Brings the other to the countertop. "If you'd rather not—"

"No. Thanks."

"It does suck. I remember that." He looks in the direction of his father's room. "The fighting. The bullshit." His gaze softens for a moment, then he brings his attention to me. "So? How was he?"

"What?"

"James? Good? Bad? Tiny? Loaded?"

"You're such a guy."

"How is that?" he asks.

"All the talk about dick size."

"Like you didn't ask Daisy about Holden's the second she told you."

I clear my throat.

"Ugh. Why did I bring that up?" His expression twists with distaste. "Don't want to know. Don't want to hear a thing about it."

"Really? So you probably wouldn't want to hear—"

He makes a show of covering his ears. "What was that? Can't hear you. Sounds like you said something about you've been with so many guys because you love dick so much."

That's ridiculous. I can't help but laugh. "That sounds like me."

"Yeah. You're on a mission to suck as many cocks as possible."

"A generous mission."

He chuckles. "It's in your nature."

"Is it?"

He makes that same *a little* motion. Half-smiles.

I half-smile back.

For a moment, the air is light. Easy. Then it hits me.

He's thinking about me.

Right now.

Picturing us—

Fuck.

There's barely any room between us. Four feet maybe.

Sure, there's a countertop, but all the better. The perfect place for him—

"Did you and James?" His gaze moves around the room. The angled stairs, the leather couch, the TV. Me.

"Did James and I…"

"Fuck?"

"Yeah." I force myself to look him in the eyes. Completely fail to hold eye contact. It's there. In my head. The image of him ordering me onto my knees. Which is ridiculous. I don't even like that. I mean, I don't not like it. But I don't—

"How many others?"

"Still none of your business." I fight a blush.

He chuckles. "Because you're embarrassed?"

"Because it's none of your business."

"Okay." His eyes find mine. No more *I'm picturing your lips around my cock.* Just *I'm teasing my friend.* "But we can agree James was a scrub."

"We were in high school," I say. "What's even the metric then?"

"Good future, I guess."

"He was a football player," I say.

"That's your type, huh? Athletes?" He chuckles. "Hot guys. You're always dating hot guys."

"What kind of guys should I date?"

He shrugs. "Wouldn't know what makes a guy appealing."

"What kind of women do you date?"

"I'm not right now."

Huh.

"Don't give me that look," he says. "It's just… a break."

"Oliver Flynn is taking a break from dating. I don't believe it."

"Believe it."

"For how long?" I ask.

"A few weeks now."

"Until…"

"Until I stop the break," he says.

"Did you lose a bet or something?"

"Or something."

Hmm. I try to find the answer in his expression, but the more I stare at his baby blues, the less I care. He really has pretty eyes. And now they're full of hurt. Regret even. "There is a reason?"

"Yeah."

"Are you going to tell me?"

He shakes his head *no*.

"So I should just watch *The Bachelorette?*"

"Probably."

I push off the counter. Move to the couch. Pull up the proper streaming service.

His gaze stays on the TV as I start the first episode. For a few minutes, he watches from the kitchen island. Then he moves closer. Sits next to me on the couch.

By the first commercial break (skipped, thank you premium plan), I have my head on his shoulder.

He's so warm and safe and strong.

And he smells so good.

Bad news—secrets and sluttiness and the ability to destroy the only stable relationship in my life. But still so warm and safe and strong.

Chapter Six

OLIVER

Luna falls asleep on the couch. Rouses when I tap her shoulder. Heads to the spare room without complaint.

She doesn't make a point of sauntering up the stairs. It's just the way she walks. With that slight shift of her hips. Like she's compelling me to stare at her ass.

Like she knows she's driving me insane.

No. There's plenty of insanity to go around here. I guess she's the cherry on top of the bonkers sundae.

I turn off the TV. Brush my teeth. Retire to my room.

This is it. My bed. The bed I've had since I was a kid. Dad paid Mom a fortune so he could keep the house. Not that she wanted to be here. Not sober.

She didn't want to do anything sober.

Look at me, following in those wild footsteps of hers. At least I'm trying. That's something. More than she can say.

I read the same sentence ten times. Give up on the book. It's good. One of those psychological thrillers with an unreliable narrator. Is this woman insane? Or is someone just fucking with her so well she thinks she is?

There are plenty of scary things in the world. Horrible shit happens every day. And losing people… it can happen so fast. So easily.

I almost lost Daisy. I know how it feels. To be there, on the precipice, not sure if your sister is going to live or die. Not sure if she'll ever be okay again.

That's the scariest thing I've ever experienced.

But this, the idea of losing touch with reality—it's up there. People have given me shit about drinking for a long time.

Just Dad at first. Then Daisy. But what do they know? They're supposed to look out for me. Remind me of limits. Act as general buzzkills.

Then other people. Like Chase, the guy who runs the shop. But Chase's brother is an alcoholic. The guy is always looking for cracks. He lives for it.

I always thought they were full of shit. I'm still young. Why can't I have fun?

If it never got in the way of my life, what did it matter that I put bourbon in my cold brew or stayed at parties until the last bottle was empty?

What did it matter that I numbed all the bad shit? It's my liver, isn't it?

Then… bam—

One stupid decision and suddenly everyone is entitled to their judgment. Suddenly everyone is right.

Suddenly, I'm Oliver, the alcoholic, the guy with a problem.

Suddenly, the state of California wants to get on board with the accusations.

The state didn't force me to do shit. But it wasn't much of a choice.

Jail time or attend a three-hour-a-week, ten-week class on "alcohol education."

Maybe I should have picked the jail time.

At least it would have been over fast.

I roll onto my back. Toss my blankets aside. Open the window. It's freezing outside—the temperature swings wildly between afternoon and night in October through May—but it's still too stuffy in here.

And I'm still wound tighter than a drum.

It's too late for coffee. I'm too tired to work. The gym isn't even open.

Which leaves sex.

Do I have shit left? I'm not sure.

I can't go there. The second I close my eyes, I think of Luna.

That self-destructive part of my brain.

Maybe I have a problem. But it's not the alcohol. The alcohol is the fucking solution.

It's this.

That match that will burn the only bridge that matters—

No, the Molotov cocktail that will burn the only bridge that matters is right there.

And it's shiny and new and beautiful.

And so fucking appealing.

Six more weeks. Then I can move out. Find some way to explain it to Daisy.

Do something, anything that won't fuck things up more.

Not this.

Anything but this.

———

THE UPSIDE OF INSOMNIA—

I'm awake before the rest of the house. I wash my hands, brush my teeth, throw on my gym shorts.

Run to a particularly miserable Bad Religion album. It's cloudy this early. We're a solid half a mile from the beach, but we still get the morning clouds.

I run in the direction of the Pacific. The air gets cooler. The smell of salt mingles with the scent of gasoline.

Mmm, Southern California, so many charms. And expensive as fuck too. It's home, yeah, but if I want to move out, I need to get smart.

Living rent free is a pretty sweet deal. Especially in this part of town.

I'm good at my job, but it's not exactly investment banking. I don't have one-bedroom-near-the-beach money.

Studio next to the freeway... maybe.

I contemplate the matter as I run along the boardwalk. This time of year, this early in the morning, it's all locals. Women in yoga pants jogging before work. Kids on bikes. Teens on skateboards.

Light sky, beige sand, miles and miles of deep blue ocean. It is beautiful. Objectively speaking. If there is such a thing.

The Pacific Ocean. The Western coast of the United States. The sea that spans half a globe.

The water I see every damn day.

I guess it's not the same water. I move onto the sand. For more resistance. Whatever it takes to annihilate my thoughts.

A wave breaks. The water recedes into the mass of ocean.

It no longer exists in that form.

It returns to the Pacific. Still water, still there, but no longer its own entity.

Is that the inspiring part? Or is it something else entirely?

It's a nice thought, the ability to shift shapes, to smooth sand, to find the path of least resistance.

Then there's the raw power of the ocean. Hurricanes, tsunamis, summer storms.

All that force daring people to fuck with it.

I make a mental note to work on a mock-up of a wave. Something different. New. Interesting.

A mermaid maybe. A Disney riff.

Daisy watched *The Little Mermaid* all the time when she was a kid. She always admired Ariel for her curiosity, her drive, her sense of wonder.

How does she do that? Find all this beauty in the world? So much she's willing to part with her fucking voice?

I mean, yeah, if I had the choice between speaking and fucking, I'd choose the latter too.

But it's more than that.

It stays in my head as I run home. Fix a dark roast. Drink two cups.

Until Luna trots down the stairs. "I smell coffee." She rubs her eyes. Brushes her messy hair behind her ear. "Please tell me there's coffee."

"I made extra, yeah." I pour her a cup.

She moves across the room, her grey eyes half open, her arms stretching over her head in a yawn. "Are you always up this early?"

Lately, yeah. "Are you?"

"I got used to sleeping in all summer. But my body remembers six a.m. practices come September. Four years do that, I guess." She sticks out her tongue *ugh*. "At least the college ones are in the afternoon. If I never wake up before the sunrise it will be too soon."

I offer her the mug. Her fingers brush mine as she takes it. It's nothing. A gesture I've repeated a million times.

But it's fucking electric.

She inhales the coffee. Lets out a deep sigh. One that's all pleasure. It spreads over her expression. Her brow softens. Her lips part.

My cock whines.

Not the time. Not the pants. I turn to the stove. Wish I didn't. The world dulls instantly.

I grab a pan. Turn on the burner. "You want eggs?"

"With garlic and red pepper? Uh, yes."

"Bossy."

"You love it." She smiles. A big, full smile that lights up her gorgeous face. "Thank you, Ollie."

"Sure." I watch her sit at the table. Groan over the coffee. Lose her joy as she pulls her cell from her pajama bottoms.

Is this really the only thing that thrills me now? My sister's best friend?

Maybe I can work with that. Maybe I can be her friend, period, the end.

It's possible to hang out with her without touching her.

No matter how much my cock protests.

Chapter Seven

OLIVER

"**Y**ou look thirsty." Holden saunters into the shop like he owns the place. He stretches his arms over his head. Lets out a yawn. "Real thirsty."

"Ignore him," Forest calls from his suite. It's with his usual *I cannot be bothered to deal with Holden's bullshit* tone.

After Chase, he's the oldest guy at the shop. The most experienced.

He's also Holden's older brother. He knows attention feeds Holden's shit-stirring.

So after an eye roll, he returns to his mock-up. An intense In Memoriam. Roses around a tombstone. Pain turned into beauty. Or maybe it's pain turned into more pain.

"I always do." I'm at the spot behind the counter. Alternating between staring at a mock-up and staring at the bright sky.

It's a slow day. I'm between appointments.

I used to savor this time. What's better than shooting the shit with friends? Even if I'm not usually the one doing most of the talking.

But now?

Waiting is a lot less fun without a buzz. Especially when you don't want to talk to any of your friends.

"You know you love it." Holden moves to the counter with those bouncy steps of his. He places his hands on the slick surface. Glances at my mock-up. Then at me. "An ode to your dick?"

It's not a ridiculous suggestion. The mock-up is badass. And incredibly phallic.

A giant octopus wrapped around a ship, tearing it to pieces, dragging sailors into the ocean.

No pretty mermaids or sweet turtles or sunny yellow fish. Deep blue and black and a red-orange that screams of destruction.

"Half-sleeve," I say.

"Should I repeat the question?" He slides onto the counter. Turns toward me as much as he can manage. "Half-sleeve ode to your dick?"

"For a client."

"I'm not hearing no."

"Why are you so interested in my dick?" I ask.

"If you're gonna wave it around for everyone." He smiles. It's bright. Pure troublemaker. Pure Holden. "I'm only human."

"Uh-huh."

"*Is* it an—"

"Get real," I say.

"Real?" He makes a show of scratching his head. "What's this real you're talking about? I'm not familiar with the concept."

"You are too."

He slides off the counter. Shrugs *maybe, maybe not.* Keeps up the shit-stirring smile. "You do look thirsty."

"What the fuck does that mean?"

From his suite, Forest chuckles. "You are obsessed with his dick."

"Look at him," Holden says. "Look at his face. Pure thirst."

Okay…

"What the hell is thirst?" Forest asks.

"Damn, you're old." Holden shakes his head *sad*.

"Not all of us can fuck eighteen-year-olds." Forest's gaze flits to me. I must look pissed—I don't need the reminder Holden is fucking my sister—because he mouths *sorry*.

Holden ignores the reference to his inability to keep his dick in his pants. He shakes his head *it's sad*. "Thirsty means in dire need of action." He nods to his crotch. "And you're wearing it all over your face." He draws a circle in the air. "You need to get laid. Bad."

Forest looks up from his spot. He's a dozen feet away. Too far for detail. But he still nods *it does look bad*.

"What's it been?" Holden asks. "Three, four days? Must be a record for you."

"Been long enough." My thoughts go to Luna immediately.

He notices the change of expression instantly. "Interesting."

"Nothing is interesting," I say.

He shakes his head. "There's someone."

"There's nobody," I say.

Even Forest nods *there's somebody*. "Don't date clients."

"You've gone out with clients," Holden says.

"You too." I need the change in subject. Or a way to speed up time. My client is due here in thirty minutes. That's an eternity. Way too long to contemplate my thoughts.

"I have to say it," Forest repeats. "With Chase on paternity leave."

Chase is the guy who runs the shop. He's a serious, no-nonsense, take no shit man who knows how to manage.

He also knocked up Forest and Holden's kid sister Ariel.

They had a baby two months ago. Charlotte. She's cute as far as kids go. I can't say I get the appeal.

Why screw up something pure and innocent? My fucked-up parents fucked up me and Daisy. They didn't mean to. They couldn't help it.

Maybe she's better enough to overcome that shit. Maybe she's okay now.

Me?

Not so much.

"Is that the issue?" Holden's grey-green eyes dart to the mock-up. "Is it the client?" He looks at me, studying my expression. "I don't think so."

"It's nothing," I say.

"How long has it been?" he asks.

Forest shakes his head *you're ridiculous*.

"That's none of your fucking business," I say.

"Excuse me?" Holden makes a show of holding his hand over his head. "Did Oliver Flynn just decline to offer details?"

I shoot him a *stop* look.

He ignores it. "The Oliver Flynn? The dirty bastard who's told me the story of the kinky yoga instructor who wanted to recreate every position in the Kama Sutra multiple times?"

Sure, I told him that story many times. Maybe I embellished a little. For effect.

The kinky yoga instructor did want to try a few near impossible positions. And it was exciting. At the time.

48

For a moment, the memory warms my skin.

For a moment, I see her. A petite brunette with flowing hair, sheer lingerie, a tattoo of Ganesh.

The two of us attempting wheelbarrow. It worked for about ten seconds. Until her wrists folded from the weight of holding half her body.

For a moment, I'm in that night, laughing and groaning and living it up.

I smell the incense. I hear the chanting music. I taste the bourbon.

Everything skips.

The light dulls. The colors grey. The fun fades.

Was it ever fun? Or was it just the booze?

"Are you seeing this?" Holden turns to his older brother. "There's something wrong with him. I think he needs medical attention."

"Are you here to work or fuck off?" Forest asks.

Holden laughs *are you really asking that question?* "This is my process."

"Get lost or get to work."

"Some brotherly love!" Holden feigns insult. "Are you seeing this? What a lack of loyalty."

Strong words from Holden. The guy did fuck my sister. After I specifically asked him to keep an eye on her.

Sure, he joked about how he was going to "introduce her to pleasure" all the time. He spent the entire summer teasing me about his plans to take Daisy's virginity.

It pissed me off, yeah, but I knew it was a joke.

And he knew how important it was to me, that someone keep an eye on her during her birthday trip to Mexico.

So finding out he interpreted that as *fuck her—*

Maybe I should cut him some slack. He says he loves

her. She says she loves him. He does treat her like a princess. And she is over the fucking moon.

Maybe I should be happy for them.

A part of me is.

This other part refuses to let go of the betrayal.

"Where are the details?" He looks to me with that same shit-stirring grin. All smiles and ease and devil-may-care.

"You remember this day two months ago? I invited you to Puerto Vallarta. You promised to keep an eye on Daisy. You did it with your dick." My voice is short. It's harder than I mean it to be, but I don't want to soften it.

"Shit, dude, you know it wasn't like that." His expression gets hazy. "I love her so fucking much. Yeah, I know I should have kept my promise. But I'm not going to apologize for falling in love with her."

Whatever.

"And you can stay pissed if you want," he says. "But it won't stop me from giving you shit."

"Of course," I say.

"And it's not what's good for her. Don't lie to yourself about it being honor or duty or loyalty. It's self-indulgent paternalistic BS," he says.

I look to Forest. He sends me a shrug.

I guess the guy knows a thing or two about holding a grudge. For years, he was totally unable to get over his ex fucking some guy behind his back.

Holden shifts into effortless troublemaker. "So… how long has it been?"

"I'm on a hiatus," I say.

His jaw drops. "No."

"Yeah."

He shakes his head, sending his messy hair in every direction. "No."

I nod *yeah*.

"Oliver Flynn is taking a vow of celibacy?"

"Don't make it into a thing," I say.

He turns to his brother. They exchange a look. A familial one that says everything. Then Holden turns to me. Shakes his head *you're full of it.* "You don't have to tell me why. But we both know it's a thing."

I shrug like I don't care.

He doesn't buy it, but he still moves to his suite.

———

My client arrives early and ready. He sits quietly as I prep him. Declines offers of distraction or conversation.

For a few hours, we work in silence. Nothing but his grunts and the energetic pop-punk soundtrack Forest favors.

Some guy whines about how he wants his ex to drive off a bridge. Even though he totally doesn't care about her. Why does she think he cares anyway?

I guess music from high school trumps newfound happiness. After a ridiculous charade—Forest and his best friend Skye pretended they were a couple, all to make his ex jealous or something—Forest is now happily dating his best friend.

He still dresses in mostly black and listens to angry assholes.

But he's over the moon.

This isn't my sound, but I appreciate the passion.

I'd kill for this kind of energy. Even if it was all anger directed at someone who didn't really deserve it.

The best I have is Holden and we have such a long history.

The asshole is right. My attitude isn't helping Daisy.

I should let it go.

I want to.

I just can't.

Eventually, we finish our set time. I clean and bandage my client. Send him home with instructions and an appointment date next week.

It's a complicated piece. Lots of detail and shading. A few more hours and we'll be done, but, for now, it's a work in progress.

The afternoon moves quickly.

A sugar skull on a tough guy's bicep.

A butterfly on a cute woman's wrist.

An invitation to her place to celebrate her new ink.

For a second, I consider it. Then she mentions a wine vintage and I invent a girlfriend.

I walk her to the door. Promise I wish things were different.

Return to the desk. This is it. After I finish some admin shit, I'm done.

I stretch my arms over my head. Consider the instant coffee maker.

No. Good coffee is one of the only passions I have left. No way am I drinking anything from a pod.

I sit behind the desk. At the shop computer. Let the sounds of the afternoon fill my head as I finish scheduling.

The buzz of a tattoo gun, the energetic guitar riff, the murmur of conversation.

The ding-dong of the bell.

Luna steps inside. She's in a trendy outfit. A white tank tucked into her pale blue jeans. Purple back pack. Pink Chucks.

Silver hair, sexy messy.

Lips a deep pink-red.

Heart-shaped sunglasses covering her pretty eyes.

"Hey." She looks to the speakers and sticks out her tongue. "He's still playing this stuff?"

That gets the attention of everyone here. The buzz ceases. The conversations shift.

Forest looks at us. Loses interest.

Holden tells his client—a cute chick who's definitely flirting with him—to take a break. When she moves toward the bathroom, he turns to us.

Looks from me to Luna, then back to me. "Always good to see you, Luna."

"Yeah. You too." She half-smiles. "Glad you took my advice."

He actually blushes.

Fuck, it's something about Daisy. About their sex life.

That's information I don't need.

"You here for me?" He holds his hand to his chest. Makes a show of fanning himself. "You know what the attention does to me."

"Ollie," she says.

He shoots me a knowing look.

"You're off now, right?" she asks.

"You know his schedule?" he asks.

"Your schedules are on your website." She looks at Holden like he's saying something stupid. Which is a pretty standard exchange for them. "I have to ask you a favor."

"A sexy favor?" Holden asks.

She ignores him. "I have to pick up some stuff. At home. And I need, uh… someone strong. Who can carry a lot of things."

"So you came for Oliver?" Holden asks.

"Don't you have a client waiting?" She gives him another funny look.

"Yeah. Just contemplating a fact I heard earlier today." His eyes meet mine. "Think I may have found the reason."

I shoot him a *don't* look.

He nods *of course not.* "Any reason you're asking Ollie?"

"Will it be faster to tell you to go away or explain?" she asks.

"Explain," he says.

"If you promise to go away after that," she says.

He chuckles, not at all offended, and makes the *scout's honor* gesture.

"I'm staying at the Flynn's place for a while," she says. "While my parents, uh, remodel."

He nods, accepting her explanation. "Staying with Ollie. Damn, good luck."

"Thanks," she says.

"And you too, Ollie." He copies her tone. "I have a feeling you're going to need it."

Chapter Eight

LUNA

Inked Love is a twenty-minute walk from the Flynn place. Since it's just north of the Venice/Santa Monica divide, just off the main drag—

There's no parking. Even in October.

He walked. I walked.

Now, we walk together. He's quiet. The usual Oliver quiet. Only it feels different.

Weighted.

He stops in front of a coffee shop. One of his favorites. Raises a brow *you in?*

"Always," I say.

He nods, opens the door for me, follows me into the tiny shop.

There's no one else here. Just the two of us and the one employee.

Oliver orders a cold brew.

I order an iced Americano. Whip out my wallet before he can swipe his card.

"I can get it," he says.

"You're doing me a favor." I hand the barista my credit card. "I'm getting it."

"You don't have a job."

"And?"

"Where do you get your money?"

Since when does he worry about that kind of thing? I try to keep the mood light. To tease him. "I'm a secret cam girl. I go by Missy MegaTits." I feign shock. "Oh no, my secret's out."

He gives me one of those long, slow once-overs. Assessing my earning potential as a cam girl? Or something else?

"Do you have experience with members of my profession?" I try to keep my tone silly, but my voice disobeys my intent. It drops to something low and breathy.

"Never paid for it."

"Just regular old cyber-sex?"

"Tried it once," he says. "Wasn't really my thing."

The barista looks at us with mild annoyance. He's not at all interested in tales of our sex life.

He wants us to shut up or get out of his space.

It's not possible. The shop is ten feet wide, at most, and the counter takes up half the space.

Still. I worked at a coffee shop all summer. I know annoying clients. I mouth *sorry*, move to the front, motion for Oliver to follow.

He does.

It only puts five feet between us and the barista, but it's the best we can do.

"You couldn't do it," Oliver says. "You have to take orders from customers."

"You think I can't take orders?" I mean to say it in a playful *fuck you* kind of way. Instead, I say it in an *I dare you to order me out of my clothes* way.

His pupils dilate. His tongue slides over his lips. He stares back at me for a second. Almost like he is going to dare me. But he doesn't. "Name one time you have."

"I listen to my coach."

"Uh-huh."

"You think I want to suffer a hundred hundreds?"

"Maybe. But you don't listen to me." He shrugs, trying to sell casual, failing to hide the desire in his voice.

Thankfully, the barista interrupts. Calls out our drinks.

I keep mine black.

Oliver lightens his cold brew with whole milk and simple syrup.

"How do you drink that?" I ask.

"I put the straw in my mouth and suck."

"It's too sweet."

"It's good."

I shake my head *no way*.

He offers me a sip.

Okay, fine. My fingers brush his as I take the cup.

His gaze stays fixed on my lips.

There's intent in his eyes. Like we both know he's picturing my lips wrapped around something else—

Or maybe I'm imagining things.

Why am I imagining things?

Oliver isn't my friend, exactly, but we're friendly. I know him well. Yes, he's sexy and tattooed and troubled.

With that dark hair and those deep eyes.

And I...

Uh...

The point is, yes, Oliver is attractive. But it doesn't affect me like this. Even if I occasionally think about him naked.

Or picture his hands in my hair.

Or his lips on my thighs.

57

I, uh… "What was Holden talking about?" I reach for some way to change the subject.

He runs a hand through his hair. Fights a look of displeasure. "Holden bullshit."

"Right." I take a long sip of my iced Americano. Let out a low sigh. Fuck, that's good. Rich and nutty and refreshing.

He looks at me funny, but he doesn't say anything.

"Anything interesting?"

"My hiatus."

"Oh."

"What?"

"I just thought… I know you guys are awkward, since Daisy—"

"Since he broke his promise to look out for her?" His voice drips with anger. In an Oliver way. Restrained. Hurt.

I want to hold him, comfort him, convince him it's okay.

And tell him he's an idiot. Daisy is an adult. She can choose to date anyone she wants. Even if it's kind of messed up dating her brother's best friend.

Not that I'm contemplating a similar idea.

I would never.

Daisy is my best friend. I'm not risking that.

Or my place to stay.

I'm just—

Ahem. "I thought you'd have told him."

"You know Holden. Makes everything into something."

True. And Oliver tends to hold his cards close. Sure, he's free with dirty stories or tales of drunken debauchery. But he rarely shares the serious stuff. "Is it something?"

He shrugs. "Just a thing I'm trying." He motions to the door. Moves toward it at a quick clip.

I rush after him. "Is there a reason? Why he thinks it's a

thing?" It's definitely a thing. If he's running away from it so quickly.

I don't mind walking fast—I have long legs, after all, and I'm in comfortable shoes—but this isn't really his thing.

He's not slow. More purposeful.

This is something else.

"You need to grab anything at home first?" he asks. "Or should we go straight to your parents' place?"

"We can go straight there."

"You actually need someone to carry stuff?"

"Kinda. I need my clothes. My makeup. Books. It's a lot."

"We can take the car."

I nod. "My car is there. And you don't have space for another."

"We can take my car."

I bite my lip. "Oh. Sure. But, uh, I didn't ask you for your biceps."

"No?"

"No." I take a long sip. Walk faster to keep up with him. "I want someone else there. In case Allison is home."

"You don't want to see her?"

"No. I can't look at her right now." My chest tenses. "She's the one... she's leaving Divya for a younger woman."

"Fuck."

"Yeah."

"I guess... if she was a guy, it would be expected. Rich business owner. Good looking. In great shape."

"And Divya isn't?" I ask.

"Are you really asking me if your mom is hot?"

"You just went on about how my other mom is hot."

He chuckles *I guess so.* "Like you don't talk about how hot Gabe is."

Okay, maybe I mention it. On occasion. But, in my defense, Gabe is smokin'. All tall, and broad, and stoic. Dark hair and clear blue eyes.

Oliver in twenty years.

Not that I—

I just notice attractive men. That's all.

And that's all this is.

Sure, I want Oliver.

But I'm an adult. Unlike Allison, I can control myself.

No matter how much my body protests.

Chapter Nine

LUNA

Thankfully, both my and Oliver's parents live in the residential part of Venice Beach.

Our place is way south of theirs, but, hey, we don't have to cross any major streets. Even with those silly apps routing people through the neighborhood to avoid traffic, the road is clear.

Five minutes of empty streets and cute bungalows.

Oliver parks right in front of my parents' place. Next to the cute lattice gate. The rows of succulents. The stone walkway.

It is a cute house, objectively speaking. Not really like either of my parents.

Allison, my biological mother, is a no-nonsense, tough as nails HBIC (head bitch in charge, usually said with love. Right now... ugh).

Before this particular revelation, I would never have called her a bitch. Okay, I still wouldn't, unless it was in a HBIC/I say it as a compliment thing. I don't care for that word.

The point is... she's tough and serious and not at all

into frills. When she isn't wearing a suit in a neutral color, she's wearing a suit in a power color. And when she's not wearing a suit, she's sipping red wine in a silk pajama set.

Her idea of a casual weekend is pairing a suit with designer flats, sipping black coffee at brunch, then reading a business book as Divya and I play.

Fun is not in her vocabulary.

I guess I found out where she gets her fun. Other women. Like so many male execs before her.

Divya is her polar opposite. Her parents moved to London when she was a baby. She grew up in a city of culture and influence and came out with an eccentric love of family and tossing aside tradition. (They were both studying at Oxford when they met).

Divya loves fun. And not the *fucking other women* kind.

She watches reality TV with me, teaches me how to cook by feel, marvels at my outfits, allows me to test makeup techniques on her.

She's the one who plays at the park or braves the waves at the beach (they're too cold for her, but she tries). She wears fun clothes at pretty much all times. (I'm not sure there are neutrals in her closet). On formal occasions, she busts out a formal Sari. And she shrugs if people look at her twice.

I admire them both.

Or I did.

Allison for her drive and ambition.

Divya for her love and warmth.

Both of them, for being sure of themselves and supportive and madly in love.

They had this plan. Both of them pregnant from the same sperm donor. But it didn't happen for Divya.

So I'm an only child.

And now I'm here. To pick up my stuff and run as quickly as possible.

Neither of their cars is on the street. No shiny black Tesla (Allison) or red convertible (Divya).

The coast is clear. For now.

Oliver studies my expression for a minute. Then he undoes his seat belt. Waits.

Slowly, I take a deep breath. Step out of the car. Onto the sidewalk.

He grabs the suitcases from the trunk. Follows me into the house.

The same as always. A mix of sleek minimalism and cheerful accents. Pristine hardwood floor, bright blue leather couch, orange accent pillows.

It's easy to see the mix of both my parents in the den. And the dining room, with its simple cherry table and its framed prints.

The kitchen. All clutter and mess and color on top of modern counters and stainless steel.

I grab my coffee blend, my chocolate (eight-five percent or bust), my *beach please* thermos, my mermaid-covered mug.

It's too much to hold already. I'm about to drop something when Oliver offers me a shoebox. An old one of his. For some pair of black sneakers, size twelve.

I swallow the joke about men with big shoes and big feet.

Is that actually true? If only I'd picked that as my project for AP statistics.

"Thanks." I set the shoebox on the counter. Carefully arrange the breakable mug in the corner, padded by the bag of coffee beans.

He takes the box from me. Holds it to his chest as he grabs a suitcase and follows me up the stairs.

Upstairs is the same. Sleek hardwood, white walls, framed photographs.

Half of them missing.

The ones of my parents' wedding, their honeymoon, the vacation when Allison was pregnant. Even the pictures of them at notable events in my life.

It's just me. My first day of school, my first swim meet, my kindergarten talent show.

Vacations, school events, the awful year of soccer (anything but running).

The awkward middle school pics. Homecoming dance. Daisy as my date. Then, later the scrubs, as Oliver called them.

My natural hair at my shoulders.

The time I cut it really short.

All the different colors I tried. Dark brown (not my look), jet black (even worse), bright red (nope), platinum blonde (not bad).

My first day of college. My hair already short. My smile wide and authentic.

Did they know they were separating then?

Were they pretending for my sake? Or was Divya as clueless as I was?

I can't say I keep tabs on my parents' love life. Who does? But I notice when they're happy. When they're loving. When they're going on regular dates or fighting nonstop.

They haven't been tense lately. They haven't been arguing about little things. Or debating big ideas.

They've just been… quiet.

Working.

Allison at her company. Divya on her cooking.

Usually, she makes traditional Indian dishes. The

recipes her mother taught her. But the last year or two, she's been expanding. Trying all sorts of cuisines and styles.

Filling the empty hours.

Just like Oliver.

I table the thought as I step into my room. It looks the same as it did this time yesterday. Before they sat me down and delivered the news. Before my family fell apart.

Posters of amazing female musicians—Lorde, Billie Eilish, Halsey, Kimbra. Bright pink comforter. Black desk. Stacks of text books. Messy makeup.

Underwear sitting on the ground. Waiting to be sorted. Shit.

"Don't look at that." I reach out to cover Oliver's eyes.

He pushes my hand away. "I've seen you in less."

His gaze moves over the pile. From the worn cotton to the new mesh.

His eyes stop on a sheer black bodysuit.

They flit to me. Then back to the pile.

It's quick. But his intent is still obvious. He's picturing me in the lingerie.

"I said don't look. Not tell me why you should look." I push him gently. "Turn around. While I pack it."

"You realize I'm here to help you?"

"Turn around while I pack it, please."

He does.

I pick up the suitcase. Lay it on the bed. Toss my underwear into it. Then my three best pairs of jeans, a cute denim skirt, a few plain tees, my favorite blouse, two casual dresses, two party dresses, another pair of Converse, gym clothes, tall boots, combat boots, heels.

Eventually, Oliver turns. Watches as I pack. "You want my biceps?"

My eyes flit to said biceps. He's in his usual arm-revealing get up—black t-shirt and black jeans. Tattoos on display.

God, those arms are sexy. I want them wrapped around my waist. Or covering my chest. Or maybe his hand on my throat—

"Luna? You invited me for help?" he asks.

"More… as a shield. But yeah, if you could pack all those textbooks." I motion to the stack on my desk. "That would help. Thank you." I grab my pajamas. Bras. Two swimsuits, one for practice and one for leisure.

He moves closer as he slips the textbooks into the suitcase. It's all one suitcase. The book is next to my panties. They're clean, but still…

He doesn't mention it. He finishes packing. Motions to the hallway. "Should I make coffee?"

"You just had one."

"Is that a no?"

"Sure, yeah. Thanks." I need a minute to myself. And if he's downstairs, he'll be the first to face the traitor. Win-win. Even if I want to ask why he's drinking so much coffee. Yeah, he loves coffee, but he doesn't love it this much. "I'll meet you down there."

"You can get that suitcase down the stairs okay?" He says it without a hint of condescension. All help. No superiority.

Even so, I don't like the implication. "You're right. I need my big, strong man to carry it for me."

"You asked for my help."

Right. I'm being a bitch. "Thanks. If you want to labor for me, you can. I'll meet you downstairs. Drink the coffee. Watch as you do my bidding."

He chuckles *you would*. Then he moves down the stairs.

I find my silver makeup bag. Gather the essentials.

Then the non-essentials in a tote. My razor, soap, shampoo, dye, hair product.

Daisy has most of this stuff, but I don't want to smell like her.

I gather everything I can in the one suitcase and two bags, then I sit on my bed. Stare at the familiar walls.

My home for the last nineteen years.

The place that's supposed to be safe and comfortable.

This place that's supposed to belong to a happy family.

And now it doesn't.

I stare until a sound interrupts me.

A door opening. Footsteps.

Allison greeting Oliver.

I guess this is it. Time to see if my shield really can protect me.

Chapter Ten

OLIVER

I 'll say this for Mrs. Locke: the woman has impeccable taste.

The wine fridge in the corner of the room is filled with good shit. Expensive bottles that make collectors ooh and ahh.

I never developed a taste for wine. I'll drink it, but I don't have the palate. It's all the same to me.

I guess it doesn't matter now.

This is one time, I don't have to find an explanation for why I'm not drinking.

Or maybe I do?

I'm twenty-one. Mrs. Locke is polite. It's not out of the question.

I hold up my mug. "I fixed coffee. Would you like some?" There. That should stop any offer.

Her gaze flits to the stairs. Luna's room. "If there's extra." She looks to me. Smooths her blazer.

She's in a deep red suit. It's dramatic, with long lines and all sorts of presence. It matches her slick straight hair and her intense eyes.

She has the same grey eyes as Luna, but her hair is almost black and her features are chiseled.

Luna has that sharpness, but she has a softness too. A perfect mix, really.

"You take it black?" I ask as I pour a cup.

"Like Luna." She nods as she takes it. "Thank you, Oliver." She holds my gaze, even as she brings her cup to her lips and takes a sip. "Excellent."

"Thanks."

"She's staying with you for a while?"

"Yeah. Dad said he called."

She nods *he did*. "I suppose she told you what happened?"

"It's none of my business."

Her lip corners turn down. "She did."

"Shit happens."

She just barely nods. "You two are friends?"

"Yeah."

"Only friends?"

"Only friends." My voice lacks conviction.

I try to find it in my coffee. Fail. I guess that doesn't matter.

Luna is my friend. And I know how it feels to want to avoid your parents because they're tearing your life apart.

Sure, as far as I know Allison is a pretty good mom. But it sounds like she's the one leaving.

She might have a good reason. But I doubt that matters to Luna at the moment.

"We promised to make dinner, actually." If I can spare her from this pain, I will. "So I should probably make sure she's ready. Head out."

Allison nods. "Luna's cooking?" Her lips curl into a wistful smile. "Divya always loved teaching her."

"Yeah. She takes instruction pretty well." My thoughts

jump to completely inappropriate places. "In the kitchen." That doesn't help. Only fills my head with images of her bent over the counter, her jeans at her knees, binding her legs so she's powerless to do anything but take me.

"Sometimes." Her laugh is sad. "She's a headstrong young woman. The same as I was at her age."

"Not anymore?"

"I guess it's the same now. But age brings experience. And experience brings certain wisdoms. Sometimes, it's easier to give up one thing to gain something greater."

Uh-huh.

"Sorry. I shouldn't go on." She looks to the stairs. "Luna, please, will you come down here? Say goodbye. I'll get out of your way after that."

Fuck, she looks like Luna did last night. Like she's about to burst into tears. It's different on Allison. She's so restrained. Seeing her on the verge of falling apart—

Maybe I shouldn't give my dad so much shit. He's trying his best. It's just his best is a lot like mine—not good enough.

Allison sips her coffee as she waits. She's quiet. Still. A rock in a river.

But Luna is just as willful. She stays in her room without a peep.

"Let me ask," I say.

I'm not sure why I'm volunteering to help with the family reunion. Some wisdom that came with experience, I guess. If I can help Luna handle her parents' divorce better than I handled mine—well, that's something.

Allison nods *thank you*.

I finish my last sip. Set the mug in the perfectly clean sink. Move up the stairs. "Luna."

"What?"

I knock. "I'm coming in."

Luna mumbles some kind of okay.

I step inside. Leave the door half-open. "There's still coffee."

"I'm okay," she says.

"Your mom wants to talk to you."

She shakes her head *I can't*. "Not right now. Please."

"Just goodbye. If that's it?"

"She's the one fucking someone else. Did I tell you that?" Luna's grey eyes fill with hurt. "Why should I absolve her?"

"Don't absolve her. Just let her know you're okay."

"I'm not okay."

"That you're alive," I say.

"What would you do? If it was your parents?"

"You know what I'd do."

"So why are you suggesting this?" she asks.

"Does what I do work out?"

A laugh falls from her lips. "I guess that's true."

"You really want to be like me?"

She shakes her head. "Just goodbye. That's it. Then I'm out the door."

I nod. Offer my hand.

She takes it. Lets me help her up. Slides a tote bag on her shoulder. A backpack (another KanKen, this one teal) on the other.

I grab the suitcase and lead her down the stairs. To the door.

She stops in front of the kitchen. In front of her mother.

Her expression hardens. She does nothing to hide the sense of betrayal.

"I love you, Luna," Allison says. "I know you're upset. I know I deserve the anger. But I do love you."

Luna nods.

"If you need anything, please. Call. Please," Allison says.

Luna nods *okay*. She stares at the floor for a moment. Then she steps toward the door. As she pulls it open, she whispers, "I love you too."

She doesn't look back to see if her mom hears it.

But I do.

I watch relief, hurt, regret spill over Allison's expression. Then I follow Luna to the car. Pack everything inside.

Drive her home.

Carry her stuff to the spare room.

She waits until I'm in the hallway to say, "Thank you, Oliver."

"Yeah. Sure." I run my hand through my hair. I don't know what to do with this kind of honest gratitude. "I meant what I said about dinner."

"You really need help?"

"Help? Fuck no. You're gonna make it for me."

She half-smiles. "I guess it's only fair." She pushes herself to her feet. Wipes her hands on her jeans. "But I am going to make what I like."

"I know."

"Unless you want to help. That's the only way you get a say."

I nod *I know*. And even though I know I should stay away—my body is already begging me to hold her—I follow her to the kitchen. Stay way, way too close.

———

Luna insists on more pasta. Arrabiata this time. With shrimp.

She asks me to prep the shrimp in a quiet voice. One that isn't at all her.

But her sadness fades the more she concentrates. She chops garlic and tomatoes, boils water, seasons sauce.

By the time we're sitting at the table, topping our arugula with Parmesan, she's at ninety percent. Not all the way to her usual badass, bossy self, but close.

Dad texts that he'll be home late. Then some shit about how I should keep an eye on Luna. And by eye he means keep the pants zipped.

For once, I think of the hurt on Luna's mom's face, and I let it go. He's trying. I'm not getting pissed about it today.

He's right.

Luna needs a friend.

And, fuck it, I do too. If I can actually help her—

That's something.

It's the best I can do right now.

Chapter Eleven

LUNA

Allison's face stays in my head as I study for my chem test. All the hurt and regret and frustration. No *I'm sorry* or *I know I was wrong* or even *I promise I've apologized to my soon-to-be ex-wife for betraying her.*

Only worry.

About my well-being? Or losing my respect?

Maybe I'm being uncharitable. It's not *just* respect with her. I know she loves me. Normally, I know my parents love me the way I know I need swimming.

My favorite dark roast.

The exact shade of eggplant shimmer of my Urban Decay *Rockstar* eye pencil.

Right now...

I finish the chapter. Check my cell.

A group text about our study group. Sure, I can do Sunday evenings.

An *I'm fine, sweetheart, I'm more worried about you* from Divya.

And Daisy, checking in, trying to pretend like she's not checking in.

Has Oliver told her anything?

Is there anything for him to tell her?

Daisy: Are you really staying in the spare room? My room has better air flow.

Luna: And everything is pastel pink.

Daisy: You bought me that comforter.

True. And it's perfect for her. She's sweet, innocent, adorable.

Whereas I...

Usually, that's something I know the way I know my purple eyeliner.

I'm Luna Locke, chemistry student, two hundred breaststroke swimmer, lover of dark chocolate.

Fashionista, punk rock pixie, take no shit badass.

All of that is true. Technically.

But I know it the way I know my parents love me.

It's fuzzy, ill-formed, impossible to describe.

Hard to believe.

Daisy: Would you prefer black? I'm sure Oliver has extras.

Mmm. Oliver's sheets. Do they smell like him?

Are they stained with his—

That should disgust me, but it doesn't.

I barely laugh at the joke. Of course, Oliver has black sheets. Of course, Daisy is teasing me about wanting black sheets.

I wear black all the time (even though it's not really my color).

It's not that I want his sheets.

Or him.

She doesn't know that.

She can't know that.

Luna: How about silver?

Daisy: Am I going to come home to find you dressed in all silver?

Luna: Down to the bra and panties.

Daisy: Why can I see your bra and panties?

Luna: Hmm. Good point.

Daisy: Are you testing your sexting material on me?

Luna: I would never.

Daisy: Uh-huh.

Luna: Scout's honor.

Daisy: Are you set on the spare room?

Luna: If I stay in your room, you'll have this obstacle between you and visiting home.

Daisy: Or I'll have an excuse to stay at Holden's.

Luna: Gross.

Daisy: You're the one who told me to fuck him.

Luna: No. Fuck him. Fuck him sideways. Then come here so we can stay up late watching Dawson's Creek.

Daisy: With chocolate?

Luna: I'll buy the seventy percent you like.

Daisy: The salted almond?

Luna: You think I've forgotten?

Daisy: Tempting...

Luna: But not compared to sleeping next to your beloved?

Daisy: It just feels so good when his arms are around me.

Luna: I know what you mean.

My eyes flutter closed. My thoughts flit to Oliver. His low grunt, his blue eyes, his tattooed biceps.

The pressure of his body against mine.

The warmth of his skin.

The hardness.

The sound of his breath—

Fuck. I'm not fantasizing about my best friend's brother while I'm texting her. That's a new low.

I'm just—

Which is worse? Thinking about Mom or thinking about Oliver?

The reason why I need to stay here.

The reason why staying here is far too dangerous.

Daisy: Are you okay?

Luna: I don't know. It's weird. I never thought it would happen to my parents. Maybe everyone says that.

Daisy: Uh, no.

Luna: I feel silly complaining. You had it so much worse.

Daisy: You're not complaining. I asked. And, sure, my parents were a nightmare. But they were always a nightmare. You're losing something real.

Luna: Am I though? Or have they been lying to me all this time?

Daisy: You really think so?

Luna: I don't know. Allison was lying about seeing another woman. What else isn't true?

Daisy: Maybe it's just that.

Luna: Maybe.

Daisy: They do love you.

Luna: Do I have to acknowledge that?

Daisy: No.

Luna: Is it really cool if I stay here forever?

Daisy: Only if you're ready to watch teen soaps every night.

Luna: Deal. Wait, does this mean I have to eat seventy percent dark chocolate?

Daisy: No. You can stick with the eight-five.

Luna: Then good luck getting rid of me.

Daisy: Why would I want to?

Luna: I miss you.

Daisy: I know. I miss you too. But I'll be home for Thanksgiving.

Luna: That's in a million years.

Daisy: I might come sooner. If I have a light weekend.

Luna: You promise?

Daisy: Yeah. But you know I'll spend half that time with Holden.

Luna: It's not "Sisters before misters unless he makes you come." It's just "sisters before misters."

Daisy: You should be proud of me for getting some.

Luna: Does that mean you have a story?

Daisy: Maybe.

Luna: Tell please.

It takes a few more requests, but eventually, she spills the details of a phone sex session with Holden.

The tattoo artist turned my sweet, innocent best friend into a sex-crazed pervert.

They're good together. She loves him. He treats her like a princess.

And I understand why she wants to stay with him. Why she'll see him first when she visits.

The girl needs to get hers.

I'm okay stepping aside.

I just miss coming first.

Even this thing with my parents…

I know it's not my fault. I know I can't control it. That she's the one who chose to have an affair.

But I miss coming first there too. Our family coming first.

Allison chose something else.

Maybe she had her reasons. Maybe it's complicated.

But she still chose to tear our family apart.

I can't look at her.

I just can't.

So I'm going to have to find a way to stay here without touching Oliver.

Even if it kills me.

Chapter Twelve

OLIVER

The next day, I fix dinner. Eat with Luna. Leave the leftovers—and the mess—for dad.

Luna studies at the table.

I fix decaf.

When I sit, she hands me her flash cards. Asks me to quiz her on European history.

When we're finished, we celebrate with dark chocolate and two episodes of *The Bachelorette*. I hate to admit it, but it's pretty entertaining watching these idiots fall all over themselves to impress a woman who clearly prefers another guy.

Anything to stay on TV, I guess.

She goes to sleep before me. I wish her good night. Inhale the familiar scent of her shampoo. Lie in my bed, trying to read, failing to sleep.

In the morning, I wake, dress, jog, shower, fix coffee for two.

She arrives just in time to request eggs. And toast. With butter, please. Real butter. None of that dairy free butter.

"Why would I have dairy free butter?" I ask.

"The place we get brunch only has dairy-free butter." She sticks out her tongue. "You know I don't mind veggie food. I'll eat dal all day. Or almond milk. Coconut ice cream. Whatever. But the fake butter…" She sticks out her tongue again. "Disgusting."

"So you want the veggie meatballs when we go to Ikea?"

Her nose scrunches in distaste.

"We are going? This weekend? To get you stuff."

"Of course."

"Am I not invited."

"No. It would be good to have your… biceps."

I actually flex for her.

She laughs. "Impressive. But we'll see what they can do."

I pour her another cup of coffee.

She sighs with gratitude. Groans through her first few sips. "You know, Ollie, for a brooding asshole, you're not too bad."

"You flatter me."

"I do try." She smiles.

And I melt.

————

QUICKLY, IT BECOMES A ROUTINE.

Breakfast and dinner with Luna.

Trashy reality shows with dessert.

The company of someone I like. Who doesn't think I'm a fuckup. Who appreciates my help.

Friday morning, I smile when she groans over her coffee. I laugh when she complains we're out of dark chocolate.

And when she stretches her arms and lets out a yawn—

Well, it's only natural my eyes go to her bare stomach. It doesn't mean anything.

It's not like I'm desperate to touch her. Not at all.

"Don't eat too much," I say as I set a plate of eggs in front of her. "You need room for the veggie meatballs."

Her nose scrunches in distaste.

"I will if you will." I hold out my hand.

"We suffer together?"

"Yeah."

"We could just not suffer."

"Where's the fun in that?"

She shakes.

Chapter Thirteen

LUNA

Mid-morning on a Friday, the traffic is light.

We zip down the 405 in Oliver's car, to the sounds of some Nirvana album, and the sights of sun-bleached concrete.

All this time to design the perfect room.

Since my bedroom—the one I designed over the last eighteen years—is no longer a perfect space.

I shouldn't complain. I'm an adult. Plenty of people leave the house the day they turn eighteen. Or sooner. When they're way too young.

Maybe I don't have my parents' emotional support, but I do have their financial support.

Physically, my house is a perfectly safe place.

Is it really so bad it's an emotional landmine?

That I have to watch my parents sell our house, argue over assets, ask me where I want to stay on Thanksgiving and Christmas?

I'm the one that gets to choose.

I'm the one that has to hurt them.

One of them.

I close my eyes. Focus on the warmth of the sun. The softness of my tank top. The steady mumble of the music.

There isn't much I'll say in favor of Kurt Cobain, but damn did the guy know how to project an uncomfortable numb.

Oliver's fingers tap the steering wheel. He's quiet.

He's usually quiet. Even now that we're spending all this time together, drinking our morning coffees, making dinner, watching *The Bachelorette*—

He's always there, quiet and steady and sure.

Only, right now, he's not.

He's frantic. Well, by Oliver standards.

He's tapping too fast. Like he's got no other way to unleash his energy.

Light floods my senses as I open my eyes. It's way too bright. Sunglasses now.

Even if they make it harder to understand Oliver's expression.

There's something on his mind. I have no idea what it is. And I want to know. Too much. Way too much.

Not falling for my best friend's brother.

My new roomie.

The only person in my life who doesn't want to convince me to let Mom's affair go.

I motion to the stereo. "Isn't this enough misery?"

"There's a limit?"

My laugh is light. Easy. "For you, no. But for me. The pain of listening to Nirvana… it's all I can take."

"You want to play Lorde, don't you?"

I press my hands together. "Please."

His eyes flit from the road to me. "Are you begging?"

"If that's what it will take." I hold up my hands. "Please, Oliver Flynn, the powerful and merciful. Please change the music to Lorde before I go insane and pick up your cell and toss it out the window because that's the only way to stop this awful grunge music."

"Well, when you put it like that." He shakes his head *you're ridiculous* and hands me his cell.

"Thanks." My fingers brush his as I take it. Mmm. His hand just feels good. Warm and strong. I already want it everywhere.

And I am not thinking about that. Nope. Music. Songs. I'm playing one. Something.

Melodrama. Right. There. I pull it up on Spotify. Cut Kurt off mid-sentence in favor of my favorite Kiwi songstress.

Green Light flows through the speakers.

"Ah... so much better, don't you think?" I hold the cell to my chest. Lean back in the chair. Let my shoulders soften. Maybe everything else is fucked up. But I have music. I have a friend who will go to Ikea with me. I even have a lunch of veggie meatballs to fear.

Oliver's eyes flit to me again. He takes in my expression with a smile. Shakes his head. "Terrible." But his smile only gets wider.

Every song, he shakes his head *terrible.*

Every time, his smile gets a little wider.

————

WE PARK, CLIMB THE STAIRS TO THE SECOND FLOOR, SCAN the fake rooms for possible furniture.

"You could take Daisy's room, you know?" Oliver steps into a fake studio bedroom. It's tiny. Only a futon, a TV, a two-person table, two chairs, a fake sink, microwave, stove.

"She said the same thing." I follow him into the space. Not that there's much of it. He's right there. Close enough to touch. Close enough to push onto the couch and mount.

"But it's hers. I don't want her to feel like she can't come home."

He nods. "I think that too. About moving."

I run my fingers over the futon. Black. Soft. Not at all supportive. "That she'd visit less."

"Wouldn't she?" His voice softens.

"I don't know. She could still see you. But she... she'd be disappointed."

"I know." He shakes his head *of course she would*. Sits on the cheap futon. Pats the spot next to him. "This is probably what I could afford. If I want to move into a place near the shop."

"You're moving out?"

"Eventually." He folds one leg over the other. Looks up to me. *Are you going to sit or not?*

I do. But he's so close. Too close. God, he smells good. Like his earthy shampoo. "Eventually, in a few weeks. Or eventually... eventually?"

"I don't know." He presses his palm into his knee, pressing his leg into the cushion. "There's shit with my dad. I'm trying to deal. To keep my promise to Daisy, to stay here all year, but he's too fucking annoying."

"New shit?"

"Kind of."

Hmm. Gabe and Oliver do have an uneasy relationship.

And the tension at any shared dinner is incredibly thick. Like, they barely talk to each other thick.

Gabe tries, but Oliver shrugs it off.

And not in his usual quiet *I'm hanging on the sidelines* way. In a more *leave me the fuck alone* way.

But what's changed? Gabe always gives Oliver shit about drinking.

Oliver always shrugs it off.

Only now Daisy is at Berkeley.

And I'm here.

"Is it me?" I turn to Oliver. "If I'm giving you grief, you can tell me."

"Of course, you're giving me grief. You're a pain in the ass."

"Hey!"

"You said I could tell you."

"Not in such a rude way," I say.

"Just acting like you."

"When am I ever rude?"

"When?" He raises a brow *really*. "What about when you threatened to throw my cell out the window?"

"I was warning you. About an involuntary response."

"When you order me to make you dark roast."

"You love that."

He chuckles *maybe*. "It's still rude."

"But you do love it."

"I might." His eyes flit to my chest. "But only 'cause it reminds me of other times with bossy women."

"You like bossy women?"

"Not going there. Not with you. Not right now."

"You brought it up," I say.

He pries his eyes from my chest. "Even so." He turns to the fake TV. "It's not you. It's other shit. Without Daisy here, it's not worth it."

"Is it really that bad? He's never home."

"I could say the same thing about your parents."

"That's not fair," I say.

"I know. That's why I didn't say it." His eyes flit to me. "Your mom looked really fucking sad."

"She's leaving for a woman half her age."

"Half? Really?" he asks.

"Close enough."

He raises a brow.

"I don't have to justify myself to you. I remember what you were like when your parents separated. You were an obnoxious shit."

"When have I ever been an obnoxious shit?"

"You were running away from it. Getting in fights. Drinking all the time. Leaving Daisy alone with it."

His lips curl into a frown. "Yeah."

"Sorry. That wasn't fair—"

"No. You're right. I did. I wasn't there for my sister and I should have been."

Is that why he's here now? Some way to erase his past sins? That's sweet, but I don't want it to be true.

I want him here for me.

Because he likes me.

Because he wants to be around me.

His eyes meet mine. "I forgot what I was going to say. You're distracting me."

"How am I distracting you?"

He gives me a long, slow once-over. Raises a brow. "Are you really asking that question?"

"What? My outfit?"

He nods *obviously*.

"What about it?"

"What about your skin-tight jeans? And your low-cut tank top? What about the lace-up combat boots that scream *fuck me in only these*?"

"The boots do not say that."

"Uh-huh." He eyes my boots more carefully. "What are those, hiking boots?"

"They're Timberland, yeah."

"Only with a chunky heel. You're gonna hike in that?"

"I might," I say.

"Yeah, hike into someone's bed." He shakes his head *get*

real. "I'm not complaining. I'm just saying, you dress to impress."

"And you don't?"

He shrugs *I guess*. "It's different for guys."

"Sure. But your jeans are snug on your hips."

"Are they?"

"And they're slung just low enough," I say.

He shrugs like he doesn't notice.

"You know they make your ass look fantastic."

"My ass always looks fantastic," he says.

"Because you spend ten hours a week at the gym."

"It's not for looks."

This time, I shoot him the *get real* look.

"It's an outlet. For my energy."

"You have energy?"

He play swats me. "See. Rude."

"You're the one listening to Nirvana all the time."

"What's that have to do with shit?"

"No energy there." I imitate Kurt Cobain's mumble.

Ollie cracks a smile. "That's fucking adorable."

"Spot-on, you mean."

"Sure." He chuckles.

I finish the chorus. Move to the verse. Get the first line. Forget the second. Go right back to the chorus.

His smile widens. "The makeup too."

"What about it?"

"What about it?" He makes a show of pouting. Blowing me a kiss. "That's *I love to suck dick* red."

"Excuse me?"

"I'm just saying."

"You are just saying?"

He nods *yeah*. "Been with a lot of women. The ones with that shade of red always..." He shrugs *what can I say*. "I don't want it to be true. It just is."

"Allison wears this color," I say.

"Well, maybe it's just a love of performing oral."

"Oh my god."

"I can see it with her. She's reserved most of the time. Always in control. When she lets her hair down, I bet she's fucking wild. But still in control. Just pinning—"

"That's my mom!"

His laugh gets big and hearty. Big enough it wipes the tension from his expression. "You brought it up."

"You brought it up."

He shakes his head *uh-uh*. Motions to my lips.

"This is not for your benefit."

"I'm the only person you've seen today."

"We're in public." I motion to a young couple walking past us. They glance in our direction. Keep their distance.

"You're scaring them."

"You're scaring them." I push him. "You know I cut my hair so less guys would get that impression."

"The impression you love to suck dick?"

"Excuse you!"

"It's what you said," he says.

"The platinum. It made them think... I guess they watch too much porn."

He nods *yeah, I see that.* "So this." He reaches out. Brushes a stray hair behind my ear. "Is all because a bunch of assholes thought you'd happily drop to your knees?"

"Kind of."

He smiles, amused. "I like it." His fingers trail my cheek. My chin. "Brings out your eyes. Your jaw. Your neck." He pulls his hand back. "It's sexy."

I swallow hard.

"And it suits you." His eyes bore into mine. "Guess I should find one of those assholes. Thank him."

"Oh my god." I push him again. Harder this time.

He grabs my arm. His fingers curl around my wrist. He looks down at me. For a second, he pauses. Just stares at me.

For a second, I pause. Just stare back at him.

He's so handsome. And so close. And so kissable.

I never thought that about Oliver. But he is.

Sexy and difficult and kissable as fuck.

I suck a breath through my nose. Push an exhale through my teeth.

Jump at the sound of a familiar voice.

"Luna? Is that you?" the voice asks.

Shit.

Oliver turns to face Sean. Ollie shakes his head *I hate this asshole*. But he smiles. "Sean, good to see you."

I clear my throat. Stand. Move away from the magnetic energy compelling me to kiss Ollie. "It's uh, good to see you."

"Oh, so you and Oliver..." Sean raises a brow. "How interesting. I wouldn't think he's your type."

"Oh, we're just..." I motion to Oliver, asking him to finish my sentence. "We're..."

He smiles at Sean and says. "We're madly in love."

Chapter Fourteen

LUNA

Sean forces a smile. "Wow, really. I can't believe it."
He offers his hand.

Oliver stands. Shakes with a firm grip. "You
look good. You lose weight?" He smiles in a knowing way.
Knowing it annoys Sean.

Sean is always trying to get built. Or he was when we
were together. I haven't seen him in months. Who knows
what he's doing.

In fact—

"What are you doing here?" I ask.

Sean looks at me funny. "Buying furniture."

"Isn't it a little... not your style?" I fail to find a polite
way to say *we both know you think Ikea is beneath you.* Sure,
Sean is a yuppie in training, down to the khakis, polo shirt,
and single visible tattoo. But he never tires of reminding
people his parents could buy theirs.

"My girlfriend loves it," he says.

"Your girlfriend?" Oliver asks.

Sean nods. "She's at the cafe. Grabbing coffee."

"Extra cream and sugar?" I ask.

"Of course." His smile stays forced. His light eyes stay smug. "You going to Patrick's birthday?"

"Huh?" I think Patrick works at the shop.

"He did that, right?" Oliver motions to the tattoo on Sean's forearm. An anchor with *carpe diem* on the ribbon. "It's pretty badass." He looks at me and raises a brow.

Somehow, that gets across his intention. *Patrick sure did what he could with that lame as fuck quote. Are you one hundred percent cliché or just mostly cliché?*

I guess Oliver really doesn't like Sean. He's always been a little irritated by Sean. Even when we were dating.

Because of how Sean treats me? Or something else?

There's plenty to hate.

Sean is spoiled, condescending, oblivious to other people's needs.

It's just… he's also handsome, smart, witty, and incredibly charming.

It took a while to realize there wasn't much beyond *spoiled rich boy* besides *spoiled rich boy*.

"Yeah. Thanks." Sean smiles. "So how long have you two… you're Daisy's brother, right?"

"Not long enough if you ask me." Oliver slides his arm around my waist. "You know Luna. She's a fucking dream."

"Uh-huh," Sean says.

"It's new," I say. "And, yes, he is. Daisy's at Berkeley. Remember?"

Sean's eyes turn down for a second. He always wanted to go to USC—it's the family school—but he still applied to Berkeley. And he still cursed the UCs for not recognizing his brilliance. "Of course. And how's your semester going? Besides your football team losing to ours?"

"Yeah. Go Bruins." I make a fake *rah* chant. As much as I love swimming, and participating in competitive swimming, I don't really care about other sports. Especially ones Sean enjoys. "Between my chem lab, European history, and Microeconomic Theory, I'm really busy."

"Really? You're taking an economics class?" He looks at me like I'm crazy.

"Yeah, who would imagine, the woman with a CEO mother might learn about money," Oliver says.

Sean lets out a fake laugh. "Right, yeah." He looks toward the stairs. The ones that lead up to the cafe.

"Need that coffee, huh?" Oliver asks.

"One of those days." Sean forces a smile. "I guess I don't have to tell you how Luna loves coffee."

Oliver nods. "I love it too. In fact, I think we should grab some." He pulls me a little closer. "What do you think, angel? You want some coffee?"

Angel. "Sure, yeah." *Angel.*

Fuck, it sounds good on his lips. It does something to me. To my chest, my sex, my legs.

They're not moving. They're stuck together. They're barely holding me up.

"You cold?" Oliver makes a show of running his hand over my side. "You're shivering."

"Oh. Okay." Conscious thought flees my brain.

Oliver slips his jacket off his shoulders. Hangs it over mine. "Better?"

It smells like him. It's so warm and heavy and safe. "Yeah. Better. Coffee?"

Sean nods. "I'll walk with you. See what Missy is up to."

Oliver shoots me a look. *Of course, that's her name.*

He motions *after you.* Presses his palm into my back as he leads me up the stairs.

Sean follows.

Somehow, I move. One step. Two. Three.

We make it to the cafe.

It's wide and bright and airy. And totally free of a woman Sean's age who isn't done with his bullshit.

Sean checks his cell. "She's in the bathroom. Loves to fix her makeup. A lot like you."

"Uh-huh." I try to ignore his *women, huh* tone.

He refuses to drop it. "You look good, Luna. Still dressed to kill."

"Thanks." I know it's not a compliment, but I take it as one anyway.

"And your hair," he says. "The silver suits you. And it looks good short too. Probably less high-maintenance."

Anyone listening would think he's doling out compliments. But I know better.

I know what he means: *Are you ever going to grow up? Act like a lady. Dress like a lady.*

Of course, I had to dump you. I can't deal with a woman who's so much. Can't you do one thing normally? One time?

Do you really have to ask so much at every opportunity?

It's just hair, for fuck's sake! Do something normal with it! You really think this punk rock pixie thing is cute?

"Yeah." Oliver just smiles at him. "I like her new cut too. Sexy, don't you think?"

Sean clears his throat.

"Mmm." Oliver makes a show of running his fingers over my neck. "I love it. Especially love it in my hands when Luna is coming on my cock."

Sean's jaw drops.

"Or, fuck—Guess I don't have to tell you how good she is with her mouth." Oliver smiles, pure serenity. "It was good to see you, Sean. Glad you haven't changed." He presses his palm into my lower back.

I'm too frozen to move.

Guess I don't have to tell you how good she is with her mouth.

"Angel? The coffee?" He presses harder. "We should grab it now."

"I want to..." Did he... Did I...

Oh my god.

Sean stares at us, dumbstruck.

"Luna." Oliver slides his arm around my waist. He pulls me closer. Pulls me with him as he takes a step toward the cafe. "See you later, Sean."

Sean stares.

I let Oliver lead me.

I...

He...

What...

Guess I don't have to tell you how good she is with her mouth.

My thighs shake. My toes curl. My breath hitches.

I don't even like—

"Luna? Do you want the coffee?" Oliver lowers his voice to a near whisper. "Your ex is still looking."

"Yeah." I keep my eyes on the cafeteria line. All sorts of weird foods. And the coffee right there. In the middle.

I take a step toward it.

Oliver follows. "Are you okay?"

"Did you really say that?" My gaze flits to his eyes. My cheeks flush immediately.

"Say what?"

"That you... that I..."

"That you're good at giving head?"

"You used different words."

"You want me to repeat that?" He chuckles, but it's not his usual above it all tone. It's almost... nervous.

"Do you think about that?"

"You don't want me to answer that." He stops at the machine. Grabs two cups. Motions to the options. Dark and light roast. "Dark?"

"Yeah."

He fills the cup to the top.

"You were just saying that, right?" My hand brushes his as I take the cup. "You don't really think about me—"

He cuts me off. "Do you really want me to answer that?"

Chapter Fifteen

LUNA

Do you really want me to answer that?

Right. We're sane people. We aren't talking about how I caught him fucking himself.

We aren't discussing what he imagines when he fucks himself.

And, really, he should be more generous in his fantasies. I mean, sure, they're his fantasies. He can think whatever he wants.

And it's not as if I dislike that particular activity.

I mean, I don't really like it. But I could. In theory.

It's just Sean was too aggressive. And I have a sensitive gag reflex. And he was never grateful. It was like he expected me to blow him just because he existed.

Is Oliver the same way?

Or does he groan a thank you so deep and needy it makes my sex clench—

"Luna." He cuts me off again. "I'm gonna stand next to you until his 'girlfriend' shows up."

"Yeah." Right. I'm standing here, holding this cup of

coffee. And Sean is sitting at a table, waiting, pretending not to watch us.

"We aren't talking about it."

"Right." I nod.

"So you should make it less obvious you're thinking about it."

"You're the one who said—"

"Pissed him off, didn't it?"

My gaze flits to Sean. He's staring at his phone, all pouty and frustrated. That *why can't you understand what I want* look of his.

Was he always this irritating? Or is it just that he decided I was too much work?

The only guy I ever loved—my boyfriend of eighteen months—deemed me difficult.

Too hard to please.

Too demanding.

Too…

I'm not even sure. Just that he did the math and arrived at the conclusion *Luna isn't worth the effort*.

Whatever.

He's not worth the effort.

"Fuck." Oliver chuckles. "He looks so mad."

He does.

"Like he wants to deck me, but he's afraid he can't take me."

"He could," I say.

"You're defending your ex-boyfriend?"

"If you're going to fight, you should know what you're up against."

He shakes his head *shameful*. "He looks pathetic."

"Because he's picturing us…" Ahem.

"'Cause he's picturing you sucking my cock?"

"Jesus, Oliver." My blush spreads to my chest. It's ridiculous. I don't get nervous. I just...

"Fuck, he's so jealous. I think he's gonna do it."

"He's in good shape."

Oliver shrugs *whatever*. Sure he can take Sean. "I would hit him. If you asked."

"Why would I ask?"

"Didn't he dump you?"

"Thanks for the reminder."

"Just saying."

"Just saying?" I swallow a sip. Mmm. Dark and rich. Surprisingly good for a furniture store. I let out a groan.

Oliver stares with rapt attention. "You like it?"

Not going there. "It's good. Thanks."

He turns to his coffee. Adds sugar and half-and-half. Takes a long sip. "I got it." He motions to the register. "Stay here."

"I can."

He shakes his head *no way*. "Please. I owe you. For the satisfaction I'm feeling right now."

Okay... sure.

I sip my coffee, trying not to picture Oliver's suggestion, half-watching Sean as he stands, greets his girlfriend, keeps glancing our way.

She's exactly what I imagine. A petite brunette (natural color and it's long and neat) in an adorable yet tasteful dress and flats.

Is she oblivious to what a dickhead he is?

Or do his other traits make up for his attitude?

Sean *is* incredibly handsome. As handsome as Oliver. In a more clean cut, future finance guy way.

No intense blue eyes. Or strong eyes.

Or tattoo just above his hip—

Ahem.

Oliver rejoins me at the counter. "Five more minutes."

"Huh?"

"Of enjoying his pain."

And that sexy, deep voice. The throaty laugh. The wicked grin.

The, uh…

God, Oliver is hot. It's wrong. It's really, incredibly wrong.

Oliver chuckles as Sean glances at us again. "Was that the thing to say?"

"Huh?"

"Did you not…?"

Not going there. "Why do you want to know?"

"Curious."

Why is he curious? We are friends. And friends talk. But this isn't friends talking.

It's something else.

"What about?" I ask.

"If you don't want to talk about it, that's fine."

"I don't *not* want to talk about it," I say.

He shoots me a *bullshit* look, but he doesn't say anything.

"I can talk about it."

"Sure."

"It's just not fair. If you're the one asking me all the questions."

"You want to play twenty questions?"

I swallow another sip. Take the dare. "Sure."

"Okay, a question for a question."

Right. A question for question. That's fair. It's going to kill me, but it's fair.

"You can go first," he says.

Right. I can go first. I can ask him anything. About his sex life. Like why he's so obsessed with whether or not I blew Sean on a regular basis. "Do you ask the women you fuck to…"

"To blow me?"

"Yeah." My cheeks flush.

His fingers skims the plastic lid. "Not usually."

"Oh."

"Oh?" he asks.

"In my experience, men are… enthusiastic about that particular act."

"You don't like it?"

That's not really answering the question, but okay, fine. It is his turn. "Sometimes… I don't like it rough," I say.

"Ah."

I ignore the implications. "I have a sensitive gag reflex. So I prefer… not too rough." I'm going to die. Literally die. "And I need him to finish somewhere else."

"Where?"

"Where?"

"Yeah." His eyes flit to my lips. Shoulders. Chest. "Where do you like guys to come?"

"In a condom."

He chuckles. "If you're sucking them off." His gaze stops on the v-neck of my tank top. "On your tits?"

"Is that what you like?"

He makes this *mmm* sound. It's music. Poetry. *Hell yes, every yes, absolutely yes.*

And now that image is in my head.

In Technicolor.

Oliver wants to come on my tits.

What the actual fuck?

He looks back to Sean, who is now only half-watching us. And half talking to his girlfriend, who has no idea we're here. "You think she's into that?"

"How would I know?"

"She looks sweet. Like she only does missionary."

"Sweet can be deceiving." I don't add details about how Daisy is a total freak now.

He doesn't ask. Just nods *true*. "When you asked him to slow down... did he not take that well?"

"I tried to do what he liked for a while."

"And when you didn't?"

"He made it clear he preferred things a different way."

Oliver's eyes narrow. "He pushed you?"

"No. It was more like... maybe we shouldn't talk about this."

"Maybe I should hit him."

"It wasn't like that."

His eyes find mine. This time, there are no nerves in his deep blue eyes. Only fire. "Seriously, Luna, if he pressured you—"

"He didn't."

He arches a brow, not quite buying it. But he still drops it. "Seems like an asshole."

"Yeah."

"Small dick?"

"Oh my god."

"Guess it can't be too small. Or it wouldn't trigger your gag reflex."

Kill me now.

"No. I bet he's one of those guys who thinks because he's big he doesn't have to try."

I clear my throat.

He chuckles, mostly at ease. "Fuck, called it."

"I thought we were—"

"Pretty sure I have eighteen questions left. Or seventeen. Unless you want to stop."

I should say *yes. Of course. This is silly*. Something to that effect.

But I don't.

Instead, I say. "It's my turn then, right?"

He nods *yeah*.

"And I can ask you anything?"

"Anything." He holds up his drink. "Lay it on me. I'm ready for whatever you've got."

Chapter Sixteen

OLIVER

Luna's blue eyes stay on mine for a minute. Then she turns her attention to her drink. Wraps her pretty red lips around her cup.

Swallows softly.

Fuck, she's gonna kill me. That smart mouth—

She doesn't like it rough. I can do that. I can go as soft as she likes.

And I'm more than happy to come on those lush tits.

Fuck—

I need to think about something else.

Like her dickhead ex.

That stupid asshole Sean is still watching us. Someone needs to punch him and his smug face.

He's looking at me like he's sure she's traded down. Like he's so special because he's a sophomore at USC and I'm a tattoo artist without a college degree.

Like he's a billionaire and I'm the fucking help.

"You really don't like him," she says.

"Is that your question?"

"No. It's just curious."

No. He's an asshole. Completely undeserving of her.

Sure, he's handsome, in good shape, on the path to riches—

But he's a dickhead.

Obviously not a generous fuck.

Obviously the kind of douche who thinks she's slumming it in a bad boy phase.

Like he's so special dating some girl who walked out of an LL Bean catalog.

If anyone is in a phase, it's him.

"You're sure he never pushed you?" I ask.

She nods.

"'Cause I would love the excuse to kick his ass."

"He has friends. And you need your hands to work."

Even so. I hate his smug grin. I hate his douchey face. I hate his stupid voice. I can practically hear him *please baby, you know I like it, if you love me you'll*—

Whatever.

If he fucks with her, I'm going to hit him. Asshole has it coming. No one fucks with my friends.

"It's my question, isn't it?" she asks.

I nod *yeah*.

"What do you normally do?"

"Do?"

"With your short-term relationships?"

That's a nice euphemism for her. I guess she's still uncomfortable.

Or distracted.

Is she thinking it too?

Fuck, if I could have my way with her, lay her on that table, roll her pants to her ankles, dive between her legs—

Goddammit. "I usually warm a woman up and get to the point."

"And how do you warm a woman—"

I hold up my right hand. "I need my hands for more than work."

She chuckles. "True."

"That's a second question, by the way."

She ignores me. "You don't go down on women?"

"Sometimes."

"You don't like it?"

"Pretty sure that's a third question." I check Sean's stare one more time.

He's looking at us. Ignoring whatever his girlfriend is saying.

I wrap my arm around Luna's waist. Bring my lips to her ear. "Want to make him jealous?"

"Why do *you* want to make him jealous?"

"'Cause he's looking at you like you traded down."

"So it's for your sake?"

"Both our sakes."

She makes that *hmm* noise that means *I'm not sure if I buy it.*

"Is it a problem?"

She leans into my touch, playing it up. "Go for it."

I make a show of running my hand over her side.

Bad idea. My entire body hums. Fuck, she's so soft and curvy. Her top is smooth and thick, but I can still feel the warmth of her skin.

I need her clothes gone.

I need her body under mine.

I need my name on her lips.

"I like it." I lower my voice to a whisper. "I just… keep it more straightforward. If it's a casual thing." Shit gets personal too fast. I can't handle personal. Better to keep lines clear.

"You do non-casual things?"

"There are degrees of casual."

Her eyes flit to Sean. Then they flutter closed.

"Was he any good at it?"

"He was. But he didn't do it much."

Fuck, I really don't like him.

"He was… well, he wasn't huge. More above average. But he… you called it." Her voice drops to a whisper. "What about you?"

"What about me?"

"Are you like that?"

I shake my head. "Always make sure a woman comes first."

"Oh." Her cheeks flush.

"It's a responsibility."

"Huh?"

"The size. With great power—"

"Oh my god." Her eyes blink open as she laughs. "You're pulling out the Spider-Man quote to talk about your dick?"

"It's true."

Her laugh gets louder. "That's… oh my god." She turns to the counter. Presses her palms into the surface. "I'm glad you think of it like that."

You'll be glad when you sit on my cock. "Don't you wish Sean had thought about it like that?"

"Kind of, actually. It just sounds…" She laughs so hard her tits shake. "It does sound ridiculous."

I pick up her cup. Shake it to check the level. Empty. "Want another?"

"Maybe. We should probably get going…" She motions to the stairs. "I do need stuff. For the spare room."

"You could take Daisy's."

She looks at me *of course I couldn't.*

It's like she's saying *of course, I can't sleep where your sister sleeps. You wouldn't want to fuck me in her bed.*

But that's in my head.

There's no way she'd go there.

Is there?

———

THERE'S NOTHING LIKE AGONY ON A DOUCHEBAG'S FACE.

It's the best thing I've felt in ages.

I help Luna without complaint. I take measurements, debate color schemes, test couch firmness, roll chairs.

Then Sean sends her a *nice to see you/stay in touch/I'm still thinking about you sucking off your boyfriend. It's going to be the go-to image in my spank bank for the next three months—*

Okay, all it says is *it was great to see you & your new man. Hope I'll see you at Patrick's b-day party. Stay in touch.*

But I don't even care that I'm going to have to see this asshole again—

Or that my coworkers' booze-soaked birthday party is coming to test my resolve.

Those are problems for later.

For now, I'm good.

Luna laughs as she slips her cell into her back pocket. She plops on a red armchair. Spreads out wide. Then sits up straight, pulls her legs onto the cushion and folds them over each other.

She looks up at me. "You think?"

"For the office?"

She nods. "I want something bold."

"It's not quite *I love dick red*, but it's nice."

Her cheeks flame. "That isn't a thing."

"You think I don't know?"

"You'd have to be with hundreds of women for an accurate sample size. And you'd have to isolate other variables. Maybe it's the type of women you're attracted to."

"Maybe it's just me."

She laughs. "Yes, they see your dick and they can't help themselves."

"Didn't consider that possibility."

She shakes her head *you're ridiculous*. Runs her fingers over the armchair. "I like it. But I don't know if I love it."

"Do you need to love it?"

"Maybe." She looks around the room. A dozen chairs on wheels on the right. Armchairs and loveseats in our section on the left. "I need to not be around Allison."

"And the armchair is going to do it?"

"I just… I want it to feel like *my* room."

"How long do you want to stay?"

Her eyes meet mine. "I don't know. I try not to think about it. They'll probably sell the house."

"They might." That might be better too. If they split the money instead of arguing over the sentimental value.

Sentimental value gets ugly fast.

"Is that what you want?" I ask.

"I want to go back in time and keep my mom from having an affair." Luna frowns. "But I can't do that, so… I want a nice room, where I can study and call Daisy and watch teen soaps on Skype and not hear Allison and her new girltoy."

"Do you need an armchair for that?"

"Maybe."

"The red suits you." My eyes flit to her lips.

She notices immediately. "Would you take the chair? If I leave. When I leave."

I shake my head. "It will be Gabe's." And who knows what he'll do with it.

"No. It will be Gabe's. And I don't give a fuck what he does with it."

She motions to the armchair next to hers. It's broad

with cognac leather. Like something in front of a fireplace on a British TV show.

I sit. Fold one leg over the other. Just barely turn toward her. We're almost parallel. But not quite.

"Are you going to leave?" Her voice is soft. A plea, but I'm not sure what she's asking. "Soon?"

"No. It's easier with you here. More space."

She half-smiles. "You'll be okay? Staying?"

"For a while. I did promise Daisy. I can save a lot more if I wait until next year. Find a better place."

"You must have a lot saved. You've been there awhile."

"I do," I say.

"How much?"

"See. Rude." I almost smile. "Always so fucking rude."

"No, if I was rude I'd say something like… hmm, kinda defensive there. It must not be very much."

I flip her off.

She smiles, almost all the way back to her usual self. "Okay, tell me this." She holds up her hand. "How many figures." She holds up three fingers.

I shoot her a *get real* look. "After three years?"

"You didn't make much apprenticing."

"What do I spend it on?"

"Uh, Daisy's birthday? Top-shelf bourbon? Friday and Saturday night?"

Those are fair points. They don't fit into my recent life, but my past… I have spent a lot of money on booze.

She holds up four fingers.

I shake my head.

Five fingers.

I nod.

"Not bad."

"Not bad. But not great either."

But, right now, I don't want to leave. I want to stay in

the room across from hers. Close to the hum of her pop music, and the warmth of her smile, and the joy of her laugh.

I like her way too much.

It's going to be the end of me.

Chapter Seventeen

LUNA

At home, Oliver builds furniture while I make lunch.

(Tragically, we compromised on buying frozen veggie meatballs. I mix them with a veggie curry. Which does a lot to enhance the bland flavor).

This is a riff off Divya's favorite recipe. One we've cooked together a million times.

It's strange, making it here, without her.

When I haven't talked to her in days.

Is she as hurt as I am?

Or is she conspiring with Allison? Was she lying to me all this time? Is she going to try to convince me to forgive her?

I don't know. So I don't reach out.

But if she is hurting...

She's losing her family and her marriage.

I swallow the thought as I finish, plate the food, call Oliver to lunch.

He steps into the hallway, stretching his arms over his head as he pulls on a shirt.

Fuck, the way the afternoon light hits him—

He's tall and broad and handsome. And those tattoos. The only insight into his head and his heart. And it's there. It's mine.

I shouldn't want that so badly.

But I do.

I really do.

"Water?" My tongue slides over my lips. God, he's so yummy. There's no better word. Just yummy.

He nods *thanks*. "It's hot today."

"Yeah." I move into the kitchen. Fill two glasses with ice and water. Bring them to the table.

"This looks good," he says.

"Does it?"

He chuckles as he steps off the stairs. Closes the distance between us. "Smells good."

"We'll see."

"Didn't you make it?"

"I have no faith." I motion to a particularly round veggie ball.

His laugh deepens. He shakes his head *you're ridiculous*. Pulls out his chair. Motions *after you*.

I sit.

He follows.

His eyes meet mine for a second, then they're on the food. He studies it carefully. Like it's a mock-up he's trying to memorize. "We had all this?"

"Yeah. I had to make a few substitutions. But it tastes good to me."

"What's the dish called?"

"Ikea is disturbing."

He laughs harder. "It's got a real ring to it." He pretends as if he's talking to a waiter. "I'll have the Ikea is Disturbing with naan please."

118

"You have naan?"

He shakes his head. "We could go to the place in Culver City—"

"We have rice."

"You prefer one or the other?"

"Rice. But I won't turn down extra carbs."

His lips curl into a half-smile. "It looks like veggie curry."

"More or less."

"Your mom taught you?"

I nod.

"She's a good cook."

"Hey!"

He laughs again. "You are too. Since you need the compliment." He picks up his fork. Stabs a veggie meatball.

"Rude."

"Uh-huh." He shakes his head *you're ridiculous*.

Maybe I am.

This is just strange. The day, the week, the month.

Everything since my parents sat me down and told me they were getting a divorce.

The familiarity of ginger and cardamom—

I need it.

Even with the strange veggie meatballs.

I pick up my fork. Taste a carrot. It's good—soft but not too soft, creamy, well-spiced.

Then half a ball.

It's actually... decent.

And it's mine. "We were supposed to go to India a few years ago. Most of our family is in London, but a few aunts and uncles live in Delhi. Only we canceled last minute."

"Who did?"

"Mom. I'm not sure which, actually. They presented a

united front. I didn't think much of it at the time, but now…"

"You keep wondering," he says. "If that was the start of it."

"Yeah." I mix my curry and rice together until it's a big mess of brown, orange, green.

Oliver brings a spoonful to his mouth. Chews. Swallows. "This *is* good, Luna. Thanks."

"Sure, yeah."

His gaze shifts to the window. He stares at the quiet street outside for a moment, then he looks to me. "Are you okay?"

"Yeah."

"Would you tell me if you weren't?"

Maybe. We're friends, but I'm not sure we're *that* kind of friend. "Would you tell me? If you weren't."

He doesn't make an excuse about how he can't, how it's different, how he's the big strong man who has to handle things on his own… but he doesn't agree either.

He just takes another bite.

Swallows another sip of water.

Changes the subject. "Is it weird? Not looking like your mom?"

"Sometimes." I stab another carrot. "When we're out, just me and Divya, sometimes people look at us funny, like they're not sure why we're together. Less so now that I'm older. But when I was a kid… I didn't really get it then. The way people would look at her like she didn't belong. Or like she was the help."

"A lot of people?"

"Enough."

"People are assholes."

I nod.

"Other times?"

"Yeah." I take another bite. "You know Divya. She's really modern. She doesn't go around wearing saris and talking about Hinduism. But there are things that matter to her."

He nods.

"And they matter to me too. Because they matter to her. But if I try to participate anywhere else… people act like I'm some dumb white girl trying to earn style points."

"You're still close though."

"I thought so." I play with my fork. "But she didn't tell me about this."

"Maybe she didn't know."

My eyes meet his. "You really think so?"

"Fuck if I know. Who understands parents?"

"Yeah." I swallow another spoonful of curry. "I keep thinking this might be it. Maybe last Christmas was the last Christmas we'll ever spend together. And tomorrow is Saturday and we're not going to our favorite brunch spot on Abbot-Kinney. And Divya isn't going to complain the place has a weak chai. And Allison isn't going to ask for three refills of her coffee. And they aren't going to look at each other like they're sharing some secret about me. About how proud they are. About how much I can accomplish."

"Fuck, Luna."

"They won't be there to marvel at my Halloween costume. I won't help Divya make Thanksgiving dinner and bring it to the table where Allison is picking out the best wine. And getting ready to deal with her parents." I stick my tongue out. "They always say something about how the food is too different. Too spicy. Too untraditional. But Divya just smiles and says we like it that way. She lets it roll off her back. I always admired that about her."

He nods.

"What will it be instead? I make dinner with Divya and Allison is off with her twenty-eight-year-old at some fancy wine bar? Drinking instead of eating?"

"Doesn't sound so bad."

"I guess not." I stab a green bean. "But it's not the same."

"It's not."

"I know it's nothing. Compared to your parents."

He shakes his head. "You thought they were happy." His voice softens. "They were happy. I saw them. They were in love. My parents... I vaguely remember Dad playing *Every Little Thing She Does is Magic*. Telling me the song perfectly defined love. Then playing it for Mom." He motions to the living room. "Taking her arm. Dancing the whole time."

"The Police, huh?" I bite my green bean in half. "I see that."

He motions *they're okay*. "I kind of remember weekends at the beach. Mom sitting on a blanket with a book. Dad gushing over her swimsuit. I didn't get it then. But the way he looked at her... it was love. I knew it. I didn't know what it meant, I still thought girls were icky, but I knew it."

"I know that look."

"They had it."

"Until recently." I try to remember the last time either of my parents looked at the other with love. Everything blurs together. A dinner alone. A quiet night. A smile as they wished me goodbye. Was that it? When they dropped me off at the airport? They had a look, but was it love? Or did they already know it was the end?

"It sucks. And..."

"It's going to keep sucking?"

He nods. "Until everything is final. And after that..."

He looks into my eyes. Looks for something. "It takes a long time to feel normal. After shit changes."

"Yeah."

"Maybe... if you want to talk, I can listen. Or... if you'd rather not think about it, I can find you a distraction."

"You can?"

"Yeah. I know just the thing too."

"You do?"

He nods *hell yeah*. "The perfect way to keep your mind occupied."

Okay, I'll bite. "What is it?"

Chapter Eighteen

LUNA

Without a word, Oliver sets his fork on the table, stands, motions to the stairs.

Uh. Okay.

There's no way he's about to take my hand, lead me to his room, throw me on his bed.

That's totally ridiculous.

So what if we almost kissed at Ikea?

Maybe I imagined that. Maybe he tries to make all his friends' exes jealous. Maybe he teases everyone about the color of their lipstick.

I should ask. To make sure.

To keep myself from crossing the line.

But I don't.

I follow him across the room, up the stairs, down the hallway.

He turns the knob, presses his door open, motions *after you*.

Really. This is a good place to ask.

To stop.

To say something that convinces him I don't want him to throw me on his bed.

I mean, I do want him to throw me on his bed.

And he wants to throw me on his bed.

Is it really so bad?

Will it really ruin *everything?*

He's so tall and broad and handsome. All shirtless and tan and tattooed.

"Let me find it." He motions *one minute*. Turns to his desk. Scans the neat array of art books, pens, paperbacks.

Sketchpads.

Something in the drawer.

"Here." He grabs a sketchbook. It's bright yellow with a tiny date penciled in the corner. "This is it."

"This is it?"

"Yeah." He flips through the pages. Smiles as he stops. "Fuck, I should make you work more for this."

How are you going to do that? Do you need me at your service, sir?

"You were so fucking annoying, begging me. Nonstop."

I suck a breath through my nose. Attempt to push my dirty thoughts out with my exhale.

It's no good. As soon as he shakes his head *you're so difficult*, my head fills with ideas. Ridiculously complete fantasies where I'm the bad girl who needs to earn his favor on my back.

Or my knees.

Fuck, I don't even like that.

Or I thought I didn't.

Maybe I do. Maybe it was just Sean. Maybe there's something about Oliver.

"You ready?" he asks.

I nod.

"You sure?"

Yes, take off your pants. I want to feel you.

"Close your eyes first."

Jesus Christ.

He raises a brow. "Close them or you don't see."

Okay. I close my eyes. Attempt to inhale calm and exhale dirty thoughts. Or maybe I should keep the dirty thoughts. I've already forgotten why Ollie is trying to distract me.

"Open on three." His footsteps move closer. "One, two, three."

My eyes blink open. Go straight to the sketch in front of me. The lyrics I fell in love with the day I heard them.

I used to beg Oliver for this. Or threaten to ask Holden instead.

God, it's even better than I imagined.

A row of trees, consumed by fire, with the lyrics from my favorite song.

The Lorde song about being too much.

The perfect claiming of an insult.

I *am* a wildfire. I *am* a force of nature. You will dance in my storm and you'll like it.

It's beautiful. Sharp and bold and perfect.

My fingers move of their own accord. They reach out. Brush the paper. Trace the lines.

He looks down at me, his expression a mixture of pride and apprehension. "You like it?"

I nod. "I love it."

His smile widens. "Yeah?"

"Yeah." I trace the lines again. "Can we do it now? Today? Please?"

"Right now?"

"Why not?"

He chuckles *you're ridiculous*. "'Cause you just saw it."

"I wanted it then. I want it now."

"Daisy will kill me."

"Is that your excuse for everything?"

He nods *yeah*.

"Can we do it tomorrow?"

His laugh gets louder. "You're like a kid."

"You're showing me this perfect, beautiful thing, this thing I've always wanted and telling me I can't have it."

"You think it's perfect?"

"It is." The thin lines, the deep colors, the vibrant orange. "Ollie, please."

"It's too soon."

"Don't make me beg."

"Don't beg. I can't handle it." He turns the sketchpad around. Studies the design carefully. "All right—"

"Yes."

"If—"

"Don't ruin it," I say.

He ignores my protests. "We'll do a trial run." He motions to the drawing. "Print a temp at the shop. Apply it today. If you still want it in two weeks, I'll do it."

"Really?"

"Yeah."

I throw my arms around him.

He takes a half-step backward. Then he settles. Wraps his arms around me. Pulls me closer.

"Thank you." I rest my head on his chest. My hands on his waist.

That's his bare skin against my palm. His body against mine.

It's not the first time we've touched, hugged, embraced.

But it's the first time I've needed to inhale every inch of his skin.

He holds me close for a moment, then he releases me. "I should finish your furniture."

I shake my head.

"Where are you going to sleep?"

"Finish when we get back."

"You know I'm doing you a favor?"

"I'll buy you coffee."

He half-smiles. "Hard bargain."

My eyes flit to his crotch.

He notices, but he doesn't call me on it. "Twenty minutes. I'm going to shower. And finish lunch. Then we walk over."

"Thank you."

He nods. "Thank me with the coffee."

"Really, Ollie."

He shrugs like it's no big deal, but the pride in his eyes betrays him.

———

IT'S A BEAUTIFUL DAY. A BRIGHT BLUE SKY, A BIG LEMON sun, a soft breeze that turns the afternoon temperate.

Ollie shakes his head *it's too fucking bright*, slips on his sunglasses, slings his backpack over his shoulder. "I should make you carry this."

"It doesn't go with my outfit."

He chuckles *of course*. "You know what matters."

"A girl's got to have priorities." I follow him down the sidewalk. "What do you think for coffee? Blue Bottle, Groundworks, Intelligentsia?"

He makes that *hmm* noise. "Good day for iced. But Blue Bottle is the other direction."

"I don't mind."

"Tomorrow," he says. "You can buy some. Bring it to the shop. Do my bidding for once."

"That doesn't sound fun."

"Huh, imagine that?" He smiles.

"You're not the only one who doesn't follow orders."

He raises a brow.

I fight a blush. "You only do things if you want to do them."

"You sure about that?"

"Yeah."

He shrugs *whatever you want to believe*. Motions in the direction of his favorite coffee shop.

For a few minutes, we walk in silence. Nothing but the breeze, the hum of traffic, the occasional rumble of someone else's conversation.

Even as we turn onto the main drag, as we move into the coffee shop, wait in line.

This place is hipster extreme. All white walls and glass contraptions. Sparse wooden seats. Rude baristas.

"What if I get a French press?" I tap his shoulder with mine.

"We'll be here for twenty minutes."

"Are you saying no?"

"It will be an extra twenty minutes before you get your fake ink."

"You can have some," I say.

"I've shared coffee with you. I know what that means."

"Fifty-fifty. I swear." I place my hand over my heart. "On the honor of the *Bachelorette* franchise."

"What honor?"

"On my obsession with keeping my hair the perfect shade of silver."

He nods *okay*. Holds out his hand.

I shake.

"Why do you do that?" he asks. "This." He brushes my bangs out of my eyes. "The silver."

"I thought we talked about this—"

"Your quest to suck as many dicks as possible?"

The guy in front of us turns and shoots us a *what the fuck is wrong with you* stare.

"Sorry," I mouth.

Oliver leans in to whisper. "I think he's volunteering."

"Oh my god." I hip bump him.

He bumps back.

The guy shakes his head *really, how rude.* He takes a big step forward. Taps his toe impatiently.

"Look at what the rejection did to him," Oliver whispers.

This time, I push him. Softly enough it's playful.

But he still wraps his hands around my wrists. Stops me.

His hands are just there. Wrapped around my wrists. Ready to guide me.

And he's standing there, all tall and strong and proud, looking down at me with eager eyes.

Eyes that scream *yes, now, let's be naked.*

I freeze.

Lose myself in his deep blue eyes.

In how badly I want to touch him.

In how badly he wants to touch me.

I'm there. Waiting. At the precipice.

Until the barista calls *next* and Oliver steps back.

Right. Our coffee.

This is a favor. I'm buying him coffee.

I order the large French Press. The single-origin beans from Brazil.

It's going to take a few minutes. They'll call us when it's done.

Right.

I pay.

Oliver finds seats in the back of the crowded cafe.

They're bench seats. Next to each other.

Sure. That's no problem. I can sit next to him without touching him.

Totally.

I'll just wait at the counter. Until the coffee is ready. For no reason.

I motion to the counter. Pretend as if I'm fascinated with my cell. Wow, Buzzfeed, can you really guess my favorite ice cream flavor?

Strawberry.

Not even close.

Coffee ice cream is the only flavor that isn't too sweet.

The French press arrives just as I start a second quiz—pick an outfit and we'll give you a celebrity to date.

I thank the barista, grab the press and mugs, bring them to the table, sit.

It's a tiny space. So small my leg is pressed against his. We're both wearing jeans, but I can still feel the warmth of his skin.

I'm still itching to touch him.

I fill both cups instead. "Cream and sugar?"

"A crime punishable by death?"

"This time, I'll allow it."

"Generous."

I nod *I know*.

He half-smiles. Holds up his tiny mug to toast. "To wanting the best."

"To wanting the best." I tap my ceramic against his.

He watches as I bring the mug to my lips. As I sip, taste, swallow, sigh.

My eyes flutter closed. I soak in the rich, deep, dark perfection of the coffee.

But still, I feel his stare.

God, I like his stare. I want more of his stare.

"It's sexy," he says. "Your hair. I wasn't just saying that for Sean's benefit."

"Thanks." Light floods my eyes. Then it's his strong jaw, his long nose, his gorgeous eyes.

"You really cut it shorter because guys thought your platinum look was slutty?"

"It wasn't just guys." I force my attention to the coffee. "People thought I was a shallow party girl. I started to look in the mirror and see that."

"You're not."

"Yeah, but I was spending the summer on bullshit. At these big events at the beach with classmates I didn't even like. Or at parties that went too long, with people who were too drunk."

His voice softens. "You weren't having fun?"

"At first, yeah. I needed to let off steam, with school ending. And Sean dumping me. I needed the attention. Or maybe I just wanted it. To feel like someone still wanted me. Like I wasn't too much."

"Is that what he said?"

"Yeah. He needed an easier girl. One who would support him. Who wouldn't ask so much."

"When you fucked?"

My sex clenches. "Yes, but I'm not sure that's what he meant."

"Of course it is. He wanted some chick who would go down on him every night without asking him to reciprocate."

"I haven't met many guys who'd turn that down."

"Maybe." He takes a long sip. "It wouldn't be my first choice."

"No? If I said *Ollie, please, I need help getting over Sean. Can I please blow you every night for the next few weeks?*"

His pupils dilate.

133

"You'd say no?"

"Listen, Luna, I know you're on a mission, but you gotta romance a guy first."

A laugh escapes my lips.

"Make him feel special. And not like he's just another notch in your bedpost."

"I guess you know a lot about that."

"Yeah." His gaze shifts to the window looking out on the street. "I always thought I was being fair. I was upfront about wanting something casual. Sex is fun. I make sure women come. Help them relax. Try new shit."

I don't know what to say, so I nod.

"It's not like it's personal. It's not like a woman is lacking in some way. I just can't handle more than casual."

"Have you tried?"

"Yeah. Sometimes shit has gone on too long. Started to get serious. Real. I just..." His shoulders clench. "I don't know. I guess it's different now." His gaze shifts to his coffee cup. "I have a lot to figure out. I don't want to put that on anyone."

"Are you rejecting my fake offer?"

He chuckles. "It's a fake offer."

"What if it wasn't?"

"Hypothetically? Or *let's go to that single-person bathroom right now*?"

"Ew. I'm not blowing someone in a single-person bathroom."

"No? Only multi-people bathrooms for you?" he teases.

"No bathrooms."

"Never?" He raises a brow, challenging me.

"Maybe... once. After some alcoholic beverages. At a party."

"Sean?"

"His birthday."

"Fuck, I really don't like him." He shakes his head.

"You wouldn't ask that? For your birthday?"

"You think I'm that uncreative?"

"You have a more creative ask?"

He nods *hell yeah*.

I motion *go on*.

"With anyone? Or you?"

"Let's say it was me."

"What are we doing in this hypothetical scenario?" he asks.

"Isn't that the question?"

"No." He refills his cup. Then mine. Like this is a normal conversation on a normal day. "Are we strangers at a party? Long-term lovers? Boyfriend/girlfriend?"

"Friends who got drunk enough they decided hooking up would be a good idea."

The playfulness drops from his expression. He gives me a long, slow once-over. Stops at my hips, chest, mouth. "It's a one-time thing?"

"Undefined."

"If I only get one chance, I'm not going to waste it on a blow job." His voice drops another octave. "I'm going to watch you come. See the way your expression changes. See your eyes fill with pleasure. Hear my name on your lips."

Fuck.

"I'm going to feel you pulsing around my cock. And I'm going to watch it happen. So, sure, we can do the bathroom at a party. But only if I've got you pinned to the counter and I'm fucking you from behind and we're both watching every second."

Oh.

Oh.

Yeah.

Pretty much all I have here is oh.

135

Chapter Nineteen

OLIVER

S hit.

It occurs to me the second the words are out of my mouth.

I need to do something, anything to slam the brakes.

Of course, I don't.

I'm not Oliver Flynn, smart, productive, well-functioning member of society.

I'm Oliver Flynn, self-destructive fuckup.

Only I don't care. The consequences are too far away. The reasons are fuzzy.

Luna is so fucking gorgeous. Of course, I want that sassy mouth on me. Of course, I want to see pleasure spill over her expression, fill her pretty eyes, soften her neat brows.

She stares at me; her grey eyes wide, her soft lips parted.

They're not that same pinkish red anymore. Half her lipstick is on the clean white cup.

Will it stain me the same way?

My neck, chest, cock—

My sheets, shirt, boxers—

Fuck, she's still staring.

And I'm still thinking about her naked.

And this is still—

What the fuck are we doing here?

Right. The mock-up. The temporary tattoo. The promise of my mark on her skin forever.

Thank fuck for dark denim. My jeans aren't doing enough to hide my hard-on, but they're doing something.

I reach for some way to slow this train. "So, uh, why silver?" It's a stupid question, but it's something.

"Huh?"

"Your hair? You changed it so you wouldn't give a certain impression—"

"Have you thought about that before?" she asks.

"Your hair?"

"Us. At a—"

"Off the cuff."

"So you…" Her throat quivers as she swallows. Her eyes fix on my lips. Jaw. Neck. Then down my torso.

"I know what I like."

"Oh."

"And you?"

"And I?"

This isn't exactly changing the subject away from sex. But at least it's not about how I want to watch her come. "What would you want? As your birthday gift?"

"It's not for six months."

"Even so."

Her eyes stay on my crotch for a quick second then they move back up my body. "I don't know. I guess I don't want sexual favors. I don't want someone to do something because it's my birthday. I want them to do it because they want to."

"What if your guy gave you carte blanche? His fantasy is filling your fantasy." Fuck, what is wrong with me? I bite my tongue. Not that it helps pull the words out of the air.

They're still there.

She's still staring.

She's still so fucking beautiful.

I need to make her come. It's the only thing in the world that makes sense.

Sobriety is a drag, work is fine, running is okay.

But Luna groaning my name?

That's better than anything.

"Just the one time?" she asks. "That's a lot of pressure."

"Whatever comes to you."

She laughs *okay* but it does nothing to ease the tension in the air. "I guess... I have this regular fantasy. We're at a party. It's a nice night, but no one is outside. So we sneak to the backyard. To one of those big lounge chairs. It's dark. Hard to see us. But if someone really looked, they could."

"Yeah?"

She nods *yeah*. "And he sits, pulls me into his lap. He's wearing jeans and I'm in a cute dress. No bra. No panties. He peels the dress down my chest. Asks if I want someone to see. If I want to get caught. If I—"

"Yeah. Right." Fuck, I'm going to come right here.

She snaps out of her trance. Blushes, suddenly self-conscious. "Yeah... you get the idea."

Fuck, do I get the idea.

She turns away from me. Stares at her cup of coffee as she takes a timid sip. "So, uh..."

"Silver."

"Silver?"

"Your hair. You changed it so—"

"Yeah." She stays at that one-hundred-thirty-five degree angle. "I was going to a lot of parties. Drinking a little too much. Flirting a little too much. Hooking up a little too much."

"You were fucking guys?"

"Not fucking them, but…"

"Working on your mission."

She blushes. "No. More… making out. Or hand stuff. When I drank too much. I thought it would make me feel wanted. But it didn't. It made me feel used."

"Did anyone push you?"

"No. It was more… it was supposed to be fun, right? But it wasn't. So I stopped telling myself it was. But when I looked in the mirror, I saw this girl everyone thought was a dumb, drunk slut."

"Yeah."

"So I cut it. To something more stylish."

"And went silver?"

"Yeah. Guys don't get it."

Maybe I don't get it, but I like it. "It's hot. In a more classy way."

Her blush deepens. "Thanks."

"It does suit you. More than the platinum."

"You're treading dangerous ground." She shakes her head. "You should know better."

I chuckle. "Probably should."

She turns so we're parallel. Then toward me. "Did you ever feel like that?"

"Like what?"

"Empty? Used? Like you were supposed to get more out of a fuck than you did?"

"I don't know," I say. "I've never… got more out of it."

She nods with understanding. "Isn't that lonely?"

"Sometimes."

"How long has it been?" She refills our cups. "Since you…"

Last time was the night of the incident. "About five weeks."

"That's awhile," she says.

"For you?"

"There were two guys after Sean. The last was July."

It's been awhile for her. Or maybe that's normal. Maybe she prefers not to let random guys stroke her to orgasm.

Fuck knows I don't want random guys touching her.

Which is some hypocritical bullshit, sure, but I don't care. I don't want anyone else touching her.

———

My cock refuses to quiet.

I try to reason with the fucker. Remind him Luna is Daisy's best friend. My current roomie.

The only person who doesn't see me as a piece of shit.

I need that.

Not that my cock cares.

My thoughts keep slipping back to her.

As we finish our coffee, bus our tables, walk the rest of the way to the shop, dance around what we're both thinking—

She's actually talking about makeup.

And I'm actually nodding like it's interesting.

Like I'm not thinking *fuck, I want that lipstick on my neck.*

Fuck, I want those nails on my back.

Fuck, I want my name on your lips.

Fucking cock.

No matter what I offer the damn thing—another woman, a threesome, any sick, twisted porn out there—it stays on Luna.

The other woman in my fantasy becomes her.

The gang bang loving school girl is Luna in a plaid skirt, begging me to come on her tits. No sign of the gang.

Just a schoolgirl awaiting the professor's punishment.

Or a secretary begging to serve her boss.

Or a tough as nails lady cop ready to interrogate a suspect by any means necessary.

By the time we get to the shop, I'm on fire. The air conditioning fails to help. Even that miserable music Forest likes warms me further.

I motion for Luna to wait. Move into the office, alone. Copy the mock-up.

Try, hard, to focus on the details.

Her favorite lyrics. Some song about a girl who's a wildfire, who people love at first, then get tired of.

Along with a forest set ablaze.

I mocked it up the day she asked for it. Even though she was sixteen and Daisy would kill me if I gave her a tattoo.

It was perfect for her.

It needed to come to life.

I guess that's a hazard of the job. I see someone; I wonder if they have ink, wonder if it suits them or someone else or who they want to be.

Like Holden with *danger is sweet*.

Or Dad with the lyrics he thinks I don't know about.

Or my Latin quote.

ex favilla nos resurgemus

From the ashes we rise.

Shit, that fits. That reminds people of who they are.

There are plenty of people who get something because it's cool. Because it's who they wish they were.

Like the guy yesterday with the dragon backpiece. He wants to be a tough guy, but he's not, and the ink only makes it more obvious.

It's his life, his body, his business.

Sure, I tried to convince him to soften it, to twist it into something that better fit his look and disposition, but that wasn't what he wanted.

Whereas this...

The printer hums as it spits out a temporary tattoo.

I cut the edges. Run my fingers over the paper.

Call Luna into the office.

She moves into the tiny space. "Where do you think?"

"Here." I wrap my hand around her right wrist. Turn her arm over. Run my fingertip up her forearm. Fuck, she's so soft and warm.

And this battle with my cock is so over.

It wins.

I lose.

She nods. Speaks softly, "There."

"Hold still."

"Okay."

I clean and dry her skin, place the paper, wet it, hold it for ten seconds.

She stares at me, watching carefully.

Then I peel off the paper and her eyes go wide.

"Ollie." She looks up at me. "It's so fucking perfect."

"Yeah?"

She nods. "If you want me to wait, I'll wait. But I know." She traces the line. "I want it."

My work on her body forever.

I'm not just losing the battle.

I'm losing the war too.

Chapter Twenty

LUNA

At home, I study, Oliver builds furniture, the stereo blasts Pearl Jam. I don't even complain about the mumbling. It's not so bad in this context.

When he's finished, I move into my new space. A new room. My new room.

It's supposed to feel like my new home.

Like a place safe from the spectre of my parents' divorce.

But it's *there*. In the white string lights, the framed mermaid print, the deep red chair.

Everything is new. Different. Wrong.

It screams *this is not my home*.

I reorganize my makeup, but that doesn't help. Nor does arranging my outfits by style. Or moving the desk.

It's a nice room. Beautiful.

But it's not mine.

It's not a new, safe place. It's a temporary fix. An escape that constantly reminds me it's an escape.

Can I really stomach that all semester?

Longer?

I don't know.

I have to face something. At some point.

Not Allison. Uh-huh.

But maybe...

I pull out my cell. Open my texts from Divya. A few jokes about *Shark Tank*. A recipe for chai cake, along with a joke about how I never eat sweets.

No *please forgive your mother*.

Maybe I can do this.

Maybe I can face her.

She must need it. She's losing her family too. Losing her wife.

As long as she doesn't ask me to forgive Allison...

Deep breath. Steady exhale.

I text my mom.

Luna: What do you say to brunch Sunday? Same place, same time, just the two of us?

I can do brunch.

It's two hours. I can face this for two hours.

No problem.

———

Huge problem.

Every problem.

I smooth my plum jumpsuit. Zip my black purse. Apply a third coat of lipstick.

It's not right. It's still not right.

I can't wear this to breakfast with Mom. It doesn't say *I'm so sorry that your wife is sleeping with her fucking secretary. I still love you but please don't make me say I love her. Please don't ask me to forgive her.*

It's too much for an outfit.

Even if it's an incredibly fierce outfit.

Maybe more eyeliner. Or blush. Or a different purse. A different face.

A more sympathetic personality?

The kind of girl Sean would like. Sweet, complacent, easy to please.

So pleasant no one would ever leave her.

That's not happening.

But I can bring someone…

He's not sweet, complacent, or easy to please.

Right on cue, Oliver's door creaks. This is late for him. It's already ten. He's usually up before seven.

I peek into the hallway.

He stretches his arms over his head, pulling his black t-shirt up his torso. "Coffee?"

"Brunch."

"Is that a no?"

"Come with me."

He looks at me like I'm crazy. "Come with you."

"And Divya."

"To brunch?"

I nod *yes*.

"Do I look like I go to brunch?"

"They have a full bar."

He shoots me a *really* look.

Yeah, really. This is Oliver Flynn we're talking about. Not uh… some bastion of sobriety. This is the guy who carries a flask and brings "the good shit" to every party.

Only—

Oliver isn't going out. At least, I haven't seen him go out.

And he isn't drinking.

Or he's hiding it well.

Is he slipping whiskey in his coffee? Sipping his flask at work?

"They have coffee." I switch tactics. I can contemplate Oliver's self-destructive choices later. After I avoid my own. "And pancakes."

He shoots me that same *really* look.

"Or eggs." I bite my lip. "Uh... did I mention the coffee?"

He gives me a quick once-over. "The place on Abbot-Kinney?"

"Yeah."

"You're dressed for it." He gives me a slow once-over. "Wearing that red again."

"The other red was wine. This is plum."

"Uh-huh." His gaze flits to my lips. "What do I get out of it?"

That isn't what he's asking. That isn't how he means it. But, damn, the ideas in my head... "Coffee."

"I have coffee here."

"Blue Bottle. On the way. And after."

"I have work at two," he says.

"I'll bring it to you."

"At five?"

"I have a study session."

"Before your study session." He holds out his hand. "And you make dinner. Whatever I want."

"Yes. Sure." I hold out my hand. Whatever it takes to make this easier.

———

THE RESTAURANT IS BUSY. WAITERS BUZZ BETWEEN TABLES of friends, couples, hipster families.

The scent of salt mingles with the citrus. The windows are wide open. The ocean air fills the room. Keeps it temperate.

Ollie presses his palm into my lower back to lead me to the hostess stand. It's a reassuring gesture. The gesture of a friend who knows I need comfort.

It doesn't matter that I want his hand under my jumpsuit.

It doesn't matter that I want his arms around me.

It doesn't matter that I want him to hold me all night.

"Locke party." He nods to the host. "Three of us."

He smiles at the hostess as she pulls menus and motions *after you*.

She leads us to a table in the back. One of those tables that's half bench, half chairs.

Divya is already here. On the bench side of the table.

She looks good. Happy even. Bright makeup, flowing maxi dress, wide smile. "Sweetie, I've missed you." She stands. Invites me into a hug.

I hesitate.

Oliver nudges me.

I give him a *what* look.

He nudges me again *get your shit together*.

Right. She's not the one having an affair. She's the one losing her wife and her family.

I move closer. Let my mom wrap her arms around me.

She smells familiar. Like the lotion she uses. The one that perfumes the bathroom upstairs.

It overwhelms me. That feeling of home, safety, comfort.

Then I hear those awful words—*we're getting a divorce*—and it disappears.

"I missed you too." I pull back. Swallow hard. I don't know if I can trust her. I want to. I really do. But what if she's been lying to me all this time?

"It's nice to see you, Mr. Flynn." Divya smiles at Oliver.

"Mr. Flynn? I could get used to that." He shakes.

149

She stage whispers to me. "He's always been a hand-some young man, but he's bringing extra effort today."

"Mom!" My voice drops to a *you're embarrassing me* squeal. It's so normal and familiar and strange.

"I'm old, not dead?" she asks.

"What are you, thirty-five?" Oliver winks, suddenly full of charm.

Seriously, he never tries to charm me. Where did he get this reserve of flirting? Is he taking lessons from Holden?

"You don't even like men," I say.

"That doesn't mean I can't appreciate a handsome man." She winks at Oliver. "She hates when I talk about her boyfriends."

"OH MY GOD, MOM! He's not my boyfriend," I say.

"I know." Her dark eyes light up with mischief. "Do you think I'd let you stay with him if he was?"

"Lots of women my age live with their boyfriends," I say.

"Eighteen-year-olds with their boyfriends?" She raises a brow. "Really?"

"Trust me. I'd never date Luna," Oliver says.

"Hey!" I bump him with my shoulder. "What's that supposed to mean?"

"Too much attitude." He motions to me. Makes a show of shaking his head. "See."

"You love my attitude," I say.

He smiles, unable to hide his affection. "It's more the looks."

"She's a beautiful young woman," Divya says. "She takes after her mother."

She means Allison. But I don't acknowledge that. Sure, I don't share any of Divya's DNA, but I take after her.

We're loud in dress, attitude, speech.

Maybe that's why...

Maybe Allison found an easier woman.

I swallow hard.

"You wear such different styles." He nods to Mom's flowing maxi dress. "But there's something about the way the look is put together. I can see where Luna gets it."

She smiles.

"And the makeup too. Did you teach her?" he asks.

"Are you sure he isn't your boyfriend?" she asks. "He's playing the part well."

He is.

He deserves a thousand coffees for this.

There's something about Ollie. His presence is comforting.

Somehow, I believe it's going to be okay.

"Are you doing okay with the Flynns?" She motions for us to sit.

We do.

I pick up the menu. Pretend as if I don't know what I want. "It's having someone my age around."

"You can come back home. When you're ready. I know you aren't, but you can." Hurt drops into her voice, but she swallows it.

"Not yet." Maybe in a few months. Or maybe less. I don't know. When this feels easier. When they're past the worst of it.

I can't watch them fight over assets.

Or divide things calmly.

Which is worse? The passion of a painful separation? Or the apathy over a mutual one?

Does it have to be apathy?

Maybe they agree. Maybe it's time. Maybe that's just how adult relationships work.

It's not *I love you forever*.

It's *I love you until it's too hard*.

They've got through hard before. They've been through so much. Why can't they get through this too?

"I know," Divya says. "Coffee first. She can never talk before coffee."

That is true.

"And she looks exhausted," Divya says.

"She does," Oliver agrees.

"Hey!" Levity drops into my voice. Maybe this can feel normal. For one hour. One hour of family brunch then back to *I have to accept my family is never a single unit again.* "I do not."

"Don't fish for compliments." Oliver nudges me toward the bench. "You know you're gorgeous."

Divya nods *it's true.*

"I didn't insist I'm gorgeous," I say. "I insisted I don't look tired. Of course, I know I'm gorgeous. I'm not blind."

Oliver chuckles.

Divya lets out her usual throaty laugh.

"Should I pretend otherwise?" I ask.

Which only makes them laugh louder.

Oliver even shoots her one of his *can you believe this* looks.

"I like him," Divya says. "Are you sure you aren't dating?"

"Gross. No," I say.

"Gross, huh? You don't like tall guys with tattoos all of a sudden?" she asks.

I clear my throat.

"Is it because he's not an athlete?" Divya's eyes flit to Oliver's arms. "He looks like he's in good shape."

"Oh my god, Mom, don't be gross!" I say.

Oliver chuckles, amused by my discomfort.

"What's gross about noticing a guy works out?" she asks.

"What if he talked about my body like this?" I ask.

"Should I try?" Oliver asks. "Say something about how much I love your shoulders?"

"You're making it seem normal." I nudge him. "And since when do you like my shoulders?"

"Since always. They're sexy. Especially with that haircut," he says.

She completely ignores his objectification. "It suits her, doesn't it?"

"Did I ask for opinions?" My voice drips with *Mom you're embarrassing me* whine. It's horrible, but in a familiar way.

It feels normal.

Like any other Sunday brunch.

Like it's surrounded by a happy, stable family life.

I let that feeling wash over me.

I let them tease me about my hair (she can't go five minutes without wondering if it's the right shade of silver), my style (she won't go out in anything that isn't intentional), my hate of vegan butter (no, I would not like vegan butter on my chocolate pancakes), my distaste for sweets (and no syrup either), my lust for coffee (the largest French press you have, please).

I tease them back.

Divya about her taste for sweets. Her insatiable appetite for chai. Her excessive use of syrup. Her obsession with coral lipstick and maxi dresses.

Oliver about his coffee addiction, his need to show off his tattooed arms (does he own anything with long sleeves), his love of grunge music.

For a while, everything is easy.

Then he excuses himself. To use the bathroom.

And Divya looks to me. "I know you don't want to talk about it, sweetie. But we have to."

153

I swallow hard.

"There's a lot going on. And it's happening fast. I know what I'm willing to do." She folds her hands together in her lap. "But I need to know… what will it take to get you back home? I want you to be okay, Luna. Tell me what I need to do to make that happen."

Chapter Twenty-One

LUNA

I want things to stay the same.

That isn't possible. I'm not stupid enough to believe it is. But that logic does nothing to alleviate the ache in my heart.

I want to feel... in the know.

And not like my parents have been lying to me for ages.

I swallow another sip of my coffee. Try to collect my thoughts. Find some reasonable response.

Fail. "Did you know?"

"Did I know?" Her eyes meet mine.

"About her affair? Did you know?"

"Luna..." She shakes her head the way adults do when they just can't explain something. "It's complicated."

"You knew she was seeing someone else?"

Divya nods. "Yes."

"For how long?"

"For a while."

"But..." Why? How?

"We... Luna, I love your mother. I always will. But we've been drifting apart for a long time."

"You knew?" I ask. "You gave her permission?"

"Not exactly."

"What exactly?"

"We both knew it was over," she says. "We want different things out of life now. With you in college—"

"You were waiting?"

Her eyes cloud. "Yes."

"So you were lying to me?"

"It's not that simple."

"You knew you were separating, but you still sat there, holding hands at graduation. You still stood there, gushing over memories on my first day of college. You woke me up an hour early to make chocolate chip pancakes. You still—"

"You'll understand one day, Luna. If you get married. It's hard. It takes work. Sometimes, it takes too much work."

"But…"

"We still love you. And we can still like each other. If we stay together, we won't." She folds her hands. "Maybe we should have told you sooner. Maybe we shouldn't have left you in the dark. But we did the best we could."

There's no apology to accept. Only the typical adult *I know better, deal with it.*

"I know it's hard, Luna. But we want to make it easy for you. We're going to split assets. Fifty-fifty. The house… we need to know what you want. Do you want to stay? Do you want to sell it? Or… if you want to live on your own. We can help. Whatever you want."

What I want? "I want you to be honest with me."

"I am."

"You kept this from me. For how long?"

"I love you, sweetheart, but this was our business. Not yours."

No. It's my business too. It's my family too.

And now Mom is coming to me, trying to make it right, saying it's all about making it easy for me.

After lying to me for months.

Years.

This is such bullshit.

I'm not.

I can't—

"Excuse me." I stand. Move toward the door. The bright street. Somewhere to breathe.

It's too hot outside.

The air is too stiff.

There's a breeze. Why is the air so stiff? Why is it so fucking hot?

I move away from the door. To the glass of the shop at the corner. The only smooth, cool thing in the entire world.

Half a year.

Longer.

How long have I missed it?

How long have I believed in a lie?

I press my eyelids together. Suck a breath through my nose.

It's too bright.

Too hot.

Too suffocating.

"Hey." Oliver's footsteps move closer. He wraps his arms around me. Pulls me into a tight embrace.

God, he feels good. Tall and safe and strong.

"It was the vegan butter, huh?" He presses his palm into the space between my shoulder blades. "Even the thought of it disgusted you."

A laugh escapes my lips.

"It's okay. You have standards. That's nothing to apologize for."

"Oh my god."

"We can go to Blue Bottle. Wash it down."

I nod into his chest.

"You should talk to her. Before you go."

I shake my head.

"You'll regret it if you don't."

"But—"

"If anyone knows, it's me." He traces the line of my shoulder blade. Down then back up. His finger against my bare skin. A million volts of electricity.

Maybe he's right. Maybe I should. But I can't. I shake my head. "Not now."

"Later?"

"Please, Ollie. I can't think about this anymore." My fingers curl into the soft cotton of his t-shirt. The firm muscle of his back beneath it. "Please. Can we go somewhere else?"

"Will coffee help?"

I nod into his chest.

"Okay." His fingers skim my wrist. My thumb. "This way." He takes my hand and moves away from the restaurant.

Toward something I can't take back.

Something I need more than anything.

Chapter Twenty-Two

LUNA

For a few minutes, we walk in silence. Along the busy street. Surrounded by conversations, music, car horns.

Then around the corner. To the overpriced grocery store with incredibly expensive coffee drinks.

It's a SoCal stereotype. Seven-dollar slices of raw chocolate cake, ten-dollar smoothies, outrageously expensive wild caught salmon.

We wait in line at the smoothie/juice/coffee bar. Behind a couple toting yoga mats, wearing designer sunglasses with their hundred-dollar leggings.

Not that I'm judging. I'm here too.

Sure, I'd rather spend my money on an entire outfit than one pair of three-hundred-dollar sunglasses, but if I had the cash to spend—

Well, I'd still buy the outfit. But I'd like to have the cash to spend.

One day.

Allison makes a lot of money. A lot. My parents are well-off. I'm lucky that way.

I guess Oliver is lucky too. Gabe must be loaded.

How else would he pay for that house even closer to the beach after splitting assets fifty-fifty with his ex?

Ollie's mom is a mess. Way worse than either of mine.

A drug addict. Usually high-functioning. Usually hopped up on pain meds but still able to hold down a job and charm doctors into writing a new prescription.

I don't really know the details of his parents' divorce. It was ugly, that they fought all the time, that his father dropped a "me or the drugs" ultimatum.

But what was going on between the two of them?

Were they like my parents? Conspiring to lie even though they couldn't stand each other?

Or were they fighting to hold on?

Were they still in love?

Does he still love her?

I don't know.

As much as Oliver would hate to hear it, he and Gabe are a lot alike. They're both strong, silent types. They keep their cards close. They keep a poker face. They keep their attention on the people they love.

They should have more common ground.

They both lost his mom.

They both almost lost Daisy.

They both love Daisy more than anything.

And I…

"Luna." Oliver taps my shoulder. "We're up."

Oh. Right. We're here. Getting coffee. I have to order. It's a sunny day and we're going outside. And my jumpsuit is not that breathable. But the breeze is cool and I don't have a jacket.

"French press." He orders for us. "The biggest one you have." He names a dark roast. Offers the barista his credit card. Takes a number.

Then his arm is around my waist and he's pulling me away. Toward the shelf of chocolate. The row with its back to the theme-park style winding line.

This place is packed. Narrow aisles, tons of people, expensive treats.

"This is your brand." He bends to grab a bar of eighty-five percent. Studies the selection carefully. A dozen flavors of this brand, half a dozen of that. The less expensive options. The mid-range. The ridiculous. "What about this?" He picks up a one ounce single-origin bar that costs... well, as much as our overpriced French press.

God, maybe our parents really are rich. If this is the closest grocery store.

How can anyone afford this stuff?

"It's too expensive," I say.

"Luna Locke thinks something is too expensive?"

"It's happened before."

"The woman who demands the best, at all times?"

"What about that bottle of bourbon?"

His expression darkens, but he shakes it off. "Do you not want it?"

Single-origin chocolate from Vietnam. With notes of fig and caramel. Still eighty percent. It's hard to find single-origin chocolate over seventy percent.

It's next level chocolate.

All the delicious, rich, creamy, fruity flavors. With a million times more subtlety.

My tongue slides over my lips.

"You want it," he says.

"It's too expensive."

"I'm going to buy it. Hope someone eats it."

"It's too much."

"What the fuck did you do with my friend Luna? The one who threatens to throw out my phone if I play music she doesn't like?" His eyes meet mine. "The girl who tells me every time I make coffee wrong."

"I just…"

"You want this."

"Yeah."

"So why are you making it hard for me to give it to you?"

"It's just… it's expensive."

"So?"

"And my parents, and I'm living with you, and you're saving to move out, and… money is fucked up."

He nods *yeah*.

"Maybe that's why it's all so fucked up. The money."

"As opposed to…"

"I know it's better to have money." I'm not that out of touch. "But the divorces… it's like your dad said. The assets make it ugly."

"Maybe. My dad didn't give a fuck about the money. He wanted custody. He would have paid anything for that."

"You're giving him a lot of credit."

A guy in board shorts tries to cut through us.

Oliver pulls me aside. Motions to the aisle across from us.

I nod. Follow him into it.

Snacks. From the organic version of the classic plain potato chip to the chickpea puff to the chip with actual chicken in it.

Don't these people know they can buy chickpea and lentil chips at the place in Culver City for half the price?

"You eat enough?" He motions to a bag of garlic and rosemary potato chips.

"Yeah." I scan the rows, looking for a distraction. A

novelty. Something. There are some unusual flavors here. Dill pickle, Moscow Mule, Korean Barbeque. All on potato chips.

But they have these everywhere. Even at Safeway.

It's the chips made out of chickpeas where things get weird.

But I don't want salty snacks. I don't want any snacks. But if I have to have snacks—

I move to the next aisle. Nuts. Expensive, organic ones. Slightly less expensive roasted versions. Flavored.

Chocolate covered almonds.

No. This chocolate is plenty. I'm not even hungry. And —"Our coffee is probably ready."

"You keep looking at food. You hungry?"

"No. I just… want something to look at."

"I'm sorry."

"Huh?"

His fingers skim my shoulder. Then his palm rests on it. He turns me so we're face-to-face. "I'm sorry about your parents. I'm sorry they're divorcing. I'm sorry they're lying to you. I know how it sucks."

"Thanks. I'm sorry about yours too."

His expression gets sheepish. "Thanks. Yeah. That was hell. But it's over. And now—"

"You get to have fucked-up relationships with both of them separately."

He just barely chuckles. "Basically."

"Do you see your mom much?"

"Birthdays and holidays."

"When was the last time?"

"I called her on Daisy's birthday. To make sure she called, left a message, made Daisy feel loved."

"Really?"

"Yeah." That same sheepish expression. "Don't give me that look."

"What look?"

"I don't know. But I don't like it. We're talking about your shit."

"I thought we were getting coffee."

He makes that *hmmm* noise.

"What?"

"It's not like you. To avoid things."

"Thanks, Dr. Phil."

"If I'm going to be a TV host, I'm Oprah."

I raise a brow.

"She's the voice of America."

A laugh escapes my lips. It's true, I guess. "Okay. You can be Oprah. Thanks, Oprah."

"She doesn't really give advice."

"Just sits there and lets other people talk."

"You could learn a lot from her," he says.

"Oh my god." I go to play hit him.

He grabs my wrist.

It's equal parts hard and soft.

And entirely *I'm going to pin you to the wall and have my way with you.*

I swallow hard.

He stares into my eyes.

For a second, I consider going for it, kissing him, asking him to take me home, touch me, fuck me, do whatever it takes to make me forget.

To make me feel good.

But that's…

I can't.

I really can't.

"You're sweeter than you act." My voice is a struggle.

"With Daisy." There. That's it. I need to remind myself why this can't happen. And him.

Daisy.

My best friend.

My favorite person in the world.

His sister.

His favorite person in the world.

"She hasn't totally given up on Mom." He releases me.

"You have?"

"I don't know." He takes a step backward. "I used to think my dad was crazy. Over-reacting. But now... I don't know. She is trying."

"It's hard."

He nods *yeah*.

Neither of us expands on *it*. So many things are hard. Dealing with parents, fighting addiction, standing here without jumping into his arms.

His mom—

There's something there, something I want to know. But there's something about his posture too. I shouldn't press it.

He motions to a box of chocolate-covered almonds. "You sure you aren't hungry?"

"Isn't that what the chocolate is for?"

He half-smiles. "True." He motions to the corner. The direction of the coffee bar. "Why don't you get a seat on the patio. I'll get these."

"Oh. Sure. Yeah."

"Should be a few minutes."

"Grab a water too maybe."

He nods *yeah*. Watches me move around the corner. Toward the door.

It's a perfectly reasonable idea. Divide and conquer.

Is that all?

Or does he need a reprieve? A chance to collect himself? And talk himself out of doing something very, very stupid.

And very, very wrong.

And very, very right.

Chapter Twenty-Three

LUNA

I stop by the bathrooms. Pee, wash my hands, fix my lipstick. The pinkish red. The one that makes him tease.

It's totally ridiculous. What woman has ever thought *gee, I better find a shade that makes me look like I love sucking cock?*

Okay, I'm sure it's happened. It's probably the number one question on porn set makeup artists' minds. *What red says ram me hard and come on my face?*

Do guys actually want that?

Does Oliver?

I'm sure he watches porn. He's a guy. Most do.

Most women do too. I watch the occasional video, but most of it is too over the top, too violent, too much.

My imagination is plenty active.

When I close my eyes, I see him behind me. Wrapping his arms around my waist. Tugging at the zipper of my jumpsuit. Whispering in my ears. *I want the entire store to hear you come.*

Fuck.

Nope.

Not going there.

Going outside. To sit. And drink coffee. And not think about my parents lying to me.

Or about Oliver.

I really need less on the *don't think about this* list.

I take a deep breath, move around the corner, outside, to the patio area.

It's quiet but crowded. A mom and a girl in a stroller. Three people in laid-back attire, talking business. A couple sharing a scoop of ice cream from the place with a pale yellow food truck.

They're pretty good. Not too sweet. With a to die for coffee ice cream.

But coffee is a lot like chocolate. Best in its purest state.

I find a seat. A small table with a two-person bench. No room for restraint.

What good is restraint, really?

Wouldn't it be better if I told restraint to fuck off? If I climbed into Oliver's lap, hooked my arms around his neck, pressed my lips to his?

Does he taste like the toothpaste in his bathroom?

Like chocolate and coffee?

Is he already sipping the French press?

Fuck. I pull out my cell. Look for a pleasant distraction. Find only a *call me when you're ready to talk* from Divya.

Ugh, no.

Forget it.

I lean back—the bench is just off the wall—close my eyes, soak in the weather. It really is nice, just warm enough, just breezy enough, just bright enough the sun feels good on my skin.

Oliver turns the corner. I can recognize his steady foot-steps without opening my eyes. Then the smell of his shampoo.

"They put it in takeout cups." He sets both on the table. Then the bars of chocolate. "Disgusting. I know."

"Only if you put cream and sugar in yours." I blink my eyes open. Watch him sit. "Because you thought I wouldn't see."

"It's my half of the coffee."

"Uh-huh."

"Shouldn't I drink what I like?"

"Sounds like crazy talk."

He chuckles *you're ridiculous*. Motions to the cups. "Only one way to find out."

It's a strange dare, but I'm not turning down the chance to sip extra java.

I wrap my fingers around the cup in front of me. A normal paper cup with a sleeve. The familiar feel of cardboard. The warmth of the liquid inside.

That hint of plastic lid. Then warm, dark, rich coffee.

Fuck. That's good. I let out a soft groan.

His pupils dilate. He watches as I pick up the second cup, taste a sip, swallow, groan.

The same coffee. No milk. No sugar. No additions but the lipstick marking the lid.

My lipstick marking his cup.

It's not enough. I want to see it on his skin.

Fuck.

I can't face my parents.

I can't stay across the hall without touching him.

I can't be anywhere.

Or maybe I can. Maybe it's worth it. To touch him and kiss him and risk everything.

"Proud of me?" he asks.

"I am."

"For once." His voice is teasing, but there's a sadness in his eyes. It hurts. That he's disappointed people.

I want to say something. To soothe him. Explain how much he means to me. How much I value this relationship. Whatever it is. But I don't know how to say that without changing everything. So I pick up the single-origin chocolate bar. "Shall we?"

He nods *go for it*.

I unwrap the paper. Then the foil. There's a long, thin bar, in four pieces. I break it in half. Then quarters. I leave three on the foil, bring one to my lips.

Fuck.

It's so good. Too good.

My eyes close.

My senses flood. Rich, fruity, chocolate. It has the intensity of dried figs. Caramel. Raisin.

The depth of flavor. One on top of another.

I groan as it dissolves on my tongue.

"Are you eating that or fucking it?" There's no irritation in his voice. Only deep, pure need.

And I need his need. I need the world to make sense. To be someplace beautiful and comforting and warm.

God, he's so handsome.

So sexy. With those intense blue eyes, that dark hair, those strong arms.

"Try it. You'll see." I take another bite. Try to focus on the notes of fig and raisin.

Watch him pick up a piece of chocolate, bring it to his lips, place it on his tongue.

His eyes close.

His brow softens.

His entire expression fills with bliss. The kind of intense, pure bliss that usually comes with an orgasm.

Or maybe he has a different look when he comes.

I don't know.

I need to know.

A groan escapes his lips. It's low and deep and hot as fuck.

My sex clenches.

My thighs shake.

My body screams *yes, now, touch him*.

He's right there. His legs are three inches from mine. I could put my hand on his thigh.

I could whisper *please* in his ear. Kiss him as I stroke him to orgasm.

Why did I wear a fucking jumpsuit?

There's no way for him to touch me in this thing.

But I don't care. I'm ready to go to the alley behind the grocery store. To do away with the whole thing. To feel my naked skin against his.

Now.

Please.

"Fuck." His eyes blink open. "No wonder you have expensive tastes."

"You insisted."

"I know." His eyes find mine. "I'm glad I did. Get to watch you enjoy it."

"Right." It's not that he wants to watch me come. It's just that he, uh...

Nope.

That's pretty much the only explanation.

He does.

And I do.

And this.

Uh...

I swallow a sip of coffee. Fight my desire to groan. It's good, yes, but it's not top-tier the way the chocolate is.

It's just good.

I don't need to groan.

I don't need to wonder if my groan makes him hard.

I don't need to think about the feeling of his cock straining against his jeans.

What would he say, if I asked?

There're too many people here.

It's not private enough.

Not here.

But at home, in his room, on those black sheets, where I can strip down to nothing and—

"Where are you going?" He groans over another bite of chocolate.

"Huh?"

"Your expression... you're thinking something."

Does he really not know?

He must. He's not stupid.

"Just thinking." I take another sip. Will it to cool me down. Or wake me into sense.

"Thinking..."

"Yeah."

"About..."

"Isn't it obvious?" My gaze goes to his lips. Chin. Chest. Stomach. The table is in the way. I can't see his crotch without turning my head. Without making it obvious.

"Luna..." There's intent in his voice. A *we can't*. And an *I want to*.

I swallow another sip. Try to bring my gaze to his eyes.

"Luna..." His tone shifts. Less *we can't*. More *I want to*.

My eyes find his.

He stares back at me.

Then he moves a little closer.

And I turn a little further.

His fingers skim my collarbone. "Luna... we can't."

"I know." I close my eyes anyway.

He kisses me anyway.

It's soft. Intense. Electric.

He tastes like coffee and chocolate and Oliver.

And home and safety and danger.

My lips part.

His tongue slips into my mouth.

He kisses me like he's claiming me.

Maybe he is.

Maybe this is the only thing that makes sense.

He pulls back with a sigh. "Luna…"

"I…"

His eyes find mine. Fill with apology.

Fuck.

"We can't."

"I know." I swallow hard.

He stands. "I, uh… I'm sorry."

What?

"But I… work." He looks at his cell. Pretends to check the time. "I can walk you back. If you want. But I can't…"

"Yeah."

"So… uh."

"Yeah."

He gives me the chance. To ask him to stay. To tell him we can, we will, we must.

But I don't.

So he leaves.

And I sit there, with my chocolate and coffee, and fall apart alone.

Chapter Twenty-Four

OLIVER

I taste her the entire walk to the shop. As I sit, prep, move through my first appointment.

Coffee and chocolate and Luna.

That red lipstick.

It's still on my lips.

On my cup.

That perfect shade on the smooth white plastic. I need it there. I need it everywhere.

We can't.

I can't.

But, fuck, I want to.

It's impossible to concentrate. She fills every spare moment.

The taste of her lips.

The need in her eyes.

The hurt in her expression.

I'm fucking this up too.

Hurting her too.

But she…

She agrees, doesn't she?

We can't.

She knows that.

She loves Daisy as much as I do.

She has even more to lose.

People don't expect her to fuck up. They won't shrug *what can you do, that's just Luna?*

The reasoning fails to stick. So what if this will hurt Daisy? Daisy doesn't exactly approve of my frost with Holden.

And she's a grown-up.

If she's old enough to fuck my best friend, she can get over me fucking hers.

But I know that's bullshit.

That it's not the same. Even if it is.

Because I'm the alcoholic fuckup who ruins everything he touches.

And she's... not.

I don't resent my sister. She's smart and sweet and hard-working. She deserves all her success. She deserves our parents' pride.

But, fuck, why can't Dad give me that look for once?

Why can't one person say *good job, Oliver, I'm proud of you?*

Am I going to be a constant disappointment until the day I die?

I'm fucking up the only good thing in my life.

And, this time, I can only blame myself.

————

I SHOULDN'T AVOID LUNA. I SHOULD TALK TO HER.

Figure out some way to reconcile this.

Act like a fucking grown-up.

But the second I get home, see her on the couch, watch hurt spread over her expression—

My body screams *bring her to your room, touch her, taste her, fuck her.*

Comfort her the only way you know how.

I can't stand here and say *I'm sorry, I was out of line, I won't do it again.*

I don't believe it.

But I can't take her to my room and fuck her either.

So I nod *hey*. Ask, "You have dinner?"

"I'm not hungry. And I have a test tomorrow." She doesn't give me a chance to respond. Pulls her textbooks to her chest. Moves up the stairs.

Okay. I have time.

An entire minute.

But it's the same problem.

I won't apologize for kissing her.

I won't tell her I don't want her.

I can't touch her.

So I let her go. I go to the gym, work out until I'm exhausted, shower, fix dinner, knock on her door to let her know it's ready.

She doesn't reply. But a few minutes later, she leaves her room. Heats up dinner. Talks with Gabe about some TV show they both watch.

She has company.

Probably better company than me.

Dad is an asshole sometimes, but he's not an alcoholic fuckup. He doesn't break everything he touches.

He isn't going to kiss Daisy's best friend.

———

ALL WEEK, IT'S THE SAME. I WORK LATE. SPEND MY evenings at the gym. Leave her dinner in the fridge.

She stops avoiding me, but she barely speaks when we

177

pass. She just nods, says something about the weather, returns to studying.

By Saturday, I'm worn thin. Work is my only distraction. Then too many cups of coffee.

The bar next to my favorite shop is already pounding. Friends out for an early night. Drinking beers or slamming shots.

Laughing.

Forgetting their problems.

Erasing the voice in their head screaming *I'm a fuckup*.

There's beer on the patio. I can smell it from the sidewalk. I don't even like beer, but I want every drop.

Every perfect, pain erasing drop.

I jog home instead. Try to scrub myself clean in the shower. Fail to erase my thoughts.

Maybe Dad was right.

Maybe I can't handle this.

Maybe I need more help. Something else. Something more serious.

Or maybe...

I don't know.

I cinch a towel around my waist. Step into the hallway. Try to think of some way to soothe myself without drinking.

The door to Luna's room opens. She steps into the hallway in a short black dress and wedge boots.

She's all dolled up. Deep red lips, dark eye makeup, shiny silver purse.

Gorgeous grey eyes passing over me.

She's not shy about checking out my shoulders, chest, stomach, hips.

Her breath catches in her throat. Her eyes move back up my body. Stop at mine. "You're not ready yet."

Huh?

She notices my dumbstruck expression. "Patrick's birthday. We said we'd go together."

Shit, is that today? The guys at the shop have been talking about it all week. But it's always in the middle of shit I try to ignore.

Booze, birthday, booze.

I bought you more Bud Light! What a present, huh? Think you'll ever be able to handle the hard stuff? Maybe in a sippy cup!

"Ollie?" Her chest rises with her inhale. "Are you okay?"

"Yeah. Just, uh, need coffee."

Her eyes flit to the window. It's already dark. Way past the usual time for coffee. "Maybe I should meet you there."

"No. I'll get dressed."

"Okay."

"Give me ten." I wait for her to tease me. *Ten minutes is a while, what do you need all that time for?* But she doesn't.

She just nods *okay* and moves down the stairs.

Of course.

This is the most we've spoken since I kissed her.

She's wearing the same lipstick. When I close my eyes, I taste it.

I taste her.

Is this really better than going for it?

Either I lose the only person who gets me.

Or I risk losing my sister.

Fucking this up for all three of us.

I can't do that.

I need to behave myself.

I dress in my nicest outfit. Slacks, a button-up shirt, motorcycle boots.

Maybe that's what I need. A fucking bike. Another way to find a thrill.

Anything that isn't touching her.

My cock protests.

I attempt to reason with it.

Yeah, Luna is dressed to kill. Yeah, she's gorgeous and sweet and sassy and I really want to hear her come, but—

Fuck, I've got nothing.

The damn thing is winning.

I don't have the willpower.

I don't have the reason.

I don't have shit.

These aren't jeans. I can't hide a hard-on.

With that outfit she's wearing—

Fuck, I don't know.

I take a deep breath. Let out a heavy exhale. Move downstairs.

She's at the counter, her back to me. A gorgeous silhouette.

Tall black boots, long legs, short black dress that hugs every inch of her curves. It's off the shoulders. Like she's in the middle of stripping.

And that short haircut—

Her elegant neck is on display. Begging for my hands, lips, teeth—

Fuck, I want to kiss her, touch her, hold her.

"You ready to go?" She keeps her back to me.

"Yeah. Sure."

"You want to call an Uber?"

"No," I say. "I can drive."

She picks up her purse from the counter. Turns to face me. "Is that a good idea?" Her voice is soft. Questioning, not accusing.

But it still gnaws at the hole in my gut. She doesn't usually go there. She doesn't usually remind me I'm Oliver Flynn, alcoholic fuckup.

"Patrick lives on the other side of the freeway," I say. "You want to walk?"

"You know what I mean." Her eyes meet mine. They bore into mine. Ask a million things I can't answer.

"Yeah. I'll be fine."

"You sure?"

No. This is going to kill me. But that's not what she means, so I nod *yeah*, and I lead her to the car.

Chapter Twenty-Five

OLIVER

Fuck. This is really going to kill me.

A fully stocked bar in the corner.

And Luna, next to me, hurt and gorgeous and completely irresistible.

I suck a breath through my teeth. Push out a heavy exhale.

This is a party. I've been to a million parties.

Yeah, this is the first time I'm attending sober. But my dad and Daisy and the state of California are wrong. I'm not an addict.

I like to drink, period, the end.

Not drinking—

Not a big deal.

I shrug my shoulders. Reach for Luna. Think better of it.

We've already suffered the world's most awkward drive.

Fifteen minutes of Lorde and Luna is still nursing a frown. I didn't know that was possible. Usually, she slips into a trance like bliss the second she hears her favorite performer.

She doesn't want me closer.

But where the fuck can I put my hands? Without a drink, they're empty and awkward.

I slide them into my pockets. Look for a better distraction.

The room is already full. Half a dozen people from the shop. A handful of Patrick's friends. Cute girls. Single ones and significant others.

Forest and his girlfriend Skye are sitting on the couch. She's in his lap in some sexy mesh and lace dress. It's as loud as her platform boots. And it shows off her massive tits.

She's some kind of influencer. Or maybe just a plus-size model. Her Instagram feed is nonstop pics of her in lingerie or swimwear. She says it has something to do with body positivity, but it's hard to see beyond her epic cleavage.

Sure, she models plus-size clothes, but she's not wearing a lot of them.

I try to hold on to that.

Stare at her lush legs, her dark hair, her huge tits.

Her hair is cut in a straight line at her shoulders. A cut Luna used to have. Now that her hair is short enough to bare her neck—

Fuck.

Patrick catches sight of us. Waves some kind of *stay there* and heads over.

"Should we have brought him something?" Luna asks.

Yeah. I usually bring a bottle to these things. But today I have nothing.

It's too obvious. Like I'm standing here naked, a blinking arrow pointing at my scars.

A bright light flashing *Oliver Flynn, alcoholic fuckup.*

Patrick arrives before I can reply. He greets me with a high five. Offers Luna a hug.

She takes it. Pulls him close.

Closer than she normally would.

Or maybe I can stand it less than I normally would. Now that I've kissed her. Now that it's impossible to deny how much I need her.

He's fucking touching her.

What the fuck is he doing touching her?

My chest eases as he releases her. Then I spot the bottle in his hand—Bud Light, of course—and it tenses again.

"Thanks for coming." His voice is happy drunk. He's already gone. This early.

It's obvious too. He's standing there, all smooth and confident, like he thinks he's smooth and sober.

Am I that obvious?

"You need anything." He points to the bar. "And you, Luna. You're Daisy's friend, right?"

"I'm Luna," she says. "No qualifier needed."

He chuckles. Leans a little closer. Into flirting distance. "Sean's ex?"

"What did I just say?" she teases.

His laugh is lighter this time. "Gorgeous goddess?"

"That one, I'll take." Her red lips curl into a smile. That same shade of deep, slightly pink red.

Fuck, I need to taste that lipstick.

"How about, Luna, mistress of the boom box?" he asks.

"Boom box?" Her brow knits in confusion.

He chuckles, again. "The music." He motions to the stereo setup in the back. "Boom box is something we used to say in the old days."

"How old are you turning?" She shoots him an *I don't buy it* expression. "You don't look forty."

185

"It's the plastic surgery. Does wonders," he says.

She laughs. "I can see that." She reaches out. Touches him. Her fingers on his jaw.

I have to press my palm into my thigh to keep from grabbing her.

"Well, give me his number," she says. "In case I need it."

"Oh no, I can't allow anyone to mar perfection." He smiles, pure charm.

She smiles back, endeared. Or pretending. Or trying to make me jealous.

Is she that petty?

Am I that desperate to believe I matter to her?

"I hope you like eighteen-year-olds singing about getting dumped," I say.

He nods. "My favorite genre." He presses his hands to his heart. "You know me. Love the pain."

I guess. He does have an ex he isn't over.

But the guy alternates between sunny and stormy like *that*. One day he's bouncing, flirting with every cute girl in sight. The next, he's hiding behind his hoodie and head-phones, completely blocking out the world.

I always noticed, but I never thought much of it. People are who they are.

They don't change.

Only I...

Fuck, I don't know.

"I better go with you." I reach for her reflexively. Try to stop myself. But I'm too slow, my hand skims her waist.

Her cheeks flame with anger.

I pull my hand to my side. "So you pick something good."

"No grunge, Ollie, we need to bring the mood up, not down." She blows Patrick a kiss. "Happy birthday."

"I hope that doesn't count as my birthday kiss," he says.

She smiles *who do you take me for?* Takes a half-step toward him. Places her hand on his chest. Rises to her tiptoes.

Kisses him.

His fucking cheek.

But still.

My fingers curl into fists. My heart thuds against my chest.

No fucking way.

Only there's every fucking way. I don't have a say. I've barely spoken to her. I don't have any right to tell her what to do.

She waves another goodbye to Patrick, turns, saunters to the stereo.

It's connected to his laptop. To some streaming service.

She bends over, places her palms on the table, focuses intently on her selection.

Fuck, she has a perfect ass. It's impossible to look away.

I try, but my eyes refuse. They stay on her as the music shifts—some popular singer who's on the radio twenty-four seven.

As she rises.

As she turns to me with a look of righteous indignation.

She *is* pissed. But that's not fair.

She's avoiding me too.

She had the chance to say *I know we can't but I don't care.* And I—

Fuck, I'm the one who kissed her then stopped it. Of course, she's pissed.

I should let her go. Let her mingle. Stay the fuck away.

For a moment, I stay in place.

She holds my gaze, waiting for me to react, say something, somehow explain.

But I don't know what she wants me to explain. So I let her move forward. Let her brush past me on her way to the bar.

My body refuses to still. I follow her. Wrap my fingers around her wrist.

She looks up at me *what the fuck?*

"Let me fix you a drink," I say.

She motions to my hand.

I release her. "A Negroni, right?"

Her posture softens. "Here?"

Somehow, Patrick has everything I need. The guy only drinks Bud Light. What's he doing with Campari *and* Vermouth?

Is it shit I left?

A million things fill my head. A night in Mexico with Luna. Daisy's birthday eve. I fixed a dozen classic cocktails. So my sister could try everything.

She didn't like this one. Too bitter. Too alcoholic.

She favored Holden's drink. Kentucky Mule. Ginger beer and bourbon. All sugar and spice. Like the chai lattes she drinks every morning.

But Luna starts her day with black coffee. Of course she loved the Negroni. The only desserts she'll consume are eighty-five percent dark chocolate and coffee ice cream.

Everything else is too sweet.

"Oliver?" she asks.

Right. I'm fixing her a drink. Like normal.

Things can be normal. For once. "We need a glass."

"This is fine." She motions to one of the red plastic cups.

I shoot her the *really* look.

"It's a party."

"You deserve the best."

She nods *true*. "You're finally making sense."

"Does Patrick really think you're a goddess?"

"Excuse you?"

"I'm not saying you're not—" I motion to the kitchen. It's around the corner. This is a one-bedroom apartment. A big den, a hallway kitchen, two doors.

"You're digging your own grave," she says.

Probably. "You are a goddess."

"Obviously."

I actually chuckle. Fuck, I like her so much. She's funny, confident, strong. "Anyone can see that."

"Not really seeing your original point."

Yeah, me either. Of course, he thinks she's a goddess. She's tall, curvy perfection. "The dress."

"Excuse you?"

I move into the hallway. Find a short glass in the cabinet. Ice in the freezer.

"You want one too?" she asks.

What the fuck can I say? It's not my drink, sure, but since when do I refuse booze? "Don't like gin."

She knows it's bullshit, but she lets it go. "What about my dress?"

"It's fucking hot."

"Thank you."

"And that lipstick."

She shakes her head *you're ridiculous*, but I can't tell if it's a good or bad *you're ridiculous*. "Oh my god, Ollie, you are not going on about the lipstick again!"

"It's a fact," I say.

She motions for me to follow as she moves back to the bar. "It's a good color for me. I'm a cool summer."

"A what?"

"It's flattering."

"It's hot."

"Yes. That's the male version of flattering."

My eyes stay on her lips. Fuck, I need to taste them. To taste her. I focus on my task. Equal parts gin, Campari, vermouth.

One shot of each.

Bam.

Bam.

Bam.

I stir with a straw. Pull it from the glass. Bring it to my lips.

A reflex.

I stop. But not fast enough.

The flavor explodes on my tongue. Bitter, herbaceous, rich. It's good gin too. Really fucking good.

"Thanks." She brings the glass to her lips. Watches me watch her lipstick mark the glass. "Fuck." She lets out a soft moan. "You're skilled."

"Thanks."

"I might let the dick lipstick thing go. This once."

"It's true."

"It's not."

"'Cause you don't like it?" I should let her go. She's more dangerous than the bottle of gin. I'm already too close—we're pressed together—but I still move closer.

She looks up at me as she takes another sip. "I didn't like it with him."

"So you do like it?" I ask.

She sets her drink on the bar.

I pick it up. Motion to the bottle of gin.

She nods. Watches me fix another.

This time, I don't taste it. I don't covet it. I don't think about how the bitter cocktail will erase the voice in my head screaming *you're only going to fuck this up worse.*

I just hand it to her. Watch her wrap her lips around the glass, sip, swallow.

Fuck, I can still taste the drink.

That's what's on her lips.

I need to taste her fucking lips.

Now.

"What if I do like it?" Her hand goes to my chest. The same way she touched Patrick. But different. So fucking different.

Her fingers brush my collar. Then my neck.

Fuck. That feels good. Too good.

"Do you?" I ask.

"What would it matter to you?" She runs her fingertip over my collar. "If we can't."

"Luna."

Her fingers brush my neck. "What if I want to like it? What if I'm just waiting for the right guy? Is that what you want to hear?"

"I don't—"

"How about I go to Patrick. Tell him I have a better birthday present for him?"

"Luna."

"You're jealous." She presses her palm into my chest. Pushing me hard.

I hold my ground. "Of course, I'm—"

"You've barely spoken to me all fucking week, Oliver. You promised to comfort me and you ran away. What gives you the right to be jealous?"

"You're doing it on purpose?"

She shrugs. "I'm single. He's single. How is it any of your business?" She takes another sip. Licks her lips. Stares at me, proud, defiant, angry.

Which only makes my cock stir. It loves this side of her as much as I do. I want that proud, defiant woman in my bed, ripping off my jeans when I try to order her out of her dress.

She shakes her head *you're fucking ridiculous*. Then she finishes her drink, turns, spins on her heel, moves to the door.

She's right.

I'm ridiculous.

I don't have any fucking right to my jealousy.

But I chase her out the door anyway.

Chapter Twenty-Six

OLIVER

Even in wedge boots, she's fast. A blur of silver hair and dark fabric.

I run after her. Down the stairs. Past a group of people smoking. Across the residential street.

"Where are you going?" I catch up to her. Reach for her.

She pulls her arm away. "Away."

"Away where?"

"Away from you."

"Luna."

"Don't Luna me." She folds her arms over her chest. "You've been avoiding me all week. Now that I might blow your friend, you suddenly want to talk to me?"

"I didn't—"

"I don't care what your reasons are. You're an asshole."

"I know."

"Then you know why I'm leaving."

Yeah, but I have to stop her anyway. "Can I explain?"

She sucks a breath through her teeth. "I'm calling an Uber."

"Please. I'll drive you wherever you want to go. Just let me explain."

"Why should I?"

"Because you want to."

Her eyes flare with anger.

"Because I'll look pathetic if I beg."

"Sounds like a reason you should."

"I will."

She motions *go ahead*. Folds her arms. Stares at me like she's sure I won't take her dare.

But I will. If that's what it takes.

Fuck, here goes nothing. I take a deep breath. Drop to my knees with my exhale. This is not how I imagined doing this.

My head is already flush with other images—

My hands under her dress.

My lips on her thighs.

My name rolling off her lips.

Not the time. Not that my cock cares.

I try to ignore the fucker. Press my palms together. Look up at her. "Please, Luna."

She looks down at me. "Please what?"

Too much. *Let me explain. Let me confess. Tell me it's okay.* "Give me ten minutes. If you still want to tell me to fuck off, I will."

She says nothing.

"If that's not in the cards, at least let me make sure you get home okay."

"I'm an adult."

"I know."

"I can take care of myself," she says.

"I know."

"Why should I let you pull that patriarchal bullshit?"

"Because I'm begging," I say. "Because I look pathetic."

"You do."

"And it's probably embarrassing for you. How pathetic I look."

She shakes her head. "I'm enjoying it."

"I'll stay here." I reach for her hand. "If that's what you want."

"It would serve you right." She half-smiles. "After all the shit about my lipstick."

"It would."

"I should probably keep you here awhile. At least until your knees are aching."

"Okay."

Her smile widens. "You think I won't?"

"I know you will. But I also know you're merciful."

She makes that *kinda* gesture.

"You didn't throw my phone out the window."

"I would have."

"Really?"

"Maybe."

"I will stay here."

She looks down at me. "Okay." For a long time, she just stares at me.

I stare back at her.

The sounds from the party mix with the street beyond.

Pop music, laughter, conversation, engines, brakes, breeze.

My knees burn.

Then ache.

Concrete is fucking hard. These pants are thin. Ruined, now, probably.

But I don't care.

I need to talk to her. To explain. To fix this.

She makes me wait through two songs, then she nods

okay, offers her hand, helps me up. "I don't want to go to your house."

Because my dad is there? Because it's where I sleep? Because we can't have loud sex against the wall with my father home? "How about we drive someplace nice?"

"Where?"

"The beach. Up in Malibu. It's a clear night. We can see the stars."

"That's a long way to go for an explanation."

"I know."

She stares at me for a moment, considering her options, then she nods *okay* and follows me to the car.

———

PATRICK LIVES IN CULVER CITY. JUST SOUTH OF THE TEN and east of the 405. It's a long way from Malibu.

She knows that.

She's willing to give me that time.

That means something.

I put on her favorite album and find the nearest on ramp.

She's quiet as I take the ten to the 405 to the one.

The freeway empties as we pass the lights and sounds of the Santa Monica pier. Nothing but open road, dark sky, miles of ocean.

She loves the beach, loves the water, loves swimming.

The way I love drinking.

The way I loved drinking.

I don't know anymore. After six weeks of sobriety, the world is a different place.

Harder, colder, darker.

But somehow brighter and fuller too.

Luna sets her purse in her lap. She plays with the edges.

She's antsy too.

Because she doesn't want to be here with me?

Or because she does?

I try to think of something to say. Some way to start. But the words jumble in my throat.

There's too much.

Way too fucking much.

Eventually, I come to a quiet stretch of beach. Turn left. Pull into the empty parking lot.

Lorde's vocals fill the space as I cut the engine.

Luna turns the mirror toward her. Pulls her lipstick from her purse. Turns to me with a half-smile, half *what the fuck is wrong with you*. "Not a word."

I mime zipping my lips.

She just barely laughs. Shakes her head. That same *you're deranged and I like it* laugh of hers.

She looks to the mirror as she adds another coat of lipstick.

It's just us, in this car, on this empty beach.

Why the makeup?

Is she teasing me on purpose? Putting on a shield?

Fucking with me?

It's too hard, understanding another person.

Impossible.

And the only thing I want.

I want to know every part of her.

She drops the lipstick in her purse. Closes the latch. Places it in her lap.

"You want to stay in here?" It's a tiny space. There isn't enough room for how much I want her. "Or the sand?"

"It's freezing."

I slide my leather jacket off my shoulders. Offer it to her.

Her eyes move to the water. The sky. "Here is okay."

I nod.

She turns a little toward me. "It's fucked up, you know. You promised you'd be there and then you ditched me."

"I'm sorry."

"But you don't even stick with that. You still fix me coffee every morning and leave me dinner every night. You still walk out of the shower in a towel that's barely cinched around your hips. You still sit there, in your room, playing your fucking Nirvana, filling the entire house with your mood."

"I don't mean to—"

"Pick a side, Oliver. Either you're my friend or you aren't."

"It's complicated."

She shakes her head. "It's not complicated."

"It is. You know that."

She turns to me. "I know you're Daisy's brother. I know you kissed me. I know you regret it—"

"I don't." I'll never regret kissing her.

"Then why—"

"I'm an alcoholic."

"What?" Her eyes go wide.

"It's the first time I've said it out loud. Like this." I swallow hard. "Even in my head, I protest. 'I'm not an alcoholic. I don't have a problem. I just like to party. So what if I drink too much sometimes? So what if it's the only thing that kills the voice in my head that tells me I'm a fuckup? Why is bourbon wrong when anti-depressants are right'?"

"Are you on medication?"

I shake my head.

"Should you be?"

"How the fuck should I know?"

She shrinks back.

"Sorry." I run a hand through my hair. "I… this isn't your shit, Luna. I'm not trying to put it on you."

"Okay."

"I shouldn't snap. It's just…"

"A lot?"

"Yeah."

Her grey eyes fill with understanding. "You're an alcoholic?"

"Is it that surprising?"

"No."

"Hey."

A laugh spills from her lips. "Ollie, we bought enough booze for a dozen people in Mexico."

"Yeah."

"And that was only half of what you drank."

"You never said anything."

"Would it have done any good?" she asks.

I shake my head.

"And like you said, not my shit."

"Yeah."

"But I… I want to be your friend." Her fingers skim the hem of her dress. "And this is not excusing you for being an asshole. Friends don't suddenly disappear. Friends don't ignore each other. You have shit to deal with, fine. But you tell me first. You tell me you need space. You tell me—"

"I like you."

"What?"

"A lot. More than I've ever liked anyone. It's not just that I want to fuck you, Luna. I do. But I want everything. Things I've never wanted before."

"What things?"

My body warms. "I want to touch you, taste you, make you come. And I want to hold you. I want to go home and cook you dinner, and help you study, and laugh at *The Bachelorette* and tease you about your lipstick. And watch you put on your makeup when we're getting ready to go out, annoyed you're taking so fucking long, but loving it too, because it's you."

She swallows hard.

"But... even if you weren't Daisy's best friend... I'm a fuckup. A mess. I can't put that on you."

"You're sober now?"

I nod.

"For how long?"

"Six weeks."

"Is that why you're always hanging out with me?"

"Not exactly."

Her voice is soft. Curious. "Why exactly?"

"Because everything is hard and dark. And you're this fucking beacon of light. You're bright and alive and you make me feel bright and alive. When you smile, the clouds part. When you laugh, I get warm all over. I think about it as much as I think about your groan. And I think about your groan all the fucking time."

"Fuck."

"Yeah." I press my palms into my slacks. Anything to keep from touching her.

"Six weeks?"

I nod.

"And you're staying sober?"

"I'm trying."

"You promise?"

I nod.

"I need a better promise. A promise on something that means something to you." She holds out her hand.

200

"What?"

"Your dick."

"My dick?"

She nods. "Swear. On your dick."

"What if I break my promise?"

"Then I break your dick."

I chuckle. "That's violent."

"I know." She motions to her hand. "Promise."

"I swear, on my dick, that I'll try really fucking hard."

"Okay." She shifts forward. "You should come over here. To this side. Because that steering wheel is going to get in the way."

"Are you sure?"

"Yeah."

"I don't have a condom."

"You have a hand, don't you?"

Chapter Twenty-Seven

LUNA

Oliver's lips curl into a smile. "I do."

"Two, actually."

He nods. "Not here."

Yes, here. No, waiting. "Now."

His smile widens. "Impatient."

"Now."

"I'm bigger than I look."

"Ollie, I'm sold. You don't have to talk up your dick."

A chuckle falls off his lips. "You're sold?"

"I already want to fuck you."

"Yeah?"

"What about *now* do you not understand?"

He laughs again. "Fuck, I really like you." His eyes brighten. He shakes his head *you're ridiculous* then he pushes his seat all the way back. Puts his hands on the center console. Slides into my seat.

Kind of.

He's only half on it.

I try to shift. To climb into his lap. But my head hits the roof and my ass hits the door.

"See. No space." He brings his hand to my cheek, his thumb against my temple, his eyes locked on mine.

God, the way he's looking at me. Like I'm the only thing he's ever needed.

He's so close. And he smells so good.

And I need him so fucking badly.

"I can't wait," I say.

"Yeah?"

"Less bragging. More making me come."

Again, he smiles. That same *I really like you* smile.

Which is sweet. Incredibly sweet.

But, seriously. "Less talking. More sex."

"Outside." He drags his hand down my side. "I'll keep you warm."

Fuck, that feels good.

Okay. Outside. I can do that. I can do anything except wait for him to touch me properly.

I nod. Reach for the door. Pull the handle.

He follows. Pushes the door closed behind him.

His hands go to my hips. In one seamless gesture, he pins me to the car door. "You're tall."

I nod.

"The angle works." He rocks forward, so his hard-on brushes my pelvis.

Yes. The angle works. Fuck, how the angle works. My body catches fire.

Cold, what cold?

I'm burning up.

"You drive me out of my fucking mind, Luna." He keeps one hand on my hip. Brings the other to my chin. "I've been dreaming about this for so fucking long."

He tilts my head so I'm staring into his eyes.

Then he moves closer.

Closer.

His eyes flutter closed.

Mine follow.

His lips brush mine. It's soft at first.

Then harder.

Harder.

My lips part to make way for his tongue.

He claims my mouth. There's no other way to describe it. Like he's never going to get enough of me. Like I'm the only thing he needs.

Like I'm his.

And he's mine.

I want that so badly. Too badly. But I don't care. I don't care about anything except the taste of his lips and the smell of his skin and the feel of his body against mine.

He pulls back with a sigh. Runs his fingertips over my jawline. "Too hard?"

"I'll tell you."

His mouth crashes into mine. No softness. All hunger and need.

He sucks on my bottom lip.

Then it's the scrape of his teeth.

My hips shift of their own accord. My hands go to his dark hair. It's too short. I can barely get a grip. But I can.

And I'm not shy about tugging.

He groans. That same low, perfect groan he makes over his coffee.

My sex clenches.

Yes. All. More.

I need to make him groan again. Now.

I rock my hips to grind against him.

He runs his fingertips down my neck. Along my collarbone.

He traces the neckline of my dress. Then he dips below it.

205

"Fuck." He pulls back. "You're not wearing a bra?"

"The dress is lined. I don't need—"

"You thought about this?" He runs his thumb over my nipple. "When you picked out your dress?"

"Maybe."

"Thought this might happen?"

"Maybe."

"Wanted to drive me crazy?"

"Yes."

"Bad girl." He rolls my nipple between his thumb and forefinger. It's hard. Enough, it hurts.

But in a way that makes my sex clench. "Bad girl? For this?" I arch my back, lifting my chest.

He gets my meaning immediately. Rolls my dress down my chest. The sleeves catch as my breasts spill from the fabric. "For teasing me."

"You don't like it?"

"I love it." He kisses me again. The soft brush of his lips. Then the rough scrape of his teeth.

I groan against his mouth as he cups my breasts.

He's slow. Patient. Too patient.

His thumb against my nipple. Up and down. Left and right. Zigzags. Circles.

Softly.

Then harder.

I pull back. "More." I rock my hips. His pants are thin. There's barely any fabric between my sex and his cock. But I need it gone. I need his body joining with mine.

And I need this.

Him teasing me, toying with me, dragging out my bliss.

He rocks his hips to meet mine. Then harder. Enough, he pins me against the car.

Enough, I'm at his mercy.

And he takes his sweet, sweet time toying with me.

Those slow rolls of his thumb.

Then harder.

Faster.

Until—

Fuck. "Ollie." My fingers curl into his hair. "Please, Ollie. Make me come."

"Soon." He brings one hand to my hip. Holds me in place as he toys with my breast. Those perfect slow circles again and again.

Mmm.

Such wonderful, horrible agony.

He winds me tighter and tighter.

I rock my hips, reaching for him.

He groans as his cock brushes my pelvis. "Not yet, angel."

Angel. Fuck. The pet name sets me on fire.

He notices. He's glued to me. Watching every breath, every groan, every shift. Staring like I'm a mock-up he's perfecting.

Like I'm the only thing he's ever needed.

He brings his hand to my outer thigh. To the hem of my dress.

He traces the line over my legs, then back again.

Again.

Again.

"Please." My voice rises to a whine. I should hate it. Hate how much I need. How desperate I am for his touch.

But I don't.

I love it. I crave it. I want all of it, all the time, always.

My eyes fall closed as he traces the hemline again.

Again.

Again.

Finally, his fingers brush my inner thigh.

The fabric of my panties.

207

"Fuck." It falls off my lips.

He lets out a grunt of approval. Shifts his hips so I can feel his hard-on. "Look at me."

My eyes blink open. Meet his.

God, his blue eyes are so beautiful like this. Filled with the perfect mix of need, anticipation, control, desire.

His eyes stay locked with mine as he slips his fingers into my panties.

The pressure of his hand overwhelms me. His skin against mine. Oliver touching me.

It's almost too much to take.

"You get this wet for me, angel?" He breathes.

The pet name sets me on fire. I barely manage to nod. I'm too lost in anticipation. "Please."

"Please, what?"

"Ollie—"

His teeth scrape my neck.

"Touch me. Please."

"Like this?" His fingers skim my inner thigh.

"Make me come. Please."

He slips two fingers inside me. It's hard and fast. Almost too much. But somehow not enough too. "More."

He slips his fingers deeper.

Deeper.

Fuck. It's too much. It's not enough. It's everything.

He watches me carefully. Waits until my breath steadies and my brow softens. Then he pulls his fingers back and drives them into me again.

Softly at first.

Then harder.

Harder.

There.

"Fuck," I breathe. "Like that."

He nods. Brings his lips to mine.

Kisses me as he drives his fingers into me.

That perfect pressure.

Again and again.

I kiss him back as hard as I can. Like *I'm* claiming *him*. Like this is all I get.

We're a perfect circle of need.

His fingers driving into my sex.

His tongue dancing with mine.

Bringing me closer and closer—

Winding me tighter and tighter—

So fucking close.

But not close enough.

He pulls back. Breaks our kiss. "Show me." His free hand finds my wrist. "Show me what you need to come, angel."

Fuck, that's so hot. The deep tone, the demand, the patience.

I nod. Run my hand over his neck, chest, stomach, hips.

He shifts enough I can cup him over his slacks.

He's so hard and warm and huge. And I need that. All of it.

I run my palm over him, rubbing him over his slacks.

His eyes close. His head falls to one side.

God, it's so beautiful. This strong, impossible, in control man lost because of me.

"You first." He breathes. His eyes blink open. Fill with demand. "Show me." He rolls my dress to my waist. "Show me how you touch yourself, angel."

The pet name makes my sex clench. I barely manage to nod.

He slips my panties to my hips.

I bring my hand to my thigh.

There's no doubt about it. I'm on display for him.

Touching myself for his viewing pleasure at this semi-private place.

It's so hot it's wrong.

"Like this." No teasing. I go straight to what I need.

My ring finger against my clit. The spot a little to the right. Those quick, tiny circles.

Fuck.

I'm wound too tight. I'm too close.

"Please." It falls off my lips again. "Please, Ollie. I want to come on your hand."

He nods. Pins me to the car as he brings his hand to my clit.

A tiny, slow circle. To the left. The right.

A little higher. A little closer.

"There," I breathe. "Faster."

My eyes flutter closed.

His touch speeds.

Until it's almost what I need.

Then exactly what I need.

My lips part with a groan. My legs shake. My nails dig into his neck.

He draws those perfect tiny circles.

Again and again.

Winding me tighter and tighter.

Until I'm so, so close.

His lips find my neck. Then it's the scrape of his teeth.

It's all I can take.

With the next brush of his finger, I go over the edge. My world goes white. This perfect, blinding, blissful light.

My sex pulses as I come.

It's intense. So much my legs crumble.

But he catches me. Wraps both arms around me. Pulls me into a slow, deep kiss.

I melt into him.

We stay locked like that, pressed together against the car, kissing like it's the only chance we have.

I pull back to catch my breath.

His eyes are still bright and vibrant and alive.

And I still need to make him come.

I kick off my panties. Right my dress.

Oliver bends to pick up my thong. He slips it into his pocket. Stands. Smooths my dress. Smiles.

"Less smiles. More taking off your pants."

His smile only widens. That same *I really fucking like you* smile. "Not here."

"Why not here?"

"'Cause I want to fuck you."

"Oh. Okay."

"Okay?"

"Less talking. More sex."

He lets out that same honest chuckle. "This is why I need my own place."

I nod. Yes. His own place to fuck me. The other details are far away.

"I have an idea," he says. "If you're game."

"You're going to fuck me?"

Another chuckle. "Yeah."

"It's not funny."

"Just... I really fucking like you." He leans down to press his lips to mine. It's soft, slow, intense. *I love you* as much as it's *I need you*. "Won't have a bed. But, yeah, I'll fuck you so hard you see stars."

"Then I'm game."

Chapter Twenty-Eight

OLIVER

L una's ex-boyfriend is a fucking idiot.

Too much? Too difficult? Too demanding?

Uh-uh.

I thought I appreciated her bossy, take no shit, *I will tell you what I want and you will give it to me and if I don't like it, I'll let you know* nature before.

But now?

As much as I need to be inside her—and I do—I want to torture her forever.

She huffs as she clicks her seat belt. Squeezes her knees together. Plays with the hem of her dress.

Her eyes flare with victory when she catches me watching.

She pulls the dress a half-inch up her thighs.

Damn, those long, tan legs. I need them wrapped around my hips. Or pressed against my cheeks.

I don't fucking care. As long as I make her come again.

She crosses her legs as I start the car. For a second, she closes herself. Fades into the bliss of her favorite album.

Then she turns to me with an expression of pure anticipation. "How long will this take?"

"We're pretty far in Malibu."

"That was your idea."

"I know."

She lets out a huff that means *oh my god, why are you so difficult.* "What's it like, being the most evil person in the world?"

"A lot of fun."

"You would say that."

My smile widens. "I would."

"How are you enjoying this so much?" Her eyes flit to my crotch.

I try to keep my gaze on the road, but it's really fucking hard.

"You're still…" She bites her lip. "Maybe it is you."

"Maybe what is me?"

"The dick lipstick."

"What?" I can't help but laugh.

"I just… I'm actually considering unzipping your slacks."

My cock whines. Fuck, the thought of Luna's hand around me—

Or her soft red lips—

I'm going to crash the fucking car. And it's just the thought. "Angel, you're gonna kill me."

"Good. You deserve it."

"And yourself. I'll drive into the fucking ocean if you do that."

She makes a *hmm* noise.

"You're considering it?"

"Well, look at it." She motions to my crotch. "It's just…"

"You shouldn't give him attention. It will only prolong the—"

"Him?" she asks.

I nod.

"You refer to your dick in third person?"

"He and I don't always agree."

"No?"

"Yeah. But we'd both like to make it to our next destination alive to fuck you properly."

"I don't know," she says. "Seems like he'd like to do that now."

I can't help but chuckle. "Do it for me then."

"You can't maintain that until we're... where are we going?"

"A surprise," I say.

"It's at least twenty minutes back to civilization," she says. "Unless you have a secret place in Malibu."

"From my secret camboy career."

She falls into her seat as she laughs. "You know men are the main audience for those things."

"And?"

"You'll fuck yourself for other guys?"

"It's for me."

She laughs *yeah, okay.*

"My personal show. Anyone can watch."

"If they pay the fee?"

"Of course."

"Must be a pretty hefty fee," she says. "If it affords you a pad in Malibu."

"That's just one of my fans. She lets me broadcast from her place if she gets front row tickets."

"She does?"

I nod *of course.*

"She must be pretty rich?"

"Oh yeah. And famous."

Luna laughs *uh-huh*. "Would you really? If someone offered that?"

"If some rich lady said I could live in her Malibu mansion in exchange for live shows?"

She nods.

"I need details. How rich? How many shows? How hot is she?"

"She needs to be hot?"

"Those are factors to consider."

She shakes her head *how ridiculous*. "She's smokin'. But older. And the place is enormous. Reality TV mansion enormous. But you're at her beck and call. You whip it out whenever she asks. As often as she asks."

"Not that different than the last two months."

"Oh?" Her eyes light up.

Fuck, she's adorable. And sexy. I want to tease her as much as I want to fuck her.

I want to talk to her as much as I want to fuck her.

About shit that matters—her parents, my sobriety, the state of the goddamn world. And shit that doesn't.

I try to keep my eyes on the road. This is a windy stretch of Pacific Coast Highway. And there's no way I'm willing to die before I fuck her. I have to pay some attention if I want to avoid driving into the ocean.

"Ollie." Her voice drops to a *why aren't you fucking me* whine. "You were saying?"

"You're fucking adorable."

"Uh-uh. Less talk about me. More talk about—"

"My cock?"

She laughs. "Basically."

"You do want to live?"

"Do I have to choose between living and fucking you?"

"How are you going to fuck me if you're dead?"

She makes that *hmmm* noise. "True." Her eyes pass over me. Stop on my crotch. "It's receding."

I chuckle. "Need the blood in my brain."

"Probably." She reaches over the center console. Places her hand on my thigh.

"I thought I was the addict."

"Are you asking me to move it?"

"No."

"Good." She smiles as she runs her hand down my thigh.

Fuck. This is going to kill me.

"Oh."

"Maybe you should—"

"Maybe." She pulls her hand back anyway. "I guess I see why you're evil. It's fun."

It is.

"You were saying. About your cock?"

I chuckle. "I was saying something?"

"About your hypothetical mistress. Giving you a nice pad in exchange for constant masturbation."

Oh. "Only change is the mistress."

"You've been…"

"Fucking myself nonstop."

Her eyes flit to me. "Because of me?"

"Yeah."

"Oh." Her cheeks flush. "Just me?"

"What if I say no?"

"That's not good for you."

"You won't fuck me?" I ask.

"I didn't say that."

"You've… increased the rate."

She smiles.

"But it was already pretty fucking high."

"Since…"

"I quit drinking."

"Oh," she says.

"Yeah."

Luna settles into her seat as the album fades. She pulls her cell from her purse. Plays an old Pearl Jam album. One I blast constantly.

"You're playing this on purpose?"

She nods.

"Damn. You must really like me."

"I do." Her smile is soft. "It feels appropriate. The way this guy mumbles. How your groan could fade into the music. I've thought about it. A lot. Since the day I caught you."

Fuck, that is not what I need to hear if I want to live. My head fills with the image of Luna's wide eyes. I need that. And I need to say anything else if I want to make it back to Venice. "You know why they call it Pearl Jam?"

She eyes me tentatively. "Do I want to know?"

"I'm going to tell you either way."

She nods *true*. "Why?"

"Another way to say cum."

"Oh." Her nose scrunches in distaste. "Gross. I've been saying I hate Pearl Jam for the last eight thousand years."

"Do you?"

"They're okay."

"No. Do you?" I motion to my crotch.

She laughs. "You didn't answer your question. Why should I answer mine?"

"Uh, in this hypothetical pad, can I fuck other women?"

"Sure."

"Does she get a free invite?" I ask.

"No. Just the masturbation."

"Then, yeah. I'd do it," I say.

218

"Really?"

"You wouldn't?"

She bites her lip. "I don't think so. Only if I wanted the guy watching already."

"You want someone watching?"

"Maybe."

"Someone else?"

Her smile lights up her eyes. "I should say yes. To fuck with you."

She probably should. I deserve it after ignoring her for the last week.

"Say I want Patrick to watch."

"We both know you're not into Patrick."

"Do you know that? He's a moody tattoo artist. You're a moody tattoo artist."

"Those are my defining traits?" I ask.

She shrugs *maybe*.

Two can play this game. "If you're into him, maybe I should drop you back at his party. Instead of taking you someplace to fuck you."

"Why not both?"

"Fuck you at his party?"

"You think I won't do it?" She raises a brow, daring me.

Honestly, I don't know what she'll do. If I can call her on it. "What about your bathroom policy?"

"Go to his bedroom."

"His bed?"

She shakes her head. "The wall. Or a dresser or something. I haven't seen his bedroom."

"Yet?"

She nods *true*. "You wouldn't do that… would you?"

"Fuck you in his room?"

"Drop me there."

"Well… if you'd rather fuck him."

"Oh my god, Ollie." She swats me playfully. "Don't be an idiot."

"You're the one trying to tease me."

"I said maybe I'd let him watch me masturbate. Not that I'd fuck him."

"It's still sex."

She bites her lip. "I guess… it would be just as intimate. More maybe."

"Can I watch?"

"Can you watch?"

"You fuck yourself?" I ask.

"Right now?"

"Angel, do you have a death wish?"

She laughs. "I meant… whenever we get where we're going. And no. You promised to fuck me."

"Tomorrow."

"I'll think about it."

"You can say no."

"Hard to tease you if I say no," she says.

I raise a brow.

She laughs. "I should make you earn it."

"How will I do that?"

"On your knees."

My eyes flit to her thighs. Fuck, I want to roll that dress to her waist, pry her legs apart, lick her until she's scream-ing. "You coming on my face?"

She nods *yeah*.

"Whatever you want, mistress."

Her cheeks flush. "I'm not sure I'm going that far."

"No? Never want to role play as a professor punishing her student?"

She shakes her head.

"What if I'm the professor?"

Her teeth sink into her lip. "Maybe."

"You'll consider it?"

She nods *exactly*.

"You still didn't answer?"

"Huh?"

"About Pearl Jam?"

"Oh." She laughs. "Do I like cum? How do I answer that?"

"With a yes or no."

"I don't like it in particular, no." Her laugh gets louder. "I'm not going to utilize it for other purposes."

"And you don't like to swallow."

"Jesus, Ollie."

"What? No shame in that," I say.

"Yeah, but, you just… go there."

"You'd rather I not come in your mouth?"

"I don't know." She laughs. "When you say it like that, it sounds kind of hot."

"But it won't be hot if you're gagging on my cock."

This time, she shakes her head as she laughs. "I guess, yes, I'd prefer somewhere else. But who said I'm sucking you off?"

"Angel, you're crazy if you think I'm doing anything but fucking you."

"Like you said. Tomorrow."

I raise a brow.

"I don't remember offering."

"You don't want to?"

Her eyes flit to my crotch. "I didn't say that."

She's teasing, I know. And I fucking love it.

As much as I want to keep the mood light, I have to set the record straight.

"If you don't want to, don't," I say. "I can live without it."

"Oh?"

"But if you do want to, then I'm happy to watch your pretty red lips stretch over my cock."

She swallows hard.

"And more than happy to come on your gorgeous tits." Say, if she peeled her dress to her waist again. And I could tug at that pretty silver hair as she wrapped her lips around me. "Dammit, angel, you're gonna kill me."

"All you this time."

"Maybe."

"You are a lot dirtier than Patrick. I'll give you that."

"Glad to take the honor," I say.

"It suits you."

"But you shouldn't test me. Might drop you at his apartment."

"You won't," she says.

"You sure about that?"

She nods.

But she doesn't bring him up again.

Chapter Twenty-Nine

OLIVER

Luna laughs as I park in front of Inked Love. "Of course."

"You object?"

"Have you ever?"

"Fucked here?"

She nods.

"No. Never."

"Then no." She bites her lip. "I don't—"

"Want to go anywhere I have?"

"Is that ridiculous?"

"No." I don't want to fuck her anywhere someone else has. Or maybe I do. Maybe I want to claim her. Erase every asshole who came before me.

No one she's dated has ever been worthy of her.

And there are the assholes who made her feel used.

Fuck. I can't add to that.

It was necessary, giving up sex for a while. The only way to sort out my thoughts.

But now that it's been two months and I can see how reckless I was with women's feelings—

I can't do that to Luna.

But I don't know to do anything else. I don't know what this is. What it means.

There are all sorts of reasons why we shouldn't.

But they're dull compared to how much I want her. Need her. And that other word that tangles in my throat.

I try to find something close as I get out of the car, lead her inside, lock the door, pull the blinds.

She looks around the empty shop with wide eyes. It's different, at night, in the dark. There's a soft blue glow from the light seeping through the cracks in the blinds.

The place is other-worldly. Like some space that only exists for us.

For her.

"You have condoms here?" she asks.

"We keep some in the office."

She chuckles *of course*. "What if you're out?"

"Then you'll have to come on my face."

"And…" Her eyes flit to my crotch. "I never thought I'd like you in slacks, but I do."

"What do you like me in?"

"Nothing." She smiles. "You set that up for me." Her eyes flit to the office door. The counter. The suite in the middle. "Where do you think…?"

The desk in the office is handy. One of those sit to stand models with all sorts of options.

The counter is always a possibility. Especially with her in those shoes.

Fuck, the thought of bending her over the plastic, peeling her panties to her thighs, driving into her until she's groaning my name—

My cock roars to attention.

I want her every way I can have her. But I need to see

her. To look her in the eyes. To watch her come. "The chair."

"Is that sanitary?"

"It's clean."

"For your future customers?"

I can't help but chuckle. "Considerate."

"Is it?"

I push my palm into her lower back as I lead her to the office. "I'll clean thoroughly after."

"Oh. Okay." She tries to turn the handle, but it's locked.

"Let me." I pull my keys from my slacks. Find the one for the office.

She sighs with relief as the lock clicks. "You really do need your own place."

"I know." I lead her inside. Go straight to the bottom drawer of the cabinet. Thank some higher power when I find a full box of condoms.

Or maybe I should just thank Chase. Or Forest. Or even fucking Patrick.

God, I already want to hit the asshole and he's not even an asshole. The hint of Luna wanting him, touching him, letting him touch her—

It makes my blood boil.

I've never cared like that before. I don't know how to handle it.

I don't know how to handle how much I need her.

But, right now, I know exactly how I need her.

I stand. Show off the foil packet.

She smiles. "Okay. Pants off now."

I can't help but chuckle.

"Less finding me amusing. More pants off."

"You first."

"We already did me first." She closes the space between

us. Presses her palm to my chest. Grabs my belt with the other. "Now."

My smile widens.

"No, no, no. Less amusement. More fucking."

"Stop being adorable."

"I'm not adorable. I'm just clear in my instructions."

"You are."

"So. Pants. Off."

I shake my head. Take her hand. Place it on my slacks, right over my cock.

Her eyes light up.

"Not yet." I wrap my arm around her waist. Lean down to kiss her.

The kiss she returns is pure need. Hard, hungry, completely lacking in patience.

I've never been into kissing. Even when I was that age where kissing is all you do.

With Luna—

I feel everything. I feel her in my bones.

I want to fuck her. I want to drive into her so hard she screams.

And I want to touch her, hold her, make fucking love to her.

How do I explain that? How do I let her know just how much I need her?

I pull back with a sigh. "I like you."

She nods. "I know. You like me, I'm adorable. Less talking, more sex."

"No." My fingers curl around her neck. "I care about you."

"You care about me?"

"Yeah. I want to fuck you, angel. I want it really fucking bad." I shift my hips so she can feel my hard-on.

"These are some mixed messages."

I chuckle. "You want me to stop?"

"God no."

"I just... I don't want to hurt you. It would kill me."

"Okay."

"And I... it's not just sex. It's more. I don't know how to do more, but—"

"I care about you too." She hooks her fingers in my belt loop. "And, really, I would love to talk about this. And it's really sweet you're trying to make sure I know where this is going before you fuck me."

"Yeah."

"But we can figure that out later. Right now, I need you to fuck me." She tugs at my belt loop as she takes a step backward. "I need you inside me."

Fuck. I can't say no to that. It's physically impossible.

She catches my change in posture. Bites her lip. Revels in her fucking power.

Luna leads me to the suite in the back. My suite. The place I spend my entire work week. "You've thought about this?"

"Fucking you?"

She nods. "Here. In the chair."

"Yeah."

"How does it go?" She shrugs the jacket off her shoulders. Hangs it on the hook against the half-wall.

It goes a lot of fucking ways. Too many to count. "Take off your dress."

She shakes her head. "You're wearing all your clothes."

"You want to come on my face? Or you want to strip item for item?"

She bites her lip.

"Really?"

This time, she's the one with that knowing smile. I recognize it. *You drive me crazy in the best possible way.*

227

I almost want to toy with her all night. To keep that smile on her face.

Almost.

"Okay. Fair is fair." I kick off my shoes. Peel off my socks.

She laughs. "I can take my boots off too."

"Dress. Off."

She holds my gaze for a moment, daring me. Then she pushes her dress to the floor and kicks it aside.

Luna is standing in front of my chair in nothing but her boots.

This beacon of light and beauty and sass.

An actual fucking angel.

One intent on driving me out of my fucking mind.

She motions *come here* with two fingers as she takes a step backward. Then another. "Off." She motions to my shirt. Then my pants.

"Sit."

She shakes her head. Repeats her command. "Pants off."

"After you come on my face."

That same smile.

It warms me everywhere. But I'm out of fucking patience. "Now." The playfulness drops from my voice. It's all demand.

She notices. Sits immediately.

I take another step toward her. "Spread your legs."

For a second, she stares back at me like she's going to say no, keep teasing, insist she doesn't take orders, request a please.

But she doesn't.

She reclines in the chair—it's already at a forty-five degree angle—and hangs her legs over the sides.

She tilts her hips up. To give me a better view.

Fuck. "Beautiful." I don't have words. Only an immense need to taste her.

I close the distance between us. Hook my hands under her upper thighs.

Then I drop to my knees between her legs.

She looks down at me, her gorgeous grey eyes wracked with anticipation. "I like to pull." She knots her hand in my hair. Tugs lightly to demonstrate. Then harder.

"Good." I press the heel of my hand into her inner thigh. Softly. Then hard enough I pin her leg to the chair. "Makes me hard."

Her teeth sink into her lips.

"It makes me so hard I can't stand it." I lean down to press my lips to her inner thigh. "So pull as much as you want, angel. But know it's gonna speed things along."

Her head falls back as I kiss her thigh.

Fuck, she's perfect like this. Not just because she's splayed out for me. Not just because I'm her entire universe.

Because she's there, lost in this world of need and anticipation.

I bring my free hand to her other leg. Hold her in place as I kiss my way up her thigh.

Closer and closer and—

There.

She groans as my lips brush her clit.

I do it softly. To tease her.

Then harder.

Harder.

Hard enough she groans.

"Ollie." Her hand knots in my hair. "Please."

Dammit, that sound is music. I need more of it. All of it. Every day. Until the end of time.

I run my tongue over every inch of her cunt. Exploring her folds. Tasting her sweetness. Testing her reactions.

She gasps as I suck on her lips. She groans as I slip my tongue inside her. And when I flick my tongue against her clit—

A little higher.

Left.

Then right.

There.

"Fuck." She tugs at my hair. "Don't stop."

Not a chance in hell.

I press my hands into her thighs as I lick her.

Right there. Exactly where she needs me.

Exactly how she likes it.

She squirms in her seat, fighting my hands, tugging at my hair, just barely rocking her hips to meet me.

I dig my nails into her thighs.

She lets out a low, deep groan.

I do it again.

Again.

Until she tugs. "Too hard."

Then a little softer.

I keep that pressure, my nails digging into her soft skin as I work her with steady flicks of my tongue.

Her thighs shake as she gets closer.

Her head falls back. Her groans run together.

Then her nails find my shoulder. And she scratches hard enough to leave a mark.

Hard enough to draw blood.

Fuck, that feels good. Like she's claiming me.

I've never wanted that before. But with Luna, I want everything.

Her breath hitches.

Her fingers curl.

One more flick of my tongue and she's there, groaning my name as she comes.

Her nails dig a little deeper.

Then everything inside her releases.

She pulses against my lips. Gets sweeter. Wetter.

Her hands fall.

Her legs soften.

Her breath slows.

"Fuck." Her voice is heavy. Strained. "You're good at that."

I stand. Wipe my mouth with the back of my hand. "Thanks." I offer her my hand.

She stands. Goes straight to my shirt.

Her eyes meet mine as she tears through the buttons. Pushes it off my shoulders.

Then the belt.

The slacks.

My boxers.

"Fuck." She wraps her hand around my cock. Pumps me with a steady stroke.

My eyes close. My breath catches. That feels too fucking good. I'm too fucking close. "Condom."

She takes the foil packet. Tears it open. Slides the rubber over my cock.

God, she's so fucking beautiful.

And impossibly sexy.

I'm not going to last long enough. And I can't find a single fucking thought to cool me down.

"This might be tricky." I climb into the chair. "Haven't tried it before."

She nods. Watches me recline. "You're going to ruin this place for me."

"Yeah?" I motion *come here.*

She does.

"Ruin how?"

"I'll think of this every time I see a tattoo."

"Think of fucking me every time you see a tattoo?"

She nods.

No way I'm cooling down now. Luna thinking of this nonstop, her face flushing as she recalls the feel of my hands, mouth, cock—

"Now." I bring my hands to her hips. "Leg here."

She swings her leg over the chair, straddling my thighs

My hands go to her hips. Slowly, I pull her into position.

The chair isn't designed for two. There's no space for her knees.

But she makes it work. She presses her hands into my shoulders. Shifts forward.

Her cunt brushes my cock.

Her eyes fix on mine.

She drives over me.

Slowly. Impossibly slowly.

So I feel every inch of her sweet softness.

Fuck.

She groans as I fill her.

Her eyes close. Her head falls to her side. Her fingers curl into my shoulders.

So fucking beautiful.

So fucking perfect.

Then she shifts her hips forward. Just enough her clit rubs my pubic bone.

Just enough she drives me out of my fucking mind.

I keep one hand on her hip. Bring the other to her chest. Toy with her nipple as she rides me.

The soft circles she likes.

Then harder ones.

Again and again.

As she rocks against me again and again.

Fuck, that feels too good. I'm too close. And I need to make her come again first.

I press my hand into her back. Pull her closer.

For a moment, I soak in the feeling of her skin against mine.

Then I bring my mouth to her chest. Take her nipple into my mouth.

She groans as I scrape my teeth against her tender flesh.

"Fuck, Ollie." Her hand knots in my hair. She tugs as I do it again. As she rocks forward, driving her cunt against my cock.

Fuck, she feels good.

Like home.

She does it again.

Again.

Again.

Finds the rhythm.

The speed.

Exactly what she needs to move closer and closer.

But I'm a greedy bastard. I want more.

I bring my thumb to her clit. Rub her exactly where she needs me.

Her groan gets lower. Harder.

She's moves faster.

Harder.

A few more rolls of her hips and she's there.

She rocks through her orgasm, pulsing against my cock, pulling me closer.

Taking me deeper.

Groaning as she comes on my cock.

Her breath catches. "Fuck." She straightens. "That's…

fuck." She pushes her palm into my chest. Rises off me. "Counter. Now."

Fuck yeah.

I follow her to the counter.

Bend her over the plastic.

She grabs onto the opposite edge. Shifts her hips. Offering herself to me. "Fuck me, Oliver."

No teasing, no testing. Fast and hard.

I hold her steady as I drive into her.

Again and again.

Until she's panting and groaning and writhing.

"Touch yourself, angel. I want to come with you." My fingers dig into her hips, holding her in place. "I've got you."

She nods. Slips her hand between her legs.

Then she's rubbing herself, her eyes closed, her lips parting with groan after groan.

I drive into her with those same steady thrusts.

Hard and deep.

Enough, she shakes against the counter.

Enough, her groans bounce around the room.

Closer and closer—

Then she's there, pulsing around me again, pulling my body into hers.

With my next thrust, I come.

I groan her name, my nails digging into her hips, my cock pulsing inside her.

Pleasure spills through my senses. Commands every ounce of my attention. That deep, perfect satisfaction. Only deeper and more intense than ever.

Because it's with her.

I work her until I've spilled every drop. Then I slow. Untangle our bodies.

Take care of the condom.

She looks up at me with a hazy smile.

I wrap my arms around her. Hold her until she melts into my chest.

I KNOW BETTER THAN TO INVITE LUNA TO SLEEP IN MY BED.

But I do it anyway.

She knows better than to say yes.

But she does it anyway.

She brushes her teeth, washes her face, changes into one of my old t-shirts and a pair of my boxers. And she falls asleep in my arms.

It's too risky. It's stupid.

It's completely impossible to say no.

Chapter Thirty

OLIVER

For the first time in forever, I sleep late. Wake rested. Easy. Peaceful.

It's a beautiful day. Blue sky, bright sun, soft breeze.

Morning light falls through the window, casting Luna in an angelic glow. With the short, silver hair, she really does look like an angel. Some spitfire pixie who takes orders from no one, higher power included.

Who is not at all interested in the task of saving my soul.

Is she?

That's a lot to ask. I'm not putting it on her. I'm not letting myself believe that's possible.

She's beautiful, smart, feisty, sexy as hell—

And dealing with her own shit. She isn't here to save me. I don't fantasize about shit like that.

Not usually.

Maybe it doesn't have to be black and white. I can lean on her sometimes. Talk to her. Listen.

Her chest rises and falls with her breath.

The breeze rustles her short hair.

This is the same Luna I've known for years. The fifth grader who rolled her eyes when I asked if she wanted to bake cookies.

Why? I like cookies because I'm a girl? I'll have you know I don't enjoy pastries of any kind.

The seventh grader who informed me I'd look much cuter if I wore tighter jeans. *Baggy isn't your look.*

The high schooler who showed up early in her homecoming dress. Trying not to cry, because she didn't want to ruin the day for Daisy. Because she didn't want to let her stupid ex-boyfriend ruin it for both of them. What kind of asshole dumps her the day before homecoming? She'd have worn a different dress if she knew she'd be single.

The young woman who watches my sister fall apart and put herself back together. Who stayed by her side without flinching once.

And now this...

I don't know what the fuck Daisy will think of it. Only that I can't fuck that up. They both deserve better.

I move through my morning routine. Head downstairs to the smell of coffee and the sizzle of bacon.

Dad's at the stove in his gym clothes. Sweaty from one of his long workouts. Cooking.

Huh. It's been awhile since we've shared a Sunday morning. Usually, I...

When I was drinking, I'd take a girl to brunch. Women love brunch. And Luna was right. It's a socially acceptable time to get buzzed.

Watch a pretty girl drink mimosas or listen to my dad's bullshit?

Easy choice.

The last few weeks...

Well, I've been avoiding him. Avoiding that judgmental look in his eyes.

The same one that's there right now.

"Breakfast?" he asks.

"Yeah. Thanks." I suck a breath through my teeth. Flit through the list of possible reasons for his judgment. There's the usual—do better at your sobriety, why did you fuck up. Then not calling Daisy enough. Not talking to him enough. Not keeping an eye on Luna.

My eyes flit to the stairs. I can't see the hallway from here. I don't know if her bedroom door is open. If it was obvious she didn't sleep in her bedroom.

If it's obvious we fucked last night.

I haven't showered yet. I didn't want to wash the smell of her off me. But, fuck, that might mean—

"Sunny-side up with toast?" he asks.

"Yeah, thanks." I move into the kitchen like everything is normal. Pour a cup of coffee. Add a little cream and extra sugar.

He watches as I add a second spoonful. "You didn't used to take it so sweet."

"Shit changes." It's true, the adage about alcoholics trading booze for caffeine and sugar.

He nods *it does*. "How is it going?"

Where the hell do I start with that? I take a sip. Focus on the rich taste. Dark and nutty with a full body.

And extra *what the fuck are you screwing up now?*

No. Maybe it doesn't have to be that way. Like the look on Luna's mom's face. She's trying her best. Just fucking it up.

Maybe Dad has good intentions.

"What do you mean?" I inhale the smell of java. Catch a hint of Luna's shampoo. For a second, my skin flushes.

My head fills with flashes of her. Then I see my dad flip a slice of bacon and take a step backward.

"It's not a trick question."

It's hard to believe that. "Been busy. Working a lot."

"Avoiding Luna?"

I shrug like that's not the case.

"Did something happen between the two of you?"

Yeah, but not what he's asking. Or maybe that is what he's asking. Either way, I can't fill him in on the details. "What do you mean?"

"Oliver, I'm not trying to trap you. I just want to know how you're doing."

"Good." I take another sip. Move to the table. Sit as casually as possible. "I'm good."

He nods *okay*. Turns his attention to his cooking. Because he accepts my answer? Or because he's waiting to strike?

I try to put it out of my mind as I sip my coffee. At the moment, life is good. I'm fifty feet from a gorgeous woman with a smile that lights up the room. And she wants to fuck me as much as I want to fuck her.

And I'm going to fuck her the second I can.

If Dad ever leaves the house.

Okay. That's a conversation. One that moves the needle away from whatever he's getting at. "Work is really good, actually. And being here so long, I have a lot saved."

He nods *sure*.

"Been thinking about moving out."

He makes that *hmmm* noise that means *I know best and we both know it isn't that*. (The man is very talented with his *hmms*. He packs a lot into them. Always something about how I'm fucking up but he won't call me on it. Yet).

"There're only two weeks now."

Another *hmmm*.

"I'm doing well."

"Staying in your room."

Yeah, but not because I can't function without alcohol. Because I can't stay near Luna without touching her. Not that I can tell him that. "Because I'm busy with mock-ups."

He says nothing. Just places the bacon on a plate. Drains the grease.

"I've been working out a lot."

He nods. Puts four slices of bread in the toaster.

"And I've been... hanging out with Luna. Making sure she's doing okay."

"Is she?"

"Mostly. It's hard. Her entire life is changing. Her normal routine is gone and she doesn't really have anyone nearby who gets it."

"It's good. That you're helping her." His voice is even. Free of implication.

But I hear it anyway. *It would be good. If you were only helping her. How did you feel when your best friend helped your sister with his cock? And now you're doing the same thing. Hmm...*

"She's a smart kid."

"Yeah."

"Majoring in chemistry?"

"And business." My voice fills with pride. "She wants to run a makeup company."

"Competitive field."

"She could do it."

He turns. Studies my expression. Notes something. "She's a lot like you that way. Headstrong. Determined."

"You don't usually say anything nice about me."

He frowns.

"Think that's the first time in... months."

"You're right."

Fuck, I'm right? That's a first.

"I'm sorry, Oliver. I know I'm hard on you. I know it doesn't help, when I make it obvious I'm disappointed. I don't know how to help you. I don't know what I'm supposed to do if you start drinking again. Or if you get into another accident. It terrifies me."

I don't have anything to say to that, so I take another sip of my coffee.

"You remember how it felt. When Daisy was in the hospital."

"Yeah."

"It's like that. All the time. But since she's been staying here, you've been different. Lighter. Easier. Like you're living and not waiting until you can drink again."

Maybe.

"And I want that for you. I want you to be happy and healthy. I want that for you and your sister. More than I want anything else."

This is too positive. He's going somewhere with it. Somewhere I won't like. "Thanks."

"Am I right? Have things been easier?"

"She's good company, yeah."

"She makes you laugh," he says.

My smile is involuntary. "Yeah."

"I don't know what to say, Oliver. Because I want that for you. I want you to have a best friend. I want you to fall in love. I want you to find someone you can count on."

"I'm not—"

"But what the hell is your sister going to say?"

"I..."

"She likes you."

"I know."

"Have you acted on it?"

I swallow hard.

"It's obvious. The way you look at each other. Your sister will see it the second she gets home."

Maybe. "She's with Holden."

"And when's the last time you talked to Holden by choice?"

It's a good point. Fuck him for making it. But it's a good point.

"I don't want her to lose her best friend."

"And I do?"

He shoots me a look. "Has something happened?"

"No," I lie. "We're just friends."

"Does she know that?"

"Yeah. That's just Luna. She likes to flirt. It doesn't mean anything."

He stares at me like he's waiting for me to give up the truth.

I stare back. Like I have absolutely nothing to hide.

The silence hangs in the air.

Until the toast pops. He turns back to the stove. Cracks four eggs onto the warm pan. "Her parents won't like it. Her staying here if the two of you are fucking."

"She's an adult."

"I don't like it either."

"We're not," I lie.

He doesn't believe me, but he doesn't call me on it.

"She's not staying here forever. Only until things settle with her parents," I say.

"It might take a while."

Yeah.

"Maybe you're right. Maybe you should get your own place."

He's never said that before.

"But not yet, Ollie. Keep the promise you made to your sister. Her first year. Both of you need it."

Maybe.

He turns to the stove. Slides the eggs onto plates. Adds the toast. Brings everything to the table. Then silverware. Coffee. Hot sauce.

A door upstairs opens. The water runs.

Dad stares at me with accusation. Can he tell that was my bedroom door? He's not a fucking bat. He can't use echolocation.

Luna's room is right across from mine.

To a human, it all sounds the same. A door upstairs. Any one.

"I'll make her breakfast." He stands. Moves to the stove. Warms the pan.

Footsteps move into the hallway. Down the stairs.

She smiles as she sees me.

Stops dead in her tracks when she spots Dad.

"Gabe." She brushes her bangs behind her ears. Smooths the Inked Love t-shirt she's wearing. "Good morning." Her hands go to her boxers. Her gaze fades.

"Glad you found the spare pajamas I left." I try to find some explanation. Something that isn't *yeah, Dad, we did fuck. Ready to kick me out now?*

"Yeah. Thanks." She pats her stomach. "Oliver's cooking is too good. Old ones don't fit."

Dad makes that *hmmm* noise. He looks to me, his eyes filled with accusation. "It has meant the world to me, Oliver. To see you doing better the last few weeks. Thank you. For trying."

"Yeah," I say.

"And thank you, Luna. For putting up with him," he says.

She laughs, a little awkward, mostly sincere. "He's difficult. But I'm used to it."

"I'm glad to see you two becoming friends. I'm sure

Daisy would be happy to see it too," he says. "She says she won't be home until Thanksgiving. But it's only a few hours on the train. And she misses Holden. She could be home anytime."

Fuck, he might as well say *I'm pretty sure you're fucking, but not a hundred percent.*

"I hope she does." Luna smiles, the picture of confidence. "I miss her like crazy. And, no offense to either of you, but I'd much rather talk to her about clothes. And hair."

He smiles, lets her change the subject. "You don't like my look?" He motions to his short dark hair.

"Same as Ollie's. You two could be twins." She smiles. "If only Ollie was a little more handsome."

He chuckles. "You're a charmer."

"I only speak the truth." She moves into the kitchen. Pours a cup of coffee. "Thank you, Mr. Flynn. For breakfast. And everything. I really do appreciate it."

"Of course." He cracks eggs into the pan. Motions to the table. "Now, tell me about the clothes you need to discuss with Daisy."

She chuckles. "It doesn't work like that. I don't have any specific clothes." This time, her laugh lights up her eyes.

Fuck, her eyes are so beautiful. Her everything is so beautiful.

He notices my stare, but he doesn't mention it. He just nods *I hope you know what you're doing* and replies to Luna.

Are we finally on the same side?

I hope I know what the fuck I'm doing too.

Chapter Thirty-One

LUNA

Does Mr. Flynn know we're fucking? Or is he just suspicious?

He lets it go pretty easily. Nods as I describe a cute dress out of my price range. And another that I want desperately, despite its lack of practical application.

A sequin Jessica Rabbit number. Gorgeous, over the top, completely unwearable.

Unless I'm going to a gala.

Or a Halloween party.

"What do you normally do for Halloween?" he asks.

"Normally, Divya helps with my costume. We find something really fabulous. Sometimes a joint costume. Then we take a bunch of pictures and hand out candy to the kids in the neighborhood." I already miss that. "Then Allison would tease her about how this is the only time she ever dresses up. And they'd get this look that meant... I needed to leave the house. And I'd go to a friend's party. But this year..."

"Doesn't Holden throw a party every year?" he asks.

"Yeah." I bite my lip. "But the rest..."

"You could wear the dress," he says.

"You'd make a good Jessica Rabbit," Oliver says.

"I feel like I should take offense to that," I say.

He raises a brow.

I fight a blush. "Is Holden throwing a party?"

"Pretty sure," Oliver says. "You know Holden."

I do. And I know he and Oliver aren't really talking at the moment. What with Holden fucking Daisy.

I encouraged him to pursue her. And encouraged her to go for it. Now that the shoe is on the other foot—

It's complicated.

"Are you going to go as Roger Rabbit?" I ask.

"The detective guy," he says. "Guy's a hard-drinking asshole. Suits me."

Gabe looks at him carefully. Trying to figure something out.

If Oliver has told me about his sobriety? Or something else?

I guess it doesn't matter what Gabe thinks. Only... I don't know what a big deal it is. If it's a big deal. If there's some insight Gabe has that I lack.

"You should talk to Holden," Gabe says to Oliver. "It's a good idea. Daisy would appreciate it. If you two made up." He stands. Motions to the now empty plates. "I should shower. You know the rules. I cook, you clean."

"I've got it," Oliver says.

"Do me a favor, Luna, and get him to dress up. It's been awhile." Gabe winks as he takes his leave.

Oliver waits until Gabe is all the way up the stairs, the bedroom door shut. "Fuck, he should just say it. That would be easier."

"Do you think he knows?" I ask.

"Maybe." He stands. Gathers the plates. "You know

what he said? It's obvious that we like each other. From the way we look at each other."

"Maybe it is."

"Maybe." He half-smiles. "I do like you."

"I do like you."

"And I want him to leave so I can make you come again." My cheeks flush.

"Still can't believe I can make you blush."

"Why?"

"You're Luna. You're not shy."

"It's not shyness. Just…"

"How badly you want me."

I nod. "I like the Halloween idea. We should find you a costume."

"And go to Holden's party?"

"He is your best friend."

His brow scrunches in distaste.

"You should get over it."

"Yeah." He places the dishes in the sink. Returns to the table for the rest. "Don't have much of a leg to stand on anymore."

"He's a good guy."

He motions *maybe*.

"He treats her well. You know he does."

"I can deny it," he says.

This time, I shoot him the *really* look.

He nods *yeah, really*. "You want to talk about Holden? Or you want to talk about coming on my face?"

"The Halloween costume," I say.

"You'd rather discuss that?"

"Your dad is still home."

He nods *true*. Drops the rest of the dishes in the sink. Motions to the coffee. *You want another?*

"Let's go out for it," I say.

I don't have to add *so we can be alone*. He gets that right away.

"And maybe… we'll look for a costume while we're out."

"Uh-huh."

"I love Halloween."

"I know."

"And I'm going to someone's party in some kind of sexy outfit. If you're not there, I'm sure——"

"Don't fucking say Patrick," he says.

"He'll be there," I say.

His brow furrows. "I have an appointment."

"After."

He shakes his head. "Can't wait until after. I need to make you come now."

"Right now?"

He nods *yeah*.

It's tempting. Very tempting. But not with Gabe upstairs. "What time?"

"Are you going to schedule me in?"

"Do you have to go to work?"

His eyes flit to the clock. "An hour. Let's go to your room. Play music. He won't hear."

"He's already suspicious. And he…" I don't know what Gabe will say, but my parents will flip if they find out Oliver and I are… involved. There goes their blessing to stay here. And here comes a bunch of extra conversations with Allison. No thanks. "My parents…"

"Yeah." He shakes his head. "You know how distracted I'll be at work? Looking at that chair, remembering you coming on my cock?"

"And I won't?"

"It's not right in your face."

"Trust me. I'll be thinking about it."

"Yeah?"

I nod.

The water upstairs runs. Oliver sighs with relief. Motions *come here*.

I do.

He wraps his arms around me. Pulls me into a slow, deep kiss. "You taste so fucking good." He shifts his hips so I can feel his hard-on.

"Ollie—"

"I know. After." His hand slips under my t-shirt. Up my side. Over my breast. "Just this."

"Fuck."

He toys with my nipple as he scrapes his teeth against my lower lip.

I reach for his hair. Tug at his dark locks as I rock my hips against him.

We kiss until the running water stops.

Then he steps back. Smiles a smile of pure evil. Pure *I have you right where I want you*.

He does.

But I do too. "After work."

His eyes stay glued to mine. "Maybe."

"Maybe?"

He nods *maybe*. "Or maybe I like making you wait until you're begging for it."

Fuck.

———

We dress. Go out for coffee. Fail to keep our hands off each other.

Ollie says goodbye with a long, slow kiss. A kiss so hard

and deep it sets me aflame. I stay at the coffee shop with my European History text book.

I struggle through my reading. Even after a second iced Americano.

Then I head home. Grab my car. Force myself to concentrate at my chemistry study group. This is my major. This is what I actually need to know.

It's just so much less interesting than Oliver's hands.

Or his lips.

Or his eyes.

Or that sound he makes when he comes.

God, I need that again. That low deep groan that's equal parts demand and gratitude.

It's different than other guys. We're different. Equal.

He cares about what I need. He's fascinated by what I need. The way he looks at me...

Shit. I completely miss a question from my lab partner. I try to stare at her. To focus on her glasses. They're a transparent red. It's a bold choice. Classic and trendy at the same time.

It suits her.

And the answer is Tin.

Somehow, I make it through our session, get into my car, drive to Inked Love.

On a Sunday evening in late fall, parking is slightly less horrible than usual. I find a spot six blocks away. Speed walk the entire distance.

My skin warms as I step into the shop. It's not the change in temperature—it's always cool in here, but it's already cold outside.

It's him.

Ollie is finishing up with a client. A short guy sitting in the teal chair. The chair where he made me come.

And there's Holden. At the counter.

The counter where he made me come.

God, the man is good at making me come.

I really want him to do it again.

But there are all these people here.

And Holden is already looking at me all... Holden like. I never know with him. The guy isn't as much of an insti-gator as he was before he started dating Daisy, but he still lives to cause trouble.

I used to think he was a fuckboy. Always starting shit, always with a new chick, never, ever serious.

I still encouraged her to pursue him. I wasn't sure he'd deliver on the fantastic lay front, but she wanted him, and she had the opportunity. Why not seize the fucking day?

Carpe cock.

Or something.

When I saw them together, saw how hard he tried to understand her, how much he wanted to know her, how quickly he set her at ease—

They're good together. It defies reasoning—the sweet, innocent bookworm and the troublemaking tattoo artist—but they really are.

And he's... well, we're not friends exactly. But we're friendly.

He nods *hey*. "Heard you're coming to my party."

"Did you?" I make my voice casual. We are friendly, and he's not the type to snitch, but Daisy is his girlfriend. And that's a bond that trumps anything.

Ollie and I need to be the ones to tell her.

Somehow.

Eventually.

"Yeah." Holden nods to Oliver. "Ollie looked at me and grunted, 'you still doing your Halloween shit?'"

"And you are?" I ask.

He nods. "Wasn't the nicest invitation request I'd ever heard, but he's always on my list."

"He never wears a costume," I say.

Holden laughs *true*. "Always brings good shit."

So Holden doesn't know. Does anyone else know?

Does Daisy know?

I swallow the question as quickly as I can, but it's not fast enough. Holden notices my change of expression.

He makes that *hmm, interesting* nod of his. The one he makes when he's figured something out.

I pretend like I don't notice. "You have a costume picked out?"

"Of course."

"Are you going to tell me?"

"Reveal my secret before the big night? I don't think so."

"It's like a wedding dress?"

He nods *exactly*.

"Only everyone is the groom?"

"And my bride already knows."

"Oh?" I ask. "You trying to convince Daisy to come down?"

He shakes his head. "We're doing a couples thing. Her at Berkeley. Me here. If she calls me from the train station to say she's on her way, I'll pick her up. But we have our deal."

Right. He agreed he wouldn't ask her to come home until after Thanksgiving. And that he'd only come up once a month her first semester. To give her time to get used to her new home.

It must be torture, being that far away from her.

I'm fifteen feet from Ollie and I can't stand it.

"And you?" Holden slides off the counter. "Have a costume?"

"Still brainstorming," I say.

"Doesn't sound like you."

"Distracting time."

"Mm-hmm." His eyes flit to Oliver. "Distracting men in here."

I clear my throat.

"I don't imagine you're here to ask about my party?"

"No. Just to see your beautiful face," I say. "It's already made my night."

He makes a show of playing shy. "Give you something to think about later?"

"Exactly. Who else would be at the top of my spank bank? Besides my best friend's boyfriend?"

"That's how you like it. Off-limits." He raises a brow, daring me to go on.

I don't. "No." I press my hand to his chest. Make a show of pretending I want him. "It's just you, baby. That's how irresistible you are."

He laughs *yeah right* as he takes a step backward. But he doesn't quite hide his discomfort.

The thought of being with another woman? Of fucking shit up with Daisy? Or is he just better on offense?

I'm not sure. But all I need is retreat.

"You here for Oliver?" he asks.

"We do live together," I say.

"How is that going?"

I shrug like everything is business as usual. "He's quiet."

"Plays all that grunge music?"

"Of course."

"Complains when you play eighties jams?"

"Haven't tried many eighties jams," I say.

"You're missing out."

"Am I?"

He nods *oh yeah*. "Great way to torture him. Play The

255

Cure. Then tell him it's way better than Nirvana. Watch him hulk out." His gaze flits to Ollie. "Well, by Oliver standards."

"Good tip. Thanks."

Holden nods *sure thing*. Motions to Oliver finishing up with his client. Then for us to move aside.

All the way to the instant coffee maker.

Okay… that's weird.

I look to Oliver for a clue, but he's busy with his client.

And Holden is here. In a semi-private space. Trying to tell me something. Or ask something. Or figure something out.

"What's up?" I ask.

"What's up?" He laughs *okay, sure*. "You think you're subtle?"

"Hmmm?"

"Luna, I know what a woman in need looks like."

"I don't know what you mean."

"You do. We both know you do."

Maybe.

"It doesn't bother me. Even if it makes him a fucking hypocrite. But we both know Daisy—"

"Yeah."

"So… how was it?" he asks.

"Excuse me?"

"Like you don't want to tell someone." He raises a brow. "I know you and Daisy. You tell each other everything. And now you can't tell her shit."

"I don't give her details about guys." Not explicit ones.

"Bullshit."

"Why do you care?"

"You must be dying to spill." He leans in to whisper. "So… how was it?"

"Are you serious?"

He nods *yeah*. "You think I can't keep a secret?"

I motion *a little*.

He shrugs *suit yourself*. "If you change your mind." He motions to his cell. Then to his suite in the front. "You know where to find me."

Holden looks to Oliver as he walks his client out. Joins the two of us.

"This guy giving you trouble?" Ollie asks.

"Just the usual." I shoot Holden a *don't* look.

He nods *of course*. For all his issues, the guy knows how to play along. "Heard you're getting some new ink. Can't believe you didn't ask me." He bows his head in the ultimate display of mock sadness. "You're breaking my heart."

"Uh-huh," I say.

Ollie chuckles. It's easy. Like he's not worried about Holden catching on.

"You gonna do it now?" Holden asks. "Can I watch?"

"How did he make that sexual?" I ask.

"It's a gift." Oliver nods.

"He's gonna hold a giant needle to your skin to mark you permanently," Holden says. "How is it not sexual?"

"It's a little phallic, yeah," I say.

"And that design… pretty badass, Luna. Is this your first?" he asks.

"Yeah." I bite my lip.

"A virgin too." Holden smiles. "Always love to see a virgin. But I'll leave you to it." He winks at me. So it's clear I know he means *to the actual fucking*. "See you Saturday night."

Holden nods goodbye to the shop and takes his leave.

The room quiets. Only the hum of Pearl Jam and the buzz of a tattoo gun.

"Patrick?" I ask.

"Angel, don't." His fingers brush my thigh. "I can't think straight when I'm jealous."

And if he can't think straight, everyone here is going to know we're fucking. And it's going to get back to Daisy.

Tattoo artists gossip like middle school girls.

"Would you do it now?" I ask. "The tattoo?"

He shakes his head. "Too tired. Won't do it right." He motions to the office. "But I do have an idea."

"Oh?"

"About how you can earn it."

Fuck.

Chapter Thirty-Two

LUNA

bout how you can earn it.

He lets it hang in the air. Expand to fill the space. To make the entire room warm and inviting.

Yes.

Hell yes.

Every. Single. Yes.

I nod.

He motions to the office again.

I motion to the still occupied suite. Patrick and a cute chick getting something on her wrist. They're halfway done. Unlikely to stop and enter the office.

But they're still here.

Oliver drops his voice to a whisper. "Would you rather wait?"

I shake my head. No.

"Good." His eyes light up. He takes my hand. Leads me to the office.

A tiny space. A desk, an ergonomic chair, and cheap white cabinet, this long stretch of empty wall.

A lot of options.

I press my back against the door. Click the lock. "I have to earn it."

"Yeah." He brings his hand to my hip. "You'll have to find some way to convince me."

My voice drops to something low and breathy. "How can I do that?"

"You're a creative girl." He slips his hand between my legs. "I'm sure you'll think of something."

He's letting me lead the... whatever this is.

A role play, I guess. I've never tried it before. I've thought about plenty of scenarios, but I've never acted on one.

"What do you want?" I drop my voice to a tone that's soft. Obedient.

"What do you think?" He rocks forward until his hard-on presses against my stomach.

My breath catches in my throat. Fuck, that already feels good.

"You did this to me, angel." He wraps his fingers around my wrist. Brings my hand to his cock. "You make me this hard."

I cup him over his jeans.

"Make me this fucking crazy." He leans down to press his lips to mine. He kisses me hard and deep.

So much I can't breathe.

So much I can't sense anything but the taste of his lips and the warmth of his body.

When he pulls back, I'm dizzy. Already lost in how badly I want him. Already fading into this game we're playing.

He takes a half-step backward. "You're wearing my jacket."

"Yes."

"Yes, sir."

My sex clenches. "Yes, sir."

"You know what that does to me? Seeing you in my clothes? When I can't touch you?"

I nod.

"Take it off."

I slide it off my shoulders. Toss it on the desk.

He takes another step backward. "Now the dress."

I reach down. Pull it over my head. Drop it on the floor.

His pupils dilate. He looks me up and down slowly, stopping to marvel at my matching bra and panties. Black mesh. The sexiest thing I own. "You wore that for me, angel?"

"Yes."

"To torture me?"

"To please you." I push off the wall. Press my body against his. One hand around his waist, the other against his cock. "That's all I want, sir. I want to please you." I rub him over his jeans. Softly at first.

Then hard enough he groans.

"Is that what you want, sir?" I keep the same pressure. "Do you want me to wear lingerie for you?"

He nods.

"To strip for you?"

He nods.

"To cause this… situation." I find his zipper. Pull it down.

"Fuck."

"I make you hard."

"And leave me that way." He brings his hand to my ass. Pulls my body into his. "Bad girl."

"What is it you say?" I almost break character. "Great power. Great responsibility."

CRYSTAL KASWELL

"Fuck." He *does* break character. He chuckles, shaking his head. "Don't make me laugh."

"Why not?"

"Bad girl." He says it in his usual voice. The one that's all teasing.

"I am." I slip my hand into his jeans. Rub him over his boxers. Only that one tiny layer of fabric between my hand and his cock. "But you already know that."

He nods.

"You love that I drive you crazy."

"Yeah."

"That I make you hard."

"Yeah."

"And leave you to wait and wait and wait... until I release you." I find the opening in his boxers. Run my thumb over his tip.

"Fuck," he breathes.

"You want this."

He nods.

"I'm doing it for you, sir." I look up at him. "Because I want to please you." I run my thumb over him again. Then I release him. Shift back enough to do away with my bra.

His eyes go wide as I slide off my panties.

"You are right. It's cruel... to cause this situation and leave you alone with it."

"It is." He nods. "You have great power—" He almost laughs.

"Great responsibility." I smile. It's funny. It's ridiculous. But there's enough truth in it it's really fucking hot.

I *do* drive Oliver wild. I *do* make him hard. And he *does* suffer with pent-up desire until he finally fucks himself.

And now—

"I've wound you tight." I bring my hand to his t-shirt. Pull it over his head.

He tosses it aside. "Made me hard."

I nod. "Made you fuck yourself thinking of me. Again and again." I find his waistband. Undo the button. "Tortured you again and again."

He nods.

"And now I'm asking for a favor. I should be asking for forgiveness." I push his jeans off his hips. Then the boxers. "I should beg you. For the privilege of releasing you."

"You should."

I press my lips to his as I wrap my hand around his cock.

He slips his tongue into my mouth as I pump him with a steady stroke.

Again.

And again.

Until he's groaning against my mouth. And rocking his hips to meet me.

He pulls back with a sigh. "You should." He motions to the jacket on the table. A cushion. For my knees. "You should beg for it."

I nod. Step back to grab the jacket. Drop it at his feet.

Bend.

Fall on to it. "Please." I run my thumb over his tip. "May I please suck you off?"

"Fuck." His hand curls around the back of my head. "Luna—"

"Please, Oliver."

"You don't—"

"I know." I look up at him. "I want to." I shift back into character. "I want the privilege of releasing you." I'm not saying it to play this game. I do. I really fucking do.

He nods.

"Of making you come."

"Fuck." His hand knots in my hair. "You lead, angel. Show me exactly how much you want me."

I wrap my fingers around his cock. Hold him in place as I bring my lips to his tip.

A soft brush. Enough to tease him. To taste him.

Salt and soap and something all Oliver.

Then a little harder.

Harder.

Enough, he shudders.

I look up at him as I wrap my lips around him.

His blue eyes fill with the perfect mix of need and satisfaction. Then his eyelids flutter closed. His head falls to the left. His fingers dig into my scalp.

I watch pleasure spread over his expression as I take him deeper.

There's something about the feel of him in my mouth. The taste of his skin. The sense of power.

Yes, I'm naked, on my knees, in the locked office at his work.

But I'm the one driving him out of his mind. I'm the one bringing him bliss. I'm the one in control.

And I...

I trust him.

It feels ridiculous, thinking it now, but I do. I trust him to care about what I need, what I want, what I'm willing to offer.

I pull back to his tip. Wrap my lips around my teeth. Run my mouth over him again.

He's big. I can only take so much, even with my hand wrapped around the base of his cock.

But he still shudders every time I run my mouth over him.

I do it again and again.

He presses his fingers into the back of my head, not pushing or pulling, just moving in time with my motions.

His free hand finds my chin, shoulder, chest.

He toys with my nipple as I work him. Softly at first.

Then harder, as I pull back to suck on his tip. To flick my tongue against him. To run my lips around him.

I gauge his reactions. He shudders as I flick my tongue against the bottom of his tip. He groans when I wrap my lips around him.

And when I suck softly—

He rolls my nipple between his thumb and forefinger.

My sex clenches.

His hand knots in my hair. His eyes close. His thighs shake.

"Fuck, Luna." He works me with that same rough touch. "Don't stop, angel. I want to come on those perfect tits."

I suck on his tip until he groans. Then I wrap my lips around my teeth. Pull back. Take him as deep as I can.

He toys with my nipple as I work him.

His touch gets rougher as I suck harder.

The two of us in this perfect cycle. Me bringing him to the brink; him teasing me, harder and harder and harder.

His breath quickens.

His thighs shake.

I bring my free hand to his hip. Dig my fingers into the flesh of his ass. Pull him just a little deeper.

It's almost too much. But I swallow. Relax my throat. Manage to take him.

For a moment, his eyelids flutter open. He looks down at me like I'm heaven-sent.

Then his eyes close.

And his groans run together.

I take him again.

Again.

Again.

"Fuck, angel." He tugs at my hair. "I'm gonna come."

I take him one more time.

Then he pulls harder. Shifts back.

Groans my name as he spills on my chest.

It's as perfect as I imagined. So low and deep it fills the room.

"Fuck." He runs his fingers over my jawline. Reaches out. Offers his hand.

I take it. Let him help me to my feet. Let him clean me up.

Let him kiss me so hard I see stars.

And when he slips his hand between my legs and groans, "You need to come now."

I have the good sense to agree.

Chapter Thirty-Three

OLIVER

Luna holds a short blue dress to her chest. A cheap polyester thing that screams *cop in a porno.*

My cock whines *fuck yes, right now.*

"It suits me." She places the hat on her head. Cocks a finger gun. "I'm going to need you to step out of the car, sir. And if you fuck with me, I'll fuck you up."

"Already abusing your power."

She nods. "You love it."

Too much. "Gonna take you right here if you keep going."

"Excuse me, sir." She slips deeper into her role. "I'm the one issuing orders here." She closes the distance between us. Places one hand on my chest. Pushes just hard enough I feel it. "And you won't be taking anything. Except your clothes. Off."

"Oh?"

She holsters her invisible gun. "So. Let's go. I need to see if you're hiding evidence."

I motion to the quiet shop behind us. Sure, it's empty. But it's still a public place.

She raises a brow, daring me.

"You think I won't?"

Luna breaks character with a chuckle. "All right, sir. I suppose, we'll have to do this at the station. I have to warn you though... I have all sorts of methods for obtaining a confession."

I grab her ass.

She gasps as I pull her body into mine. "Ollie."

"One more word, angel." I press my lips to hers.

She sucks on my bottom lip. Pulls back with a sigh. Makes that *shh* motion as she returns the costume to its rack.

"How much is that?"

She makes the *shh* motion as she points to the price tag.

It's way too much for the quality. But the logic fails to appeal. There isn't enough blood in my brain.

There's an entire wall of this shit. Outfits more lingerie than costume.

A French maid, a school girl, a sexy space cadet— anything and everything.

And I want her in everything.

Only—

"No offense, Luna, but isn't this place... not up to your standards?" I ask.

She makes that *shh* motion again.

"I will fuck you senseless if you say another word."

She raises a brow.

"But I'll wait."

"No fun." She smiles. Turns to the wall. Picks up a Tinker Bell lookalike. "Of course. Cheap material, poorly made, obvious. I usually buy something custom. Or put together a look myself."

"That sexy devil thing you wore last year?"

"You liked it?"

"Fuck yeah."

She returns the costume to the shelf. Slips her hand in my back pocket. "How much did you like it?"

"Did I fuck myself thinking of it?"

Her cheeks flush as she nods.

"Yeah. Fuck, still remember when you stormed inside. And gave me that *where the hell is your costume* look. But all I could see was legs… Fuck, did I really say I'd wait until we're home?"

"We just went."

"So?"

"You're that insatiable?"

I nod. Slip my arm around her waist. "You still own it?"

She sighs as I pull her closer. "Of course. I don't waste."

"Will you wear it for me?"

"I'll think about it." She smiles, reveling in her power. "I was seventeen last Halloween."

"I know."

Her smile widens. "Dirty boy."

"You've doubted that?"

"No… Oliver Flynn, there are three things I know about you."

"Only three?"

"Three I know for sure." She scans the row of lingerie-like costumes. Turns to the next aisle. All angels and devils.

My gaze goes straight to a fallen angel costume. A short black dress, tattered wings, fishnet tights. Sexy as fuck. And perfect for her.

"One." She holds up a finger as she motions to my wide eyes. "You're a sex-crazed pervert."

My lips curl into a smile. "Guilty as charged. What's my punishment officer?"

She laughs. "Exactly." She holds up a second finger. "Two, you're painfully stubborn."

That's not what I expected for two. But I can't exactly argue.

She holds up a third finger.

My breath stops. This is going somewhere I can't stomach. Some shit about how I bring a bottle everywhere. How it's a miracle I'm six weeks sober.

But she doesn't say any of that.

She brings her other hand to my forearm. Traces the rose tattooed to it. "You're a fantastic artist."

My shoulders relax. "You think so?"

"Yeah." She traces the line up my arm, over my elbow, all the way to my shoulder. "I always have. Since the first time you showed me a drawing."

"The pinup?"

She laughs. "You remember that?"

"Of course." I was a dickhead teenager. Thought I could simultaneously shock and impress Luna by showing her my first attempt at a pinup tattoo. After all, the work was badass, and the babe was naked. Win-win. "It was supposed to be you."

"Really?"

"Yeah."

Her nose scrunches. "I was like… fifteen."

"I know."

"Pervert."

"Did it to rile you."

She raises a brow. "You didn't think that would backfire?"

"You can stop at 'didn't think.'"

She laughs. "You're not bad for a brooding asshole, Ollie, but you are still a man." She hooks two fingers into my belt loop. "Still—"

"Think with my dick?"

"Yeah." Her laugh gets louder. Heartier. "You can admit that?"

"Like you said, sex-crazed pervert."

She smiles. "True." She traces a line up my body. Stomach, chest, shoulders, chin, eyes. "You still have it?"

"Somewhere."

"It was really me?"

I nod. "Thought it would get under your skin."

"I kind of wondered..." She almost blushes. "But I was too enamored to ask. I couldn't believe it. Someone I knew was going to be a tattoo artist. It was like meeting a movie star. I didn't think... well, I guess..."

"People with rich parents usually go to college?"

"It was already absurd. A high school student who didn't plan to attend university. Unthinkable."

"You told me that."

She laughs. "I know. I was in awe of you. Going after what you wanted. Not caring what anyone else thought. Giving your dad that huge middle finger."

I make that *kind of* motion.

"Is that why you started?"

"To say *fuck you* to my dad?"

She nods. "You two were already at war."

"Yeah." I pick up the fallen angel costume. Focus on the slick plastic. Instead of the ugly memories. I like Luna. A lot. I want to know her. And I want her to know me. But I can't go there. Not right now. "We have been. Since I can remember."

"Since your mom—"

"Yeah." There's too much to say about her. And how I'm walking in her footsteps. "That was part of the appeal at first."

"Very Holden of you."

Fuck, it is. I shake it off. "I'm not sure when I fell in love with drawing. Maybe the day I picked up a pen. I was always doodling. In class, after school, on those boring trips to see relatives."

"The ones where your parents leave you in a room with all the other kids? Even though they're three years older and they think you're a lame baby?"

"Yeah."

"I hated those."

"It wasn't as bad for me. I had Daisy. But she already kept to herself."

"Always had her nose in a book."

I nod. "So I had to entertain myself. And drawing felt right. It made sense. I could take what I saw and explain it. Or think up something else. Or take the ugly shit in my head and put it on paper."

"How old were you?"

"When I figured that out?" I ask.

She nods *yeah*.

"Nine or ten, maybe. My parents meant well. Even my mom. But I still knew I had to be strong. Quiet. To keep my problems to myself. Only... there was so much shit in my head. It was tangled. I couldn't make sense of it."

"Until you started drawing?"

"Yeah." I run my hand through my hair. "It always helped. Even now... when my head is a fucking mess and it hurts to close my eyes. I pick up a pen, find a paper, let my thoughts flow onto it... and it's still fucked up, but it makes a little more sense."

"It's easier?"

"Yeah." I bring my index finger to her forearm. The place she wants her new tattoo. "I'd always thought tattoos were cool. Since the first time I saw one."

"Your dad at the beach?"

"No." I chuckle. "He kept his under wraps for a while." Wait a second. "Fuck. You imagining my dad at the beach?"

"If I am?"

"Can't think straight when I'm jealous, angel."

"Jealous of your father?"

"Are you kidding?" My other hand finds her hip. "You talk about how hot he is all the time."

She smiles. Runs her fingertips over my jawline. "I shouldn't like you jealous. But I do." She leans in. Presses her lips to my cheek. Chin. Lips. "Gabe is attractive, sure, but I'm not interested."

"Yeah?"

She nods. "I don't want to fuck anyone but you."

"What if he offered to join so we could double-team you?"

Her head falls forward with her laugh. "Oh my god."

"You'd say no?"

"I'd still be fucking you. It's a grey area."

"Uh-huh."

"Yeah-huh."

She nods into my chest. Hooks her arm around my neck. "You know you don't fool me, Ollie."

"You think I won't get pissed?"

"No… changing the subject. There's something you don't want to say."

Maybe.

"You don't have to tell me." Her fingertips dig into my skin. "I know keeping things to myself. Dealing on my own."

And I hate the thought of it. Of Luna, alone in her room, trying to stomach all the pain she can swallow. Trying to carry her burden all alone.

I want to help her.

I want it too fucking badly. If I'm asking that...

It's only fair, I guess.

Even if that means—

Fuck.

One thing at a time. At least this part is easier. "Would you lean on me? If I offered?"

She bites her lip. "Are you bargaining?"

"If I am?"

"I don't know. I do like a deal."

"I know."

She looks up at me, considering it. "Okay. A story for a story? You go first."

I nod.

"Every detail on your ascent"—she raises a brow, asking if it's the right word. When I nod, she goes on—"to brilliant tattoo artist."

"Brilliant?"

"You think I'd let some wannabe put ink to my skin forever?"

"You haven't done it yet."

"Even so," she says.

I trace the lines onto her skin. It's easy to forget how important this job is. Yeah, I'm not a doctor or a teacher or a cop. But I leave people with a permanent mark.

Sometimes it's nothing. A design they like. A lark. A fun way to show their personality.

But sometimes it's everything. A way to cope. Or reclaim a scar. Or survive.

I know that too.

I've been there too.

"Okay." I kiss her softly. Taste every inch of her sweet lips. "After the costume."

She nods. "I do have an idea..." She motions *follow me*,

takes my hand, leads me through the aisles. Past the careers, the super heroes, the decades.

All the way to a wall of supernatural creatures.

Zombies, witches, sorcerers, vampires.

Straight to "Vampire King." A velvet cloak. Black on the outside. Wine on the inside. Matching vest. Fangs sold separately.

"Angel, I'm not sure what this implies, but I know it's not good."

"Something about being an emotional vampire?" Her smile is soft. "Maybe when you play too much grunge. But no, it's not about the blood sucking or energy leaching. More that... this guy, he's a brooding bad boy—"

"He's a bad boy?"

"Of course. Vampire lore is all about older men taking advantage of nubile young women." She raises a brow. *You can't really deny that?*

"Did you just call yourself nubile?"

She laughs. "You're the one who was drawing me naked when I was underage."

Fair.

"He wants to toy with beautiful women. Otherwise, he's hiding in his castle, avoiding the light."

"Fuck."

"Too much?"

Maybe. But right too. "I'm not... I'm trying to do better."

"You are."

"I just—"

"It's only a costume, Ollie. If you don't like it, I'll think of something else. But, uh..." She blushes. "It is kind of hot. The vampire king claiming me."

"You have a thing for vampires?"

"Have you never heard of *Twilight*?"

"You hate *Twilight*."

"Yeah, but..." She bites her lip. "It still infected my brain. And..." She steps backward. "If you don't like it, we'll find something else. There are lots of other hot options. Or—"

"You're really into it?"

"No." Her blush deepens. "Maybe."

"You've never asked me to bite you."

Her blush spreads to her chest.

My balls tighten. "Angel, you're making it impossible to have a fucking conversation."

Her hair falls over her eyes as she shakes her head. "That's you. Being a dirty pervert. But. Yes... next time. You should." Her eyes meet mine. "Next time."

It's too much fun teasing her. I love it as much as I love her teasing me.

In fact—

"I have a better idea. For Halloween." I motion to the velvet cape. "But I'm happy to buy this if you want to use it later."

"I don't need the costume."

"I don't *need* to buy you that cop costume, but I'm still going to do it."

Her cheeks flush. "Yeah?"

I nod *hell yes*.

"Only if we use it right away."

"You took the words out of my mouth."

Chapter Thirty-Four

OLIVER

The drive home takes too long. Every note of Luna's music—that teenager who whisper sings —mocks me.

Is this really about fucking her?

Or is it about avoiding the question?

Do I have to choose?

I *need* to fuck her. To pin her to the wall, touch her, taste her, bury myself inside her.

To feel every inch of her skin against mine.

That makes sense.

The rest of this? Not so much.

The art, I can discuss. Even if it's tangled with ugly history.

But the reason why I'm here, sober, living by the terms of the deal I made with my father?

No way in hell.

Finally, I pull onto our street. Park in front of the house.

Luna looks to me with a smile. One that's pure *I need you* and absolutely not *you're an alcoholic fuck up.*

She knows and she sees me as more than that.

If she knows everything…

She undoes her seat belt. Grabs the bag from the costume shop. "Gabe's car isn't here."

I nod.

"Is downstairs too risky?"

My head screams *yes*. My cock whines *there, now*. It's a terrible idea. Stupid. Hot as fuck.

Luna's smile gets wicked. "Okay. Give me five minutes to change. Then meet me inside." She leans over the center console. Presses her lips to mine.

It's supposed to be a quick kiss goodbye, but I still bring my hand to the back of her head. I still hold her mouth against mine. I still kiss her like the ship is going down.

Because it is.

Sooner or later.

When she realizes the truth—

Fuck. I'm not going there. Not yet.

Maybe this is a ticking clock. Maybe it's completely fucked. Maybe it's the stupidest thing I've ever done.

I still need her right now.

Like I need oxygen.

She pulls back with a sigh. "Fuck. You're going to kill me."

"Death by orgasm?"

She nods. "A good way to go." She runs her fingers over my jaw. "Five minutes. Then sit on the couch."

"You're issuing orders?" I try to make my tone light. To slip into something easier. The familiar casual routine.

I've used sex as a distraction for a long time. But it feels wrong with her.

Impossible.

I have to be there with her, watching her eyes fill with

bliss, listening to her breath quicken, feeling her thighs shake.

Maybe I'm an alcoholic fuck up. Maybe I'm a piece of shit.

But I know how to make her come.

I'm going to make her come.

I nod and I watch her slip into the house.

Five minutes. That's too much time to think. I close my eyes. Try to step into the scene.

Luna as a bossy cop who isn't afraid to use her handcuffs—

That's pretty fucking hot.

It fits. Too well. There is shit I need to tell her. Shit I'm hiding.

I can make that work.

Or throw her on the couch and fuck her senseless. One of the two.

I step out of the car. Lock the door. Check our surroundings.

Our place is a lot like her parents'. The opposite side of the same neighborhood. A row of bungalows and renovations on a quiet street. Parked cars. No traffic.

An oasis in the middle of the crowded beach and the traffic hell that is Lincoln.

I step inside. Move to the couch. Try to find some kind of peace. Calm. Anticipation.

Whatever is going on with my head needs to stop. Or at least ease. I need to feel her.

I'm enjoying this.

Period. End of sentence.

A door upstairs open. Heavy footsteps move down the hall. Her boots. The ones she was wearing when I fucked her.

My balls tighten.

My thoughts drift to dirty places.

She steps into view. In that tight, impossibly thin blue dress, cap askew, boots to her knees, smile wicked.

"Ah. I see you've been waiting." She cracks her knuckles as she moves down the stairs. "This is interrogation room one." She steps onto the main floor. "I wasn't expecting so little resistance."

"Is that right?" I raise a brow.

She nods. "You seem like a difficult suspect."

"What have I done, Officer?" The list is too fucking long.

"We'll discuss your charges after a thorough strip search." She smiles, reveling in her power. "Stand up."

"Here?" I play dumb.

"Right there." She moves to the front of the couch. The spot in front of the TV. "I need to see if you're hiding anything."

"What would I hide?"

"A weapon. Or some other tool you could use against me." She draws a circle in the air. Points to my t-shirt. "Take that off."

"This?"

She nods. "To start."

I stand. Pull my t-shirt over my head. Drop it on the floor.

She makes a loud *hmm* noise. "This..." She crosses the distance between us. Presses her hand to my forearm. Traces the lines of my tattoo. The Latin quote.

ex favilla nos resurgemus

Her fingers curl over my arm. "It might be some kind of gang sign."

"A gang with Latin quotes?"

"Are you questioning me, sir?"

"It sounds unlikely," I say.

"Then I'd like to hear your explanation." Her voice softens. Almost breaking character. "What's the meaning of this?"

Haven't I told her? I still remember the day I got it. When I saw her next. She couldn't stop staring.

Daisy was mortified—why did I have to cause fights with Dad—but Luna was transfixed.

"Ex favilla nos resurgemus. Could mean anything," she says.

"From the ashes we rise," I say.

"You're an arsonist."

A laugh escapes my lips.

"There's nothing funny about crime, sir."

"You think I'd advertise?"

"You need clients, don't you?" She traces the lines back up my arm. "What's the meaning, then? If it's not about your love of setting fire?"

"That's kind of personal."

She raises a brow.

"I'm not sure it's any of your business, Officer."

"No?"

"No." I slide my arm around her waist. "But it can't hurt to explain the story."

Her hand covers mine. She looks up at me, considering whether to stay in character or break. Nods *go on*.

I'm not sure what that means for the role play, but this is something I want to tell her. Something I can tell her. "It sounded badass when I was a teenager. Like the kind of beautiful self-destruction that sounds good in a song. I thought about burning my life to ashes. Becoming something better. And I thought about watching something ugly set fire to everything that mattered and coming out better for it."

"Something specific?"

"My parents. Myself. My friends. I didn't like myself then. I didn't hate myself yet, but—"

"You hate yourself?"

"Not exactly."

Her fingers curl into my arm. "Something close?"

I swallow hard. "Maybe. I'm trying to get past it. To figure it out. It's complicated."

"From the ashes we rise." She traces the lines again. "It's about burning down what you don't want? Coming out better?"

I nod. "And about surviving."

"Hopeful."

"Or self-destructive."

"Or both." Her eyes meet mine. "Ollie—"

"Angel, we're supposed to—"

"Next time." She slips her arm around my neck. "Right now, I want me and you. Right there." She motions to the couch.

"You don't get to issue orders in this—"

"Take off your pants." She presses her lips to mine. Kisses me hard and fast. "Now."

Fuck, I like her bossy. Roleplay or not. And I want to feel her body against mine.

To make love to her.

Be one with her.

All that cheesy shit.

"You have a condom?" I ask.

She nods. Pulls something from the TV stand. "No pockets."

Fuck, she's a genius.

"Pants. Off. Now."

I kick off my shoes and socks. Undo the button of my jeans. Push them off my hips.

"Sit."

"Yes, ma'am."

She laughs. "Just me and you." She leans down to unzip her boots. She slips out of them, one at a time, then she pulls the tiny blue dress over her head.

Fuck. She's not wearing anything under it.

She's standing in the living room, completely naked, looking at me like I'm everything she wants.

It's hard to believe.

But this is one place where I know what the fuck I'm doing. One of the only places.

"Sit." She closes the distance between us. Presses her hand to my chest. Softly. To issue the order. Then harder. Hard enough to nudge me.

"Sit?"

"Now." She pushes me again.

I pull her with me.

She shifts onto the couch. Onto my lap, her knees outside my hips, her cunt inches from my cock.

"Fuck." Her eyes flutter closed. Her fingers dig into my neck. Her thighs spread.

She shifts lower.

So she brushes against me.

Fuck, that feels good.

Too good.

I'm not—

"Luna—" Fuck, I want to forget. I want for it to not matter. To feel every inch of her against me, nothing between us. "Condom."

"Oh. Fuck." She presses the packet into my palm.

I tear it open. Lift her hips. Slide the rubber over my cock.

She shifts back into place. Her fingers dig into my shoulders as her cunt brushes my cock.

Her eyes meet mine.

She stares at me as she lowers her body onto mine.

Fuck, she's already wet. And she feels so fucking good. Soft and warm and mine.

I bring my hand to the back of her head. Pull her into a slow, deep kiss.

She kisses back as she rocks against me.

We stay locked like that, pressed together, moving together, the world a place that makes sense.

Then I bring my thumb to her clit. Rub her until she's groaning against my lips.

Until she's there, pulsing around me.

It pulls me over the edge.

I hold her close, kissing her hard as I spill inside her, pleasure flooding my senses.

Everything bright and beautiful and easy.

She collapses against my chest. And I hold her there for a long time. Until her breath steadies and the air shifts and the world returns to normal.

No, not normal.

Still brighter and warmer and a million times more beautiful.

She is a beacon of light.

I have to tell her. Soon.

Right now—

I need to take her upstairs and clean up and hold her until the world makes sense.

Chapter Thirty-Five

OLIVER

Dad gets home early. Joins us for dinner.

She discusses Halloween costumes with him, cleans up, goes straight to her room, texts that she can't stay close to me without touching me.

That we have to wait until he leaves.

Of course, he doesn't.

He gets home early Monday.

Leaves for work late Tuesday.

Drops by the house for lunch Wednesday.

Okay, he knows. And he's fucking with us. Fair enough.

But I can't go another day without kissing her.

After work, I pick her up from school. Take her to the shop. Fuck her brains out in the office.

Then we head to her favorite organic coffee shop. Well, her favorite expensive coffee shop with parking.

It's still hip to the extreme—expensive single origin beans, white and teak furniture, baristas with beards and tattoos—but it's more spacious. There's room between the tables.

Room for my secrets to spread. To fill the space. And pollute the air.

It's obvious the second I walk in the door. There are no more excuses. I have to tell her.

Fuck.

I run my hand through my hair. Suck a breath through my teeth. Try to find some place to start.

This conversation heads somewhere rough. But there's plenty of light in it.

And she's full of life and joy and pride. For herself and for me. I'm not sure what I did to deserve it, but I'm holding onto that too.

Luna is already sitting at a white table in the corner. She has a giant French press, no doubt filled with some dark roast, and two little ceramic cups. Plus one of those expensive tiny chocolate bars they sell at the counter.

I join her at the table. "Eighty-five percent?"

"Of course." She unwraps the paper. The foil. Breaks off a tiny square. "You want some?"

"Not sure I'm worthy."

"You might find a way to convince me." Her eyes flit to my crotch as she places the square on her tongue. She lets it melt, closes her mouth, licks her lips.

My body begs me to chase the trail. To wrap my arms around her, kiss her, demand I lick chocolate off her thighs.

I want to touch her, taste her, fuck her.

Make fucking love to her.

I want every sweet sensation. The physical and the emotional.

The closeness. The distraction.

The chance to flee.

But now isn't the time. I need to tell her this. Sooner rather than later.

She offers me another square.

This time, I take it. Let it dissolve on my tongue. Focus on the flavor. Fruity. Like figs or caramel. Only rich and decadent. And far less sweet.

Intense.

Like her.

"You like it?" she asks.

"Not as much as you do."

"Too much to handle?"

"I can handle a lot."

Her eyes meet mine. They look for something. Some reason to believe I'm talking about her, maybe.

She's a lot, sure, but in the best fucking way. "I like that about you."

"Oh?"

"You're like the chocolate."

"Expensive and delicious?"

My laugh eases the tension in my shoulders. "Intense. But, yeah, delicious." My eyes flit to her hips. My body begs me to continue. To find some way to express this without words. But that's impossible. Some shit has to be said. "Sean is an idiot."

"True."

"You're demanding, yeah. You're difficult sometimes. And you have high fucking standards. But that's what I love about you."

"Thank you." Her finger skim her mug. "We... uh... if this is some way to change the subject... you don't have to talk about anything."

"No." I pick up the French press. Motion *shall I?* When she nods, I fill her cup. Then mine. "We never really finished our conversation."

"Which one?" Her eyes flit to my crotch. "A lot of conversations end with our clothes off."

"About art."

"How you got into it?" she asks.

"Yeah. This part is good. Funny."

"It gets better than you drawing me naked?"

I chuckle as I set the carafe on the table. "I've drawn you naked a lot, angel."

Her cheeks flush.

"You have any idea what you did to me, running around in that black bikini all summer?"

Her eyes spark. She knows what she did to me. And she's reveling in it. "Maybe."

"Tease."

"Right back at you."

Fuck, it's too easy to flirt with her. I want to do it forever. And I can. I will. After this.

If she still wants anything to do with me.

I swallow hard. Try to find a place to start. Say the first thing that comes to mind. "Thanks." I pick up the mug. "For the coffee."

"Of course." She picks up her mug. Holds it up to toast. "To intense."

"To intense." I tap my cup against hers. Bring it to my lips. The warmth of the coffee is soothing. And the taste is familiar. Intense, yeah. Rich, nutty, and bitter too. "I don't remember the first tattoo I saw. But I remember the feeling. Of seeing this mark on someone's skin. This art, there, forever. It was scary. And thrilling. I was still a kid. A year felt like forever. An actual eternity—"

"Or at least as long as you have skin."

"Morbid."

Her laugh is soft. "You know what I mean."

Yeah, I do. "It's with you." My fingers go to the ink on my forearm. My first. "Your entire life. Whatever happens after... that ink is still there, on your body. What else lasts that long?"

288

"Love?"

"Maybe." My shoulders tense. "The idea stuck with me for a long time. At first, it was a fascination. With the idea of forever. Then the ink itself. The art of tattooing."

She traces the line.

Fuck, that feels good. Too good. "When my parents announced they were finally splitting... I was pissed. Angry. Self-righteous. How could they lie to me? Tell me they loved each other, that they would be together forever, that our family was forever? And now they were changing it. Tearing it apart. And it's not like it was mutual. It was another ultimatum from Dad. After a bunch hadn't worked."

Her eyes fix on me.

"I'm not sure I got it then. How bad it was. How often Mom was using." My fingers curl into the ceramic. There's something soothing about the warmth. The smoothness. "At the time, I thought he was a merciless asshole. She was trying. Why was he so hard on her? Why was he telling her she needed to be better? Why couldn't he love her the way she was?"

"It's a fair question."

"Maybe. I don't know. Maybe she was always like that. Maybe he should have known better... accepted her, flaws and all."

"Was she?" Luna asks. "Always using?"

"I don't know. When we were kids, she was always around. I don't remember a lot. But I remember that sense of love. Patience. Warm days at the park. On the beach. A trip to fucking Disneyland."

"You hated it?"

"Yeah." I run a hand through my hair. "Already brooding and difficult. Even as a kid."

"Even when you thought both your parents loved you?"

"I know they love me. It's more... If I can trust Mom to stick around. To be there. To be coherent. To be the fucking parent." My chest tenses. "I'm not sure when it started. At first, it was quiet afternoons. I'd get home from school and she'd be fuzzy. Like she wasn't there."

"High?"

"Yeah. But I didn't realize at the time. She just seemed... calm. But too calm."

"Yeah."

"Then... it was all night. All day. And she started missing shit. Forgetting to pick me up from school. To get groceries. To make dinner."

Luna takes a long sip. Folds her hands around her mug. "You picked up the slack. I remember that."

"For a while, that was enough. It was hard, but it felt good. Taking care of Mom and Daisy. Making sure they were okay. I didn't think about how I was obscuring the truth. I was just—"

"You stepped up, Oliver. You don't need to feel guilty for that."

"Maybe." My head is a mess. This shit is too tangled. There are years of it. "I did my best. I just... I'm like my dad. My best isn't good enough."

Her lips curl into a frown.

"That was when I really got obsessed with art. It was the only time I had space for myself. You know?"

"Yeah." She nods. "Other times... what everyone else needs is in the way."

"Exactly. It was like an affair."

"Have you had an affair?"

"I'm sure I've been with married women. No. It's not the odds. I remember a few. Hell, I remember this one woman... she was older. She was at a bar. Upset about something her husband did. She straight up told me. 'I'm married and I need one night to get back at my husband. Will you help me?'"

"And you did?"

"Yeah. She was gorgeous. And she had this sense about her... like you, actually."

"I'm like a married woman looking for a revenge fuck?"

"She knew what she wanted. But she was more shy about it. Like she wasn't used to anyone giving a fuck about her desires. I was already loaded when she asked. But then... I was always a little fuzzy. I've been drinking morning to night for a long time."

"Bourbon in your coffee?" she asks.

"That obvious?"

She shakes her head. "I only caught you doing it a few times. I always figured... it was the weekend or vacation or whatever. A special occasion. But part of me wondered."

"Now you know." I tap my chest. "Oliver Flynn. Dirty pervert, stubborn artist, alcoholic fuckup."

Her brow furrows. "Ollie..."

"Wait until I've told you to argue."

"Told me?"

"What happened... that got me into this stupid fucking program."

"It's helping, isn't it?" she asks.

"Yeah. But... fuck, if I have to drink one more shitty cup of drip." I shake my head. "I hate that place."

"Where you go for your classes?"

"It's antiseptic. Like a hospital wing. Like some place people go to die. The air is too still. The walls are too bare. Everything is this ugly shade of beige. No color. No life. No brightness."

"There must be other places," she says.

"Yeah. I just... I don't know. It's still hard. Sitting here. Trying to talk about this. Trying to face it. I still want a fucking drink. Something sweet and rich and strong enough to dull the ache."

Concern fills her eyes.

"I haven't, but... Dad thinks I'm trying to white-knuckle it. Maybe I was. But you... you've got me all fucked up."

"Is that a compliment?"

"I meant what I said the other night, Luna. You're this beautiful splash of color in an ocean of grey. You're so bright and alive and you don't look at me like I'm a fuckup or a lost cause or a ticking clock. Daisy and Dad... I know they love me. I know they want the best. But the way they look at me—"

"Yeah." She nods. "She does mean well. She just worries. But..."

"Yeah."

"I've done that too." She reaches out. Places her hand on my wrist. "I'm sorry."

I shake my head. "Don't be. You were right. You are right. I am an alcoholic fuckup. I just... I'm trying. But it's really fucking hard."

"It must be."

"Fuck, I lost track of my story."

Her smile is soft. "You were in high school, right? When things got really bad with your mom?"

I nod. "Yeah. It took a year, maybe, for Dad to really catch on. To really see it. Then there was another year of fighting. And trying. Or pretending to try. Ultimatums. Lies. Secrets." My throat tightens. "You were around. You saw some of it."

"They tried not to fight in front of me." She takes a long sip of her coffee. Stares at the empty mug for a moment. Then reaches for the French press. Refills both our cups.

"They tried not to fight in front of me and Daisy too. But that was almost worse. It was obvious something was there. But they pretended like it wasn't. And I... fuck, I didn't know how to handle the tension."

"But you were still drawing?"

"Yeah. It kept me sane. And when I started hanging out with Holden—"

"And his older brother was already a working tattoo artist?"

I nod *exactly*. "It became an obsession pretty fast. And it was an escape too. I'd go to their house after school. Avoid the fucking war zone."

"I always wondered how you two became friends. He acts like he doesn't care about anything. Like everything is light and easy. And you're... the same, but the opposite. You sit on the sidelines, like you can't be bothered to deal with anyone. But it seems like everything is so... heavy, I guess."

"It is."

"Is that why you started drinking?" she asks.

"Trying to make this story coherent."

She half-smiles. "Life isn't coherent."

"It all blurs together. My parents fighting. Then trying not to fight. Trying to take care of Daisy and Mom. Then rebelling and avoiding everyone. Trying to find an alliance with Daisy. But she went the other way. Wanted to be the good girl. So she didn't cause any more conflict for them. So shit wasn't harder for anyone else."

"You both decided to shoulder everything on your own."

"Yeah. And then they announced the divorce to us. They'd already started the legal process, but it got ugly. All these lawyers. And the same arguments over whether or not Mom could really handle taking care of us. In the end, a judge agreed with Dad. Gave him full custody. And Mom... I don't know. She proved him right, I guess. I can't remember the last time I saw her sober."

"You see her a lot now?"

I shake my head. "Holidays, mostly. Every so often she calls. To meet for coffee or dinner or whatever. Sometimes, she's doing better. Sometimes, she's not. I... I don't know. I guess, when I was still drinking, I thought I knew better. I thought I had it together. That I'd found a way to self-medicate in moderation. So why the fuck couldn't she get with the program?" I run my hand through my hair. "Fuck, I was an asshole. I am an asshole."

"That is true."

My laugh erases the tightness in my chest. Fuck, she's funny. And she's trying. She really is. "Hey."

"Was I supposed to argue?"

I nudge her.

She nudges back. "You did hide it well. Sometimes... I guess I thought you just liked to party."

"Yeah."

"It's not like you'd be the first twenty-year-old guy who drank too much for a while. Got over it. Grew up."

"That's what I thought too."

"Did you know you were self-medicating?" she asks.

"Maybe not in those terms. But I knew... shit was hard, and I needed it to be easier. I needed to stop feeling so heavy. And it worked. Food tasted better, music sounded catchier, even the air smelled sweeter."

"It was easier?"

"Yeah. At first, that was it. I drank a little. At parties. Just enough to make it easier. Then enough to stop caring my life was out of control. Enough to feel less lonely."

"Is that why you fucked everything that moved?"

"Only women."

Again, she laughs. "High standards."

"Yeah."

Her voice softens. "Is that different now?"

"Sex?"

"Is it... less?"

"Fuck no." There's no way to put it into words, but I try. "Maybe if I'd tried to keep up with my old routine. To find women who were just as lonely and empty. To fill a few hours—"

"A few hours?"

"You don't think I'm good for it?" I ask.

"No, I just mean—"

"From seduction to satisfaction."

"Still."

Fuck, she makes me laugh. I can't help it. "Angel, you have a one-track mind."

"I know. Just... that's a long time."

"It is."

"You've never given me a few hours," she says.

"You want me to?"

Her nod is coy. "Later... when things are less complicated."

If things are less complicated.

"But, uh, you were saying."

Right. "Maybe if I'd kept that casual shit up. But with you... it's different. I guess it's always different. Now that I'm sober. Food is more bitter, yeah, but it's more every-thing. I can taste all the notes of the coffee. The bitter. And the nutty, rich toffee."

"So... it's more?"

"More of everything."

"Oh." Her eyes meet mine. "And that's good?"

"Angel, are you asking me if more intense is better?"

"I guess I am," she says.

"If anyone should know, it's you."

"So I... with your newfound sobriety, you're basically a virgin."

I chuckle. "Basically."

"So I popped your cherry."

"Don't get ideas about it."

She shakes her head. "I have all the ideas about it." Her fingers brush my wrist. "But, uh, you still didn't answer the question."

"About tattoos?"

"Yeah... how you really started. And why you're sober. What happened? I'm not stupid, Oliver. I know you didn't wake up one day and decide to quit drinking?"

"I didn't."

"So... what was it? Was it really that bad?"

Chapter Thirty-Six

LUNA

Oliver motions to my car, parked on the street. "If you want to run the fuck away from me after this, you can. But I'll go. You stay. Wait until you're calm to drive."

"It's that bad?"

"I don't know. I don't have a sense of it anymore." He places his hand over mine. His fingers curl around mine. "Come here." He pulls me closer.

His eyes flutter closed.

Then mine.

Then it's his mouth against mine.

His kiss is hard and rushed. Like he's trying to soak in everything he can get. Like it might be the last time.

Is it really that bad?

That's hard to imagine.

But I can't stand the thought of this being the last time. So I knot my hand in his hair and I pull him close.

I kiss him back with everything I have.

I inhale every ounce of him. The taste of coffee on his

lips. The smell of his shampoo. The warmth of his fingers on my skin.

When he pulls back, I'm dizzy.

He pours the last few drops of coffee into my mug. Motions to the counter. "One more?"

"Sure." More coffee is always a good idea. And as much as I want to know, I want to wait too. To stay here. In this beautiful, clean, white space where he's pouring his heart out.

Where I understand him and he understands me.

"I got it." He motions for me to stay. Places the French press in the bus tray. Orders another. Waits at the counter.

The sounds of the cafe fill the space. One of those soft rock indie bands. The click of typing. A quiet conversation. Two friends laughing over a TV show. The hiss of the espresso machine.

Finally, the barista finishes with the French press. Ollie drops it at the table. Then he brings over a side of half-and-half and two packets of Sugar in the Raw.

"You used to take it black," I say.

He nods *I know.*

"Because everything is more intense now?"

"And I don't have the same taste for bitter."

Is it a psychological thing? Or a physiological? Is there a meaningful difference? I know a lot about chemical bonds. But almost nothing about how they affect human behavior.

Maybe next semester. When I take bio-chem. At the moment, all I have is instinct.

It makes sense. Everything more intense. Including the bitter notes in the coffee. And without the rush of neuro-transmitters the booze provides—

Sugar is a weak substitute, but it's something.

"You managed half the last one." I pour two cups. Wait until he's fixed his. Hold mine up to toast.

"What to this time?"

The bitter truth? The sweetness of his lips? Softening a blow? I don't know, so I say, "Coffee."

He chuckles. "I'll toast to that." He taps his cup against mine. Takes a long sip. Groans with pleasure.

"That's not fair."

"Oh?"

"This whole—" I try my best imitation of his low, deep groan. "Right before you're supposedly dropping news that might scare me forever."

"I want the odds in my favor." His eyes fix on mine. "I really like you, Luna."

"Thanks."

"And I… you are this bright, beautiful oasis in a land of grey. You are. But it's not just you. It's caring again. Wanting something. Trusting someone."

"You mean I'm not special."

His smile is sad.

"No… I'm glad. That you don't think I'm going to save you."

"You might. But not the way you mean."

"Oh?"

He nods. "You make me want to try. Not just because you're bright and beautiful. And not just because I want to fuck you."

"Only mostly?"

His smile softens. "Because you're a fucking role model. You face shit head-on."

"Uh? No. I'm pretty sure I ran to your house."

"Sure, but did you get wasted and sleep with the nearest hottie?"

"Kinda."

He chuckles. "My ego." He presses his hand to his heart. "That hurts."

"Don't get all Holden on me."

"Okay." His eyes find mine. His smile widens. It's that same look. *You're ridiculous in the best possible way.* "Was that really why you fucked me?"

"If it was?"

"I'll never get over it." His voice is teasing, but there's a hint of truth in it.

"It didn't hurt. But, uh… I like you too. A lot. So whatever this is… don't fuck it up."

"I'll do my best." Hurt seeps into his voice. He did something bad. Or he thinks he did.

I don't know. Ollie is self-destructive on his best day. And it sounds like this was his worst day.

It must be something. If he stopped drinking.

It must be big.

I swallow a sip of my coffee. Focus on the rich flavor. Yes, it is a little bitter. But what can I say? I like the taste.

The robust, nutty, deliciousness. And the bite of bitter.

"Forest was the first tattoo artist I met, yeah." Oliver jumps back into his story. "But you know Forest."

"All brooding like you?"

His laugh softens the furrow in his brow. "Yeah. And just as take no shit. He pointed me to a figure drawing class and told me to ask again when I was eighteen. Guy wouldn't give me the time of day. But I was obsessed. And that made it feel possible. So I started hanging out at Blacklist. Hoping one of the guys would take pity on me. Teach me something. Show me something. Fill an hour with a free tattoo."

"Did they ever?"

He nods *yeah*. Stands. Places his foot on the chair. Rolls his jeans up and his socks down.

There. A tiny diamond. It's messy. Asymmetrical. Imperfect. "I reminded one of the guys of his younger brother. So, one day, when he had a free afternoon, he grabbed his tattoo gun and some gloves and said, want to see what you're getting into?"

"And he did that?"

"No. I did it."

"He just let you do it?"

"Fuck no. He took out a box of fruit. Asked me to try ten on a banana. Then a grapefruit. An orange. But he left me alone with it, so..."

"You just did it?"

Oliver nods. "I was sitting there, on his desk, sure I was a tough bastard. But the second the needle hit my skin—" He motions to the point on the right. It's messy. Skipping spots. "I thought I was gonna die. It hurt so bad. I'm not sure what I expected. Maybe that I'd shrug it off... but fuck. It was miserable. I almost screamed. But I pushed through. Finished before he caught me."

"What did he do?"

"Shook his head *stupid kid, you gotta live with that.* And told me to go."

"It is crooked."

"Yeah. But that's what makes it mine. That's what makes it perfect."

"That's life, isn't it?" I ask. "The messy shit is what makes it yours?"

"I guess it is." He drops his jeans. Sits. Turns all his attention to me. "After that, I was addicted. Saved all the money I had to get new work. Went straight to the figure drawing class—"

"Naked chicks?"

"Yeah. It sounded hot. But even at sixteen... don't get me wrong. I'm always happy to see a naked woman."

"Excuse me?"

He chuckles. "But when I learned to turn on that artist sense... to see lines and shapes. It's different. Abstract." He reaches out. Runs his hand over my chin. Down my neck. Along my neckline. "Right now, when I look at you, I see Luna. This gorgeous badass with sexy short hair, and red lips, and striking features. But if I pick up a pen, try to put you on paper. I see a strong line." He traces my jaw again. "A long, sinuous line." Then my neck. "A red that's almost pink." His thumb catches on my lips.

"And you think *dick lipstick*."

He chuckles. "Dick sucking lipstick, but yeah." He raises a brow. "Tell me I'm wrong."

I suppose I can't really claim that. So I flip him off.

He wraps his hand around my wrist. Brings my finger to his mouth. Sucks softly on the pad. "You're distracting me, angel."

"You're the one talking about naked people."

He nods *true*. "When I shift into that mode, it's just lines, curves, shapes. I can break down the entire world into these tiny pieces that make sense."

"That must feel good."

"It does," he says.

"I wish I had something like that."

"Don't you?" He releases my wrist. "The way you talk about music... it reminds me of learning to draw. You feel that somewhere deep?"

"Sure. I soak in a song. I feel it everywhere. And sometimes it makes me feel understood. But that's it. I might think about the lyrics, but I can't dissect them."

"That's a lot."

Maybe. "There's this Lorde song. About how her boyfriend dumped her because she was too much and he couldn't handle it. I played that a lot after Sean and I ended."

"How did you feel?"

"Better. But worse too. Like I went inside it." My eyes meet his. "I guess... I felt understood. And that helped."

"It always does."

Yeah. And he had all this art. This new obsession. It should have been perfect. "How did you get from that— from this new skill that opened your eyes—to drinking the way you do?"

"I felt better when I drew. And sometimes I held on to it. But sometimes I didn't. Or I'd fixate on it. Like you did, with the Lorde song. Obsess over something that hurt me. Something that fucked me up. Some pain I felt. And... I don't know. I wish I had a good story. That there was this one moment when I snapped. But there wasn't. For a while, I just drank at parties. Bought stuff for friends. Then I started buying for myself. Drinking at home alone. Some nights, when I was bored. Or lonely. Then every night. And when I found out Daisy—"

"Yeah."

"If there was a moment, it was that."

"You couldn't deal with the guilt?"

He nods. "And then I'd drink and hate myself for it. For numbing my shit instead of being there to help her. For being a fucking hypocrite. For lacking the willpower. And it just grew from there. Before I knew it, I had a flask in my pocket at all times."

"You've defended the hell out of that flask."

His chuckle is weary. "I thought it was normal. It was for me."

"Until... something happened."

He nods *yeah*. Takes a long sip of his coffee. Swallows hard. "I drink like a fish, sure, but I'm usually smart about it. Only this time… I was at a woman's house. Doing my usual—"

"Yeah."

He continues, "she wanted to have a nightcap. Then it became two. Three. She nearly fell asleep in my arms. I had to get the fuck out of there. I knew I should call a car, but I didn't."

Oh.

"It happened fast. A bright light, honking horn, brakes squealing. Then I was in the hospital in handcuffs." He holds up his left wrist. "Sprained some shit, but nothing that wouldn't heal."

"The other car?"

"He broke a few ribs. But he didn't want to press charges. And since it was a first offense, and I wasn't quite at twice the legal limit… a four-figure fine, a shit ton of community service, and this bullshit program."

"Oh."

"Yeah."

"But he is okay?"

He nods. "I could have killed him. Fuck, Luna… I don't know. I thought I was better than that. I thought I had shit under control, but… no wonder Dad looks at me like a lost cause."

My inhale is shallow. My exhale is heavy.

"You probably… I can't blame you. If you think the same thing. Everyone else does."

"Ollie—"

"Yeah?"

"It was stupid."

He nods.

"Really stupid."

"I know."

"You could have killed someone."

"I know," he says.

"You should have known better."

The hurt in his eyes deepens as he nods.

"You fucked up, yeah. But feeling sorry for yourself doesn't help."

His eyes fill with surprise.

"I'm not saying *get over it*. Because I know it doesn't work that way. And who am I to talk. But... stewing in guilt isn't an apology. It doesn't make things right. I know it's not as easy as—"

"You don't hate me?"

I shake my head.

"You don't want to run a million miles away?"

"No."

His voice cracks. "You're sure?"

"I'm sure."

He sighs with his entire body. His shoulders fall. His grip softens. His eyes fill with relief. "Luna, I..."

I don't let him finish his sentence. I hook my arm around his neck and I bring my lips to his.

I kiss him like I'm claiming him.

Maybe I am.

He is offering his heart.

I'm taking it.

And I'm not letting go.

And I'm totally fucked, because there's no coming back. And there's no going forward. Not without losing my best friend.

But I can't stop.

Because, more than anything, I need him to be mine.

Chapter Thirty-Seven

LUNA

I lose my ability to think straight. Or make intelligent decisions. Or do anything except fuck Oliver senseless.

It's a good word for it.

I don't have a hint of sense.

And I don't care.

After I drive home, I take Ollie to my room, strip him out of his clothes, fuck him senseless.

Join him in the shower.

Linger for far, far too long.

Somehow, we elude Gabe.

Every day, it's the same. I wake to coffee and breakfast and Oliver dripping with sweat. I ogle him as I sip my java. Then I dress, fix my hair and makeup, ruin it by making out with him.

I go to class, I study, I meet a friend for coffee or swim laps or listen to music in my room. Then I make dinner with Ollie. Eat with him and Gabe. Stay on the couch, watching trashy TV until Gabe goes to bed.

Join Oliver in his room.

I should say no, I should stay quiet, I should—at the very least—insist we drive to some distant spot where no one will catch us.

Instead, I slip out of my pajamas, groan into my hand as Oliver strokes me to orgasm, fall asleep in his arms.

So, on Friday morning, when I wake to a text from Holden—

Holden: Put on your pants.

Luna: Huh?

Holden: We're coming over.

Luna: It's like seven a.m.

Holden: Yes.

Luna: We?

Holden: Patrick and I are gonna double-team you. Get the lube ready, baby. It's gonna be crazy. Who do you think we is?

Then a picture. Him and Daisy at a coffee shop, a pot of tea on the table, early morning light surrounding them in a soft glow.

She's in a new outfit. A peach sweater dress and tall brown boots.

This is from today.

Luna: Where are you now?

Holden: On our way.

Luna: What train leaves this early?

Holden: She caught a ride with a friend. A ride. To my place.

His place is ten minutes away. On foot. In a car—

Shit.

Holden: Hope you're about to confess or you have a good cover story.

Luna: I'm getting dressed.

Holden: Tell your boy toy to get his shit together too.

Luna: I got it.

Holden: Until then.

I slip into my t-shirt and boxers. Tap Oliver on the shoulder.

He rouses. Looks up at me like I'm an angel. "Hey." He smiles. Reaches for my arm.

"Not now." I turn my cell to him.

He reads the message on the screen. "Fuck."

"Yeah."

"Get dressed. I'll make the coffee." He presses his lips to my wrist.

Neither of us asks if we should tell her.

———

I SHOWER. IN CASE I SMELL LIKE HIM. THEN DON A POWDER blue bodycon dress. Combat boots. Leather jacket.

The pink-red lipstick that drives Oliver insane.

Holden and Daisy arrive around my first coat of mascara. I listen to them greet Oliver with a *surprise*. Launch into conversation about an expensive but delicious tea place in San Francisco.

I give them a few minutes alone. Buy time to think of a story.

To-may-to, to-mah-to.

I move downstairs.

Easy breaths.

Steady steps.

I'm seeing my best friend in person for the first time in nearly two months.

I'm excited about that.

I'm not terrified she's going to find out I'm fucking her brother.

Not. At. All.

There. My feet find the ground floor. My lips curl into a smile. My heart thuds against my chest. "Hey."

Daisy jumps out of her seat. She turns to me. Claps her hands together. "Oh my god, Luna. I missed you so much." She practically leaps from her spot at the table— next to Holden, across from Oliver, who's got a perfect poker face.

I wrap my arms around her. Pull her into a tight hug. "I missed you too." So much. Too much. I'm already melting into the familiarity.

Daisy is family. For the last ten years, this place has been my second home. But, really, it's her.

The shy girl who comes alive when she listens to music. Who insists she will never, ever read me her "terrible poetry."

Who loves tea, and tries to make everyone happy, and looks far too adorable for her own good.

She releases me with a happy sigh. "I haven't seen your hair in person, yet." She flips a few strands. "It's fierce."

"Thanks."

"Perfect on you." She turns back to Holden. "Doesn't she look good?"

"This is a trap," he says.

"Oh please." Daisy laughs. "He's not shy about pointing out cute chicks."

He nods *maybe*. "Luna looks amazing, baby. She knows that. Don't you, Luna?"

"Sure, but it never hurts to hear it," I say. "Tell me more, Holden. What do you find most beautiful about me?"

"Your humility," he says.

I laugh.

Daisy does too.

Even Ollie joins in.

"I know my personality is perfect, yes, but we're not on that yet," I say. "Tell me more about my outer beauty."

310

"You're very tall," he says.

"Is that even a compliment?" I ask.

"It's not your best work," Daisy says.

Holden's laugh gets louder. "You want me to tell your friend she has a great rack? She knows she has a great rack. She shows it off all the time."

"God, he turned that into an insult almost," I say.

Oliver nods. "You used to have more game than this."

Holden's expression gets knowing. Something about how Oliver and I are fucking, so of course, Oliver enjoys my rack.

But he says nothing. Just smiles. "Maybe you should show us. So we can judge properly. Is that better?"

Daisy play swats him. "Don't even."

"No? Just you, baby." He motions *come here*. When she does, he pulls her into a slow kiss.

I groan reflexively.

She pulls back. Turns to me. "Sorry. He's just so incor-rigible."

He smiles. "Baby, you know what those big words do to me."

She laughs, charmed. I guess she would find her boyfriend charming. And, really, I should thank him for playing up the Casanova thing. He's doing it to distract her from the Oliver and I are fucking thing.

Or maybe he's doing it because he's Holden.

Either way, it works.

I mouth *thanks* to the trouble making tattoo artist. Turn to my best friend.

"What were we… your hair. It really does suit you." She smiles. "I cut mine a little." She motions to her wavy blond locks. They're still long, but now they fall at her shoulders, instead of halfway down her back. "You like?"

"You look grown-up." It's overwhelming. Daisy is the

311

sister I never had. She's sweet and well-meaning and incredibly easy to hurt. I'm protective of her.

So seeing her bloom—

I blink back a tear.

"Oh my God, Luna, don't. Or I won't stop." She squeezes me again. "Come on, Ollie made coffee."

"You look so grown-up."

"I do not." She leads me to the table. To the spot next to Oliver.

"You do, baby." Holden leans in to kiss her.

"Why?" Daisy's voice fills with curiosity. "I'm the same."

"No." He shakes his head. "You're carrying yourself differently. With more confidence. And this—" He runs his fingers over the hem of her dress.

Oliver practically growls.

Holden turns to him. Shoots him a *really* look. "Down boy."

"You really want to say that to *him*?" Daisy asks.

Oh—

Ew. I clear my throat.

Holden chuckles. "Okay. No funny business at the table. I don't like those rules." He kisses Daisy again. "But I can live with them."

"Can you?" Oliver asks.

Daisy mouths *sorry*. "It's surprising, actually." She smiles. "I got to his place at six a.m. Woke him up. And then—"

"Fuck, no details," Oliver says.

She blushes. "I'm just… surprised you have so much energy." Her eyes fill with affection as she looks at her boyfriend.

"For you? Always." He pulls her into another soft kiss.

Yeah, it's adorable. They're in love. I'm happy for them.

Just maybe… "Save it for later."

Her blush deepens. "I better keep him busy." She squeezes his hand. "Make me a chai? Pretty please."

He nods *sure*. Kisses her again. Like he's making a show of it.

Maybe he is. It's not like either one of us can object.

Even so, I thank some higher power when Holden finally moves to the kitchen.

"She's right," Oliver says. "You look grown-up."

"Why?" Her hand goes to her heart. "My hair is four inches shorter and I'm wearing a sweater dress. It was cold this morning."

"It's one of those things." His expression fills with pride. "Obvious but impossible to explain."

"A good thing?" she asks.

He nods *yeah*.

"Okay, I'll accept it. But stop bringing it up." She looks to me. "And, I guess Luna hasn't been a guest for a long time. And she's definitely not a guest now. But why is she without a mug of coffee when yours is full?"

"I'm a bad host?" he asks.

"A bad roomie, I guess." She looks to me. "Is he?"

"Only if you mind listening to *Smells Like Teen Spirit* fifteen times a day," I say.

His hand brushes my lower back as he stands.

"Only fifteen?" Holden chuckles. "He's losing his touch."

Oliver grabs a mug from the top shelf, fills it to the brim, drops it at the table. "Black?"

"Of course." I wrap my hands around the ceramic. "Thanks."

"Don't thank me. You asked for this." He pulls out his cell. Taps the screen a few times.

And bam—*Smells Like Teen Spirit* fills the room.

"No. It hurts." Holden clutches his stomach. Doubles over like he's suffering a fatal dose of poison. "Anything but this."

Daisy giggles.

I shake my head. "Truly, cruel and unusual punishment."

"This is one of the most popular songs of all time," Oliver says.

"For psychological torture," Holden says.

"Please. You listen to KROQ," Oliver says.

"It's this, the Foo Fighters, and Red Hot Chili Peppers," Daisy agrees.

"And it's torture." Holden holds his hands over his ears. Makes an expression of mock pain.

"Is this really better?" Oliver taps the screen a few times and the room fills with *The Cure. Lovesong.*

"Thank god." Holden falls to the ground in a show of relief. "The torment is finally over."

Daisy's laugh gets louder.

Oliver looks to me. *You believe this shit?*

"They could work on their routine," I say. "It's a little obvious."

"Excuse you?" Holden jumps—actually jumps—to his feet. He raises a brow in mock outrage. "You're calling my material stale?"

"Very stale," Oliver agrees.

Holden looks to Daisy. "Baby, say it ain't so."

"I love it." She blows him a kiss.

He catches it. Presses it to his heart. Shoots me a glance I can't begin to understand.

It's something about me and Oliver. Being hypocrites? Needing to keep this a secret?

Doing a good job playing along?

I haven't got a clue.

But, god, it feels good seeing them. Even Holden. He's actually... funny. And sweet.

And it's incredibly obvious he makes her happy.

She's beaming.

"I hate to say it, Oliver, but this is so much better." She shoots her brother an apologetic look. "Go easy on Luna. A girl can only listen to so much mumbling."

"Yeah, Ollie." Holden scoops leaves into a mug. "You don't want to go too hard on Luna."

Daisy doesn't catch on. Not this time.

But his intent is clear.

It's only a matter of time until she sees it too.

Chapter Thirty-Eight

OLIVER

Daisy gushes as she sips her chai latte. First, about the tea itself. Then the man who made it. *Isn't Holden the best? Cute, funny, an excellent tea-rista. What more could you want in a man?*

Then her classes. Berkeley. The ice cream place down the street.

Back to Holden and his party and his gorgeous green eyes. Have we ever seen eyes that beautiful?

"Is that what brought you here? Holden's rager?" Luna asks.

"Well... it was more a crime of opportunity," Daisy says. "My friend Sarah is obsessed with Disney. And they have some Halloween thing. It's huge. So I seized the day." She laughs. "And, I, uh..." Daisy turns to Holden. "I forgot my costume."

"No." He presses his hand to his heart with mock hurt.

"Sorry." Her expression is apologetic. "I'll make it up to you. I promise."

"Stop there." Before I need to bleach my brain to remove the mental images.

Holden stands. Offers her his hand. When she takes it, he pulls her into a tight embrace. "That sets our plans for the morning."

"Oh?" she asks.

He nods *yeah*. "Gonna buy you a costume. And I get to pick."

"You get to pick?" Daisy's expression fills with horror.

Luna chuckles. "She picks. But you can have veto power."

"How is that fair?" Daisy asks. "It's *my* costume."

"You know you want to wear something sexy," Luna says. "You only have—"

"We're leaving Sunday night." Daisy looks up at her boyfriend. "It's not enough time."

"Not even close," he says.

"And you two can go fuck at his apartment after we hang out," Luna says. "Costumes. Then lunch. Then—" She motions *whatever you want to do*.

"Okay." Daisy blushes. "I'll be good."

"I'm not making any promises," Holden says.

For once, it barely annoys me.

She's here and she's happy.

That's fucking everything.

————

"WHAT WAS THE ORIGINAL PLAN?" LUNA SCANS A ROW OF supernatural costumes. Angels, devils, witches, vampires. She nods to the vampire king. Winks at me.

It's not the time or the place, but my cock doesn't give a fuck. It already wants more of her.

Here. There. Anywhere.

I have some self-control. I can wait until we're alone. Even if it's been hours.

The incredibly long breakfast. An endless stop for tea. Yes, the coffee was great. I can still taste it on my lips.

And even though my sister is four feet away, all I can see is the lipstick marking Luna's takeout cup.

Red on white.

The taste of mint and coffee and Luna.

"No one knows the plan until the big day," Holden says. "Since the plan is off..."

"No, will you really take this secret to your grave?" Luna holds her hand over her heart, mock hurt. "I can't live like this. Always wondering... what were Holden and Daisy really doing for Halloween?"

Daisy chuckles. "Don't make me laugh. I have to focus."

"Don't focus." Holden pulls her closer. Motions to the wall to our left. The lingerie costumes. "Dress as a nurse."

She blushes.

Luna chuckles. "If you're going for porno costume, you can do better than nurse."

"I'm only getting started," Holden says.

"What about a school girl?" Luna points to an impossibly short plaid mini skirt, button-up crop top combo.

"How is school girl better than nurse? It's even more obvious porno?" Holden asks.

"But it suits Daisy so much better." Luna motions to my sister. "She's so sweet and innocent."

"And she never stops talking about books," Holden says.

"Uh, isn't this *my* costume?" Daisy asks. "What makes you think I want your opinion?"

"Ouch," Luna teases Holden.

"I'm pretty sure she meant you," Holden teases back.

"Both of you. Cut it. Or I'll send you to the corner," Daisy says.

"Are you going to punish me for that?" Holden asks.

Luna chuckles. "He really is incorrigible."

"I'm right here," I say.

Daisy turns to me and mouths *sorry*. But she still nestles into Holden's chest.

From a certain angle, they're adorable. And it's obvious he loves her.

But I'm not ready to give him credit for more than that.

"Well, I'm sure we'll never match the glory of your original idea," Luna says. "Both of you going as Robert Smith." She winks at Holden. "You would have looked fierce in black eyeliner."

"I was going to do charcoal," he says. "More my color."

"Sure," Luna agrees, "but the whole point of the goth aesthetic is that it's not your color."

"Smart friend," Holden says.

"I don't see you as Robert Smith," Daisy says. "No matter how many times you play *Lovesong*."

"Can you believe this." He releases her. Reaches over his shoulder. To his back. "This knife... you're twisting it."

"Don't even." Daisy laughs as she moves to his other side, takes his hand, slips it over her shoulders. "I'm exhausted, and I just got here. I want something easy."

"Easy and sexy?" he asks.

"The sexy ones are easy," Luna says.

"What do you like, Daise?" I ask. "What would you do if Holden wasn't in the picture?"

Holden makes a noise that can only mean *bet you love that possibility*, but he doesn't say anything. Just shrugs. "Besides cry into your pillow from the loneliness?"

"Could I really get past that?" She smiles.

He gives her that *I love you and I'm going to make love to you* look.

"Ugh, save it for later," I say.

"I have to second that," Luna says. "Although... maybe we should stop expecting otherwise." She turns to me. "Can you distract him?"

Distract Holden?

Fuck.

What can I say to the guy? *Yeah, it's obvious I'm fucking Luna, so I can't really give you shit for fucking Daisy, but I'm not over it?*

Is it obvious?

Does he know?

I can avoid the topic for five minutes. "You need a costume too, don't you?" I ask him.

"Uh-uh. Me and you, kid." He holds Daisy close. "Joint costume."

"You trust me?" She looks up at him. "I'll pick something you'll like."

He pulls her into a tight embrace. Thankfully, it's a fast kiss. He releases her. Motions *five minutes*.

Follows me to the other side of the shop. The superhero aisle. Not that either of us is in need.

He studies me. Looking for something.

Cracks maybe.

Or maybe it's friendly. Maybe I'm the asshole here.

"She's doing well," I say. "It's good to see."

He nods *yeah*. Motions to Luna and Daisy as they squeal over skimpy costumes. "They're the same as ever."

"Happy."

"They're good friends."

"Yeah."

"She needs that."

Fuck. He does know. Or he suspects. I'm not sure. I swallow hard. Try to ignore the implication. There's something else on my mind. And I need Holden on my side for it. "Remember that keychain you gave Daise?"

"Luctor et emergo? Of course. Gotta tempt my girl to the dark side." His eyes flit to the Latin on my forearm. He taps the spot on his chest that reads *danger is sweet* in Latin. Covered by his t-shirt at the moment. "I won't even show mine off."

"Latin quotes or tattoos?"

"Both." He looks to Daisy with a proud smile. "She wants it. She's just not ready."

"What if she is?"

For the first time in forever, we exchange the kind of look we used to. Like we're partners in crime. "What do you have in mind?"

"I asked my two o'clock to move. And I promised Luna I'd give her the real thing—"

"You think she'll do it if her friend is doing it?"

"Worked for you, didn't it?"

He laughs *yeah, right*. "You couldn't have kept me away." His gaze fixes on Daisy. "She'll probably say no. But she'll love that you offered."

Probably.

But a deal's a deal.

Chapter Thirty-Nine

LUNA

After we pick out the perfect couple's costume for Daisy and Holden (Hogwarts's students, from Ravenclaw and Gryffindor, respectively. Okay, so it's not a perfect costume, but options are limited here. This is solid). We pile into Holden's car.

Drive in the direction of the house.

Turn at Ocean.

Stop in front of Inked Love.

"No." In the front seat, Daisy squeezes Holden's arm.

I turn to Oliver. Raise a brow. *Really?*

He nods *really*.

Fuck, I want to touch him. To undo my seat belt, climb over the middle seat, slide into his lap.

He stares back at me, his clear blue eyes equal parts dare and demand and *don't even think about it*.

We can't.

Of course we can't.

No matter how much I want to.

"I don't know, Holden." Daisy's voice softens. "I'm not sure—"

"Just try the temp," he says.

She bites her lip, considering it. She wants it, but she's scared. Of the permanence, the pain, the possibility for irony.

Luctor et emergo

I struggle and I emerge

It's powerful and beautiful and tempting fate.

I guess Oliver knows that better than anyone.

But—

"It's been two weeks." My eyes fix on Oliver's. "You promised."

"Fuck, he did promise. I was there," Holden says.

Was he? I don't remember. I don't care. I don't care about anything but marking my skin forever.

Oliver marking my skin forever.

"Please." My voice drops to the tone I use when we're naked. It's too much. Too needy. Too desperate. But I don't care. "You promised."

"Oh. The Lorde lyrics." She whispers something to Holden.

He whispers back.

"No, it does not mean I also have to get a tattoo." She laughs. "But nice try."

"Just the temp. See if you like it." He leans over and kisses her.

But I barely notice. I'm too glued to Oliver. "You promised."

"Fuck, you said it three times. That's the magic number." He chuckles, but it doesn't ease the tension in the car.

It's too small a space. I want to touch him.

I need to touch him.

And kiss him.

And scream *yes, every yes forever* to the entire world.

"Okay." She kisses him again. "Just the temp."

Oliver turns to them. "This sounds way too familiar."

"You think I've pulled that *just the tip* shit?" Holden asks.

Oliver's face turns red.

Daisy reaches for the door. "Do you really want to continue this conversation?"

"Honestly, that doesn't sound like Holden," I say. "Sure, he's incorrigible."

"Is that the word of the day?" he asks.

"But he's upfront. More likely to say *baby, sit on my cock*." Shit. Why am I still talking?

"Oh my God." Daisy steps out of the car. Shoots me an *I told you that in confidence* look.

Holden laughs, proud of starting a scene, as usual. And proud of his uh… virility. "Thanks for believing in me." He steps out of the car. Goes to his girlfriend.

I shoot Ollie a *sorry*. "It's true."

He nods *probably*. "But not another word or—"

"You're blackmailing me because you'll do it? Really?"

"A promise is a promise."

I throw my arms around him. It's reflex. I can't help it.

"Luna—"

"I know. But it's… I would hug you here. Normally. And they're not."

"Fuck, I miss you. How can I miss you when you're right here?" He holds me close for a second. Then he releases me. Stares into my eyes with a look of pride and affection. "You're really sure?"

"I've never been more sure."

"Then you're on."

———

I'M NOT SURE.

325

I'm not even a little sure.

The needle is enormous.

It's going to hurt. I've been here enough times to know that. I've heard enough low grunts to be sure.

"Damn, Luna," Holden leans against the wall, not at all reassuring. "That's a lot of shading. It's going to be a bitch."

"He's been trying to sweet talk me for the last twenty minutes." Daisy shakes her head. She holds up her arm. Marvels at the temporary tattoo on her skin. "A lot about how I can handle it."

"You can." He squeezes her hand. "You can handle a lot, baby."

Oliver cringes. "One more word and you're leaving."

He didn't mean it like that. It's sex on the brain.

Although it is Holden. Maybe he did.

According to Daisy, he is massive. Sure, she was a virgin. She didn't have a frame of reference.

But I trust her take on it.

And I—

"Don't move." Oliver presses his palm into my shoulder, pinning me to the chair. He's not doing it as some kind of role play. Or because he's going to fuck me. Or make me wait as he strips.

We're not going to fuck in this chair.

Or in the office.

Or on the counter.

Or at all. Until Daisy is back at Berkeley.

I'm not here to have my way with him.

I'm here because this is really happening.

Oh my god, it's really happening.

"Are you sure?" Daisy's gaze flits to the needle. "It's forever."

"I know," I say.

"And it hurts," she says.

"Like a bitch," Holden adds.

"Don't scare her," Daisy says.

"You're scaring her," he says.

"Am I?" she asks.

"A little." My gaze shifts to Oliver. "But I'm sure. I've wanted this for a long time. I know. The way I know I love you." I blow her a kiss.

Oliver pins me to the chair. "Don't move."

"He likes to get bossy," Holden says. "You should know that. Being here so often."

"Go easy on her," Daisy says.

He shakes his head. Releases my shoulder. Picks up his tattoo gun. "You ready?"

I nod.

The machine turns on with a loud buzz.

Fuck. My eyes press together. I don't have to ask him to count me down.

He does it.

Three, two—

Bam.

I know he's going to do it—all of the guys here play the same trick—but it still takes me by surprise.

Fuck.

There's a needle against my skin.

Marking me forever.

Stabbing me too many times a second.

It does hurt. But it's bearable. I squeeze the chair with my free hand. Close my eyes.

Oliver mumbles something.

Daisy whispers a reply. "After I sleep all afternoon, we're going to marathon some TV tonight."

"Yeah?" My voice is weak. Too focused on the needle

on my skin. The whir of the air-conditioning. The low grumble of the music.

Grunge.

Of course.

Not Nirvana or Pearl Jam. Some other band that was huge in the '90s that barely exists today.

Fuck.

"Of course," Daisy says. "I've already asked Holden to bring four bars of chocolate."

"You do errands for her?" I ask.

"I'll do anything for her," he says.

"Don't continue. I want Oliver to do this right," I say.

Ollie just grunts. He's focused on his work. The needle jabbing my skin. Leaving a permanent mark.

I can't check his expression.

I can't look.

It's already too—

"We need something really trashy," she says. "*Dawson's Creek* level. But new."

"The new season of *Riverdale* is supposed to be trashy perfection." I try to focus on potential shows. There are so many. Teen soaps rule the world. "And we never finished *Gossip Girl*."

"Which is the one with the bad boy and the cute blonde?" Holden asks.

Daisy laughs. "They're all the one with the bad boy and the cute blonde."

"So there are a lot of people to thank. Better get writing." He whispers something in her ear.

She whispers back.

They're adorable.

It's sickening. And sweet.

"The bad boy in Riverdale isn't even that cute," Daisy says.

"He's like a discount Oliver," I say.

"Without all the tattoos," she says.

"And way shorter," I say.

"I'm not hearing a lot about how beautiful I am," Holden says.

"You know, you really didn't finish going on about Luna's beauty," Daisy says. "Maybe I should."

"Do." The stab of the needle calls my attention. It's more a dull ache now. I'm used to it.

"Tall, with those amazing shoulders. You really wear a halter," Daisy says. "You wear everything, really. You have such an amazing sense of style. You always look like a badass."

"You always look adorable," I say.

"I thought this was going somewhere dirty," Holden says.

"You did not." Daisy laughs.

"That's all the black." The needle stops. Oliver leans back. Switches pads of ink. "You okay?" His eyes meet mine.

I barely nod.

"You're almost there. You've got it." His is steady. Reassuring.

I believe him.

Even so, when Daisy offers her hand, I take it. I squeeze her so hard she yelps. But she doesn't ask for release.

She stays there, watching her brother work, watching that needle mark my skin again and again.

Until, finally, it stops.

The buzz ceases.

The pain ends.

My heart thuds against my chest. It's right there. The lyrics from my favorite song. Beneath a flame.

There. On my arm. Forever.

My message to the entire world: I'm a fucking forest fire.

Some people think it's too much, but I won't apologize for it. For demanding a lot, wanting the best, standing by my convictions.

"I love it." My eyes find Oliver's.

He's beaming with pride. Too much. Enough to give us away.

But I don't care. "It's perfect, Ollie. Thank you. It's..."

"Still can't move." He pins me to the chair again. "Not until I clean you up." He nods to Daisy. "Give us ten, okay?"

She nods, sure. Squeezes my hand one more time. "It is perfect. You." She shoots Oliver some kind of look, but I can't see it.

I'm too in love.

I know there are risks around the corner.

I know I'm already being stupid.

But I can't bring myself to care.

Chapter Forty

OLIVER

Usually, it would irritate me that most of Daisy's attention is on her boyfriend.

All right, it's still annoying. But it's a relief too.

It's strange, watching them flirt over lunch, watching them gush over Luna's new ink, watching him fuss over her when we search for a coffee shop with a proper tea selection.

He's obsessed with making her happy.

I hate to admit that it's sweet.

That he's good for her.

He puts her needs first.

So when she starts to yawn over her second steep of Yunnan Hong Cha, he wraps his arms around her, and insists she come home. To rest.

He whispers something, no doubt about how she needs all the energy she can for later, but, hey, I'm going to pretend it was *man, these two really don't get tea.*

A FEW HOURS LATER, DAISY KNOCKS ON MY BEDROOM door. "Hey." Her voice is soft. Somewhere between tired and gentle. "I brought coffee."

"You made coffee?"

"No." She laughs. "We stopped at that place you love. With the six-dollar cold brew." She knocks again. "I have to say, I don't get it. They don't have a single tea."

"Better than bad tea."

"Maybe." She knocks again. Softly. Daisy is too polite to say *open the damn door* or *what's the hold up, are you naked or some shit? Put your dick away.*

That's firmly Luna and Holden territory, respectively.

I want to talk to her. And I am ready for visitors. Dressed in my usual jeans and t-shirt. At my desk, working on a mock-up. But I can't stop thinking about Luna.

The sound of her groan.

The taste of her lips.

The look on her face when she saw her new ink.

Her first.

And it's mine.

Fuck, this is not the time. I'm talking to my sister. Without her boyfriend around. That's important.

More important than my dick.

Not that it cares.

I close my eyes. Think of baseball.

Only I know jack shit about baseball. So I think about my dad shaking his head *Oliver, I wish you weren't such a disappointment.*

Bam. Desire gone.

"Come in." I swallow hard. The room is clean. Everything is in place. I made sure of that as soon as I got home.

But what if I missed something?

What if Daisy can smell Luna's soap? Or she spots a black bra and I have no explanation?

What if it's obvious?

Daisy turns the door. Moves inside with gentle steps. Holds up the cold brew like it's a trophy.

"Is that a bribe?" I ask.

She bends. Picks up a takeout cup of tea from the floor. "If it is?"

"If it's a bribe, you want something. What is it?"

"How are you, Daisy? I've missed you. It's nice to see you. I like your haircut."

"We covered that."

She nods *maybe*. Moves to the desk. Sets the takeout cups on it. "I missed you too."

Okay, I'm being an asshole. It's not her fault I'm tense. It's not her fault I'm fucking her best friend. That's firmly between me and my dick. "I miss you like crazy, Daise. I look at apartments in Berkeley three times a week."

"Really?"

"Yeah."

She picks up her tea. Motions to the bed. *Can I?* Or maybe *is it clean?*

Either way, the answer is yes. "Changed the sheets when we got in."

"Forward thinking."

"Or I want everything fresh when I find someone at Holden's party."

Her face scrunches with distaste. "Are you still… doing that?"

"Doing what?"

"Sleeping with every pretty girl you meet?"

"Not every one." That's technically true. Even if it's not what she means.

"Holden says you're on a sabbatical."

"Does he?"

She nods. Takes a long sip. "He misses you too, you

know. I get why you're pissed. I'd be pissed too if I found out you were dating someone behind my back. Say... Luna. I guess that's the only person it could be."

"Yeah." I swallow hard.

"But... give him a chance, okay?"

What can I say? *No, I'd never do that and he shouldn't either?* "We talked today."

"More than I expected."

More than I expected too. I guess it's harder to stay angry when I'm doing the same thing. "I'm trying. I'm just..."

"Not over it?"

"Yeah."

"How are you going to get over it? Sitting here in your room and stewing?"

"Talked to him today, didn't I?"

She nods. "Even worked together." Her gaze shifts to the temporary tattoo on her forearm. *Luctor et emergo.* I struggle and I emerge. Optimistic, empowering, perfect for her.

"It looks good on you."

My sister smiles. "Are you going to make me promise you can do my first?"

"Is that in the cards?"

"Holden wants to do it."

Usually I'd say *bad idea, you shouldn't let your boyfriend do your ink.* But it's not like I can talk there. "I *am* a better artist."

"I'll consider that." Her voice shifts to a serious tone. "I'm proud of you."

"You're proud of me?"

"For letting me go. Not treating me like a vase that's going to break if anyone handles me roughly."

"Is someone handling you roughly?"

"You know what I mean?"

"Did someone hurt you?" My big brother sense kicks in immediately. Fuck hypocrisy or fair or letting her bloom on her own. If someone is fucking with her, I'm stopping them. By any means necessary.

"No, Oliver. Oh my god! I'm trying to tell you I appreciate you treating me like an adult. And this—" She motions to my fists. "I'm good. I'll let you know if I'm not."

"You sure?"

"I am."

"You're eating okay?"

She shoots me a *don't look*.

"I haven't asked yet."

"You ask every week."

"But I haven't asked today," I say.

She shakes her head *you're ridiculous*. "Okay. I'll answer that question, but I won't allow any follow-up questions."

I want to be proud of her for setting boundaries—and I am—but fuck, I don't like the deal.

"And, in exchange, I won't ask how much you're drinking. Or if you have any flasks in here. Or if I need to worry about how you'll handle Holden's party." She bites her lip. "It's going to be… less crazy. Chase and Ariel are bringing Charlotte. For the first hour, at least."

Charlotte is a few months old. She's going to be out cold by the time a non-family member arrives. Then Chase and Ariel will leave and the party will be business as usual.

Too many people drinking and fucking around and expecting me to offer a sip from my flask.

"Deal?" She offers her hand.

Fuck, there's too much in my head. Too much shit I should tell her. But that's a concern for later. Right now, I need to know that she's okay. "Deal." I shake.

"It's been hard. Really hard. With everything changing... that voice in my head that wants to control my body because I can't control the rest of my life... it's louder than normal. But I'm seeing my therapist. I'm sticking with a routine. I'm taking time to feel and enjoy."

"How hard?"

She shoots me that same *don't* look.

"Are you going to—"

"Oliver." Her tone hardens. "No. You agreed. No follow-up questions. It's my recovery. I'm in charge of it. If I need your help, I'll ask."

That's fair. I hate it, but it's fair. "Okay. But if you seem like you're not doing well, I've already got an apartment lined up."

"You have not."

"Want to bet?"

Her laugh eases the tension in her shoulders. "What about a job?"

"Open my own shop. Specialize in college students. You know how many English majors come in wanting the quote from *The Handmaid's Tale*?"

"It's a good quote."

"Badass, yeah." My lips curl into a smile. "I can see you with it." I motion to her temporary tattoo free forearm. "If you want to jump in headfirst."

Her smile is easy. "Are you okay?"

"I miss you. And Dad drives me crazy."

"He means well."

"Even so."

"You're the same way, you know," she says. "Worried and over-protective."

I can't deny it. "Yeah, but he looks at you like you deserve protecting. He looks at me like I'm the guy about to smash the vase."

"Either way... he looks at you like you might break."

"Yeah." Her eyes meet mine. "You're really okay? When Holden told me about your… sabbatical, I had to wonder. That's a big change for you."

"So's you leaving."

"You're not convincing me."

How can I explain it without telling her? I want to tell her. I will.

But not yet. Not until I'm on steady ground. Until I can tell her without a *maybe it won't stick, maybe I'll fuck up soon, maybe I'll be back to Oliver Flynn alcoholic soon* asterisk.

Will I ever get there?

Or will I be like Mom? Flitting in and out of sobriety for the rest of my life.

Trying and failing.

Trying harder and still failing.

Is anyone ever recovered?

If anyone understands, it's Daisy. But I can't put that on her. I'm her big brother. I'm the one who protects her. Not the other way around.

And I…

Fuck, it's bad enough seeing the disappointment on Dad's face. I can't take it from her too.

"Was there a reason?" she asks. "I mean, there's always a reason. But… did something happen?"

Yeah, but I can't tell her yet. Maybe it's not for her sake. Maybe it's for mine.

Maybe I'm a fucking coward.

Either way—

"My last tryst was business as usual. But at the end… I hurt someone." That's close enough to true. "I didn't feel good about it. Started to think about all the other people I've hurt. I'll spare you the details but… I always thought it was okay that I was casual with people's feelings if I was upfront. But I didn't feel good about it anymore."

She nods, not completely following. "How long has it been?"

"Two months. Give or take."

Her eyes fill with surprise. "That's a long time for you."

"Hey." I grab an old stuffed animal from my bookshelf —the teddy bear she gave me a million years ago—and toss it in her direction.

She catches it.

"You've been practicing?"

"Pure luck." She places the bear in her lap. "You're sure that's it?"

"It's complicated."

"Isn't everything?"

"You can say that again."

She does.

I can't help but chuckle. "That's a Holden joke."

"Oh God, it is." She smiles. "I guess that's what happens when you spend time with someone."

"You grow together."

She nods. "You and Luna?"

Not going there. "She's got me watching *The Bachelorette*."

"And you got her tattooing her favorite lyrics to her arm."

"She's been begging me for that tattoo forever."

Daisy laughs *true*. "*The Bachelorette* is a big win for her. You swore you'd never watch such awful trash."

"It is awful trash."

"But fun."

"It is. And speaking of fun—" I need to change the subject immediately. "I haven't finished my costume." I reach into my bottom drawer. Pull out the only item I have. "I figure, with jeans and that oversized sweatshirt she wears."

"Oh my god." She laughs. "That's perfect."

"You have a sweater like that?"

"No." She pulls her cell from her purse. "But Holden might."

"When has he worn an orange hoodie?"

"Okay, he might know someone who does. Or... I'm sure there's something at Santa Monica Place."

"A hundred-dollar hoodie from Nordstrom?"

"Twenty-dollar hoodie from H&M?" She taps a text to her boyfriend. "If you ask nicely, he'll probably grab one for you."

"That's okay." I don't want to owe him a favor. "I'll go before work tomorrow."

"You sure?" Her eyes flit to the wig. "It would be a tragedy if you didn't complete your costume."

"I'll make it happen."

She laughs *it's perfect*. But there's something else in it too. This knowing smile.

Like she knows I'm doing it because I'm fucking Luna.

But that's ridiculous.

How could she know?

Chapter Forty-One

LUNA

Daisy sits on her pink sheets. She falls onto her back. Spreads out. Sighs like she's completely out of energy.

I get the feeling.

I'm equal parts adrenaline and exhaustion. We spent the entire night watching *Riverdale* and molding chocolate into inappropriate shapes. (Yes, I have vulva molds, who doesn't?)

Every few minutes, I looked at my new tattoo and thought *oh my god, I did that.*

I really did.

It's really there.

God, it's awesome. There's no better word. Amazing, beautiful, powerful, cool.

Totally and completely awesome.

Daisy yawns. "How am I going to a party in two hours?"

"Your boyfriend's party."

"I know." She lets her eyes close. "What if I sleep instead?"

"He'll leave, come here, climb into bed with you."

She lets out a murmur of approval. "Sounds perfect."

It does. I already miss Oliver's touch. The feeling of his body wrapped around mine. It's only been a day, but that's a day too long.

I need to hold him and kiss him and fuck his brains out.

"I'm talking about him a lot, aren't I?" She rolls onto her side. Reaches for a pillow. Slides it under her head.

Yeah, but it's good to see her happy. "Is he a good cuddler?"

"Mmm."

"I would think he can't sit still."

"Sometimes. But not if I've worn him out."

"Daisy Flynn, you minx."

She giggles. "I think it's more biology."

I take a seat at her vanity. It's so her. Pretty and white and clean. "You drain every drop he has. Even his energy."

"Gross."

"What if he said it?"

"You know, Oliver accused me of making a Holden joke yesterday."

"Did you?" I ask.

She pushes herself up on her elbows. "Kinda."

"He's funny."

She raises a brow *since when?*

"Hey! Who told you to go after him?"

"Yeah."

"Even when you protested that he didn't see you that way. Even when you said it could never be anything serious. Even when you said Oliver would kill him."

"Oliver barely talks to him."

Not. Going. There. "He'll get over it." I try to ignore the matter completely. "Who encouraged you?"

342

"It was you."

"So don't give me that *you don't approve* look. I approve."

"Do you?" She shoots me exactly that look.

"Okay, sure, he's a bit of a fuckboy—"

"Hey."

I laugh. "Okay, he was a bit of a fuckboy. I admit it. I didn't have faith in him. I pushed you for you, Daisy. Because I wanted you to seize the cock."

"My new tattoo."

"Right here." I motion to her pelvis.

"More visible." She holds out her arm.

"I will if you will."

"Usually, I'd call that bluff. But right now." Her eyes go to my new tattoo. "I can't believe you did that."

"Isn't it amazing?"

"It is." She studies the lines. "And you let Oliver... I thought you'd ask someone else."

Right. That would be smart. Someone who isn't emotionally involved. But she doesn't know how emotionally involved we are.

It's not completely and totally obvious.

I think.

I hope.

"Do you like him?" she asks.

"What?" I swallow hard.

"Holden."

My shoulders fall with relief. "He treats you well. I like that."

"You don't?" She sits up straight. "Still?"

"Daisy, I like him. I don't want to be his best friend, but I like hanging out with the two of you. Well... not alone. You're a little..." I make a *kiss-kiss* sound.

She blushes. "I know. I'm terrible. I just... I haven't

seen him in forever. And he's so cute. And his lips are so soft. And he tastes like my favorite tea."

"You don't have to justify yourself. I'd do the same."

"Yeah? Were you and Sean ever that... insatiable?"

"At first." I unzip my makeup bag. Sure, we have two hours. But I need a distraction. Or I might confess everything. I'm bursting at the seams. I want to tell someone. No, I want to tell her.

She's my best friend.

I want to tell her everything.

I hate that I haven't been able to tell her everything. It's so much more obvious with her right here.

But I can't. Not yet. So I stay on Sean. "He was always a dick. But it was only to other people at first. And it made me feel kind of special. That he was only nice to me."

She nods with understanding.

"And, god, he made me feel like, well, a minx. He always wanted to touch me, kiss me, take off my clothes." I didn't mind that it was always what he wanted, when he wanted it, on his terms. Not at first. "After a while, it was... a little pushy. But at first, I liked that he'd pull me aside at a friend's house and roll my dress to my waist."

"Yes, I remember that party."

This time, I blush. "Oh god."

"At least it wasn't the first time I saw your boobs."

"Are you still shy about that?" I ask.

She motions *a little*. "Not all of us have spent our lifetime on the swim team."

True.

"But now that I have a roomie who, uh... is not at all shy." Her nose scrunches. "I had to talk to her about overnight guests."

"Really?"

"Yeah. She would start things when she thought I was asleep."

"But you weren't?"

"Or it would wake me up! She's loud."

I can't help but laugh.

"Not funny!"

"Kinda funny."

"Where's the karma? I never subjected anyone to making out my entire life and—"

"Now you do," I say.

"Okay. Now I do." She laughs. Motions to the lipstick on the desk. "Do you need help?"

"I've got it."

"Do you need makeup?"

"Not need makeup?"

"I'm pretty sure your artist never wore makeup."

True. But I can still look amazing. "Do you?"

"Okay." She stands. Fights a yawn. "God, I am tired."

"More tea first?"

"I don't think it's working. My last cup made me more tired."

"Aww, I'm the one who wore you out. Will Holden get jealous?"

"Probably." She takes two steps to the vanity. Pulls her desk chair over. Sits. "Make me beautiful."

"You're already gorgeous and you know it."

"Make me…"

"You want actual schoolgirl or schoolgirl in a porno?" I ask.

She laughs. "Not that."

"Holden would like it."

"Maybe."

I raise a brow.

She blushes. "I think he prefers me adorable."

"Good for both of you."

"Ollie said I should throw this out. Pick up something against type. A doctor. Or a cop. Or something."

My chest flushes. "A cop?"

"Yeah. He has an extra. But I think it's used." Her face scrunches. "There isn't enough laundry in the world."

I laugh like I'm equally disgusted by the thought of Oliver's used cop outfit. And not like I'm the one who wore it. And like I want to wear it again. And actually finish that particular roleplay.

"I never thought… oh my god, no. I can't go there."

Good. "Close your eyes."

She does.

I brush shadow over her lids.

"I just… never thought he'd want the, uh, other party to be the one punishing him," she says.

My head fills with mental images of Oliver handcuffed to his bed. Watching as I ride him.

My cheeks flush.

Thankfully, her eyes are closed.

"Speaking from experience?" I ask. "Do Flynns need to stay in control?"

"Oh my God, my dad too. Gross."

"I meant you."

"Oh. No. I like when he's in control."

"Go on." I move to the highlight color.

"I've said enough."

"He seems open-minded."

"Dad? Or Ollie? Never mind. I don't want to know." She makes that *ugh, gross* sound. It's normal. The same one she would have made six months ago.

Before I was fucking her brother.

She doesn't know.

Or suspect.

Does she?

"Holden?" That's totally
Totally.

"Would he want me
roleplay?"

"Would he?"

"Probably." She laughs. "I
As you say."

"Would you?"

"Hmm… Maybe." Her cheeks flush. "It could be fun."

"Minx."

"Oh my god. Like you haven't."

"I plead the fifth."

"Really?" She opens her eyes. "Since when?"

"Since… recently."

"Luna Anushka Locke! You've been holding out on me."

"Maybe."

Her eyes fix on mine. "Who? When? Why haven't you told me?"

My chest swells. I want to tell her everything. Right now. To climb onto the bed, and find more chocolate, and trade gossip all night.

But I'm not ready for everything to change.

And when I tell her—

"It's new," I say. "I don't know. I want to keep him all to myself, you know? If I tell someone, that makes it real, and if it's real, it can disappear."

She nods. "And you two are already doing sexy role play?"

"A little."

"And…"

"And…?"

"Do I need to say your entire name again?"

347

Only my evil parents would name me
cke. What the fuck does that even mean?
t *actually* Moon Grace. There are some small

y stomach twists. I miss them too.

Even though I'm mad.

Even though they're liars.

And now I'm…

Being an adult is hard.

"He's a gentleman. Very giving," I say.

"Luna Anushka Locke."

"Ugh."

"You call those details?" she asks.

"Now you really sound like Holden."

"You can't distract me with that."

"I just… I don't want to scare him. I really like him,"
I say.

"How will telling me scare him?"

That's a good point. "Putting the energy into the
universe… He's just… he's so difficult and sometimes he's
grumpy and bossy but when he smiles…"

"You do seem lighter."

"Really?"

"Yeah. Even with everything with your parents." Her
voice softens. "I'm sorry about them."

"Thanks. They, uh… let's not discuss that."

"Uh, let's talk about Mystery Man. And why you
haven't told me every detail!"

"*Every* detail?" I ask.

"Of course."

"Even about his assets?"

"Especially about his assets."

"Daisy Flynn, cockwhore. It's got a nice ring to it."

She laughs. "I hate you."

"I love you too."

She smiles. "I missed you. I'm going to miss you."

"Me too." I squeeze her.

She squeezes back. "Now. Details. As many as possible."

"Are you sure?"

She nods *hell yes*.

And even though I know she'd be mortified to hear my thoughts on her brother's sexual abilities, I share them anyway.

I want to tell her everything.

But I can only tell her this.

Chapter Forty-Two

LUNA

Two hours later, we don our shoes, grab our chocolate, and walk to Holden's place.

His dad's place, I guess. Their mom died when Holden was a kid. I don't know Forest or Ariel enough to know the gritty details. But I know it messed them up in different ways.

Forest is all brooding and quiet.

Holden is a ridiculous troublemaker.

And Ariel is, uh, lacking in social graces. Not that it hindered her happily ever after. She and her baby daddy Chase are the only other people here.

Well, besides their daughter Charlotte and the host. Who's playing with his niece.

Poor kid. They put her in the worst outfits. Sure, she's a few months old. Does that mean she can't have style?

Daisy joins her boyfriend.

I give them space. The kid is cute, yeah, but it's their family, not mine. No matter what Daisy or Ollie or even Gabe says about how I'm part of the family, it's not all the way true.

No matter how much I hate it, my parents are my family.

I have to sort that out eventually.

Soon.

But not today. Today, I'm at a party with my best friend. I'm enjoying that. No matter how much I want to find Oliver and mount him.

Ariel spots me. Motions to the bar. *Want a drink?*

Uh, yeah. My heart is already racing. My head is a mess. I want to be here, hanging out with Daisy, like everything is the same.

And I'm terrified she's going to realize the guy who drives me wild is her brother.

But then...

It's different, drinking around Oliver now. Wrong.

I meet Ariel at the bar anyway. It's not like the new mother is going to give me shit about skipping booze.

She's in a mermaid costume. It's pretty racy, considering. (Or maybe not. What do I know about postpartum fashion?)

A purple bikini top and a high waist skirt that hugs her stomach and hips. She's still pretty small—she was really skinny before she got pregnant—but she's softer around the middle now.

What is that like? Seeing your body change?

Scary or thrilling?

I've never had strong feelings about kids—maybe one day—but pregnancy freaks me out.

"You look hot," I say. "Total MILF material. I'm sure Chase appreciates it." Not that it matters. But she's just like Daisy. Mentioning her boyfriend keeps her distracted.

She smiles *oh my God, I love him so much.* "He looks good, huh?"

The same costume he wore last year. A black ninja

outfit. Supposedly, he's some brooding super hero, but I can't say I keep track of the Marvel films or TV shows. "He's kind of tall for a ninja."

She laughs. "Yeah, but look at his ass."

"You won't threaten to drop me if I touch him."

"Could I intimidate you?"

Well, no. "Maybe your baby daddy has been training you in the art of karate."

"The pregnant woman learning self-defense?"

"Maybe it's a cover."

She laughs. "Well, thank you. For assuming I'm capable. People like to fuss."

"Him especially." I follow her gaze to her boyfriend. "His ass does look great."

"Doesn't it?" She turns to the bar. "What are you drinking?"

I'm not even sure what's in my usual drink. Oliver always mixes it for me. I have my cell and Google. And I really do need some calm. But…

"Luna? You okay?"

"Uh, do you know how to fix a Negroni?"

"No. But I'm sure Holden does." Her smile shifts. Still one of love. But more *I love my ridiculous, difficult brother*. "Or are you avoiding him?"

Only Ariel would just say that. "Not avoiding."

"You're looking around. Waiting for someone?" She surveys the room. "Oliver?"

Since when is she perceptive?

"Is there something—"

"Give a girl a second to make up a lie."

She laughs. "Sorry. It's none of my business." She pulls out her cell. Taps a few words into the screen. "I'm not a bartender, but I can make it happen."

"I can—"

"No. I've had people do everything for me for the past year. I'm fixing your drink." She picks up a bottle of gin, measures a shot, pours it into a plastic cup.

"Thanks." I guess pushiness runs in the family. "Is it hard?"

"Pregnancy?"

"More, the way people act. But yeah."

She nods. "I was sick for two months straight. Then constantly tired. Then... incredibly horny." She laughs as she uncaps a bottle of Vermouth. "And still tired." Her eyes flit to her baby daddy. It's like he has an Ariel sense. He's watching her. Curious. Concerned. Somewhere between. "He's so over-protective."

"You don't like it?"

"There is something sweet about it." She waves him off. Adds a shot of Vermouth. Then one of Campari. "But not twenty-four seven."

All these obscure liquors. Did Holden buy them for me? For Oliver? For the sake of... something only Holden would consider?

I guess it doesn't matter. Ariel is kind enough to fix my drink.

I'm wise enough to accept it. "Thank you."

"What's it like?"

"Bitter but sweet. Balanced."

She nods *interesting*. "He's going to come over here. Act like he's trying to say hello. But really it's about the——" She motions to the bar. Starts fixing another Negroni. "Like I can't pump and dump."

Uh... sure, whatever that means. I guess motherhood adds an extra complication to partying. And isn't Chase's mom an alcoholic?

God, he and Oliver would have a lot to talk about. If either of them was the type to talk.

Sure enough, Chase notices the drink in her hand. Moves toward us.

Ariel shakes her head in that *I love how ridiculous he is way*. "Before he whisks me away... whoever it is you're looking for... Holden's room is clear. And you know Holden... he cleared it on purpose. So 'he can imagine beautiful women naked in his bed.'"

"You know Daisy is my best friend," I say.

"And you know Holden is full of shit." She finishes mixing. Takes a long sip right as Chase wraps his arms around her. Mouths *told you so* to me.

"Hey, Luna. How are you?" He pulls her closer.

"Good." I take a long sip. Mmm, herbal and balanced and inhibition relieving. "Your girlfriend is a good bartender. When are you going to put a ring on it? She's the mother of your child, you know?"

He just smiles. "She's the one making me wait."

"Oh?" I ask.

"I'm too busy with school," she says. "Maybe after."

"Maybe? Brutal." He presses his lips to Ariel's cheek. "She's getting tired."

Ariel nods. "Fifteen minutes and we'll go." She turns to kiss him properly.

And, damn, neither of them is shy. Their kiss screams *and after we go, I'll have my way with you.*

I guess that's nice to see. They're still madly in lust. Even with a tiny baby draining their energy.

Kids change things.

If my parents...

The buzz of my cell steals my attention.

Oliver.

Oliver: You look ridiculous.

Luna: I think you mean amazing.

Oliver: Meet me upstairs.

Luna: Where are you now?

Oliver: Backyard. I'll come up a few minutes after you. So no one notices.

Luna: And what will we do upstairs?

Oliver: I need to fuck you.

My sex clenches. Oliver is never coy, but this—

Luna: If I say no?

Oliver: You won't.

Luna: It's risky.

Oliver: I know.

It's stupid.

But I guess I'm completely without sense.

Luna: Five minutes. That's all I'm waiting.

I wait until all attention is on Charlotte, then I sneak upstairs, slip into Holden's room.

Chapter Forty-Three

OLIVER

Thank fuck for small children. When Ariel and Chase leave, everyone insists on walking them to the car. For one final goodbye to Charlotte.

And one final goodbye to calm.

The second the three of them are gone—

I know Holden. I know where this party is going. Even with Daisy here.

Sure, he's not as bad as I was. But the man isn't known for staying sober and keeping everything relaxed.

More for drinking and fucking and fucking shit up.

I push it aside as I climb the stairs. Knock on Holden's bedroom door.

For a moment, my hypocrisy overwhelms me. I'm avoiding the guy for fucking my sister. And now I'm sneaking into his room to fuck my sister's best friend.

It's bullshit.

I'm an asshole.

But I need Luna. And, more, I need to be away from that space. From all these people who expect me to live up to my role. Oliver Flynn, alcoholic fuckup when you want sobriety...

But when you want a party—

I swallow hard as I turn the handle.

Luna is sitting on the bed in a white t-shirt, flannel button-down, and jeans. Oily hair, light makeup, picture perfect grunge musician. "Well, well, well, if it isn't the not new thing." She motions to me. To my costume.

Daisy put most of it together. Bright orange sweater, baggy jeans, black and green wig. That pop star the two of them love. The one who can only whisper.

"You're looking gorgeous, baby. Are you finally legal?" she asks.

I'm not sure how old this chick is, but I nod anyway.

"And what's your name? Do you even know it?" She laughs. "How much have you committed to the character?"

"This thing is itchy as fuck." I motion to the wig.

"So take it off."

"Take it off?" I raise a brow.

She nods *absolutely*. "All of it. Now. For my viewing pleasure."

"Excuse me." My eyes flit to the plastic cup on Holden's desk. Is she drinking? Does she taste like gin? I need away from those thoughts. I need the world to make sense. "I'm the hot new thing. I'm not doing anything for your viewing pleasure."

"I'm an icon."

"Oh?" I raise a brow. "Or are you so desperate to stay relevant that you'll do anything for me?"

She bites her lip. Considering it. Then she nods, motions *come here*. "Nice try, kid, but I think we both know who's in charge here."

"Oh?"

She nods *yeah*. Motions *come here* again. "Now." She

unbuttons her jeans. "Why don't you show *me* how much you appreciate that?"

I move closer. Between her legs. "And how should I do that?" My hand brushes the inside of her knee. Then up her thigh. Higher and higher—

"Fuck, Ollie." Her eyes press together. Her head falls to her side.

"Like this?" I rub her over her jeans. Softly.

Then hard enough she groans.

I shift onto the bed. Pull her body into mine. Kiss her as I slip my hand between her legs.

Into her jeans.

Then her panties.

She groans as my finger finds her clit. "Ollie." Then her eyes fall closed and her lips find mine.

She kisses me like the ship is going down.

Maybe it is. At the moment, it feels like it.

But this is the only thing I can do. Claim her mouth, her cunt, her bliss.

Her heart.

———

After, we separate.

She leaves first.

I wait five minutes. To give her time. But it's too long. My thoughts grow with every second.

Her plastic cup is still on the desk. There's a drop left.

And there's her lipstick. Marking the cup the way it's marked me. I know that taste. That mix of Luna, mint, gin, Campari.

There's no reason to bring the glass to my lips.

Even if it's a drop.

Even if it's nothing.

I've been solid for six weeks. I can make it through the next four.

I'm okay.

I'm surviving this.

But my shoulders still ease the second I move into the hallway. I clean up in the bathroom. Slip downstairs.

The party is already booming. Not full swing, but close. Two dozen people are packed into the massive living room/den. A couple making out on the arm chair, friends smoking in the backyard, people dancing by the speakers.

And the bar. Right there. In its usual spot next to the kitchen. Packed with every liquor and mixer imaginable.

I taught Holden well. Too well.

Now, I—

"Interesting look for you." Holden nods hello. Like my irritation summoned him. "I like the red. Brings out your eyes."

"The red?"

"Your lipstick? New shade. A lot like the one Luna wears. Maybe you borrowed it."

Shit.

"Suits you. Really does."

I wipe my lips with the back of my hand.

"You still smell like pussy."

"Whatever you're going to say—"

"What I'm going to say? To try to help you get away with your hypocritical bullshit? How about *thanks for not ratting me out?*" he asks.

"I need to thank you for not snitching now?"

"After all that shit you gave me about solidarity? Right here. At the fucking party? Do you want her to walk in on you?" He shakes his head. "I've been trying, Oliver. Trying to let you have your fucking space. To have time to get over your shit. Yeah, I made a promise. I shouldn't have broken it. At least, I should have told you. But Daisy's an adult. She can make her own choices. And this is what she wanted."

"Holden——"

"Don't *Holden* me. You're full of shit."

"I want to be over it."

"You think I'm stupid? That I don't know you were upstairs fucking *your* sister's best friend?"

"Can you not?"

"She's outside," he says. "So's your... Fuck, I guess I know why you're so pissed. Because I want to slap you right now. What the fuck is wrong with you? Do you know what it would do to her? If she lost her friendship with Luna."

"I know," I say.

"Do you?" He shakes his head. "Guess I'm the same as you. A fucking hypocrite. But... stop it. If it's something real, if it's serious, if you love her... okay. But tell Daisy. Before someone else does." His eyes flit to the backyard. It's too dark to make out details. But Luna's silver hair catches the light. Daisy must be next to her. "And if it's not serious... well, fuck you, for playing with her feelings."

"Your Luna's defender now?"

"Saying what your sister would."

I swallow hard.

"She deserves better. You know that, Oliver. You've been around her for a long time."

"I'm not playing with her feelings."

"You love her?"

"It's none of your business," I say.

He shakes his head *exactly*. "You think I like being this guy?"

"It's not like that."

"Do you love her?"

I do. It hits me all at once. A truth I can't deny.

And another one.

One just as obvious and a million times worse.

He must notice the revelation on my face. Because he softens. "Fuck. I don't like being an asshole."

"You don't?"

"Not this kind of asshole. Just… figure it out, okay. And try not to hurt her. Please. For her sake. And Daisy's."

"Yeah."

Is it possible? To do this without hurting her?

No.

But in the long run…

This is for the best in the long run.

Chapter Forty-Four

LUNA

Between the post-orgasm glow and drinks with my best friend, I ease into the party. I don't even mind when Holden pulls her away with a promise to *satisfy then send her home at a reasonable hour.*

Or when Patrick and Dare make it their personal mission to tease me until they earn Oliver's attention.

I can see why they're friends with Holden. They're troublemakers, through and through. And they have a rapport. Like the one Holden and Oliver have.

Or had. I'm not sure anymore.

Okay, so, maybe I flirt with Patrick. Maybe I want to see if we can make Oliver jealous. Maybe I'm too low on inhibitions to care that it's immature and silly.

It's too hard, keeping this to myself. I want to tell the entire world.

Oliver Flynn is... maybe not my boyfriend. But something.

Handsome, difficult, caring, protective, hot as hell.

Sure enough, Patrick's flirting earns his attention. The

second the troublemaking tattoo artist pulls me into his lap, Oliver appears outside.

Like he really did materialize from the ether.

Even in the costume (really just an orange hoodie and jeans now that he took off his wig), he looks stern.

Upset.

About this? Or something else.

Patrick turns to Oliver and raises a brow.

Oliver shoots him a *get lost* look. "I'm gonna go."

"Now?" I ask.

His eyes flit from me to Patrick. Then back to me. "Yeah. There's too much shit going on."

With Holden and Daisy?

With us?

With the party atmosphere?

Everyone is drinking and cavorting and he's sober. Fuck. I should be holding his hand. Not out here, trying to make him jealous.

"I'll go with you." I rise to my feet. "I'm pretty beat."

"Uh-huh," Dare says, shaking his head *yeah-right*. "This might be the worst come-on I've ever seen, but, somehow, it's working." He turns to Patrick. "Or maybe she wants to get away from you that bad."

"Maybe she wants to get away from you that bad," Dare returns.

"Maybe it's 'cause you didn't offer to double-team her." Oliver rolls his eyes. "Get some new material."

"I'll go too," I say it again.

He shakes his head *don't*. "Stay. I'll see you—"

"I don't want to stay."

"You should." His expression hardens. "That's for the best."

He moves away from the guys. Toward the corner.

I follow him into the side yard. "Ollie…"

"Luna, don't."

"Don't what?" I reach for him. Get his hoodie. "I'm sorry about Patrick. He was flirting. I knew it would annoy you, but—"

"It's not Patrick."

"Then what?" I tug at his hoodie.

"I'm sorry."

"You're sorry?"

His shoulders fall. "I can't."

"You can't?" My fingers close around his wrist. "Are you fucking kidding me?"

"Luna, don't."

"Don't what? Call you an asshole? Tell you to fuck off? Ask where you get the nerve? You can't? Uh-uh. You can't leave me with such a weak explanation. We talked about this. We agreed. We knew it was fucked up and that we'd have to tell her eventually and we still agreed—"

"I'm sorry."

"No." I hold on to him as tightly as I can. "You don't leave with *I'm sorry, I can't*. You do better."

He says nothing.

"Oliver. At least look me in the eyes."

He turns to face me. Looks down at me with all this hurt in his eyes. "I wish things were different. I wish I was someone else. Not your best friend's brother. Not an alcoholic fuckup. Not someone unable to reconcile this. But—"

"Ollie, you're not—"

"I need to be someone who deserves you. And I'm not. It's just a matter of time until you figure it out. Why break Daisy's heart in the process?"

"But—"

"I'm sorry, Luna. Really." He slides his hand into his pocket. Takes a step backward.

"You think that matters?"

"No. But this is the best I can do."

I wait for him to explain, to expand, to realize he's being an idiot.

But he doesn't.

He leaves me there in the cold, dark side yard.

Alone with the hurt welling in my chest.

Chapter Forty-Five

LUNA

"Luna?" Daisy's voice echoes against the stone wall. She whispers something to someone. Then her footsteps move closer. "Luna." She rushes to me. "What happened?"

I shake my head.

My best friend drops to the ground. Sits next to me. "Did someone—" Her voice drops off. That unthinkable tone. *Did someone hurt you?*

Not the way she means. I shake my head again.

"Talk to me." She turns to someone. A tall figure cast in shadow, standing at the edge of the backyard. "You're not hurt?"

"Only my heart." My laugh cracks. My throat is sore. Raw.

"You don't have to tell me what happened."

"Good."

"But you do have to move."

"No deal."

She half-smiles. "You're going to stay here all night?"

I nod.

"Aren't you cold?"

I motion to my flannel shirt.

"They're prepared for cold weather in Seattle."

"Exactly."

"I'm not." Daisy motions to her bare legs. "And I'm not going to leave you here."

"Okay."

"I'll have to ask Holden to bring a blanket."

I shake my head.

"How about we go home?"

"I can't go there."

She makes that *hmm* noise. It's different than Oliver's or Gabe's. But it carries the same implication. *I see what's going on here, even if you don't want to admit it.* "You can go to Holden's room."

I shake my head.

"The couch."

"Is everyone gone?"

She nods.

"It's not a problem?"

"Is Holden going to be upset I'm hanging out with you instead of fucking his brains out?"

"No. I don't care if he's upset."

She laughs.

"But... if you are..." Finally, I look at her. "I'm sorry."

"Don't be."

"But I... I broke the girl code."

"I know."

"You do?"

She nods. "You always look at Oliver like you want to fuck him—"

"I do not."

She nods *you do.* "But yesterday... it was different. Like you knew what it was like to fuck him and needed it again."

"What does that look like?"

"You two dressed as each other's favorite musicians."

Fuck, it sounds obvious like that. But I didn't think...

I guess I didn't think.

He just... the way he smiles when I tease him about his love of Nirvana—

It's such a beautiful smile.

Even if he's an awful asshole for leaving me here.

"Holden has had this self—righteous look every time he glanced in Oliver's direction. I asked him about it. And he tried to lie, but... he's not as good at playing coy as he thinks." She offers me her hand. "Come on. Couch. Blanket. Dark chocolate. Coffee."

"Coffee?"

She nods. "Coffee."

I take her hand.

She pulls me up.

I follow her into the house.

It's night and day. No longer party central. Just a quiet remodeled bungalow with an empty couch and a huge TV and a few too many bottles on the counter.

Daisy sits me on the couch. Pulls a blanket over my lap. Whispers something to Holden. "He's going to make coffee."

"Oh no."

She laughs. Sits next to me. Rests her head on my shoulder.

Guilt wells in my chest. "I'm sorry."

"Don't be sorry."

"Are you mad?"

"Not mad… just…"

"Disappointed?" I ask.

She doesn't say, but it's all over her face. "More in him. Especially with…" She motions to Holden.

"But in me too?"

"You could have told me, you know? You could have trusted me to act like an adult. To handle a surprise without breaking."

"I didn't think you'd break."

"Maybe, but I… I love you, Luna. You're my best friend. I'm not mad you slept with Oliver."

"Not at all?"

"No. It's kind of weird. But I can get over that… but you could have told me. I wish you had."

God, it's worse that she's not mad. That she's disappointed. "I'm sorry. It wasn't that it would hurt you. I just… didn't want things to change."

"Me either."

"But they… they already have."

"Yeah."

"It sucks."

"In some ways." She looks to Holden. "But in others…" She half-smiles. "You look more grown-up too."

"The hair?"

"And the clothes. And the makeup. And the way you sit tall."

"I always sit tall."

"Yeah, but you're sitting taller. There's something about you. Like you know how to handle everything the world throws at you."

"Yeah?"

"Yeah. Or maybe it's just the hair." Her laugh is soft. "It is really fierce."

I blink back a tear. "I wish you'd seen it sooner."

"Me too." She rests her head on my shoulder. "I miss you all the time. I'll still miss you. Even if you keep sleeping with my brother, you'll always be my best friend."

"What if I kill him?"

"You can try. But I'm going to kill him first."

Chapter Forty-Six

OLIVER

The buzz of my cell interrupts the grunge anthem bouncing around my room.

Holden: You're a fucking idiot.

No argument here.

Oliver: And?

Holden: Is this your idea of making things right?

Oliver: Do you have a point?

Holden: Do you love her?

Oliver: What does that matter?

Holden: Daisy already knows.

Fuck.

Holden: Yeah, dumping her best friend at a party she's attending... not the most subtle move.

Maybe.

Holden: Pretty fucking stupid. Even for you.

Oliver: Learned from the best.

Holden: I'm flipping you off.

Oliver: It's true.

Holden: Okay. I did this first. I'm a disloyal bastard. But now you're a disloyal bastard too. So we're on even ground.

Oliver: Yeah.

Holden: I risked fucking up Daisy's relationship with you. You risked fucking up her relationship with Luna.

Oliver: I get the point.

Holden: You're fucking stupid.

Oliver: I got that already.

Holden: Do you love her?

Oliver: Still don't see how that matters.

Holden: Yes or no?

Why does he want to know?

And what does it matter? This is what makes sense. No matter what anyone else thinks.

Oliver: This is what's best for her.

Holden: Because...

Oliver: Do I have to spell it out for you?

Holden: Yeah. You know I'm barely literate.

I don't want to chuckle, but I do.

Holden: Does it go. I-A-M-A-N-I-D-I-O-T?

Oliver: You got it.

Holden: What? Some bullshit about how you're a fuckup and she deserves better and whatever?

Oliver: Yeah.

Holden: You're probably right.

Oliver: Thanks.

Holden: But shouldn't that be her decision?

Whatever.

Oliver: Is she okay?

Holden: No. You dumped her in the backyard. And she sat there for like three hours. You're an asshole.

Oliver: But she's safe?

Holden: Staying here for the night.

Oliver: Oh.

Holden: Daisy's pissed at you.

Oliver: Really?

Holden: No. It's worse. She's disappointed.

That is worse.

Holden: Get the fuck over yourself, Oliver. I didn't tell you to pull this martyr bullshit. I said if you love her, go for it. You love her. So go for it.

Maybe it's good advice. I don't know.

It's too late.

And I'm too fucking tired.

I lay my cell on the bed. Close my eyes. Try to picture something besides the hurt on her face.

Fail entirely.

———

I SLEEP IN FITS. A FEW MINUTES HERE. HALF AN HOUR OF listening for the door there.

I'm not sure what I want to hear. Silence. Daisy's light footsteps. Luna's steady ones. Her storming into my room to tell me I'm an asshole.

That she isn't taking my bullshit at face value.

That she isn't going to leave until I do better than *I'm sorry.*

I am sorry.

And I can't do better.

Holden's voice echoes through my head.

If it's something real…

Fuck you for hurting her.

Shouldn't that be her decision.

I pick up my cell. Check for any word from him. Or her. Or Daisy. Or anything.

Holden: She fell asleep on the couch. Looks peaceful. Like she's dreaming of kicking your ass. Did I mention that you're an idiot? And you need to fix this?

This is supposed to fix it.

To keep them from crumbling completely.

What is it they say? Cut off the arm to save the body? Some shit like that.

But maybe it's something else.

Maybe it's not that I want to hurt her less in the long run. Or save her and Daisy's friendship.

Daisy already knows.

And—

Maybe it's not about her.

Maybe it's about me.

A knock on the door interrupts me. That can't be her. Unless Holden fell asleep too. Unless she found his phone and sent false information to launch a stealth attack.

"Oliver." Dad knocks again. "Can we talk?"

Fuck, how did he get involved? I pinch my forearm. Will myself to wake up from this nightmare.

No good. I'm still sitting on my bed, my fan muffling the rest of the world but failing to cool me.

I'm hot all over. But it's not because I'm filled with thoughts of fucking Luna.

It's something else.

"Yeah." I pull on a t-shirt. Sit up straight.

Dad opens the door. Flips the light. He bends, picks up two mugs of coffee, holds them up like beacons of light.

Like father, like daughter. I guess she learned that from him.

"Is that a bribe?" I ask.

He half-smiles. "It's more that you look terrible."

"It's the middle of the night."

He nods *even so*. Moves into the room. Offers a cup to me.

"Thanks." I take it. Drink with greedy sips. It's not as good as the coffee I make, but it's strong and dark and hot.

He sits at the desk. Sips slowly. He's still in his pajamas.

A t-shirt and long pants. No robe today. It's too hot up here. Or maybe he knows it makes him look like an old man.

He's not the most stylish guy, but he usually looks pretty good. He's a lot like me, really. Keeps it simple. A suit or part of one or jeans and a t-shirt.

Though that's rarer.

Seeing him casual. Open. With his guard down.

I haven't given him a reason to let his guard down in a long time. It's on me. But... it's on him too.

"Here to ask me to turn down the grunge?" I take another sip. Will the coffee to ease the knot in my stomach. It doesn't. That's not one of coffee's strong suits.

"I know better."

"And you like it."

"Where do you think you first heard it?" He raises a brow. "I was never as cool as you, Oliver, but I was with it once upon a time."

"Were you?"

He chuckles. "Went to all the local shows. Knew all the best artists. Had the prettiest girl on my arm."

"Was that what you loved about her?"

His eyes turn down. "I was young. It didn't hurt. But even then, fuck, you might not remember what your mother was like before she started using. She was a force of nature."

"A wildfire?"

He nods. "I thought of her as a hurricane. And all I wanted to do was dance in her storm. She was so vibrant and alive. I didn't know that was possible."

"Did you come here to reminisce?"

"Maybe." He folds his hands in his lap. "Luna reminds me of your mom. When she was that age."

"You're telling me I have an Oedipal complex?"

"You do want to kill me."

I can't deny that.

His eyes meet mine. He studies me for a moment. Considering something. Then he says the last thing I expect. "I owe you an apology, Oliver."

What? *He* owes *me* an apology?

That's a first.

"You're a lot like your mother," he says.

"A drunk?"

"A force of nature. A stiller one maybe. But just as stubborn and tough and strong."

"Dad, I hate to break this to you, but this is the worst apology I've ever heard."

He chuckles *it is*. "You do remind me of her. And I've... I've let that get to me. I've let that weariness grow. It's hard, trying to get through to you and failing. It's impossible sometimes."

He's right, but... "This is still a terrible apology."

"It's not an excuse. That's what I'm saying. That it's hard. That it's Sisyphean."

"You're talking to me, not Daisy."

"That it feels like I'm pushing a boulder uphill. I was. There was a long time that you didn't hear me."

"There was."

"But lately... you have. And I haven't caught up with that. I haven't stopped to appreciate it. To sit down with you and say thank you for trying. To tell you how proud I am. That you are trying. That you're fighting. That you're so stubborn and tough and strong." He blinks and a tear catches on his lashes. "Fuck, I know you and your sister hate it when I'm like this."

"You're proud of me?"

He nods. "I'm sorry I haven't told you that enough. I'm sorry I haven't shown you. It has been hard, Oliver. I've spent the last few years terrified I'd never be able to help you. But that's no excuse."

He's apologizing.

He's proud of me.

What the fuck?

"You're a good kid. Even if you lied about fucking your sister's best friend." He laughs. "When your mom told me she was pregnant, I never thought one day, I'd be marveling at how similar my kid's "oh shit, Dad realized I'm fucking my sibling's best friend' face is."

"They don't talk about that in parenting books?"

He shakes his head. "But it is. You and Daisy. You two are so similar."

"Fucked up with an unhealthy relationship to control."

"You're doing better."

"I am?"

"You spent the entire night at a party," he says. "How did it feel?"

"Awkward."

"Did you want to drink?"

"Yeah."

"As much as you did at first?"

"No. But... I think... maybe you were right."

Surprise registers over his expression. "I was right?"

"Don't rub it in."

He chuckles. "I guess that's fair. If you'll do the same."

I offer my hand.

He shakes.

"I wasn't trying at first. I was just trying to wait it out. Go back to drinking again. And now... there's all this shit in my head. This shit I tried to block out. And other stuff. That I couldn't access before. But I... it's too much. I think I need help. Dealing with it."

"Okay."

"Maybe... that class is stupid," I say. "But the meetings are okay. And maybe I need..."

"A professional?"

"Yeah." I run my hand through my hair. Fuck, this is awkward. I've never asked for help before. I've never admitted I need it. But I do. "It's really fucking hard."

He nods.

"But it's good too. Like the world is in color again."

"Love does that to you."

"Yeah. It does... but it's not just her. It's everything."

He nods. "You love her?"

"A lot."

"I'm your dad. I'm legally required to repeat the wisdom about not starting relationships right out of rehab."

"I didn't go to rehab."

"Maybe you should."

Maybe. Or—"Maybe that's moving backward."

"I'll trust your take on it." He looks me in the eyes. "I should say wait. Don't risk latching onto her. Making her your new addiction. But I've seen you two grow up together. Since long before this. She's always been good for you. And you've been good for her too."

"I ended things."

"I know." He pulls his cell from his pocket. "Your friend Holden spilled all the details."

I can't help but chuckle. "Of course."

"And a few I really didn't want to hear. Kurt Cobain seducing a young pop star." He shakes his head *how wrong*.

"Does it help that she was Kurt?"

He chuckles. "I am proud of you, Oliver. For trying. And for trying to do what's right by her and your sister."

"Yeah."

"I'm sure they'd both prefer if I lobbied for love. Said

something about how it conquers all. How you two can get past this. But I—"

"Why would you think love conquers all?"

"I know it doesn't. You know that too. But sometimes it tips the scale. Sometimes it's enough, to have a reason to try."

Maybe.

"And sometimes... you're not ready. Sometimes, you need to figure your shit out before you can be with someone else. So, I won't tell you what to do with this girl. But if you want to talk, I'm here."

"What do you know about girls?"

"Enough."

"How? There's Mom and..."

He chuckles. "There are others."

"There are not."

"Not compared to you, maybe."

I can't help but laugh. "Are you calling me a slut?"

"I'm just pointing out the numbers." His gaze shifts to the desk. A sketchbook in the corner. "You're a tough guy, Oliver. You followed your own path. It scared me sometimes, but that's what I've always wanted for you. And your sister. I want to see you healthy and happy." He looks to me. "So, whatever I can do to make that happen, tell me, and I'll try."

Maybe.

Maybe there's something he can do.

And Holden.

If I'm ready to fight for her. For us.

For myself.

Am I?

Chapter Forty-Seven

LUNA

I wake on the couch. Next to the still sleeping Daisy. With the familiar lull of *Dawson's Creek* in the background.

And Holden upstairs. He actually gave us space. And did who knows what to Oliver.

I'm not sure what to expect. Or when I can face him. Right now...

I leave a note for my best friend and her boyfriend. Find my things. Slip out the door.

It's still early. The sun is just starting to rise. The sky is a glorious shade of pale blue. The cold air smells like salt.

Everything is fresh and clean and new. A classic morning by the beach. My wake-up call nearly every day of spring all through high school.

Ah, six a.m. practices, how I don't miss you.

But I do miss this. The feeling of being the only person awake. Of seeing a different side of the world. This delicate beauty. This awe-inspiring power.

The roar of the ocean.

The glow of the moon.

The light of the sun.

What does Oliver see when he runs along the board-walk? Is he early enough to see the sunrise? Does he think about the beauty in the universe or the pain in it?

There's so much of both.

And he…

Maybe he's right. Maybe this isn't going to work. I don't know.

Mom always said, when someone tells you who they are, believe them. But he's told me in so many other ways.

Fixing me dinner.

Holding me close.

Making me coffee.

God, I need coffee.

The place on the way home isn't open yet. Not until seven a.m. Damn lazy hipsters.

But Allison…

I guess I have to forgive her too. Or at least, find a way to make peace with my parents splitting up.

It is their marriage.

It is their business.

They should have been honest with me—

But I can't really talk about keeping secrets right now, can I?

I slip inside. Inhale the familiar scent. The lemon cleaning supplies. The basil plant in the kitchen. The beautiful bag of coffee.

There. I set the kettle, grind the beans, fill the French press.

For a few minutes, routine takes over. Then footsteps move closer. A light turns on. A familiar voice greets me.

"Luna?" Allison asks. "You're home?"

"Yeah." I am. This is home. I don't know what's

happening to the house. If it will still be ours. Or Allison's. Or Divya's.

It will always be home.

But it will never be *mine* again. I'll never be the little girl who accepted my parents protecting.

Who spent all her free time on the couch with her best friend. Joking about boys and wondering what I'll do when I grow up.

That phase of my life…

It's not over. But it's in the rearview mirror. I'm growing up. With all the good and bad that comes with it.

Including seeing my mom as the flawed, well-meaning person she is. "I'm home." I turn to her. "Do you want coffee?"

"Please." She cinches her robe. The same wine shade she always wears.

Only now, my head immediately goes to Oliver's claim. God, I am not thinking about how much my mom enjoys oral sex.

Gross.

It's a stupid claim anyway. He's ridiculous. And sweet. And handsome. And sexy as fuck.

And an asshole for running away.

But I'm not sure I'm capable of hating him for it.

"Give me a minute." Allison moves up the stairs. Knocks on a door.

Uh… is she bringing her girl toy down here? No thanks.

I'm not that mature and grown-up. I mean, maybe I'll meet her one day. But not right now.

I close my eyes. Focus on the coffee. On filling two mugs. Both black.

Familiar footsteps move down the stairs. Two pairs.

"Sweetheart." Divya moves into the kitchen. Wraps her arms around me. "We've been so worried."

"We?" Since when are they still a *we*?

She nods. "Your mother and me. Your friend called us. Told us you might be coming home soon. We wanted to make sure we were both here for you."

"My friend?" I ask.

"The blond guy," Allison says. "With the pretty eyes."

"The other one has prettier eyes," Divya says.

"But this one is Daisy's boyfriend. The other one…" Allison raises a brow.

Divya laughs.

They're actually… joking.

"Aren't you supposed to hate each other?" I asked.

Allison motions for me to sit.

Okay. I could sit. It's way too early to stand. I take my coffee. Move to the table.

Allison does the same.

Divya fills the kettle. Starts fixing a chai.

Like a normal morning.

Like everything is the same. Even though it's not. Even though it's never the same.

"Wait? Holden called you?" When did he do that?

Allison nods. "He didn't tell us what happened."

"You look horrible," Divya says. "Don't tell me it was a boy."

"Is telling me I look horrible your new thing?" I asked.

Allison chuckles.

"Hey. You don't laugh," I say. "You explain."

"I told you, sweetheart. I'll always love your mother," Divya says.

"And I'll always love her too," Allison says.

"And we'll always love you," Divya says. "I'll always be grateful to Allison, for being half of what makes you amazing. You're just like her. Strong and smart and resilient."

"And you're just like Divya," Allison says. "Bright and funny and charming."

They're… complimenting each other?

Allison continues. "I don't want to spend my life with her anymore. But I still want to be your mom. And we're still going to be co-parents."

"Okay." I swallow another sip of coffee. "So you're… you're really friends?"

Both of them nod.

"And you're friendly enough you'll spend Thanksgiving together. And Christmas? And you won't make me choose who gets what?" I ask.

"I think this is emotional blackmail," Allison says.

Divya nods. "Asking when she's hurting. When we want to soothe her. Ruthless. Like you."

They're almost flirting. But it's different. Removed. Like they're appreciating each other from afar.

Appreciating a movie they've finished.

"We can do that," Divya says. "For a while."

"Forever?" I ask.

"We'll see." Allison takes a long sip of her coffee. "Now. Tell us what happened. It was the one with the pretty eyes. Who was here to pick up your stuff?"

"He does have pretty eyes," I say.

"And tall. Straight girls are obsessed with that," Divya says.

"Only straight girls?" Allison challenges her.

I think Divya blushes, but I'm not sure.

Whatever it is—"Too much information."

"It was him?" Allison asks. "Oliver, isn't it?"

I nod.

"I told you she liked him," Allison says.

"I never doubted she liked him," Divya says. "He's very handsome."

"She isn't shallow," Allison says.

"She's eighteen and he's a tattoo artist," Divya says.

"Ah, like mother like daughter?" Allison teases her again.

"Aren't you supposed to be comforting me?" I ask. "Not flirting."

Allison smiles. "You're right."

"But you should have seen your mother in college," Divya says. "She *wore* that leather jacket."

"You've never worn a leather jacket," I say.

Allison nods *I did*. "I'll find it. Leave it in your room. If you're ready to come home."

"No... I think... I think I need my own space," I say. "My own place. If I can afford it."

Allison nods.

"But... I want to keep something. If you really are friends. If you're really okay. Brunch. Can we still have brunch?" I ask.

They exchange a look. Nod, yes, of course.

"It's Sunday," Allison says.

"But the restaurant isn't open for another two hours." Divya finishes her chai. Sits across from me. "Now. Tell me. What happened with Oliver?"

"You can call him by name?" I ask. "And not by eye-color or job title?"

Divya chuckles.

I don't even know how to explain. I don't know why he ran off, but I know he did. "He ended things. But I... I don't know if he really wanted to. Or if he was over-whelmed by seeing Daisy. Or by Holden realizing it. I think he realized it a while ago. But maybe Oliver didn't—"

"Baby girl, slow down," Divya says. "Start at the beginning."

"You're going to give me advice?" I ask.

"If you want," she says. "Or I can listen and make more coffee and fix chocolate chip pancakes."

Like when I was little.

Maybe…

Maybe this is okay.

I take my last sip and I start at the beginning.

———

THROUGH THREE CUPS OF COFFEE, I SPILL THE DETAILS. Staying with Oliver. Finding comfort in his steady presence. Even running into Sean, pretending we were an item.

And falling for his honesty and his strength and his heart.

And the look in his eyes when he told me it was over. Like he couldn't stand that things had to be this way.

Maybe they don't.

Maybe he'll see that.

But I can't do it for him.

When I run out of story, tears, energy, I climb into my bed, close my eyes, fall asleep.

A few hours later, a knock wakes me.

"Luna, your friend is here to say goodbye," Divya says.

Right. Daisy is leaving. It's still light out. But maybe her ride changed the timeline. Or maybe…

"Okay. Tell her I'll be five." I change into the first thing I find—a simple black sweater dress and boots—then I pee, wash my hands, wash my face, brush my teeth.

Move downstairs.

Only it's not Daisy waiting at the door.

It's Oliver.

389

Chapter Forty-Eight

LUNA

H e's too handsome.

Even with dark circles and weary eyes.

He's still so tall and broad and safe.

"Hey." He runs his hand through his short hair. "I, uh… can I have a minute?"

I look to Mom. Nod *it's okay*. Step outside. "Only one."

"Fair." He slips his hand into his front pocket. Waits for me to pull the door closed. Move onto the front step. "I'm guessing you don't want to hear *I'm sorry* again."

"It depends what you say after."

"I am sorry," he says. "For getting scared. For running away. For leaving you at that fucking party by yourself."

"Was that it? The party?"

"Part of it." His eyes fix on mine. "It's complicated."

Is it? Or is it simple? He left.

I pull my hands over my chest. Rub my upper arms. It's a cloudy afternoon. Cool. Or maybe it's my body begging for his warmth.

Oliver slips his leather jacket off his shoulders. Slings it over mine.

"Thanks." I pull it tighter.

"I, uh, I was going to wait for this part, but since we're here—" He holds out his left arm.

Part is covered in plastic.

A fresh tattoo.

An addition to his Latin quote.

ex favilla nos resurgemus
From the ashes, we rise.

The same thin black words.

And a crescent moon.

"Oliver…" My hands go to his skin reflexively. "You…"

"Yeah."

"For me?"

He nods.

"But… what if I tell you to fuck off?"

"Oh, it's temp. I'll just wash it off."

"Really?"

He chuckles. "No. I called Holden. Did it first thing."

My fingers brush the plastic wrap. "Can I?"

He nods *yeah*.

I unwrap. Run my finger over the familiar letters. The moon. "It's beautiful."

"I thought about a wild fire. Because that is you. You're a force of nature. Strong and beautiful and dangerous."

"Is that a compliment?"

"Let me finish."

I shake my head. "You used your minute."

"This didn't buy me another?"

I can't help but laugh. "Maybe five."

"That's it?"

I nod. "Go bigger if you want more."

"Okay. Five minutes." He takes my hand. Looks into my eyes. "I better cut to the point."

I nod *you better.*

"I love you."

"You love me?"

"Yeah. I love you so much it scares me. It did scare me. Thinking of the way you brighten every fucking room you're in. And the way you smile. And that perfect energy that radiates from your eyes. And thinking of being the reason why it faded… But it's not just that. I was scared of everything else. Losing you. Falling harder. Getting hurt."

I swallow hard.

"It's hard for me. Feeling everything. Seeing in color. I'm not sure I can do it. I'm not sure I can be the guy you need. I've never done that before. But I know I love you. And I want to make you happy. And I'll try my fucking hardest, every fucking day, to make that happen. To be the guy you need."

"Yeah?"

"Yeah," he says. "But I'm not there yet." He swallows hard. "I'm not drinking and I'm trying hard, but I'm still an alcoholic fuckup."

"Oliver—"

"Don't argue, angel. You spent the night crying because of me."

The pet name makes my heart thud. My body doesn't care about hurt or betrayal or any silly practicalities. Only about his strong arms and his soft skin and his gorgeous eyes.

That feeling when he holds me.

The taste of his lips.

But this is important. And he's right.

He's trying, but he's not there yet. He might never be there.

I nod *okay*.

He continues, "I'd love to tell you I'm past that. That I'm healed. But I'm not. I'm still fighting. I'm going to be fighting for a while. And I'm going to fuck up again. And get scared and run off again. And you're going to have to wait."

"Okay."

"I want to be everything you need, Luna. I want to be the guy who deserves you. I'm not there yet. And I'm going to work to get there every day, but I can't promise I will. I can't promise I'll stay sober. Only that I'll try."

"Really hard?"

"Yeah."

"You're sure that you'll try really fucking hard?"

He nods.

"I love you too." I don't give him the chance to respond. I kiss him like the ship is going down.

Epilogue

LUNA

Who needs peppermint cake when single-origin Kenyan beans are an option?

Dark, rich, bitter perfection.

Ruined by cream and sugar. Or almond milk and honey. Or the way too sweet cake.

Sure, it's Christmas. And the four of us are here for a new tradition: post dinner chocolate and coffee.

Yes, peppermint is really festive.

But so is the raw tiramisu I made. And no one is touching that.

I expect this from Holden and Daisy, but Oliver?

"You'd like this better." I dig my fork into my slice. Bring a bite to my lips. Let the flavor dissolve on my tongue. Chocolate and coffee. Truly the greatest tastes in the world.

"I'd rather watch you groan over it," he says.

Holden makes an *ick* sound. "And I'm the one who needs new material?"

Daisy nods *kind of*. "That's what it's like when it's new."

"And you'd know? Now that you've been together for four entire months?" Oliver challenges.

"Beats six weeks." Holden chuckles.

"Seven weeks," Oliver says.

Holden presses his hand to his chest. "They're still counting weeks."

"And you aren't?" Oliver asks. "You think I don't see you doodling in your notebook?"

"Drawing naked pictures of my girlfriend? Of course," Holden says.

Oliver shakes his head *no*. "Mock-ups of couple's tattoos. And hearts with her name. Or *Daisy and Holden Forever*."

For a second, Holden blushes. Then he jumps back to troublemaker. "That's a cover. So you don't realize I'm drawing her naked. I don't want to disturb you."

"You don't want to rile someone?" Oliver asks. "That's your story."

"Yeah. Of course," he says.

"Really?" Daisy asks.

"Of course." He picks up her hand. Places a kiss on the inside of her wrist. "I want to make you in every way." He draws a line over her forearm. Which once again bears a temporary version of the tattoo she wants.

I struggle and I emerge.

Only in Latin.

Everything sounds better in Latin.

"You really draw hearts with my name on them?" she asks.

"Fuck, now he doesn't know what to do," Oliver says. "Play up the bullshit. Or admit he loves her more than anything."

"I love you more than anything." Holden leans in to

press his lips to Daisy's. "And I love fucking you more than anything."

She smiles, charmed.

In love.

Blah, blah, blah. It's not that cute the ten millionth time.

Don't get me wrong. I love hanging out with my best friend. Even with her and her boyfriend. Or as a foursome.

It's our new unit. The best friend double date slash double date.

This perfect mix of friendship and family and love.

But, seriously, I don't need to see them make out anymore.

Really.

Never again.

He teases her. She giggles. Whispers back.

They smile at a shared joke. Or maybe a secret. I'm not sure anymore.

It's their own private world. I'm not in it.

A part of me aches. A part of me misses the way things used to be. But most of me—

I'm happy for her. For them. To see her soar and grow and fall in love.

To let go of what used to be and embrace what is.

Because... I'm the same. Me and Oliver. Sure, it's new and a little fragile. We're still building our private world.

But we are.

No one else teases me about the shade of my lipstick (really the only shade I wear around him now), or my idea of "sharing" a French press, or my obsession with the exact shade of my hair. (Still silver, but a little darker).

No one else knows exactly where I hurt. How I can't stand when someone calls me difficult. Or how I struggle to say nice things about Allison's new girlfriend. Or how I both love and hate the new Sunday brunch, because I get two hours with my parents. And then I have to see them say goodbye again.

And go to their separate lives again.

And leave the world that's ours again.

"Angel, you there?" Oliver releases my hand.

My gaze shifts to him. God, he has such beautiful blue eyes. It defies reasoning. And that strong jaw, those broad shoulders, the tattoo peeking out from his v-neck. "Was I saying something?"

"About the cake." He motions to the slice on his plate. Pink frosting on chocolate cake.

Poor innocent chocolate, ruined by all those extraneous ingredients.

"This is better. It has coffee in it." I push my plate toward him. "Coffee."

He chuckles. "I have coffee right here." He picks up my mug. "Do you need more?" He leans in close enough to whisper. "Or do you need to go upstairs and come on my hand?" His fingers skim my thigh.

The edge of my dress.

Then under it.

This isn't the right outfit—a sheath with a sheer embellishment, a sharp Peter Pan collar, and a very snug skirt—or the right place, but I still let my eyes close.

Let my body fill with pure need.

Yes. Now. We haven't had enough time together. Not since Daisy arrived home last week.

I spent most of the week with my parents. One, then the other, then the two of them, together today.

For chocolate chip pancakes and presents and a long walk along the beach. Like when I was a kid. But better. Because now there's coffee.

It's strange, seeing them live separate lives. But I'm getting used to it.

"It's better than it looks." Holden, now finished with making out for the moment, scoops a slice of chocolate peppermint cake onto a plate. Offers it to me. "You might like it."

And I really should stop thinking about taking off my boyfriend's clothes. "It has light pink frosting."

"We made that frosting together," Daisy says.

"And what did I say when I tasted it?" I ask.

"Oooh, can I do the Luna impression?" Holden asks. He doesn't wait for a response, he stands up. Cocks his hip. Places his hand on it. "It's disgusting. Like injecting sugar in my veins. Everyone will love it."

Daisy laughs.

Oliver too. "Sorry, angel, but that's dead-on."

"Betrayal," I say. "Ultimate betrayal."

"How will I make it up to you?" Oliver runs his fingers over my inner thigh.

God, yes.

But not here.

Not in front of her.

"Coffee." I barely get the word out. I don't want coffee. I want his body pressed against mine, his cock buried deep inside me.

But I can't have that yet.

So coffee has to do.

"Coffee." He presses his lips to mine. A quick, easy kiss. We have a lot of those now.

Hello, goodbye, see you later, you look adorable when you're working, oh my god I love that mock-up, you're way cuter than the girl on *The Bachelorette*.

Some of them become more.

A long, slow kiss that screams *I love you*.

A hard, deep kiss that screams *I need you.*

Or the crashing, frantic smashing of our lips that, uh—

He slips his hand a little higher.

My eyes flutter closed. Desire overwhelms my senses. He won't go for it. He knows better. But, god, the dare—

My sex clenches.

My brain fights for control.

Loses.

I kiss him hard.

He kisses back, the perfect mix of *I love you* and *I need you,* then he releases me. "Coffee." His fingers trail my thigh as he pulls his hand away.

Oliver winks. Stands. Moves to the kitchen.

We're here, at the Flynn place. Oliver is still honoring his promise to Daisy—her first year of college, he's here—but he's making plans to move out in June.

And who knows?

I'm not ready to live with him yet. Not the two of us, sharing a lease, acting like actual adults.

But maybe by this summer.

Maybe...

Or maybe my parents will kill him. They like Oliver. A lot. I thought they'd freak when he told them about his sobriety, but they loved it. Called him "a positive influence." "A fighter." "A survivor."

And a bunch of stuff about how he's more than pretty eyes and strong shoulders and tattoos.

They're right.

But they don't have to act like I'm driven solely by my libido. Yes, Oliver is too handsome for words, and sexy as fuck, and I do want to come on his hand and his face and his cock—

But I love him for all sorts of reasons.

His ability to make me come is only one of them.

And…

Shit, Daisy and Holden are still right there.

And I, uh…

"Luna." Daisy pulls me back to Earth. "Let's send the boys to make drinks. Talk." She motions to the couch.

It's not far from the table. Ten feet maybe. But it's enough space we can whisper.

It's familiar. The place we watched a million hours of TV.

The place I fucked Oliver too many times to count.

Ahem.

I stand. Grab my coffee and follow Daisy to the couch.

She folds one leg over the other. Smooths her skirt. She looks the same as always—a coral dress, tan boots, flowing hair—but different too.

A little more grown-up.

A little more worldly.

And—"The ink suits you." I motion to the temp on her forearm. "You should do it."

"I will." She runs her fingers over the letters. "Just not yet." Her gaze shifts to my tattoo. "I still forget. Then I see it. And it's just…"

"This reminder that everything is different."

"I can't believe you let him do it. You were already together."

A laugh escapes my throat. "You wouldn't let Holden?"

"I don't know." Her gaze shifts to her boyfriend. He and Oliver are teasing each other about something, fighting over who uses the kettle first.

It's so much like old times. Like six months ago, before Daisy and Holden kissed, before I fell in love with Oliver.

But it's different too.

She's just visiting.

And, after this—

Well, after this, I'm going to fuck Ollie senseless. And maybe I'll spend the night. But, at some point, I'm going back to my place.

The room I rent in Brentwood, a fifteen-minute walk from school. It's small and crowded and shared with two other college students, including one who plays Beck constantly (it's even worse than Nirvana), but it's mine.

"I did try the tiramisu." She takes a long sip of her chai. "It is good."

"Too strong?" I ask.

She nods. "Dessert is supposed to be sweet."

I laugh. "We'll have to agree to disagree."

"You eat one hundred percent chocolate when I'm not looking, don't you?"

"Ninety is as high as I go."

"Uh-huh." She laughs too. "Ollie join you?"

"He lost his taste for bitter. Now that he's sober."

She nods, accepting the explanation, not looking to elaborate.

It's weird. This is common knowledge now. Oliver is an alcoholic. Oliver is sober. Oliver is trying.

Sometimes, it steals all the focus in the room.

Sometimes, it's too much for him. Or me. Or everyone else.

But it's easier. Not keeping it a secret. Putting it into the universe.

"How is he?" She drops her voice to that tone that means *not drinking*.

He told everyone at Thanksgiving. When he felt confident, he was going to make it to three months.

"He's good," I say. "Really."

Her eyes flash with a familiar expression—*what, no way* and *of course*.

That was everyone's reaction to Oliver's news.

No way did you stop drinking. No way was it that bad. No way were you really more than a guy that liked to party.

And, *of course, you stopped. Of course, you had a problem. Of course, you needed to figure out your shit.*

I guess it explained a lot. About why he'd been avoiding everyone and everything for two months straight.

He's eased into the world. But...

It's different. Everything is different. The world isn't built for sobriety. Hell, when I go to a party with him, and choose not to drink—

It's really no fun, at all, hanging out with drunk people. I've tried it.

And I don't have that extra *who did I used to be, what am I doing, can I really do this forever* baggage.

"We're good," I say. "And I'm good. Thanks for asking that last."

She smiles. "You look good. I don't have to ask."

"Tell me more about my beauty."

"Happy. But that dress is fierce. And with the combat boots." She makes a show of fanning herself. "We're going dancing this weekend, right?"

"Of course," I say.

"You're going to have to bat the guys away," she says.

"I like it. I get to come home. Tell him. Make him jealous and protective."

She makes that *too much information* face. Moves on from the topic of her brother's primal need to claim me. "So I can lock down the whole we're really going to be sisters thing?"

"I have to promise to marry him?"

"How else will we be sisters."

I laugh. "Maybe one day."

"No. Promise. I, Luna Anushka Locke, will marry Oliver Gabriel Flynn."

"He hasn't asked."

"Minor technicality."

My laugh gets louder. Wider. So it fills the backyard, the sky, the world. "You're more like Holden every day."

"Probably. But I'm going to keep asking."

"I know. I love you for it." I hug her.

She hugs me back.

"Now. Tell me everything about last night. Did he actually give you—"

She nods *yes*.

"Details. All of them. Right now."

"He's going to come out and bring you coffee."

"So make it fast."

She blushes. But she still slips into the story of her and Holden celebrating Christmas Eve at his place. He bought her lingerie (really, a present for him) and a new rabbit style vibrator (still kind of a present for him, but I appreciate the devotion to her orgasm).

And, of course, they tried both out right away.

He really has turned her into a filthy pervert.

I don't tell her that I bought Oliver my own set of lingerie (for myself. It's a present for him).

Or that I found a way to get Gabe out of the house for the rest of the night.

With Holden and Daisy on their way out (their next stop is Chase and Ariel's place, though I'm not sure why. Isn't it late enough the kid is asleep?)—

Well…

Daisy doesn't need to know about my plans to fuck her brother senseless.

So I listen to the rest of her story. Trade my own gossip (the Beck loving roomie also loves loud, dirty talk). Let Oliver and Holden join us with fresh coffee.

Then I walk my bestie and her boyfriend to the door, wish her goodbye, take my boyfriend upstairs.

Make do on my plans to fuck his brains out.

After, I fall onto the bed next to him, curl into his chest, let my eyes close.

He traces the lines of my tattoo. The one he did two months ago. And the new one.

ignis aurum probat

Fire tests gold.

Because I'm fighting too. For myself. For him. For us.

Because I'm wildfire and he's strong enough to take it.

I don't know if we'll get married, if I'll end up Daisy's sister, legally speaking. But I know I want him by my side.

For now.

And for later.

And... maybe we'll talk after college.

But, first—"You have another round in you?"

"Already?" He presses his lips to my neck. "I'm not that fast."

"You have a hand, don't you?"

"Two. Last time I checked." He presses one palm into my stomach, pulling me closer. Slips the other between my legs.

"Ollie—"

"Yeah, angel?"

"At least two orgasms, okay?"

He chuckles. "Fuck, I love you so much."

———

Want more?

Sign up for my mailing list for the exclusive extended epilogue to *The Roomie Rulebook*.

In the mean time, watch Holden and Daisy fall in love in *The First Taste*, a sexy forbidden romance.

Already read The First Taste?

Go back to the very beginning of the Inked universe with *Tempting*.

If you've already read all the Inked books, and you're looking for something like *The Roomie Rulebook*, with a feisty heroine, a broken hero, and a whole lot of heat, then check out *Dirty Desires*, a virginity sale romance with a twist.

When tech mogul Ian offers Eve six figures for her virginity, she jumps at the chance to dig her family out of debt. But how is she supposed to spend thirty days in his bed with him without falling in love?

Author's Note

For every girl who's ever been told she's too much.

I have a mission with most books. An idea I want to express or a concept I want to explore. Most people would call that theme. Well, most English teachers. It's not a trait unique to my books—all art (or media if you find art too loaded a word) has a theme—but it's something we rarely discuss in the indie romance world.

Many people see romance, label it genre fiction, assume there's no deeper meaning. Plenty of books are written without a strong theme. Plenty of books read like someone put a bunch of romance tropes in the blender and made a trope smoothie.

Those books may have less to contemplate, but they still have a message. It's probably whatever message is popular in the genre. In romance, that's usually some mix of love conquers all... and a whole lot of other incongruent ideas. The strange relationship between romance novels, feminism, and sexism is a conversation for another day. I'm trying to practice the wisdom of accepting the things I can't control—other people's books and reading experiences—and focusing on the things I control:

My books.

The more I write, the less I'm willing to compromise on my ideals. When I started writing seriously, as a teenager, I had two goals: to express myself (and find some understanding in the process of sharing my work) and to show people how beautiful and fragile relationships are.

In my now thirty book career, I've accomplished that teenage goal, and I've articulated new ones. I want to push romance conventions, especially when it comes to gender roles, I want to explore ideas about relationships, trust, love, intimacy, and I want to highlight characters with baggage, mental illness, and trauma. To make people feel seen and understood.

In romance, damaged heroes usually go over better than damaged heroines. People love hanging out in the head of a truly miserable, fucked up guy. I'm not sure why. I'm not sure why I enjoy it so much either. I loved writing Oliver, diving into his messed up head as he struggled with recovery.

But that wasn't my mission with this book.

It was the line in the Lorde song Luna quotes, the one about people loving a girl with enough passion to burn a forest down, then leaving when the excitement fades and the passion is "too much."

I've been in that place too. Made friends who loved my passion and conviction, only to have them flee when that passion or conviction no longer aligned with theirs.

I've had people claim my standards are too high.

I've had people tell me I'm difficult.

I think most women have. Not just the firecrackers like Luna. The shy girls like Daisy too.

Women who ask for what they want, who demand respect, who express their beliefs—

They're told they're too much.

They're encouraged to tone it down, lower their volume, take up less space.

And I'm here to say:

Fuck that.

Turn up your passion. Say it louder. Make it bigger.

Burn so bright you set the world on fire.

You deserve it.

Love,
Crystal

P.S. I'm talking a metaphorical fire here. Please don't set the actual forest on fire. We need trees if we want paper for books. Also for breathing.

P.P.S. Seriously, no literal fires!

Acknowledgments

My first thanks goes to my husband, for his support when I'm lost in bookland and for generally being the sun in my sky. Sweetheart, you're better than all the broken bad boys in the world.

The second goes to my father, for insisting I go to the best film school in the country, everything else be damned. I wouldn't love movies, writing, or storytelling half as much if not for all our afternoon trips to the bookstore and weekends at the movies. You've always been supportive of my goals, and that means the world to me.

Thanks so much to my amazing audio narrators, Kai Kennicott and Wen Ross. You always bring my characters to life in a way that blows my mind.

A big shout out to all my beta readers. And also to my ARC readers for helping spread the word to everyone else in the world.

To all my writer friends who talk me down from the ledge, hold my hand, and tell me when my ideas are terrible and when they're brilliant, thank you.

Thanks so much to my editor Marla, my assistant Gemma, and to my designer Gel.

As always, my biggest thanks goes to my readers. Thank you for picking up *The Roomie Rulebook*.

Stay In Touch

Sign up for my mailing list to get exclusive bonus scenes, and be the first to know about new releases.

- Like my page on Facebook
- Join my Facebook fan group
- Follow me on Instagram
- Follow me on Twitter
- Friend me on Facebook

Also by Crystal Kaswell

Inked Love

The Best Friend Bargain - Forest

The First Taste - Holden

The Roomie Rulebook - Oliver

Inked Hearts

Tempting - Brendon

Hooking Up - Walker

Pretend You're Mine - Ryan

Hating You, Loving You - Dean

Breaking the Rules - Hunter

Losing It - Wes

Accidental Husband - Griffin

The Baby Bargain - Chase

Dirty Rich

Dirty Deal - Blake

Dirty Boss - Nick

Dirty Husband - Shep

Dirty Desires - Ian

Dirty Wedding - Ty

Dirty Secret - Cam

Pierce Family

Broken Beast - Adam

Playboy Prince - Liam - coming soon

Ruthless Rival - Simon - coming soon

Sinful Serenade

Sing Your Heart Out - Miles

Strum Your Heart Out - Drew

Rock Your Heart Out - Tom

Play Your Heart Out - Pete

Sinful Ever After – series sequel

Just a Taste - Miles's POV

Dangerous Noise

Dangerous Kiss - Ethan

Dangerous Crush – Kit

Dangerous Rock – Joel

Dangerous Fling – Mal

Dangerous Encore - series sequel

Standalones

Broken - Trent & Delilah

Come Undone Trilogy

Come Undone

Come Apart

Come To Me

Sign up for the Crystal Kaswell mailing list

Made in the USA
Las Vegas, NV
02 May 2024

89434575R00246